Shady Lady bored through the clouds steadily. Tension began to ease. *Maybe we'll make it without being attacked,* Brent thought.

Then the shock came . . . the tail gunner, Corporal Efrayim Mani making the first sighting. "Two fighters— five o'clock high. Diving!"

Immediately, Captain Ware commanded: "Fine pitch, full rich, emergency boost. Pour the coal to her. Give me everything she has!"

Brent searched the sky above and to the rear. Quickly he found them, two tiny crosses high above and plunging down out of the sun like darts. . . . *Shady Lady* was the dart board.

He felt his nerves tighten, heart a snare drum; the old familiar drumbeat of fear was back.

Brent recognized the first fighter. It was red; a solid blood-red Messerschmitt Bf-109. And his wingman was black-splotched with big yellow marks. Shark's teeth adorned the underside of the cowling and the oil cooler.

Colonel Kenneth "Rosie" Rosencrance—it was rumored that he had over sixty kills, his wingman, Lieutenant Rudolph Stoltz, twenty. They were Kadafi's favorites. . . .

SUPER

The Ultimate Secret Weapon

CARRIER

Peter Albano

ZEBRA BOOKS
KENSINGTON PUBLISHING CORP.

ZEBRA BOOKS are published by

Kensington Publishing Corp.
475 Park Avenue South
New York, NY 10016

First Printing: March, 1994

Printed in the United States of America

For Bernard L. Irvin, once misspelled but not misremembered.
A special welcome for Ryan Donald Ogren who reported aboard Yonaga for his first assignment.

Acknowledgments

The author gratefully acknowledges:

Master Mariner Donald Brandmeyer for his advice concerning nautical problems;

Dale O. Swanson who completed 30 missions over Germany as the pilot of a B-24 Liberator. His 31st and most exasperating mission was trying to teach this ground-bound writer how to pilot B-24 *Shady Lady* through the pages of this book;

Harold W. Garvin, veteran of 38 missions on a B-24 Liberator, who contributed his expertise as a waist gunner;

Major Robert L. Kingsbury, USA (Ret.,) for his expert advice on all matters pertaining to armored warfare;

Patricia Johnston, RN, and Susan A. Johnston, RN, who advised on medical problems;

Airline pilot Captain William D. Wilkerson for his generous explanations of modern navigational aids and airport procedures.

Mary Annis, my wife, for her careful reading of the manuscript.

William Byer and Otto Schnepp who contributed their knowledge of Yiddish, Hebrew and the state of Israel.

Chapter 1

Moored at Yokosuka's Dock B-2, carrier *Yonaga* dwarfed everything around her. Although the tide was out and she rode low against her moorings, her freeboard was so great not one crane could reach her flight deck. Over a thousand-feet long, the leviathan soared over the Tokyo Bay like Fujiyama over Lake Kawaguchi. Men working on the giddy heights of her scaffolding were as small as insects. Some at the very top of her mountainous island were obscured as torn streamers of low damp clouds blew in from the bay, cloaking her radar antennas, directors and sometimes the navigation bridge.

With high flared bows and good lines that met the challenge of the most violent seas, she showed her battleship antecedents, powerful and deadly. Viewed from the dock, her massive funnel seemed to lean over the spectator, as indeed it did with a typical Japanese 26-degree tilt to starboard. And the wings of her navigation bridge jutted out over those below, too, molded steel and glittering armored glass. But the greatest armor was low on the hull at the waterline, her sixteen-inch belt of hardened steel bulging out like a ledge on a sheer gray cliff.

Workmen swarmed over the behemoth. Most were repairing the last vestiges of battle damage inflicted by Arab aircraft during the bloody battles in the Mediterranean six months earlier. Their hoist systems and scaffoldings formed an almost impenetrable forest about the hull, flight deck and superstructure. The noise was numbing: hammers pounded; pneumatic tools exploded like Nambus on full trigger; power cranes squealed on their rails; heavy steel transporters rumbled; automatic electric running welders hissed and crackled. And everywhere scurrying forklifts wheezed and roared, belching blue smoke as they unloaded supplies, parts, and ammunition from an endless line of patient trucks, trundling their burdens to waiting hoisting blocks like ants feeding their queen.

The warship's great cranes drooped over the swarming ants like arthritic old birds, whining, straining and creaking as they labored their burdens from the dock and swung them aboard. Most unloaded on the hangar deck, passing through openings in her sides created when rolling steel shutters were raised. And here, too, four cranes working from the dock raised their burdens. Punctuated by the shouts of men, the cacophony assaulted one's ears like a Schönberg symphony played by drunken musicians; some voices exploding angry orders, others defensive, and others raised to a high pitch just to be heard over the bedlam.

High above the din in Yonaga's "Flag Country," the noise was lessened by the armored steel of the island, but still audible in the cabin of the commanding officer of the great warship, Admiral Hiroshi Fujita. No one knew the age of the "Iron Admiral." However, it was well known the tiny, withered warrior had passed the century mark. Despite the shriveled, five-foot body, a face with so many seams and rifts it looked like the map of a devastated countryside, there was an arcane, charismatic aura of power that emanated from him. His eyes were arresting, enigmatic. In their depths lurked a mystic's luminous mysticism combined with the skeptic's pragmatic view of human nature. His men not only respected him, they feared him.

Seated behind his massive oak desk, he stared at the two officers sitting erect before him. He addressed the first, a bearded Mossad (Israeli Intelligence) officer incongruously dressed in desert fatigues. "Colonel Bernstein," Admiral Fujita said in a thin yet forceful voice, "you claim this meeting is of critical importance." The old admiral nodded at the second man, a young, blond giant who sat with his arms folded over his broad chest. Even when seated, he looked tall. Fujita continued, "And you insisted that Commander Brent Ross be present."

The Israeli rubbed his nearly bald pate, the motion exposing six blue numbers tattooed on his right forearm. He sighed, his wrinkled face falling into the anxious patterns of a man who was about to test ice which he knew was too thin. "Yes, Admiral. Zahal, ah—I.D.F. has made an unusual request."

"And what does the Israeli Defense Force want?"

"An exchange, Sir. Officer for officer—a liaison."

"You are Mossad. Are you not enough? You have been with me for ten years. This is a liaison."

The Mossad agent turned his lips under and his face appeared as crumpled as yesterday's newspaper. "No, Sir.

This comes from the Israeli General Staff. They are very anxious to start an exchange program."

The ancient sailor glanced at the blond giant and then back at Bernstein. He had already read the Israeli's mind, scanned the pages like a child's basic reader. He gestured at Brent Ross, "Sacred Buddha. We have already done this—almost lost Commander Ross in that battle on the Ben Gurion Line. We cannot throw away such valuable officers in these incessant ground battles every time those fanatical Arabs decide to attack."

The Israeli's mouth settled back into a thin, nervous line. He said, "They specifically request Commander Brent Ross."

A sense of expectancy hung in the room, as palpable as the smoke of a hundred guns. Fujita's dark mesmeric eyes glowered at Bernstein. He waved at Brent Ross. "Yes. I would expect this." "But why? He is one of my most experienced officers. Skilled in intelligence, commanded a submarine, a destroyer, can stand deck watches and he is a member of NIC."

Every man in the crew knew Brent Ross occupied a special place with the old man. In fact, the senior officers often compared the American to Fujita's dead son. But military imperatives took precedence over everything. Every officer knew this, lived by the code.

Bernstein was no different, he persisted, "I know, Sir. Naval Intelligence Command is aware of the request and has approved. In fact, they feel having a NIC officer working in close liaison with the Israeli Army would be very advantageous." He turned to the American, "Brent distinguished himself, was mentioned in reports, saved the life of Colonel David Moskowitz, fought well and hard in

10

the attack on *Bren ah Hahd* and he has the vast, varied experience you just described."

Brent looked down at his bulging thighs and felt heat on his cheeks. He had been taken aback by the indirect praise from both men; especially the Admiral's. Compliments from the "Iron Admiral" were scarce. But he *had* spent a decade on *Yonaga*, learned her most intimate secrets from foretop to keel. Knew her better than most men knew their mistresses. Here, with the guidance of Fujita, he had matured as an officer. A mere stripling of an ensign when he came aboard, he had worked his way through the ranks to commander. He could understand Fujita's concern. *Yonaga*'s old senior officers were dying off and new experienced officers were scarce. Yet, the prospect of returning to Israel was appealing. He admired the tough Israelis. Had fought side—by—side with them in the Sinai. And there was that Ruth Moskowitz. How could a man ever forget that one glorious night? He sighed inwardly. He suspected Fujita would leave the final decision to him. That was his usual practice. He had already made it.

"There is a small army of American officers in Israel," Fujita scoffed.

"Respectfully, not NIC, Admiral," Bernstein insisted. "And not one member of your staff. After all, Sir, only your forces and the Israelis are actively, openly fighting Moammar Kadafi's *jihad.*"

The old man placed his bony, knobby hands on the desk as flat as his arthritic joints would permit. Moving his eyes to Commander Ross, he said, "Brent—san, it would be your posting. You have fought on the Ben Gurion Line, met Kadafi's wrath face—to—face and survived." He

11

sighed and sank back, his fingers grasping and tugging a single white hair dangling from his chin. "It must be your decision. I cannot, will not, order you to risk more." He turned to Bernstein, "I suggest you find another. There are many . . ."

Brent Ross knew it was time to speak, "Sir, I would be pleased to volunteer."

"Pleased!" The old man came erect.

Brent had tactfully debated the old man many times before. He would take the best approach, wear the face of the warrior. "Yes, sir. The Israelis are brave, resourceful people, fighting a savage enemy who outnumbers them fifty-to-one. I would be honored to return." Bernstein beamed.

The old man shook his head. "The risks are great—those desert battles bloody."

Brent had the perfect counter, "You claim I have the heart of a samurai, Sir."

A shadow of a smile crossed the thicket of wrinkles at the corners of the old man's pencil-thin lips. "Throw my own words at me, Brent-san."

Brent smiled. He had scored and everyone knew it.

Bernstein interrupted, "I will see to it that Commander Ross is assigned exclusively to staff work—in rear echelons."

Brent's square jaw hardened. "Then, I will not volunteer."

Fujita said, "You wish to return to the desert?"

The young man brushed a lank of hair off his forehead with the back of his hand and knuckled his temple as if he were trying to break loose a logjam of thoughts. Again, the warrior spoke, but, this time from the heart, "I wish

12

to see first-hand what an observer should see." His blue eyes, cold as ice, threw a hard look at Bernstein. "Anything less would defeat the purpose of the assignment and would be degrading."

Fujita beamed at his young officer. "Spoken like a *samurai*, Brent-san."

"All right, Brent," Bernstein conceded. "With the Admiral's permission, we'll leave that open."

Brent sank back, satisfaction easing the set of his jaw.

Fujita drummed the oak with twisted tendrils. "Brent-san has made his decision. And who will we receive in exchange, Colonel Bernstein?"

The Israeli pulled a document from his pocket, scanned it and said, "Captain Uri Afek, a company commander in the First Armored Division."

"They supported us at *Bren ah Hahd*," Brent said. "Tough outfit. They attacked with old M-60s and captured T-72s. Took heavy casualties but drove the Arabs off—saved my bu . . . ah, I mean, they saved my neck."

Smiling, the Israeli nodded. "Captain Afek's company is now equipped with the new American M1A1 Abrams. They are the first unit equipped with this new tank."

"Great piece of equipment," Brent offered. "Probably the best tank in the world."

"And how would you know, Brent-san?"

"I received Navy SEAL training at Camp Pendleton when I graduated from the Academy, Admiral. M-60s and the M1 Abrams."

"This does not make you a tank expert, Brent-san."

"I know, Admiral."

"You will function as an observer, only. Do you understand, Commander?"

13

"Yes, Admiral. I promise not to lead any cavalry charges."

Bernstein laughed, Fujita snapped, "Do not jest, Commander."

"Sorry, Admiral. I meant no disrespect."

"This is a serious matter. Any time I put one of my line officers at risk, the consequences can be injurious to *Yonaga*."

"Of course, Admiral." *Yonaga* came before everything. Everyone knew that.

A sudden ache brought Brent's hand to his neck, thick as a redwood. He rubbed the tight cords thoughtfully. Bernstein glanced at his watch and said, "With your permission, Admiral, I will report to the Israeli Embassy. I have been requested to give Captain Afek his pre–boarding briefing."

"Very well. You are dismissed, Colonel Bernstein."

The Israeli stood, bowed, and left.

The two men sat silently for a moment, listening to the din seeping in from the outside; yard noises, the blowers, the faint rumble of auxiliary engines. Slowly, Fujita's hand embraced the leather bound copy of the *Hagakure* (handbook of *Bushido*) which was always on his desk. Brent could sense the old man's mood change like tectonic plates shifting under the earth's crust. Fujita said, "Brent–san, you have served *Yonaga* well for ten years."

"It has been an honor, Sir."

"You have been shot, burned, stabbed."

"All in a good cause, Sir."

"You have become one of us. Some call you, 'The Yankee *Samurai*'."

"True, Sir. You know I have tried to live by the Code

of *Bushido.*" The young American nodded at the *Hagakure*, "The book tells us, 'In war, merit lies in striking down the enemy and in dying for one's master'."

"You have never hesitated to strike down the enemy, and I know, Brent–san, you have risked your life many times for me and your comrades. Your *karma* shines bright and clean."

"We have all shared those risks together, Admiral."

"But only you in the desert." Fujita hunched forward, toying with the single hair, eyes mere slits and piercing. His voice was low and harsh, "A barren, hideous place for man of the sea to find his end."

Brent gestured at the book. " 'A man who forgets the Way of the *Samurai* and does not use his sword, will be forsaken by the gods and Buddha'."

Despite the grim topic, the old man smiled. He leaned back. "You know the book better than most *samurai.*"

"You have been an excellent teacher, Sir."

"Then remember, Brent–san," he held up the book, "it also teaches,' If one thoughtlessly crosses a river of unknown depths and shallows, he will die in its currents without ever reaching the other side or finishing his business'." He dropped the book, its flat side slapping the oak loud and hard, as if providing its own exclamation mark. "The desert is a strange river for you. Never forget this."

"I am not a stranger there, Sir."

"Nor a *bedouin.*"

"True, Sir. I promise to exercise the ultimate in discretion."

"And Brent–san."

"Sir?"

"Control your temper."

The young man grinned. His Vesuvian temper was regarded with awe by all who knew him. In fact, it had been reported with relish by the world's tabloid press along with his many amorous escapades—real and imagined. Many times—in fights with *Rengo Sekigun* (Japanese Red Army) and other thugs—his shipmates had to pull him off of beaten foes before he pounded them to death with his big fists. On three occasions he had killed with his bare hands. In two other fights, he had blinded his adversaries; the first with a broken bottle, the second with a pipe wrench. "I promise, Sir, to make a strong effort."

"Remember, Brent–san, the warrior who cannot control himself, does his enemy's work."

"I'll remember, Sir."

Grim and intense, they stared into each other's eyes while between them flowed such a current of feeling that words became redundant.

With an effort Fujita broke that silent rapport, "You are dismissed, Commander."

The young American rose, his six–foot, two–inch frame towering over the little admiral. Because Fujita followed the British tradition of not saluting below decks, and Flag Country was considered below decks, Brent Ross did not salute. Instead, he bowed and the admiral nodded stiffly. The young man left.

The old sailor stared after him for a long moment, the brown of his eyes heightened by a patina of moisture. His mind stumbled back erratically into the murky catacombs of the long dead past. He saw his big, strapping son, so long ago vaporized at Hiroshima. "Kazuo, Kazuo," he said softly into his bent palms. "Do not die again. Come back."

Slowly, with his bony palms covering his face, the "Iron Admiral" melted, bending forward until his head rested on his desk.

Chapter II

Over eighteen-thousand B–24 Liberator bombers were built during World War II. The origins of the historic aircraft date back to January, 1939, when General "Hap" Arnold invited the Consolidated Aircraft company to prepare a design study for a bomber of superior performance to the Boeing B–17 Flying Fortress. The basic specifications called for a range of 3,000 miles, a speed of 300 miles–per–hour and a ceiling of 35,000 feet. At the end of March 1939, the US Army Air Corps awarded a contract to Consolidated to build a prototype.

Under the pressure of war looming on the horizon, work progressed swiftly. The maiden flight was made on December 29, 1939. This was a revolutionary aircraft. Designed around the Davis high–aspect–ratio high–lift wing, its airfoil section allowed a smaller angle of attack. This unique airfoil produced less drag and gave greater range. Mounted high on the deep boxy fuselage, the Davis wing had an outstanding wing loading capability of over sixty–pounds–per–square–foot. In deep elliptical nacelles, the wing held four turbo-supercharged Pratt and Whitney Twin Wasp engines.

The Liberator's armament was similar to the B–17's. Dictated by defensive tactics, head–on and rear attacks were met by nose and tail turrets. Ball turrets were added and in combat the engineer manned a power turret. Two waist guns made the total of ten fifty–caliber machine guns.

Over the war years, many models were built by four manufacturers: Consolidated, Douglas, Ford, and North American. The major production series was the B-24J. A total of 6,678 were built. One, was *Shady Lady*.

Shady Lady's career was short. On her second mission—a rare low–level raid on shipping in the Palau Islands—anti–aircraft fire shot out two engines and damaged a third. Almost miraculously, her pilot made a perfect landing in a clearing on the big island of Babelthuap. The crew was taken prisoner by the Japanese garrison and held until the end of the war. Then, *Shady Lady* was promptly forgotten with the thousands of other relics of the conflict that littered the jungles of the 70–mile archipelago.

If it had not been for the Chinese, she would have remained in the clearing until finally crushed by the weight of time. However, in December of 1983, the Chinese orbited their laser system. Ten weapons platforms orbited on different azimuths so that every square inch of the planet was under constant surveillance. Not one jet, not one rocket could be fired without drawing a lethal lightning bolt from the sky. Overnight, the hegemony of the Soviets and Americans was broken. The reciprocating engine was supreme and the race for old World War Two ships and aircraft began. *Shady Lady*'s future was assured.

Eagerly, the jungles, forests, even the caves, of the Pacific islands were searched. When *Shady Lady* was found by a Japanese search team she was still balanced perfectly on her tricycle landing gear, although her tires were flat. On her nose, her logo—a shapely blond in a white bathing suit—was still quite distinct. Her bubbly buttocks looked very much like those of the favorite pinup of the day, Betty Grable. Under the picture, the words *"Shady Lady"* were clear.

Pratt & Whitney and Browning were not as durable as Betty Grable, the engines and guns hopelessly rusted. Miraculously, the old radio still worked. The serial numbers were checked and the Pentagon confirmed that *Shady Lady* had been listed as missing on June 11, 1944.

Nakajima rebuilt the old plane. It was not as difficult as most engineers had expected. The aluminum construction of the forties was amazingly durable. However, her main wing spar, stringers, formers and longerons were strengthened or replaced. A new skin was stretched over the old bird. New more powerful Pratt & Whitney engines were ordered and installed. Browning shipped in new fifty-caliber guns and modern radio equipment was brought in. Within eight months the old bomber was better than new, including Betty Grable, who had been resurrected by a clever artist. Then, after lengthy discussions and a few heated arguments, the Israeli government bought *Shady Lady*. It was rumored Emperor Akihito and Admiral Fujita had intervened and forced the decision.

With its range of over 3,000 miles, the B–24 would be invaluable in flights deep into Arab territory. The Israeli

Air Force had four Boeing B–17s and two Avro Lancasters. However, none had the range of the Liberator.

Brent Ross first saw *Shady Lady* on the tarmac of Tokyo International Airport. She had Israeli markings. Despite the early hour, a curious crowd had gathered around her. Armed guards kept them at a distance from the aircraft. He stopped in his tracks in the crowded echoing main concourse and stared through a huge window. Gaping at the awesome, unleashed power of the ungainly bird, he sucked in his breath. "Magnificent! Magnificent!" he said to himself.

An excited Colonel Irving Bernstein walked up beside him. "Have you ever flown on a B–24, Brent?" the colonel asked.

"That old warhorse?" Brent stabbed a finger. "Out there?"

"Yes. They need a gunner."

Brent rubbed the slight stubble on his chin which no razor on earth could ever remove. "And I'm the gunner." He eyed the barrels of the fifty–caliber machine guns jutting out from the bomber. "Like a porcupine," he said almost to himself, chuckling.

Bernstein did not share Brent's humor. Instead, his lips took a grim set. "Mossad has good reason to believe the Arabs are aware of our plans and, remember, Moammar Kadafi has placed a million–dollar bounty on your head."

"Yeah, I'm worth big bucks. Raise the ante high enough and I might commit suicide."

Bernstein grabbed the young American's arm. "Brent, this is serious!"

"Okay. Okay. I'm listening, Irving."

"An El Al Douglas DC–3 was attacked by fighters this

21

morning. Seven passengers were killed. We have good reason to believe Moammar Kadafi suspected you were on board."

Brent's droll mood vanished. "Christ, no."

"Yes." The old Jew sighed. "Luckily, one of our patrols happened to be in the vicinity and drove them off." He shrugged and turned his palms up. "Or else, they would have all been slaughtered."

Brent shook his head. "That's the first attack. We've left their commercial flights alone and they've done the same with El Al." He pounded his big knuckles together. "There was some kind of understanding."

"You know better than that, Brent," the Israeli chided. "We're dealing with Arabs. Honor, integrity, humanity are strangers to them."

"Of course. What's wrong with me?" Brent tapped his temple thoughtfully. The prospect of flying with civilians, being helpless and at the mercy of the decisions of an unseen stranger sitting in the cockpit, never appealed to Brent. And a commercial airliner was nothing but a defenseless target for a fighter. If he were to be thrown into harm's way, he preferred to meet any challenge face-to-face, with a weapon in his hand. To fight, and if he died, at least have a chance to punish the enemy. As an aerial gunner, he had shot down a Douglas DC-3 and three Messerschmitt Bf-109s. In the maelstrom of frenzied terror and near hysteria of combat, he had found a heady level of excitement, thrill of the kill that was nearly sexual in intensity. The thought sent crosscurrents of emotions crashing through him, an amalgam of revulsion and fascination. How many times could he risk his neck and survive? Every gambler knew that someday he would crap out. But the prospect of flying in the storied bomber of World War II fame was irresistible. He said matter—of—factly, "Then, the Liberator is a good choice, Irving."

"Of course. You know it's heavily armed." Bernstein tugged on his gray, Leninesque beard. "It's a make—shift crew they're assembling to fly her to Israel, and they need a waist gunner. You have had a lot of experience in the second cockpit of an Aichi."

Brent's smile revealed his eagerness. "Can't argue with that," he said. "When do I meet the crew?"

"Now. This way." Bernstein pointed to the door of a VIP lounge. "The pilot, Colonel James R. Ware, is waiting for you in there. He's going to give his pre—flight briefing to the whole crew."

"And you, Irving?"

"Got to leave. Report to Admiral Fujita. This whole thing was his idea."

"The old man's always thinking."

"Yes. He never overlooks a thing." Bernstein's lips turned up with a slight smile. "By the way, Brent, they call Colonel Ware 'Bull'."

" 'Bull'! Why?"

"You'll see." He grabbed Brent's hand, reverted to Hebrew. *"Mazel tov,* my friend." The smiles vanished and they gripped each others hands firmly, the handclasp of friends who had entered hell together many times and survived all nine rings.

"Good luck to you, too, Irving, and *sholom aleichem."*
"Aleichem sholom."

The two old comrades grasped each others shoulders for a moment and then the Israeli disappeared into the crowd. Brent turned toward the door.

Standing on a small dais, Colonel James R. "Bull" Ware was just starting the meeting when Brent entered. At first glance, Brent became aware of how the colonel had earned the sobriquet, "Bull." A big round man with no neck and a bald cannonball head, he looked like a heavy-weight wrestler.

One glance at the commander in dress blues with a DOP patch on his shoulder and the Imperial sixteen-petalled chrysanthemum badge on the cap was enough to identify Brent to Colonel Ware. The Department of Parks shoulder patch was worn only by forces under the command of Admiral Fujita and the chrysanthemum identi-fied *Yonaga*'s officers.

"Welcome, Commander Ross," Ware said with a voice strident enough to be heard over the roar of a Pratt & Whitney. Nine other men turned toward the newcomer. All were in flight suits. "Yankee Samurai," and *"Yonaga,"* were whispered around the room.

Brent felt uneasy. "Sorry I'm late, but I was just in-formed."

Ware's smile was friendly. "You've missed nothing, Commander—except your flight clothes." He gestured to the back of the room where a young corporal sat alone at a table. A flight suit was on the table. "Corporal Knudsen has your suit—extra large." There were chuckles. "He's the other waist gunner. You'll be flying butt to butt."

Everyone laughed at the plane commander's wit. Brent found his seat next to Corporal Knudsen.

Then gesturing and speaking rapidly, Ware introduced the crew. Although most appeared very young, they were all experienced professionals. It was then Brent realized there were only nine men in the crew. The copilot was a woman; a lovely woman with fine skin and delicate features. Her name was Devora Hacohen and she was a lieutenant in the Israeli Air Force. Devora appeared very young and slender in her clumsy flight suit. Yet, when she stood, there was something irrepressible in her that announced, "I am a woman!"

Brent's eyes riveted on her face. It was breathtaking. Pale, her skin shone like mother-of-pearl, features reminding him of the serene beauty of a Vermeer portrait. Adding to the allure were the high cheekbones and classic lean planes of the Semite. Her luminous brown eyes were so large and elfin, she brought to mind a Walt Disney fawn. *That face could stop a man in his tracks—launch a thousand ships and sink them,* Brent thought. Suddenly, he wished he were the pilot.

There were more excited rumbles when Ware explained Brent's exploits and he felt especially disquieted when the big luminous eyes focused on him for a very long time. More whispers of, "the Yankee Samurai," and *"Yonaga,"* floated around the room.

"This is the first time in the history of military aviation that a naval commander has flown as a gunner on a Twenty-Four," Ware concluded, beaming. "And we appreciate your volunteering, Commander. I know you had very little notice."

At that moment Brent knew "Bull" Ware would be

easy to like. "I'm happy to be a member of your crew, Colonel," Brent said simply.

"Hear! Hear!"

Brent felt relieved when Ware moved on to other members of the crew. Although they all wore Israeli Air Force uniforms, it was an international group. "Men who fight for freedom, know no borders," Admiral Fujita had said many times. How true.

Ware stumbled over some names and referred to notes. In seconds, Brent understood that Ware only knew his copilot, engineer, the other waist gunner, and navigator–radioman. The other five members of the crew had been hastily assembled to ferry the big bomber. There would be no dead weight. The plane carried a full load of ammunition for its ten fifty–caliber guns and its bomb bay was loaded with four large auxiliary fuel tanks. Every person on board would have a function. Typical of the Israeli mentality, rank was of secondary importance.

"We may need every drop of fuel and every round of ammunition before we land at Ben Gurion Airport," Ware warned. He told them of the Arab attack on the DC–3.

Bombardier Lieutenant Horace Burnside, a thirtyish Englishman with horsy teeth and scrubby mustache, waved a hand. His melodic East Newham accent put a heavy bias on every word he spoke, "I say, Colonel, that's not sporting. I thought there was a gentleman's agreement to leave the commercial airlines alone."

"We're not dealing with gentlemen," the engineer, Sergeant Michael Shaked, a young Israeli from Haifa spat bitterly.

"Hear! Hear!"

Colonel Ware nodded agreement and continued with the briefing. "Most of you are new to this bird. I flew 25 missions in Twenty–Fours as a nineteen–year–old shave–tail in 1945. All my flying was from the right–hand seat, except on my last mission when my pilot was killed over Berlin. The Twenty–Four is not an easy plane to fly. They used to call it 'the flying boxcar' but she's a durable old bird and can bring you home with a lot of her tail feathers plucked." High–strung laughter. Pride crept into his voice, "In its day, it was a revolutionary design." Gesturing at a large schematic on the wall, he explained the Davis wing, its advantages, the great range of the bomber. "This bird fought in every theater in World War Two and more were built than any other bomber. Even Winston Churchill had his, the "Commando," for long flights," he concluded, beaming.

"I hear there was a problem with the fuel tanks," Sergeant Oren Smadja, the small, bright Israeli ball turret gunner said in a guttural accent. A student of aeronautical engineering, he knew the Liberator better than any person in the room except Colonel Ware.

"Usually, the wings contained all the fuel," Ware said. "Self–sealing."

"And self–leaking, Sir."

Ware studied the young gunner. "Can happen."

Smadja was not finished. Gesturing at the schematic, he said, "The wings slope down, so the leaking fuel must end up in the fuselage." He rose, stabbed a finger at the midsection, "And here, there are hydraulic accumulators and a lot of electric gear. With all that fuel, one spark and we could be," he turned his palms up, *"kaput."*

Ware shook his head. "Fuel can leak. "I've seen it happen in more than one aircraft."

Smadja showed his hours of study, "They called the Liberator 'the cremator'. I read a report that said the Luftwaffe preferred to attack Liberators because they caught fire quicker than the B–17 and blew up."

Ware reacted as if his own child was being unfairly criticized. "Nonsense, Sergeant. If there's any kind of fuel leak all we have to do is crack the bomb bay doors—blow the fumes out." His jaw hardened. "Sergeant Smadja, if you're having second thoughts, I will be happy to remove you from the crew."

The young gunner pulled his lips back in a tight line as if they were made of elastic. He retreated quickly, "Ah . . . no Colonel. I wish to remain."

"Very well. Then let's continue." Ware turned to the schematic. "With our new turbo–supercharged, 2,800 horsepower Pratt and Whitney engines, our cruising speed has been raised from 193 miles–per–hour, to 220 and our range with auxiliary tanks in the bomb bay will be 4,900 miles." Some of the men whistled. Picking up a pointer, he turned to three maps mounted next to the schematic. "This is our flight plan." He traced the pointer across the Pacific, indicating a landing in Hawaii. Then to Dallas, Fort Lauderdale, Gibraltar and finally Israel. "We'll have plenty of fuel."

"We won't stop at Wake Island or Midway?" the tail gunner, Efrayim Mani, asked. He looked young enough to lead a high school cheering section.

"Not necessary." Ware glance at his navigator, a Japanese lieutenant named Kennosuke Torisu. Torisu stood. He was very thin and slightly stooped. His face was as flat and expressionless as that of a stone temple icon. Uneasy in the limelight, he gestured at the charts as if he were trying to divert everyone's attention from himself. When he spoke, he squeaked out his words in a timbre that rolled with typical southern Kyushu inflections. "On a lean mixture and at our best cruising speed we can make Hawaii non–stop with fuel to spare." He looked at "Bull" Ware who moved his head affirmatively like a great white bowling ball. Gaining confidence, Torisu proceeded, "Our new engines are misers, but we can always use Wake or Midway in case of an emergency."

The Japanese began to return to his seat, but the commander stopped him with a raised palm. He looked at the new men. "Lieutenant Torisu has some new gizmos that would make James Bond jealous."

"Ah, yes," the navigator said. "The newest IRS—Inertial Reference System—has been installed in our aircraft. The IRS has laser gyros that measure the rotation of the earth and the vertical and horizontal movements of the aircraft. This information is fed into a computer and the aircraft's position is continually displayed digitally on a CRT." He ran a hand over his bony chest and a slight smile finally cracked the stone. "Actually, there isn't much for me to do except to program in our starting position and destination and monitor the equipment."

"The latitude and longitude of Tokyo?" Efrayim Mani suggested.

"No, Corporal, the latitude and longitude of the end of the runway." There was a surprised buzz and the newcomers looked at each other.

Ware gestured and the navigator sank into his chair. "And I can assure you," the plane commander said, "we have the latest radio equipment, radar and transponders. And Lieutenant Torisu told you our new Pratt and Whitneys are misers and we have more than enough fuel to make Honolulu easily."

"And *munitions, mon* Colonel?" the nose gunner, a young French sergeant named Philipe D'Meziere inquired. Swarthy, with a scarred, pockmarked face and burly build, D'Meziere looked like a brawler who had just stepped out of the alleys of the Left Bank. His accent was thick, but still quite understandable. Brent guessed scars on his knuckles matched those on his face.

Ware said, "A full load and we have been promised fighter escort by the British at Gibraltar. Two squadrons of the new Grumman FX–1000 are based there."

The gunners looked at each other. A few nods were exchanged.

Brent intruded smoothly, "They're American manned."

"Right."

"They can't make Israel. I operated with them last year. Arab radar will pick us up when we make Gibraltar and there's a good chance Kadafi will send out a welcoming committee of his own."

"True, Commander," Ware conceded with obvious deference. "We've been promised Israeli fighters will pick us up when the FX–1000s turn back."

Brent stabbed a finger at a chart, "The Italians have denied us their airfields, so there's a gap—east of Sicily and extending to Benghazi—where we won't have any escorts. Maybe four–, five–hundred–miles." There anxious mumbles from the new men.

"True, Commander. You anticipate me. I was just

30

about to discuss the 'Mediterranean gap' for the benefit of the new members of the crew. True, we may meet some bandits." He looked around, smiling reassuringly. "However, I'm confident that with this crew—you're all hand picked—we can storm the gates of hell and drag the devil himself out." He turned back to Brent. "And now, Commander, you know why I put a gun in Colonel Bernstein's ribs and recruited you for the starboard waist gun."

There was laughter, the jittery high–pitched giggling of a crew about to be exposed to mortal danger. Brent had heard it many times before. Colonel Ware scanned the crew, moving on to new topics. In detail, he reviewed radio procedures, reporting of sightings, gunnery discipline. "No long range miracle shots! Lead them, gunners! Lead them! Track your tracers and don't forget deflection and bullet drop!"

Then there was more talk about the new heated flying suits—there had been some problems with faulty circuits—the best cruising altitude which was usually about 24,000–feet, and the various radio channels available, their use and more emphasis on radio discipline.

While "Bull" spoke, Lieutenant Devora Hacohen passed out schematics of the bomber with a long list of specifications. Standing close to Brent, she leaned over him to hand Roland Knudsen the documents. Brent drew in his breath sharply when a pointed, hard breast, which only showed as a small mound under the shapeless flight suit, pressed against the side of his head. He nearly groaned when the copilot moved to the next row.

"I know all of you are experienced bomber crewmen. But most of you have never flown in a Twenty–Four," Ware continued. "You know it takes a long time to train

31

a crew, to know each other, to coordinate, to avoid snafus."

"Snafus?" Mani, D'Meziere and Smadja chorused.

Ware looked around disconcertedly like a man who realized the had almost stumbled into a gaffe. "Ah, *snafu* is an old Air Corps word that means, 'Situation normal, all . . .'" He glanced at his copilot and blurted, "All fouled up."

Everyone laughed and Ware smiled self-consciously. Brent liked the way Ware had respected the girl by avoiding the most common of military obscenities. However, he would soon learn that this was the only epithet the plane commander would concede to his female copilot. To him, she would become, "one of the boys." There was no room for special treatment, regardless of rank and gender. Everyone knew this. Ware had a crew, but he was building a team. The ideal commanding officer. There was some of Admiral Fujita in the man.

Ware moved on swiftly, all business, "But we have no time. Study your schematics and remember flight discipline. Your are all professionals, conversant in English, and I am convinced you sure as hell know your jobs." He smiled broadly, "After all, *Shady Lady* is still just an airplane." Everyone nodded. A few chuckles. He glanced at his watch. "We take off in an hour-and-a-half, at ten-hundred-hours. We'll assemble here at zero-nine-one-five." He glanced at Brent. "Commander, you can change in there." He pointed to a door. "Corporal Knudsen will assist you."

"Thank you, Sir."

"You're dismissed."

Everyone came to attention as the plane commander

32

left the room. Then, carrying Brent's flight clothes, Knudsen led Brent into the small room. It was a storeroom, piled with boxes. A small table and two chairs were pushed into a corner. Knudsen placed Brent's flight gear on the table. Brent dropped his small suitcase on the floor.

When Brent shrugged out of his tunic, the gunner pointed at Brent's shoulder holster and said, "Isn't that a Beretta, Commander?"

Brent ran his fingers over the soft leather, "Right. You know your pistols. The Beretta M951, Brigadier. Ten round magazine. Fast."

"Same action as the Walther P–38." Knudsen patted his armpit.

"You carry a Walther?"

"Right next to my deodorant."

"Good weapon." Brent dropped his tunic on a chair and bent over to untie his shoes. "You know the colonel well, Corporal?"

"Met him a couple weeks ago."

After placing his shoes under the chair, Brent pulled an electrically–heated flight suit over his shirt and trousers. "He's a good pilot?"

"One of the best, Commander. I've made a dozen test flights with him in *Shady Lady*."

Brent zipped up the suit and reached for a pair of lined zippered flying boots. He sat and tugged one on. "He said the Twenty–Four was a hard plane to fly."

"These old birds have no power assist, Commander."

"I know." Brent zipped the boot and reached for the other one.

"They're flown with biceps and leg muscles. The colo-

33

nel's in great shape. They don't call him 'Bull' for nothing, Commander."

Brent pulled hard on the other boot. "I was wondering about our copilot."

A smile crinkled the freckles sprinkled like gold flecks across the young gunner's nose and cheeks. "She's a fox."

Brent laughed. "She's your superior officer."

The freckles bunched as an Alfred E. Newman, "Me Worry?" grin spilled across Knudsen's face. Knudsen liked to live dangerously. He said, "Not biologically, Sir."

Brent zipped up the other boot and became serious. "You've flown with them. Can she handle the bird?"

"No worry there, Commander. She's good."

Brent remembered the slender frame. "She doesn't look very strong."

"Her appearance is misleading, Commander."

Brent stood and pulled on his B–15 cloth jacket. "Good." And then a new thought struck him, "What is a female, Israeli Air Force pilot doing in Tokyo?"

"She flew in some Israeli officers—a liaison team. I hear one was her boyfriend."

"We're not taking him back?"

"No, Sir. He has duty here."

Brent packed his tunic and shoes into his suitcase and picked up three pairs of gloves. Already warm and uncomfortable, he decided not to put them on. He stuffed his wool scarf into his pocket. "And you, Corporal, why are you here? You're flying for the Israeli Air Force, but you're an American, aren't you?"

Knudsen laughed. "Raised right in the heartland, Commander. My father owns an Iowa wheat farm."

Brent looked the young man up and down. Short, he

was broad with a look of strength about him, his shock of thick curly hair the color of his father's crop. His face was lean but his jaw was squared by determination, eyes a weird reddish–blue with a devilish glint to them as if he found the whole world one big macabre joke. There was something unsettling in those depths. "Why did you enlist?"

A rare grim expression crossed his face. "For the same reason you fight them, Commander."

"That takes in a lot of territory."

"I know I look like the all–American boy, Commander, but there was a Jew in my family woodpile. My maternal grandmother was a Russian Jew." Knudsen palmed some errant strands of hair away from those strange eyes. "You've heard of Babi Yar, Commander?"

Brent knew what was coming. He said simply, "A ravine outside of Kiev."

"The German's helped landscape it with my grandmother, her two brothers, a sister, and six of their children. They shot them and threw them in with 33,000 others. Did a nice job of leveling and grading."

"Your grandfather?"

"He was a gentile."

"That never meant much to the Germans. They slaughtered millions of Russians. Slavs. *Untermenschen.* "He must've been Russian."

Knudsen nodded. "Right. My grandfather worked his way south to Yugoslavia with my mother—she was only six or seven. He fought with Tito and at the end of the war, they immigrated to the U.S."

Brent locked his small suitcase with two sharp snapping

sounds. Without looking up, he said, "You never knew your grandmother."

"True."

"But it's enough."

"Yes. It's enough. My mother never let me forget. Hers was a livid, undying kind of hatred that consumed her like acid till the day she died. I'm sure it killed her as dead as Zyklon B, just another dead *juden* for Hitler." He fingered his jaw, long and hard, pulling his mouth to the side. "I want to do something, anything to help Israel. It's the Jews'—no, it's our only hope. If the Arabs win, there'll be more Babi Yars."

Brent looked the gunner in the eye. They were fiery, the red hue crowding out the blue. It was like looking into the open doors of a crematorium.

Chapter III

It was not easy to enter the Liberator. "Bull" Ware, Devora Hacohen, Horace Burnside, Michael Shaked, Kennosuke Torisu, and Philipe D'Meziere entered the forward part of the aircraft by climbing through the bomb bay. With the curtain–like bomb bay doors rolled up, the six crewmen hunched down almost double to clear the low–hanging belly, and then entered by grasping the bomb bay catwalk and pulling themselves up. Clearing the catwalk, they moved forward on a narrow deck above the four auxiliary tanks which were mounted in pairs on each side. The space was so cramped, they were forced to hold their parachutes before them.

Brent, Roland Knudsen, Efrayim Mani, and Oren Smadja entered through a door in the rear of the aircraft. There was a lot of huffing and puffing as the men, burdened by flight clothes and parachutes, went to their stations.

Brent dropped his parachute on a small stool that folded out from the side and sagged down. He was sweating.

"You'll cool off, Commander," Knudsen said, grinning. Obviously, his good humor was back.

"I know." Brent squirmed on the little seat. "Not very comfortable."

Roland laughed. "Hell, Commander, that stool has been added and so has the safety belt."

Brent shook his head. "I can't believe it. Then during WW–Two they stood up? No belts?"

"I guess, so, Commander. Or sat on the floor."

"I'll be damned." Brent fingered the belt. "No good in a scrap."

"Get in the way. Got to take it off, anyway, Commander. Guess that's why they never bothered to wear them."

Brent ran a professional eye over the loaded fifty–caliber Browning which was inboard, pointed aft and locked down. There was a windowed panel in the gun–port. He checked the breech by pulling the cocking handle back slightly and assuring himself a round was in the firing chamber. The safety was on and the lay of the flexible metal feed belt in its 110–round box was perfect. A snag meant a jam. A jam could be fatal. He hoped he would leave the panel in place and never swing the gun out. But, he was ready.

He tested the four locks on the panel. Brent sighed with relief. Soon, winds of Arctic temperatures would be storming past the bomber and he would be happy for the smothering flight clothes and the panel. But now he was hot and uncomfortable. Carefully, he adjusted and fastened his parachute and seat belt. Watching him, Knudsen smiled his approval.

"You've been this route before, Commander. You know the Browning."

"We're well acquainted, Corporal." Knudsen nodded and turned to his own equipment.

Brent stared at his hands. He was confused by the gloves. First he had pulled on a pair of thin silk gloves, then wool gloves and finally leather gloves over all. When he had flown on *Yonaga*'s Aichis he had worn a single pair of wool–lined gauntlets. "Why three pairs of gloves, Corporal?" he asked.

Busy checking his electrical and oxygen leads, Knudsen looked up. "If your gun jams, Commander, you have to peel off the first two pairs because you just can't work on one of these Brownings with all those bulky gloves."

"Good idea. We should do that with *Yonaga*'s gunners." Brent tapped his head in mock frustration. "Of course. Of course. What's wrong with me? Must be my age." They both laughed.

Brent plugged in his leads and checked the oxygen pressure in his emergency bottle. If the plane's supply failed, he would need it. Even the Liberator could reach altitudes where a man without oxygen could lose consciousness in seconds and be a corpse in minutes. Then he pulled his earphones over his head, covering only his right ear. He noticed Knudsen did the same with his earphones. This way, the gunners could talk to each other, yet hear the pilot or even transmissions from other aircraft if they wished to switch circuits.

Brent threw a switch marked "Number One" and immediately Ware's voice filled his right earphone. "Start the lawn mower!"

There was the sound of a tiny Briggs and Stratton engine coming to life in the front of the plane.

"Lawn mower, Sergeant?" Brent asked.

"That's the 'putt, putt', Commander. It's a small generator that feeds juice to the energizers. It'll be secured when the engines kick over."

Devora's voice obviously reading a check list: "All switches off, fuel quadrants off, throttles full back, fine pitch, full rich mixture."

Ware: "Engineer?"

"Instruments normal, Colonel," Sergeant Michael Shaked answered.

There was a whine of an energizer. Ware's voice: "Standby to goose the old bird." There was a pause. Then Ware returned, "Okay! Start her up!"

Brent could hear Devora's high voice over the whining energizer. She was shouting out her window at some of the ground crew. "Stand clear of Three! Stand clear of Three!"

Leaning close to his window, Brent saw a man with an extinguisher run clear of the engine. Corporal Knudsen said to Brent, "They'll start Number Three first. It has the generator that powers the whole aircraft."

Brent nodded and tightened his seat belt. There was a long pause and silence in the intercom.

Ware's voice: "Kick her in, damn it, what in hell are you waiting for."

"No way to talk to a lady," Knudsen said. Brent laughed.

The copilot's voice, "Starting Three."

With a bellow of throaty power that shook the aircraft, Number Three engine roared to life. Then quickly tamed by a reduced throttle, the big Pratt and Whitney dropped to a pulsing idle. More commands, whines, explosions of brutal controlled power as the other engines burst into life. Brent could see blue smoke and an occasional back-fire shoot back from engines Three and Four. The noise was thunderous, but not overwhelming. The panel helped.

Knudsen yelled, "They always start a Twenty–Four in the same order—Three, Four, Two, One."

"Got it."

"We'll probably warm up as we taxi. That's what Ware usually does. Saves fuel."

Ware's voice: "Tower, this is *Shady Lady*. Request taxi-ing instructions."

"*Shady Lady,* make a sharp left. Taxi to the end of Runway 22."

Brent heard Ware repeat the instructions and suddenly the big bomber began to crawl across the ground. She moved slowly, bobbing on her tricycle landing gear much like a small boat at sea. The simile brought a smile to Brent's face.

Finally, after at least six minutes of taxiing, Ware stopped the bomber and fixed the brakes. During their long run down the strip, a DC–3 and two Constellations took off, racing just a few feet from Brent's window.

Ware's voice: "We're next. Run 'em up and cut in the turbos."

Slowly, Number Three was run up to full throttle. When it seemed the engine was about to burst, the turbo was cut in, whining like an afflicted banshee. The pilot's voice: "Check magnetos!"

The copilot: "One and Two okay."

41

"Good."

Then, the other three engines were run up and the same procedure followed.

Brent tapped his left ear and shook his head. Knudsen laughed. "It'll be over in a minute, Commander."

Suddenly all four engines were throttled back and the screeching turbos fell silent. Ware's voice: "She's a ready teddy."

"Okay here," Devora said.

"Gauges normal," Shaked said.

"Okay," Ware said. "Copilot, cowl, 'putt putt' and the rest of it."

Again, it sounded like Devora was reading a check list: "Putt putt off, cowl flaps closed, bomb bay doors closed, 40–degrees of flaps, fine pitch, full rich."

Ware was all business: "Good. Tower, this is *Shady Lady*. Ready to take off."

"You're cleared for Runway 22, *Shady Lady*."

Brent felt the big plane move ahead and pick up speed as they turned sharply to the right, crawled forward for a moment and made another right turn. The big bird paused as if gathering herself for her final leap into the heavens.

"Pilot to crew!" Suddenly, Ware's voice became a burlesque of all concerned fathers: "Buckle up for safety, kiddies." Then he barked, "Tighten your seat belts, assholes and any other part of your anatomy you may be concerned about. Hang on! Here we go!"

Ware pushed all four throttles forward and the four engines snarled in happy unison like a dog guarding a bone. The pilot released the brakes, the bomber lurched and then bustled down the runway. Gaining speed, *Shady*

Lady skimmed over the concrete. She began to lighten as her Davis wing cut into the air, and finally became unstuck from the ground.

Brent watched as the land pulled away, houses and roads appeared, cars, people looking up. Some pointed. There were thumps as the gear was pulled up and locked into its wells. They were on their way.

Ware's voice, singing in a croaky basso profundo, "Off we go, into the wild blue yonder . . . ."

Brent and Knudsen looked at each other. Then they both broke into laughter.

"He's happy," Knudsen finally managed.

"He's nineteen again."

"Still living it, isn't he?"

"They all do," Brent answered. He turned to the window.

Chapter IV

On a southeasterly heading, *Shady Lady* lumbered higher and higher. "Bull" Ware's singing carried him only through the first few bars of "Wild Blue Yonder" before he was interrupted by an air traffic controller: *"Shady Lady, contact departure control on one–two–five–point-two."*

Ware's voice: "This is *Shady Lady,* opening frequency one–two–five–point–two." Then the circuits became busy with the instructions of controllers and the responses of Ware and Devora Hacohen.

Passing over the great sprawl of Tokyo, Brent's mind was filled with thoughts of this strange land, his second home. He was looking down on a city of 12,000,000 souls, Japan's New York, Washington, Chicago, Los Angeles and San Francisco all rolled into one. This was the seat of government, nation's business capital, center for international finance, education, communications, transportation and fashion.

Staring at the great green swath of gardens surrounding the Imperial Palace, he remembered something fascinating Oscar Wilde had written many years ago: "The whole of Japan is pure invention." Brent chuckled. He agreed. He had learned during the first months of his duty on *Yonaga* that Japan was a product of the imagination, and the country you saw was the country you had been trained to see. Furthermore, Wilde held that the Japanese were very much like the British. At first reading, this had surprised Brent.

Brent knew that Americans' view of Japan was distorted by the faith that, deep down, the Japanese wanted a society and economy modeled after their own. Brent saw this as nonsense. Every important American–style change in Japan had been made while staring into the barrel of a gun or under the threat of trade sanctions. Wilde's curious contention that the Japanese were not unlike the British began to ring true for Brent.

Both were tea–loving nations with a devotion to gardens, both drove on the left and were damp islands studded with green villages. Further similarities were found in rigid class systems, advocacy of a code of stoical reticence, and pride in their isolated monarchies with more than a touch of xenophobia.

Brent grinned, thinking of both peoples' proclivity for not meaning what they said, the vast distances that separated politeness from true feeling, and the way everything was couched in a kind of code in which nuances were everything. He had found these commonalities in two nations on the opposite sides of the planet. How ironic.

He chuckled out loud. But Knudsen could not hear him over the noise of the engines and the rush of slipstream.

Of course he had found differences, too, unique and eccentric traits that set the Japanese as a land apart. It seemed to Brent the Japanese were pathologically attached to the status quo and irresistibly drawn to disaster, accidents, quixotic gestures and generalized foul–ups. He had dealt with Japanese businessmen who were as reluctant as a nun on a date simply because they were dealing with an American. And, certainly, they were not always cool and in control. Every day some Japanese fell into a volcano or was swept off a beach by a wave. The inevitability of fate was accepted without a step back from the rim, a quick retreat from the shore.

And he had learned almost immediately that the Japanese lived in a jungle of inconsistencies. Here was a people who fawned politely when sipping tea with you, yet in the commuter trains would run you over like stampeding cattle; said yes when they meant no; read their books back to front; wore white to funerals; were born to Shinto rites and interred to the chants of Buddhist monks.

At first Brent had been shocked by the way the Japanese actually thrived on contradictions. "The more the contradictions, the stronger the man," Brent had heard Fujita and many of the senior officers say. Protean contradictions were part and parcel of their philosophies, religions, burnishing their karmas so that the warrior could more easily pass through the gates of the Yasakuni Shrine and reach the highest planes of nirvana.

A controller's voice jolted Brent out of his musings. "*Shady Lady,* right to heading 280. You are entering *Yonga*'s air space. Her CAP will intercept you. I repeat, turn right to heading 280 immediately and maintain an altitude of 4,000 feet."

Brent had just heard Ware's acknowledgment, when the three fighters shot into view. The tail gunner, Efrayim

Mani, was the first to spot them. "Three fighters, five o'clock high, diving, coming in at a high speed."

"Gotcha," Ware said. "We'll fly circles around the ass-holes." The big pilot's laughter filled the intercom.

Looking through the window, Brent craned his neck. Then he saw them; Yoshi Matsuhara, Claude Hooper-man and Elwyn York. Unmistakable. Yoshi's red, green, and white Mitsubishi A6M2 Zero with its brute of a Wright Cyclone R–3350 engine. Hooperman's and York's Seafires clinging to the Zero's elevators. They were diving in a "Vic" like the sharp edge of a wedge.

Now Brent knew why the enemy feared the trio more than any other pilots of Fujita's forces. It was like watching the head of a lance bolting down, a weapon hurled by a vengeful Almighty. Moving at a speed that was at least twice that of the bomber's, they flashed past the Libera-tor's tail. Perfectly synchronized, they pulled up sharply, and shot skyward, twisting into a slow roll as they passed Brent's window. They held their formation flawlessly as if one mind were controlling all three. As a youth, Brent had seen the Navy's precision team, the Blue Angels. Yoshi and his Englishmen flew with even greater precision. Then, as they turned, Brent saw the three pilots grin and salute the bomber.

Brent felt elation swell warmly in his chest and clog in his throat. Swallowing was a struggle. His best friend, Commander Yoshi Matsuhara, making a final gesture of farewell. Yoshi an original member of *Yonaga*'s crew and the oldest fighter pilot on earth. But, still youthful in appearance, lightning quick in reflexes and arguably the best fighter pilot on earth. He was certainly the most feared in Fujita's forces. His 71 kills infuriated Kadafi and he, too, carried a $1,000,000 bounty.

Brent waved and shouted, *"Banzai! Banzai!"* while the three fighters climbed into the sun and vanished into a sheet of high clouds. Losing sight of the fighters, Brent felt his joy slough away, replaced by a great sadness as if he had lost his friends forever. Of course, the feeling was nonsense, but the depression remained.

Knudsen looked at him curiously. "Friends of yours?"

"The best in the world."

"Queer looking Zero."

"It should be. It has the same engine that powered the B-29."

"Heard about it. Shouldn't fly. Should be nose heavy." And then slyly, "Your friend rewrote the textbook of aeronautics, Commander."

"He knows the Zero better than any man alive." Brent explained how Yoshi Matsuhara had personally supervised the rebuilding of the Zero, the strengthening of the airframe, installation of armor and an additional fuel tank behind the cockpit to counterbalance the brute in the nose.

Knudsen shook his head and shrugged. "Must work and work real well. Shot past us like a rocket."

"He was only idling. Should see it when he opens the throttle."

Knudsen laughed. "Those Seafires couldn't keep up with him, Commander."

"Nothing can."

"Glad they're on our side."

"Amen, Corporal."

The young gunner rose against his belt. "There's the

carriers and *New Jersey,*" Knudsen said excitedly, pointing down.

Brent unlocked his belt and stood behind Roland. Clearly visible far below at their moorings at Yokosuka was Fujita's battle group; carriers *Yonaga* and *Bennington,* battleship *New Jersey,* and eight of the thirteen destroyers of the escort group. Brent felt pride swell and the warm feeling returned. He was looking at his home—the place where he had found camaraderie with some of the finest men on earth. Suddenly, the bomber seemed very alien.

Knudsen said, "Took a little mauling in the Med, last year, Commander."

Returning to his seat, Brent cleared his throat and said, "Most of it's been repaired. They're almost ready for sea." Knudsen nodded silently.

Brent's glimpse of *Yonaga* opened the gates of nostalgia. *What an incredible odyssey,* ran through his mind. *Yonaga's* forty–two–year entrapment in an Arctic cove; the breakout in 1983; the carrier's attack on Pearl Harbor; the triumphant entry into Tokyo Bay only to learn the war had ended 37 years earlier; the outright hostility when he and Admiral Mark Allen had reported aboard as NIC liaison officers in 1983, the same day the Chinese orbited their laser system. The chaos, the emergence of second and third world powers. Kadafi literally floating on oil dollars and building his mad *jihad.*

A new voice on the intercom intruded. Apparently, they had been passed along to other controllers. "*Shady Lady,* turn left to heading 080, flight level two–four–zero. Good luck, *Shady Lady,* and *banzai!*"

"*Banzai* yourself! Ware said, voice bubbling with good humor. He repeated the order and then the big bomber banked and began a steeper climb. "Bull" began to sing, "We're off to see the wizard . . . ." Fortunately, he only knew the first line, but he repeated it three times.

"A Judy Garland imitation," Knudsen chuckled.

"Flying Officer Hooperman told me RAF pilots used to sing 'Oz' after a scrap during WW–Two," Brent explained. "Ware must've learned it when he flew with the Eighth Air Force."

Knudsen nodded. "He's sure in a good mood."

"He's back home." Brent pinched his nose. "But, what's this flight level two–four–zero, Sergeant?"

"Oh, that means twenty–four–thousand–feet, Commander."

"Why don't they just say so?"

"They're aviators."

"Of course."

Devora's voice: "Altitude seven–thousand."

Ware's voice: "Pilot to crew. We're going upstairs. Better check your masks."

Again, Brent inspected his connections and pressure. Suddenly, sharp pains in his ears caused him to yawn and pound the sides of his head. Small popping sounds brought swift relief. Climbing steadily, the temperature dropped.

He looked down and then into the distance, trying to distract himself. By now, he estimated they were at least 9,000–feet high, giving him a horizon of over a 100–miles. The view was majestic. With the Bōsō Peninsula below, he could still see as far north as Tsuchiura, west to the Izu Peninsula, observe all of Tokyo Bay with the congestion of Odawara, Yokosuka, Yokohama, Chiba and Tokyo crowding the water. Rows of houses lay like tiny boxes packed together, roadways glistening with cars like crawling insects. A pall of smoke hung over the ant heap.

Over it all towered Fujisan, stoic and regal in the distance. There was a refreshing breath from the mountains, looming behind the cities and running the length of island like a spine with broken vertebrae. Here there were tall, green, thick stands of trees, deep valleys, rugged outcroppings of rocks. And the air was clear and clean. Brent looked ahead to the sea and sky.

Raising himself from the small seat as far as his safety belt would permit, he stared down. Ravaged by wind and tide, the seashore looked like a broken sawtooth. White beaches marked the division of sea and land as if a drunken giant had drawn a chalk line between worlds of white and blue. To the east the Pacific matched infinity with the sky. The ocean was dark blue, nearly cobalt, and the curvature of the earth was quite apparent on the unbroken horizon.

The sun played tricks with the sea, reflecting from the corrugated surface in isolated flashes, patches, and sometimes long trails. It was like looking at a blue-velvet tray of gemstones held by a salesman with palsy. Brent chuckled at his fanciful notions and looked up. The sun was playing games with the clouds, too.

Above, a milky scum of thin cirrus glared white in the sun like ripped gauze, while far below small gobs of cumulus hung motionless as if they were puffy, permanent fixtures. Despite the high cirrus, the sun was a bright ball of fire, casting shadows of the low clouds, making dark footprints on the sea. At times like these he knew why Yoshi and the other pilots loved the sky.

The hazy white clouds seemed to intensify the glare of the sun. An ideal hiding place for fighters. A Messerschmitt Bf-109 had a service ceiling of almost 40,000-feet. Brent sighed. There would be no fighters here. But, over the Mediterranean there was a good chance they would lurk high in the sun. "Look out for the Arab in the sun," he had heard Yoshi Matsuhara warn his pilots many times. Soon, it would be his turn to heed that warning; especially, in "the gap."

The plane droned on, gaining altitude steadily. Insidiously, the cold crept in and Brent turned up the rheostat on his suit. He thanked a variety of gods for the electrically-heated suit and boots. Without them, he would be freezing to death. Yet, he was not as warm as he felt he should be. Time crawled. Brent's brain felt the fatigue that ached the rest of his body. It had been a very long day, starting before dawn. His chin dropped to his chest. Devora's voice broke through: "Sixteen-thousand-feet, Colonel."

Brent felt a draft. Air was leaking in from somewhere. *Shady Lady* was also *Drafty Lady*. Despite the suit, he could feel the clammy hands of freezing air beginning to grip him. Shaking the malaise away, he rubbed his arms and his legs, trying to massage the aches away. It was useless, and he knew it, but he did it anyway out of habit. He felt slightly giddy. Took deep breaths.

Roland's voice: "Cold, Commander?"

"A little. But it would be a lot worse without this suit."

The young man laughed. "It's only 40-degrees below zero, Sir. A man could freeze his balls off—clank right across the floor like Queeg's ball bearings."

Light-headedness brought on whimsy, "Is that all.

Forty—degrees. I thought it was cold." Then seriously, "Aren't there any heaters in this old bird, Corporal?"

"Seven, Commander. But none of them work."

"Naturally. Don't want to spoil the crew with too many creature comforts."

Devora's voice: "Seventeen—thousand—feet."

Ware's voice: "Pilot to crew, better put on your masks and breathe the sweet ambrosia, unless you want to take a permanent nap."

Slipping the mask over his mouth, Brent snapped it in place and adjusted it. He turned the valve to "On." Immediately, his mouth was filled with the harsh metallic taste of pure oxygen. He disliked the mask. Oxygen always irritated his throat and the plastic warred with his stubble.

The plane plodded higher, the temperature plunged. Passing through 20,000—feet the cold struck with new vengeance like a death wish. It seeped in under his scarf, up his sleeves, even seemed to penetrate the zippers. He turned the rheostat up. He was still cold. Either the suit was defective or the plane's electrical system was malfunctioning. Brent queried Knudsen.

"My suit's okay," the gunner answered. "Check your connections, Sir."

A quick check showed every connection properly made. Brent shook his head in disgust. He would not whimper anymore. "Okay. Okay," he said to a concerned, puzzled Roland. If the young gunner could take it, so could he.

Gripping his arms, he squared his jaw and leaned against the panel, pressed his boots against the boards. The cold made his exhaustion more than painful, it drained the strength he needed to concentrate. Suddenly, he found the idea of flying in a warm, pressurized commercial airliner with cushioned seats very appealing. He tried to take his mind off his misery. *Think of something warm*, he told himself.

He concentrated on the subject most distracting to men. Nothing was warmer than Ruth Moskowitz. How could a man forget that night in Tel Aviv's Maxim Hotel. Maybe he would see her again. He would certainly look her up. He shook his head and chuckled, remembering how shocked he had been to discover Ruth was the niece of Sarah Aranson. Sarah Aranson. He had bedded Sarah for a record-setting night in 1984 only two blocks from the Maxim. The two women resembled each other, but he never suspected. He laughed into his oxygen mask and immediately regretted it.

His fast–growing whiskers rubbed against his mask, producing an itching he could not reach without removing the mask. He pulled the mask aside and scratched his jaw with long, luxurious strokes like a dog pursuing an annoying flea. He sighed, long and happily. Replacing the mask, he sank back while Knudsen nodded, pulled his mask aside, grinned and scratched his own jaw.

They were headed east and north on a great circle course that would terminate at Oahu. But they would spend at least twenty hours in the air. He looked at his watch. Only an hour–and–a–half had passed. It was going to be an ordeal, a very boring, frigid ordeal. He ran a glove over the barrel of the Browning. He almost wished there were some Arab fighters around. And then he laughed and said to himself, "No. That's no way to fight boredom. Better to be bored to death than shot to death."

He looked to the north. Now his horizon was almost 180-miles, but there was nothing out there but empty sea. From here, a man could only begin to grasp the enormity of the world's greatest ocean—over 68,000,00 square miles of it. Iwo Jima was up there, somewhere. Just south of the island, they had met an Arab task force. Here they had sunk carrier *Al Kufra* and lost hundreds of their finest men.

To the south was Tomonuto Atoll and off her entrance submarine *Blackfin* rested. Entombed in her were Commander Reginald Williams and 83 other fine young men. South and west they had fought enemy battle groups in the Malacca Straits and the South China Sea where a damaged *Yonaga* engaged two cruisers in a surface battle. Here, Captain Fite led his destroyers in a desperate torpedo attack to save the carrier. *Yonaga* was saved, but Captain Fite lost four of his *Fletchers*.

The battle had been carried all over the world. North Korea, off Gibraltar, the Mediterranean twice, the Carolines, Marianas, Sea of Japan, Yellow Sea. Brent shook his head despairingly. The battles had been sprawling, bloody, incessant and it looked like they would never end. Thousands of the world's finest young men rotted in the black depths; the bright, the witty, the brave. They were always the first to fight, the first to go. It seemed war fed on war, a cancer that grew without bound and fed on itself in a perpetual circle like a snake devouring its own tail.

He settled back against the gun. The breech was hard and uncomfortable. Funny, a gun made him uncomfortable. But, then, guns made the whole world uncomfortable. Chuckling at his wit, he leaned his head against the window. It vibrated. He sighed, a deep rasping sound, pulled his legs up and wrapped his arms across his chest. He was desperately tired and the cold made him drowsy. Despite the vibrations, the cold, the gun, the harsh thoughts faded and his eyelids became very heavy.

He fell into a light, uneasy sleep.

Chapter V

Brent was thankful when Ware dropped *Shady Lady* to 14,000–feet. This was too low to benefit from the prevailing jet stream, but the westerlies gave her an added boost, increasing her cruising speed to almost 250 miles–an–hour. Following Roland Knudsen's example, Brent unclipped his mask and let it dangle on his chest, breathing sweet, clean air. Happily, he scratched both cheeks and rubbed his jaw. Then fatigue took over. Completely exhausted, he drowsed for hours, turning and grunting to near wakefulness only once when a strong hand pulled him back and something soft was pushed between him and the Browning. Finally, when he did awaken, the magic aroma of coffee did it. He stretched, trying to ease the aches that seemed to sting everywhere.

The cold was still severe but not nearly as brutal as it had been further north and at 24,000–feet. He mumbled thanks to God. Still, he felt as if he had submitted to cryogenics and was just being thawed out. "Need a microwave," he muttered to himself.

He had been tempted to complain to "Bull" Ware, but

decided against it. He was the "Yankee Samurai" and samurai did not whine about temperature. The other members of the crew must have been cold, too. He would not, could not, show weakness. He rolled to the side, raised his head. It was then he realized someone had placed a pillow between him and the hard breech.

"Thanks, Corporal," he said to Knudsen, coming erect and trying to yawn the drowsiness away.

Knudsen shook his head and said, "Don't thank me, Commander. Lieutenant Hacohen passed them out." He held up his own pillow. "And she made you comfy."

Brent smiled. "I'll be damned. The feminine touch."

"Every war should have it, Commander."

"Can't argue with that."

In his other hand the gunner held a mug of hot coffee. A thermos was on a small plastic tray at his feet next to two sandwiches in plastic wrappers. "Coffee, Sir?"

"Please, Corporal. Black."

Roland poured the coffee and held it out. "Yours, Commander, and an egg–salad sandwich."

"No ham?"

"Not on this flight, Commander."

"Just the coffee, Sergeant." Taking the mug, Brent sipped the black liquid and sighed. He felt the cold dispel. "Lord, like a transfusion." He held the mug up, "That thermos couldn't keep it this hot all the way from Tokyo."

"We have a hot plate up front. Lieutenant Hacohen made it and served it."

"I'll be damned, first class service."

"And a stacked flight attendant, Commander."

Brent had an impulse to upbraid the corporal for his candid remark about a superior officer. This was the second time it had happened. True, the Israelis were very informal and far more democratic than the Navy or *Yonaga*. But, sometimes, Knudsen balanced precariously on the line. However, at the moment, he felt more like a fellow gunner than the "by-the-book" officer. There was a tangible ambience of parity in the big bomber. He felt it the moment the wheels left the ground and he was sure it would persist as long as they were airborne. Up here every member of the crew was completely dependent on the others for his survival. Ware was indisputably in command. There had been no disrespect; not a hint of insubordination. But, the rigorous formality of *Yonaga* was missing. Brent smiled to himself. He rather liked it. And the copilot *did* have a great body. He unwrapped his sandwich.

Ware's voice, aping the oily condescension and aplomb of the professional airline pilot: "Aloha, this is your captain speaking. Our ETA in Honolulu is 2245 local time, yesterday. So, relax in your luxurious accommodations and let us pamper you with our gourmet cuisine and peerless service. You'll be delighted to know weather reports are good, skies clear, so we should have a lovely flight. The surf is up, beaches crowded with maidens sporting their bikinis and the natives are friendly. Aloha!"

"Liberte pour the crew, no?" Philipe D'Meziere chided.

"All hands. Unrestricted leave for two full hours and you can go anywhere you wish as long as you don't leave the base."

There were desultory cheers. Brent chuckled. The man was a master psychologist. The entire crew was relaxed, confident and as comfortable as the miserable conditions would allow.

The voice of Lieutenant Horace Burnside: "I say, Colonel Ware. We have a bit of a tail wind."

"Right you are," Ware answered, mimicking the Englishman's accent.

"Well, Sir, by your leave, I suggest ETA 2235."

"Sorry, old chap," Ware said, continuing his crisp imitation. "I swear on the strength and vigor of Charles' and Di's conjugal bed, 2245."

"Respectfully, Sir, I beg to differ—2235."

"For a buck? A quid?"

"Righto, Sir. A wager. One dollar American."

Efrayim Mani's eager voice. "A pool, Sir?"

"Why not. It'll cost you a buck?"

"Twenty-two-thirty," the tail gunner said.

"You're on and *mazel tov*—good luck. Anyone else."

Quickly, every member of the crew picked a time. Brent chose 2237.

"Okay," Ware finally said. "The copilot has recorded all the bets and placed them in a sealed envelope. The payments will be made when we land at Honolulu. Welshers will be thrown out at 20,000-feet."

There was a chorus of approval.

Brent finished his sandwich and glanced at his watch. They still had about 10 hours of flying time left. He felt an urgent pressure low in his abdomen and looked around anxiously.

Knudsen smiled and pointed to a tube held against the side of the aircraft by a bracket. "It's there, Sir." He stood and pulled his own tube free and unzipped his flight suit.

Grunting, Brent stood, ran his zipper down and pulled

the tube to his groin. Then he discovered how cold it could be at 14,000–feet. Roland chuckled good–naturedly. "Hurry, Sir. A guy could freeze off his social life up here."

Brent felt relief immediately. Steam rose from the tube as 98–degree liquid was whipped into the slip stream. Brent began to chuckle. The situation was ridiculous and Roland's mood infectious. Hurriedly, the young gunner pulled up his zipper. "Almost lost Queeg's ball bearings, Sir."

"Frostbite could disappoint a lot of women, Corporal," Brent said, running his own zipper up.

"A multitude, Sir."

"According to Wilt Chamberlain, 20,000."

"Is that all, Commander? Those basketball players are undersexed."

"Obviously. They run it off on the court."

Laughing, they both returned to their stools.

Brent sank back against the pillow and closed his eyes, relieved by the discarded mask, full stomach and empty bladder. Gradually, he slipped into a fuzzy realm somewhere between sleep and sentience. The steady pounding of the engines was almost hypnotic, however, the persistent cold and cramped position made a true deep sleep impossible. Time droned on with the engines.

Ware's voice broke through: "This old time machine just crossed the International Date Line. Set your watches back 24 hours."

Brent smiled and dozed. Knudsen was making strange noises. Then, Brent realized to his amazement that the gunner was snoring. "Incredible," he said to himself. "A miracle."

The hours dragged. Brent curled with his knees pulled up. "Haven't been in this position since I left my mother's womb," he told himself. It was not nearly as cold as it had been just an hour earlier. He managed to drop off, sleep falling like a dropped shroud. Time crept by, interrupted by another sandwich—melted cheese—but served by the Englishman, Lieutenant Horace Burnside.

"I say, a bit of refreshment for you chaps," he said, handing the sandwiches to the waist gunners. This time the mugs steamed with hot chocolate.

"Better than the Savoy Grill," Brent said, unwrapping his sandwich.

"Kosher?" Roland asked with mock gravity.

"Blessed it myself," Burnside answered.

The gunners finished their snack. Brent looked out, but found nothing but blackness below. He looked up. With the air clean and crystalline clear, he saw a wondrous panoply of glistening stars. It was spectacular, reserved only for those who dare to venture high above the foul air. Andromeda blazed just south of Cassiopeia and between Pegasus and Perseus. His old friends Sirius, Betelgeuse, the Dippers, and Polaris were easy to pick out. Venus glowed with a steady light. He smiled to himself sardonically. The stars and planets were wasting their light. Navigators didn't need them anymore. Machines were even eliminating the cosmos.

He shifted his weight. He was sure the Browning had forged a groove in his buttock. "Turn the other cheek," he told himself. Twisting, he finally found a semblance of comfort. Whiskers, mask, cold vibrations, boredom. He found himself wishing he were back on *Yonaga*, anywhere except in this terribly uncomfortable war bird. He nodded off again and the hours dragged by.

Ware's crisp order to Devora, "Open circuit HF 406.5," brought Brent out of his stupor.

Copilot: "Ready to transmit on HF 406.5."

Ware's voice became unequivocally military, jarring Brent into full wakefulness: "Honolulu Radio, this is *Shady Lady*. Longitude one–five–eight, altitude one–four–thousand."

"*Shady Lady* this is Honolulu Radio, squawk 2468."

Ware: "Honolulu Radio, this is *Shady Lady*. Adjusting transponder to 2468."

"*Shady Lady*, this is Honolulu Radio. I have you on radar at 140–miles."

"Roger."

Brent twisted in his seat, eager to catch a glimpse of one of the islands. Maybe the big island, Maui or Molokai. They were in the tropics and flying at a lower altitude. Now he knew why he felt warmer. Still, he saw nothing but the stars above and the blackness of the sea below. Thirty minutes passed before the anxious American commander heard the radio come to life with Ware's voice: "Honolulu Radio, this is *Shady Lady*. Request lower altitude."

"Thank God," Brent muttered. In the east he could see the lights of Honolulu and Waikiki sparkling like a swarm of fireflies.

"*Shady Lady*, this is Honolulu Radio. You are cleared to descend and maintain one–one–thousand. Contact Approach Control on VHF 119.5."

"Roger Honolulu Radio. *Shady Lady* descending to

one–one–thousand. "I'm 20–miles out. Have airport in sight. Request visual approach."

A new voice rasped in Brent's earphones, *"Shady Lady,* this is Approach Control. Turn left to heading zero–eight–zero. Descend to 4,000."

Brent sighed with relief as he felt the big bird drop her nose and lose altitude in big chunks. And the beat of the engines slowed. He said to Knudsen, "Visual approach. I thought we had the best instruments in the world."

The gunner shrugged, "He's old–fashioned. Still likes to fly by the seat of his pants."

Only minutes passed before a controller's voice returned to his earphones: *"Shady Lady* this is Approach Control. You are cleared for visual approach on Runway Eight–Right."

"Well, they trust him," Brent said.

Knudsen chuckled, "He's good, Commander. Very good."

Brent looked down. He saw the lights of several ships. They were very low.

Ware repeated the command. "Eight–Right, I'm 8–miles out." The engines were throttled back to a slow burble and the big plane continued to sink.

Now the lights of Honolulu and Waikiki stretched like a sparkling sea of polished mica below and to the east. Nearly a million souls lived on this island and they could easily be counted by their lights.

Ware's voice: "Pilot to crew. Prepare to land. The navigator's watch will give the official landing time. So get your money out and get ready to pay off. I can use the money." His voice became professional again as he talked to the copilot, "Fine pitch, full rich."

Brent heard the burble change to a whine as the propellers' pitch was changed to fine and the rpms increased. The aircraft banked. Ware's voice: "Turning into final approach. Gear down. Forty–degrees of flaps."

Devora repeated the orders. Brent felt two thumps as the landing gear was lowered. Devora's voice: "Down and locked."

"Okay. We're going to flare this baby out like a pigeon coming home to roost and then grease her in." A short pause. "Landing lights."

"Lights on."

Now Brent could see runway lights flashing past like a row of bright, glowing sentinels. They were only a few feet from the ground and moving at well over a 100–miles–an–hour. He held his breath.

There was a squeal of tortured rubber contacting concrete and the big plane settled down to earth so gently, Brent could scarcely believe they had made the transition from sky to earth. Without a doubt, he had experienced the smoothest landing of his life. "Great pilot," he said.

"The best," Knudsen agreed. "And that, Commander, is 'greasing her in'."

Brent smiled and nodded. "Got it."

The controller's voice: "*Shady Lady*, contact Ground Control on 118.3.

Ware's voice: "Ground Control, this is *Shady Lady*. Request clearance to taxi to Air Force ramps."

"*Shady Lady* this is Ground Control, your are cleared for Air Force ramp. Taxi to end of strip. Make a sharp left and taxi to Air Force Spot 3."

"Roger, Ground Control." And then to the navigator, "Official time of landing, Lieutenant Torisu?"

"We touched down at 2233."

Ware's voice came directly from the Academy Awards, "Lieutenant Hacohen, the winner in the landing time category, please. Open the envelope, please?"

"Ah, I'm afraid I'm the winner."

There were roars of mock anguish in a variety of languages. There was relief in the voices, the gleeful sound of men who had completed the longest leg of their journey in the ancient bomber and were somewhat surprised to find themselves alive. "Rigged!" *"Shlemiels,"* "It's a scam!" *"Yakuzas!"* "We've been had!" "Mafia conspiracy! We have a godfather and godmother up there." *"Mon dieu!"*

"Okay. Okay, you guys," Ware said in an avuncular tone. "So a woman whipped your butts. It's all equal now, so get used to it. Anyway, the winner has to buy drinks at the local pub."

Cheers.

The big bomber wobbled its way to the end of the runway and then turned sharply to the left.

Chapter VI

A lieutenant named Jack McMurtry followed by four enlisted men met the crew when they disembarked. Though of average height and unremarkable features, McMurtry's mouth was wide and friendly, his smile easy as he saluted Colonel Ware. After introducing himself, he said, gesturing, "We have a conference room reserved for you, Sir."

"Chow?"

"Yes, Sir. The best." He looked at the Israeli Air Force shoulder patch on the colonel's jacket. "And kosher, Sir."

"Good. Good. Some of the crew are devout."

At that moment a gasoline truck rumbled up followed by a six-by-six carrying a half-dozen men. Ware watched as the vehicles stopped next to *Shady Lady*. "Fill her up. Check the oil, water, tires, transmission, differential, clean the windshields and empty the ash trays," Ware said in a grave monotone. "And the air-conditioning needs work. It was entirely too warm up there."

McMurtry narrowed his eyes for a moment, not quite able to pierce the colonel's dead-pan humor. Then he smiled like a man experiencing a revelation, "Of, course, Sir. You did pull into the full–service island."

Ware chuckled and slapped the lieutenant on the back. "Check the heaters," he said, military again. "None of them work. And don't forget our auxiliary tanks in the bomb bay."

"Yes, Sir. Got it."

While *Shady Lady* was gassed and serviced, the crew filed into a small conference room at the base's main building. The crew paid Devora a dollar each and then rushed for the men's room. Brent, faster than the others, managed to use the facilities and return to the conference room where he seated himself at the room's single, long table. Everyone was famished, and by the time the men returned, waiters were waiting with menus. Devora found a chair opposite Brent.

Everyone ordered—steak was the most popular entree—and in a few minutes the meal was consumed. With contented sighs, most of the crew sank back while the table was cleared. Burnside dabbed at his scruffy mustache with his napkin and said, "I say, Colonel, I thought Lieutenant Hacohen was to buy drinks for the whole lot of us with her new–found wealth. I have an insatiable thirst for Dom Perignon."

From the head of the table, Ware stared at the Englishman and smiled, "True, she is the big winner. But, no liquor here, Lieutenant. The payoff will have to wait until we reach Israel."

While most of the men moved to easy chairs scattered around the room, Brent dabbed at his chocolate mousse and stared at Devora. They were the last two at the table. She wore an enigmatic, Mona Lisa smile that made her even more mysterious and attractive. She avoided his eyes and finished the last of a single scoop of sherbet.

"Dom Perignon," she said, smiling guilelessly. She raised her eyes to Brent. "And what would you like, Commander?"

Although the face was a mask of candor, there was something in her expression, the timbre of her voice, that challenged the innocence of the question. Beaming through those marvelous eyes was something unfathomable, enigmatic. He sensed a trap. The question was too heavily ladened with Freudian innuendos. A slow smile spilled across Brent's face. He sidestepped adroitly, "I'll take a Coors Light, Lieutenant."

"Nothing more?"

"I can't think of a thing."

"According to the media, the 'Yankee Samurai' is a . . . ." She paused, studied him for a moment, and then called on a Yiddish word, *"Chutzpanik."*

"Chutzpanik!" He laughed. "I have gall, nerve?"

"Right, and a voracious appetite."

"For what?"

She ran the point of her tongue over her full lips. "For anything hedonistic."

He spoke before thinking, "And you're hedonistic, Lieutenant?"

The great eyes narrowed and Brent regretted his words. "Respectfully, don't be presumptuous, Commander."

Ordinarily, the remark would have had little effect on Brent. He would have turned his back and shrugged it off. However, fatigue and aching muscles had honed his temper, frayed his nerves. His spine stiffened and motes of anger played leapfrog with his vertebrate. He knew she had deliberately tried to lead him on. Nothing could anger him more. "Don't overestimate yourself, Lieutenant," he retaliated sharply. "And don't believe everything you read in those cheap tabloids."

"Pulling rank?" she countered, unperturbed.

Brent showed his knowledge of Yiddish, "Not with an obvious *nudnik*," he retorted, rising and turning his back. She stiffened at the snub and the lovely face hardened.

Colonel Ware called out to Brent, "Commander Ross. Corporal Knudsen told me you were cold."

With Devora's eyes burning into his back, Brent walked to the colonel's easy chair. "Wasn't everyone?"

"No, Commander. You must have one of those defective suits."

Lieutenant McMurtry rushed up. "Colonel, we have spares."

"Extra–large?"

McMurtry looked Brent up and down and nodded affirmatively. "We should have one that will fit the Commander." His eyes narrowed. "Respectfully, Sir. You're Commander Ross, the 'Yankee Samurai'?"

Still smarting from his exchange with Devora, Brent replied bluntly, "Yes, that's what the damned media call me."

McMurtry backed off hastily. "Have the new suit here in a few minutes, Commander." He tried to retrieve the situation with a stab at humor, "This one would fit the Jolly Green Giant, Sir." He looked around. No one laughed.

Brent nodded. "Very well. Get it."

McMurtry left hastily.

* * *

The flight to Dallas began uneventfully. The new flight suit functioned perfectly and Brent knew he would fly in relative comfort regardless of altitude. Thoughts of the smirking Devora Hacohen haunted his mind. He sensed she disliked all Americans. Like many Israelis, she was probably convinced the United States was not providing enough help in their battle against the *jihad*. She had tried to take it out on him. Completely unacceptable. Ironically, he sensed he had aroused her sexually. This could only complicate matters. He was determined to avoid her, snub her whenever he had the chance. She was a bitch with an acid tongue.

The ball turret gunner, Sergeant Oren Smadja, had flown the first leg of the trip in the cockpit where he had sat on a small padded stool next to the engineer. Now, Ware ordered him to a position closer to his gun station, a stool between the waist guns and his own. Soon, he would be forced to spend torturous hours in the cramped ball turret. Brent, Roland Knudsen and Smadja spent the first hour talking.

The ball turret gunner was bursting with questions about *Yonaga*, the battles, life in Japan. He was particularly interested in Brent's face–to–face meeting with Colonel Moammar Kadafi in the dictator's tent the year before. "Lucky you got out of there alive," Smadja said in his guttural English. "You could have been drawn and quartered, skinned, had diseased rats fed up your—ah."

"I know. I know. They did that to Captain Henri DuCarme. Put a 3–inch pipe up his butt and pushed in rats. The gunners grimaced and shook their heads. "But we had to try to negotiate," Brent said. "Hundreds of prisoners' lives are still at stake."

The two young gunners nodded grimly. "You did secure the release of two prisoners," Smadja noted.

"Man—for—man, quid pro quo. A lousy trade. There are hundreds left."

"We have thousands of Arab prisoners."

"I know, Sergeant," Brent said. "But, not even their own leaders place much value on them."

"Makes it hard to negotiate," Knudsen observed.

"And the Arabs have no honor, no integrity," Smadja added. "We Israelis have an old saying, 'One quiet word with a wise man is better than a year of pleading with a fool'."

"How true, Sergeant. Duplicity and dishonesty are not in short supply in the Arab's tent." The enlisted men chuckled.

Brent asked Smadja about his background. "I'm a *sabra*—native Israeli—born in Kefat, a small village about 15 kilometers from Haifa," the sergeant answered.

"*Sabra* means prickly pear," Brent offered. The two young men looked at him in surprise.

"Not many people know that," Smadja said.

"Thank you, Sergeant," Brent said. "I spent a lot of time in Israel on two different assignments. And my friend Colonel Bernstein once told me, 'The fruit of the cactus is hard and prickly on the outside and soft and sweet on the inside. That's a *Sabra*'." Brent glanced at the ball turret gunner.

"Thank you, Sir. I hope the Arabs never find me too sweet." Everyone laughed.

"You were in aeronautical engineering," Brent noted.

"Yes, Sir. In the Weizmann Institute of Science in

Rehovot for four years and I was sent to your MIT by the government for graduate work. I spent a year there."

Brent whistled. "Certainly, you could've been commissioned."

The young man shrugged. "It makes no difference, Commander. I am a good gunner and learned my trade in the turret of a North American B–25 Mitchell. I have two-and-a-half enemy fighters to my credit." He waved. "And I love these old planes." His tone became wistful, "When I was very young, I built a scale model of this very same bomber and it could fly."

"And you never dreamed you would fly in one?"

"Not in a million years. And you, too, Commander."

"True."

Ware's voice interrupted: We're going upstairs." Everyone groaned. "Sorry. Lots of Commercial traffic. We've been ordered to 26,000. Check your masks we're passing through 17,000."

The order effectively put a halt to the conversation. The three gunners adjusted their masks and leaned back. Brent took a deep breath and almost gagged. He sighed it out and slouched back against the machine gun. He enjoyed talking to the young men. Time passed faster that way. But now, nothing—nothing at all to break the boredom. There was still sea and sky, but they always looked the same. Anyway, it was still dark outside. At least his suit worked. He was actually warm. He began to doze off.

An unscheduled stop was made at the Los Angeles International Airport. Ware called it LAX. *Shady Lady* had hit a head wind, her speed had been reduced and fuel consumption increased. Torisu recommended landing and refueling. It was 1400 hours when they approached the California coast with the chatter of controllers in their ears.

During the approach, Brent stared hungrily down at Southern California—at his country. He had not seen his homeland since 1989 when he flew across the continent to New York to report to submarine *Blackfin*. Memories of his dead shipmates made an acid mixer of his stomach and he found himself sniffling into his mask. He pushed it aside and wiped his nose.

They flew over Santa Barbara, inland and turned south and then west. Brent thought he recognized San Bernardino and then the great urban sprawl of Los Angeles began sliding by beneath them. And what a spectacle it was. Millions of people lived below. Their houses clumped like warrens, cars, freeways, parks crowded the landscape. There was power there. Vitality. He suddenly felt very proud and terribly homesick. They touched down at 1500 hours.

The stopover at LAX was for less than two hours. Brent did not say a word to Devora. They were in the air by seventeen–hundred–hours on a course for Dallas. Again, they were assigned to 26,000–feet. Brent remained glued to his window as long as the light held out. That was his country below and he stared like a starving man surveying a gourmet meal. He noticed Roland doing the same. He was sure they shared the same feelings.

When they arrived in Dallas, it was almost 1900 hours and dark. Again, a quick meal, refueling and they were in the air by 2100.

Ware's voice: "Next stop Fort Lauderdale. It's smaller

than Miami and much more convenient. We'll have a six-hour layover." Brent found himself cheering with the rest of the crew. "Our ETA is 0130."

Immediately a new pool was created. Brent chose 0123. They landed at precisely 0135."

"And the winner, please."

"Ah, I'm afraid I won again, Colonel," Devora said as the big plane taxied to a far corner of the airport.

More screams of anguish and claims of fraud.

While the bomber was being serviced, the crew was led to a room adjacent to the main concourse where there was a dining area and cots. Despite the hour, a small kitchen was fully manned and everyone ate. The rest rooms were in the main passenger concourse. Most of the crew filed into these facilities before seating themselves at one of the five tables. Brent sat with Smadja and Knudsen at a table far removed from Ware and Hacohen. Everyone ate and then most of the crew stretched out on cots which lined the walls.

Brent dropped on a cot and drowsed for nearly two hours. However, deep sleep was impossible, denied by gnawing aches and persistent restlessness. He had to move, stretch his bunched muscles. Stiffly, he sat up and came to his feet.

Pushing his way through the swinging doors, he entered the main passenger concourse. A cavernous, high-ceilinged building with shops and restaurants surrounding the waiting areas. It was almost deserted. A few passengers could be seen walking briskly, carrying the usual carry-on luggage. Others dozed in chairs. Only a few shops, a bar, and a single fast-food restaurant were open. A sprinkling of white-clothed maintenance personnel were at work, cleaning, mopping, emptying ash trays and tending to the hundreds of tasks left by sloppy, careless travelers. One, a large blond woman, was scrubbing the tile floor just outside the lady's room.

Yawning and stretching, Brent stared at a rack of newspapers from all over the United States. Every one was emblazoned with headlines screaming of the Arab attack on the DC-3 "Brutal," "Savage," "Murder," were spread across the papers.

He bought a copy of *USA Today* and began to scan the story. Then, two things distracted him: Devora entered the lady's room and a dark, husky maintenance worker joined the blond Amazon. Brent turned to the sports section. The Naval Academy had lost to Notre Dame by a spectacular score. He shrugged. Yawned. Same old story. Some things never changed. Inexplicably, he felt a stir of discomfort.

He looked around. The Amazon had disappeared and the swarthy maintenance worker had been joined by another man in white. He was a negro, so black he seemed to glow blue. Both were busy working, but both were glancing at him from the corners of their eyes. He caught their looks and new circuits switched on, memory banks stirred, alarms rang.

Abruptly, a cabalistic faculty bred by years of fighting sprang to life. It was something primeval, the stalking sense of the hunter or hunted. He was an animal who had caught the scent of a predator. Adrenaline chased fatigue. His faculties tightened like taut violin strings—vision concentrated to crystal clarity, hearing amplified and finely tuned, even his sense of smell became so acute he could detect the faint odor of stale cooking oil drifting from the fast food restaurant across the concourse.

Tucking the paper under his arm, he began to walk casually toward the lady's room. Sweeping and mopping, the two men backed away from the door as if they were deliberately flanking it. Then, Brent noticed a sign had been hung on the door. He could not read it. He quickened his pace.

Two over–dressed and heavily painted women approached the door. Both were middle–aged and hard–looking, like madams who had just stepped out of their bordellos. Their hurried, erratic steps spoke of a dire need for the facilities and a few drinks too many. Swaying, they stopped in front of the door, blocking Brent's view of the sign.

The first, plump with bloated cheeks and stringy bleached blond hair, cursed, "Jesus Q. Christ, of all times. They're cleaning the goddamned place." She steadied herself with a hand to the wall.

The other woman, about sixty but who was obviously trying to look 30, slurred her gripe, "My, god. Those bastards! I never knew they cleaned those sewers! I'm gunna wet my pants!"

At that moment Brent arrived at the door. The sign read, "Locked For Cleaning."

He pushed the women aside. "Hey buster, keep your goddamned hands off," the fat blond roared, breath a fetid gust of whiskey fumes. "We've got to go, too, and this ain't yours, anyway."

The skinny brunette brushed some irritating strands of dyed brown hair from her heavily made-up eyes. She cried out, "Yours is marked 'Men', idiot. Can't you read, or are you a Rock Hudson or somethin'." She and her companion cackled and rocked on their high heels.

The blond fired another barb, "Don't get your balls in an uproar, sonny, if you have any." More laughter. More weaving.

Brent ignored the drunks. "Devora!" he called, pounding.

Nothing. "Maybe she's busy, you dumb shit," the blond said.

"I've got to find a 'john'. I don't care if its marked 'Fagots'," the other woman pleaded.

Through the corner of his eye Brent could see the maintenance men. Perfectly positioned, they were stationary and about 30–feet to each side. He could hear running footsteps behind him. *"Jesus, more of 'em,"* he said to himself. He was as trapped as Devora.

"Devora!" Silence. He put his shoulder to the door. Pushed. It budged, but did not give. The women watched him curiously. "She must be one helluva piece of ass," the blond noted.

"Hey, man," the black maintenance man shouted, a warning in his voice. He and his companion began to move toward Brent. The tactics were familiar. He couldn't kill them both and there was another killer inside. A team of assassins. He had been ambushed before. Knew their tactics. They had begun killing the women. Last year it had been Tomoko Ozumori, raped and strangled with a wire. He must act fast. Devora was in danger. She could be dead already.

In three quick motions, Brent pulled down the zipper of his flying suit, reached in, and jerked out his Beretta.

"Let's get the fuck outta here," the skinny brunette

screamed, suddenly sober. There was a clatter of high heels.

Two shots blew the lock off. There was no hesitation. He could see the maintenance men stop. Reach for their belts. He would be an easy target if he charged through the door but he was a target standing in front of it. He had no choice.

Running in upright was out of the question. Instead, he crouched and leaped in low, like a linebacker making a tackle. He landed on the tile floor on his stomach, slid across the tiles, pistol extended. Behind him, there was pandemonium echoing in the main concourse.

The rest room was silent and appeared deserted. He scooted against the wall where he could survey the entire room and watch the door at the same time. He expected to see the two maintenance men come bursting through the door. Or, maybe, it would be a grenade this time. His stomach dropped and he felt sick.

But where was she? Neither Devora nor the big blond were anywhere to be seen. He studied the seven stalls on the opposite side of the room. All the doors were closed. Looked for feet, skirts, panties, panty hose. Nothing. He was too late. He was sure of that. But people could be hiding. Crouching on the toilets. "Devora!" he shouted. His voice bounced off of the hard tile walls.

Devora's head peeked over the door of the middle stall. She was resting a pistol on the top of the door. The great eyes found Brent and widened. Her voice quivered, "What in the world's going on, Commander. You shot your way in."

Brent came to his feet. "The cleaning woman. She's an assassin." He kept an eye on the door.

"Gevalt! An assassin?"

"Yes."

"How do you know?"

"She locked you in."

"She was cleaning the place. Said I could finish before she mopped."

"Where is she?"

"I don't know."

Ware's voice from just outside the door: "Brent, what in hell's going on—the gun shots?."

Devora said, "Guard me while I pull up my skirt and zip my suit." She jumped down from the toilet and her boots clumped on the floor with a rumpled flight suit draped over them.

Brent let his breath explode in a rush of pent-up air. "They're trying to kill Lieutenant Hacoheri, Colonel."

"Is it safe to enter?"

"Are you armed, Colonel?"

"Yes."

"Then enter carefully, Colonel. The assassin could be in one of the booths and cover those two maintenance men. They're part of the team."

"Roger. They're covered."

Colonel Ware, Horace Burnside and Philipe D'Meziere stole in slowly and cautiously. Each clutched a pistol. Then Brent saw an airport security man in a blue uniform steal in behind the aviators. A toilet flushed and Devora stepped out of the booth. She, too, was holding a pistol.

"Where's the cleaning woman?" Brent asked. "She's the number one shooter." Quickly, all the doors were yanked open. Nothing. There was one more door in the far wall next to the row of sinks. Ware nodded and D'Meziere approached it slowly. Jerking it open, the French-man leaped to the side. Five pistols were trained on the doorway. It opened on a small dark storeroom. Warily D'Meziere peeked in like a man who feared stepping on a cobra. Incongruously, he began to giggle. "She is in here, *monsieurs*." The men crowded behind him. The Frenchman jerked a finger over his shoulder. *"Merde!* She needs a *toilette*, no?"

"I say, old boy," Burnside said. "You threw a bit of a scare into her. It's become quite obvious—rather." He shook his head and held his nose. "Frenchy's right."

Brent stared over D'Meziere's shoulder. Terrified to the point of hysteria, the big blond cowered on the floor of the tiny room. Trembling and crying, she clasped her hands and pleaded, "Please don't kill me—please, please." The front of her white uniform was wet and there was a small puddle on the floor.

The security man, fiftyish and round with his stomach hanging over his belt said, "That's Hilda Ladermann. She's worked here as long as I have—over twenty years. She's a grandmother. Couldn't hurt no one." He shook his head incredulously, stared at Brent. " 'Number one shooter', huh? That's crazy. What kind of shit are you nuts pulling?" All heads turned to the commander.

Holstering his pistol, Brent turned away. His face felt as hot as the surface of the sun. He heard Devora mutter, "I'll never go to the bathroom again."

Giggles bounced off the walls.

Brent stalked from the room. Pushing himself past the two maintenance men, he saw communicators in their hands. No guns. Both glared. He heard the white man say, "Some Rambo!"

The black man snorted, "That cat's more like a white 'Shaft' with shit for brains." Laughter.

"Poor Hilda, she'll never get over this."

"She'll need new panties."

"Ain't that the truth."

The entire crew of *Shady Lady* was standing a few feet from the door in a semicircle. Every man held a pistol. Brent quickened his pace, pushing his way through, almost racing to the door to the conference room. There was a chorus of, "What's happening? Who's shot? What's up?"

Then he heard the security man shouting, "Who's gunna pay for the door?"

Ware answered, "Send the bill to the Israeli ambassador."

"You bunch of fuck-ups. If you don't fight the Arabs better'n this, we ain't got no chance."

"Join up fat-ass," Ware retorted.

"Fuck you."

"Up yours."

Brent approached the doors, muttering, "Paranoid, stupid, son-of-a-bitch. Son-of-a-bitch!"

Storming through the doors, he struck one with a roundhouse punch, knocking it from its hinges and sending it clattering across the floor.

Chapter VII

Brent sat sullenly as the big bird gained altitude. The flight to Gibraltar was over 4,000 miles. It would be very, very long. After storming out of the lady's room, he had raced to the bomber and taken his station without speaking to anyone. Knudsen and Smadja had tried to engage him in small talk. It was useless. Drowned in the morass of his own mortification, he could only relive the most humiliating moment of his life. He was positive the entire crew had been amused by his bizarre antics.

Had he become paranoid? A psychopath? He trusted no one. Suspected the innocent, the harmless, even old ladies. Maybe he had fought one battle too many. Been ambushed too many times. In World War I they called it "shell shock." In World War II "battle fatigue." After Vietnam there was the "post traumatic stress syndrome." Maybe he was suffering from a "current traumatic stress syndrome."

Certainly, the pressure had been brutal and relentless for over a decade. There had been no liberties, no "R and R." The only relief he had found had been with women, and two had turned out to be traitors. He had killed them both—Kathryn Suzuki with a bullet between her eyes and Arlene Spencer with his blade to her neck. Beheaded with one stroke. Blood spurting. Head rolling. Ghastly. Sickening.

Today, he had seen an ambush where there had been none. Could have killed a helpless old cleaning lady. Played the fool better than any circus clown. "Pagliacci" without music. The humiliation would reach all the way back to Admiral Fujita, Yoshi Matsuhara and his shipmates. They would all suffer. And *Yonaga*'s enemies would revel in his disgrace.

Snorting his frustrations into his mask, he tried to shake the torturous thoughts from his mind. Nothing worked. Relentlessly, the kaleidoscope rolled on.

"Lord," he muttered to himself, voice muffled by the roar of the engines and whine of turbo-chargers. "Wait'll the media grab this." He closed his eyes tightly but nothing could blot out his mortification. Again and again the whole wretched scene replayed like a VCR programmed to repeat. His stomach contorted as if giant hands were twisting, pulling, kneading. A foul, sour taste of bile crept up into his throat and he was afraid he'd vomit into his oxygen mask. *"That's all I need, now. Gag on my own vomit."*

He pressed his big hands against his temples. It was no good. The same appalling scene was the only show in town. The tabloids would have a field day. He began to see headlines: "Yankee Samurai Rescues Girl From Defective Toilet!" "Yankee Samurai Shoots Way Into Lady's Room!" "Yankee Samurai Flushes Grandmother Out of Lady's Room!" "Rampaging Grandmother Sub-

84

dued By Courageous Yankee Samurai!" "Yankee Samurai Flush With Victory!"

Ware's voice distracted him for a moment. Apparently, Devora was flying the bomber: "Give me a little more pitch and thin the mixture, copilot."

"The props are set coarse, now, Colonel, and I think the mixture's about as lean as she can take," Devora answered.

"I know. But, it's a big ocean. Let's push her a little more—a little more blade and a little less gas. See if the old girl can take it. Can't hurt anything."

"Roger, Colonel."

Brent felt the engines slow slightly and then a new vibration shook the aircraft. "Two's a little rough, Colonel."

"I can feel it."

Sergeant Shaked's voice: "Manifold pressure's dropped in Two, Colonel."

"Roger. I've spotted it. Okay. Up one notch on the mixture, Copilot, a little more boost and synch the props."

"Up one notch, Colonel, and a little more throttle—synchronizing the props." The vibrations faded.

"Pressure's normal, Colonel," Shaked said.

"Roger. Very good. We've backed her off a little and she's taking it. We'll leave her there, copilot. Put her on 'auto'."

Devora's voice, suddenly softer and hesitant. "Ah, Sir, I have something to say."

"Say what you like."

"It's personal, but I want the whole crew to hear this."

Brent came erect. That bitch was coming after him.

More humiliation. He clenched his jaw, ground his teeth until they pained from the pressure. He would take no more. If she disgraced him on the intercom, he'd tear off his mask and charge the cockpit. Anoxia be damned. Discipline be damned.

"Commander Ross," she began, voice husky and unsteady. "I have something to say to you and I want everyone to hear this." She paused. Both Smadja and Knudsen looked at Brent. Brent stared toward the cockpit angrily. Her next words stunned him, "I want to thank you, Commander. You had every reason to be suspicious back there and I am complimented—no, flattered you showed so much concern for my safety you were willing to risk your life for me." Brent looked down and shook his head with disbelief.

Disbelief turned to incredulity as Devora rolled off intimate details of his history. "I'm guilty of forgetting you have fought this war harder, seen more of your friends killed, lost dear ones to assassins even in a park, a restaurant, fought them hand–to–hand in alleys and God knows where else. You've fought our enemies from *Yonaga*, from aircraft, from a submarine, a destroyer, a block house in the Sinai defending Israel, in Libya where you put your life on the line in Kadafi's tent to bargain for our boys. True, we have all fought, but none like this, seen that much carnage, lost so much, so many dear ones. This, I did not appreciate." She paused. Brent was unable to look at his companions. "I was rude to you back in Hawaii. I apologize. And, Commander, I want you to know it is an honor to serve with you."

Cheers. Knudsen and Smadja nodded. Knudsen grabbed his arm.

Brent wanted to answer Devora, but could not trust his voice. Never had he been so surprised, so wrong in his expectations. And she knew so much. From the media? The tabloids? She sounded as if she had studied him. And he had thought Devora had been amused by his mad antics. Instead, those beautiful words that flowed across his ears like honey. She had thanked him, and, in a way, humbled herself in doing it.

Clearing his throat, he switched on his throat microphone, "Ah, Lieutenant Hacohen. You are very kind. However, I was still an ass back there."

"No! No!" rang in the intercom.

"Yes. I made a mistake in judgement—embarrassed the whole crew."

Ware's voice: "Nonsense. I would've done the same—if I had the guts."

"Hear! Hear!"

Burnside's voice: "Respectfully, Commander, poppycock! Please don't talk tosh, old boy. You were bloody boffo—sterling."

"Oui, Commandante," Philipe D'Meziere said from the nose guns. "You showed grand courage—*magnifique!"*

"Kol ha cadod!—you did a great job!—" Efrayim Mani enthused from his tail turret. "Real *Chutzpa,* Commander."

"Banzai, Commander Ross. Great *Yamato damashii*— Japanese spirit—!" Lieutenant Torisu said.

Brent shook his head. Knudsen and Smadja nodded and smiled into their masks. He wanted to say more but was incapable of speaking without embarrassing himself.

Fortunately, Ware interrupted. "We've been cleared for 14,000."

A chorus of approval and Brent was relieved attention had been diverted from him. *Shady Lady* sank steeply, and in a few moments the crew was able to remove their masks.

Feeling relieved and pleased, Brent adjusted his pillow and sank back. He knew there would be more bad moments, but for now, the horror movie had spooled out its last reel. He turned his rheostat up, tightened his scarf and tried to relax. He had become accustomed to the noise, the vibrations. Realizing the naval officer did not wish to speak, Smadja and Knudsen turned away and sought their own comfort where little was to be found. They all dozed off fitfully.

Hours later Brent was awakened by Ware's voice: "We've crossed the fortieth meridian. Our Arab friends could have fighters based in the Azores and Morocco. Gunners, quit dreaming horny thoughts about your girl friends and open your eyes. Sergeant Shaked up into your turret, Sergeant Smadja into your hole. Swing out the waist guns. Some uninvited guests could drop in."

Quickly, Brent and Roland unbolted their panels and dropped them into their slots. A blast of frozen air struck like a bat to the solar plexus, involuntarily constricting his lungs and punching out his breath in tattered banners of vapor, causing his eyes to water. Lowering his goggles, he gritted his teeth, unlocked the Browning, pulled it up, and swung it out. A quarter turn of the locking handle secured it in place.

Tightening the harness of his back–pack parachute, Smadja moved to the Briggs-Sperry ball turret which was only 4–feet from the waist guns. Knudsen and Brent stood over him. Bending over stiffly, Smadja lifted the cover and tried to lower himself in. His chute caught. *"Scheisse!"* he grumbled. Hunching forward and almost doubling up, again he tried to force his way in. No good. The chute caught again. Cursing in a guttural mixture of German, Yiddish and Hebrew, he released the chute and threw it up on the floor. Then he slipped down into his tiny hemispheric compartment.

Plugging in his leads, he wiggled against the padded seat in a futile attempt to find a comfortable position. He braced his feet against the foot rest and wrapped his hands around the pistol grips of the twin fifty–calibers. Then, pushing to the right and then to the left, up and down, he tested the power. Rolling on its ball bearings, the turret answered perfectly. Nodding with satisfaction, Smadja looked up. "Close it, Rollie."

"Your chute?" Knudsen asked.

"Choleria—the hell with it—it gets in the way." A slow smile turned the young face into an elfin grin. "Tell 'Bull' not to get shot down. He could embarrass me." He looked up at Brent and then back at Knudsen. "Okay, close and lock. *Sholom aleichem."*

"Aleichem sholom." Knudsen dropped the lid and latched it shut. Of heavy construction, it had to be strong enough to withstand the slipstream and the weight of the gunner's body when the ball was rotated. Rollie looked at Brent. Both knew that if the big bomber was shot down, Smadja had little chance of bailing out. And both had heard stories of ball gunners trapped when bombers were forced to make belly landings. Invariably, the ball gunners were left as long smears on the runways. It was said ground crews had to use shovels to scrape up enough remains to send home. Brent shuddered as he returned to his post

and stared out over the barrel of the machine gun. He knew another command was coming.

Ware's voice: "Clear guns!"

Brent unlocked the Browning and switched the fire control lever from "Safe" to "Fire." Then gripping the two wooden handles, he peered through the ring sight at a passing cloud outlined by the brilliant moonlight. Gently, he pressed down on the butterfly trigger with his thumbs and felt the weapon blast to life. The entire airframe vibrated as ten guns spit out short bursts. Brent fired four rounds and watched a single tracer smoke out nearly horizontal at first and then arc down toward the earth in a perfect parabola until it disappeared into a smear of milky clouds barely visible below. Switching the gun back onto "Safe," he locked it.

Ware's voice: "Are you guys all set? Start at the ass-end and call in."

Corporal Efrayim Mani: "Tail gunner ready, Sir."

Silence. Then Brent realized all hands were waiting for him. Years of naval training took over: "Starboard waist gun manned and ready, Sir."

He heard Ware chuckle and kid good-naturedly, "Avast and ahoy, we'll keel-haul the commander yet."

Brent smiled as the rest of the crew chuckled. Then, the remaining gunners reported ready.

Then, in the impetuous style Brent had learned to expect, Ware's voice abruptly segued into that of the commanding officer, "Sergeant Shaked. How's the fuel."

"Good, Sir. More than half left and all tanks even. Haven't had to transfer a gallon."

"Good. We're balanced—haven't had to touch a trim

tab. Good job, all of you." The wag returned, "We may survive this flight, yet."

There was a chorus of half-hearted cheers.

Lieutenant Torisu said, "Good tail wind, Sir."

"I know. I can feel it. Maybe twenty, thirty miles-per-hour."

"I figure 30, Sir."

"Ground speed?

"Maybe 260."

"ETA Gibraltar, Navigator?"

"I estimate 2330."

Immediately, the crew clamored for another pool. "But, Lieutenant Devora cannot be in it, Colonel," Efrayim Mani insisted. "She cheats."

"Yeah, she rigs it." "It's a scam!" rang through the intercom.

Brent found himself laughing. He had never experienced a group of military personnel like this. Sometimes he felt like he was back on the Annapolis football team, preparing to play Army. In a way rank had vanished, yet in other ways subtle hints of recognition and respect for rank was still there, like obeying the coach, or the quarterback in the huddle. There was a line and it was never crossed. And, certainly, Colonel James Robert "Bull" Ware was completely in command. The very tone of his voice could sway the mood of everyone on board.

"It'll be an honest game. I'll watch her, anyway, I want to get even. Two bucks this time," Ware said.

There were shouts of approval. Within a minute all bets were made. Brent's sailor's instincts told him the tail wind was not as strong as the others believed. He took 0010.

The chameleon changed colors again. "Don't forget,

91

night fighters prefer to attack from behind or below," Ware warned. "You guys back there, keep your eyes peeled if you want to collect your winnings." There was no laughter, only a few grunts of acknowledgment.

Ware had good reason to be concerned. The bright moon was almost directly overhead like a fixture in a ballroom, glaring in an almost cloudless sky. The few clouds Brent could see scudded along beneath them. Ware's generation had called it, "Bombers' Moon." Brent chuckled laconically. "More like 'Night Fighters' Moon' " he said to himself. However, he knew there was little chance Arab fighters would be prowling. He had heard their radar was poor and there had been few reporrts of effective enemy night fighter attacks. Yet, they had several old British Mosquito fighters and a few Junkers Ju-88s that had been equipped with new radar. Ominously, at least two Israeli night prowlers had been lost in mysterious circumstances. It was up to the waist, ball and tail gunners to be most alert. And Ware's warning had been based on his own long experience.

One of the favorite tactics of the night fighter was to creep up on the bombers—even when unseen in weather—until the backwash of the slipstream could be felt. Then, the pilot would open fire, usually with multiple 20-millimeter guns. This tactic was preferred by American Northrup P-61 Black Widow pilots during World War II. The attack from below was the other favorite tactic, mainly used by the Germans against the great RAF night raids. In this approach, the enemy plane dove beneath the target, pulled up sharply and then fired all its armaments into the belly of the bomber until the fighter stalled out. Either attack, if carried out with panache and verve, could be devastating. The very thought of these tactics made Brent twitch nervously.

Brent hunched forward and stared out and back, down, and occasionally, up. Nothing but the brilliant stars and glaring moon and the few clouds below. "Just stay that way," he muttered to himself.

Hours slipped by and Brent found it difficult to maintain a high level of alertness. His neck was cold and the big corded muscles stiffened and then ached. He forced himself to turn his head and watch. Luckily, Lieutenant Horace Burnside brought back thermoses of hot coffee. The copilot remained at her post. Brent could understand this.

Finally, Brent heard Ware begin to communicate with the controllers at Gibraltar. Everyone began to loosen with relief. Relief became joy when Gibraltar radar reported no unknown aircraft in the area. In fact, *Shady Lady* was the only aircraft on their radar. Quickly, the transponder setting, frequency, approach vector and altitude were given.

Ware's voice: "Stay alert, gunners. Could be a snooper hanging around 'Gib' to pick us off. By now, they must know where we are and where we're going. Don't forget, no radar is perfect and he could fly low enough to stay under it or mask himself inland behind some hills. The Spaniards hate our guts, you know."

But the landing was uneventful. *Shady Lady* touched down at precisely 0010.

There were groans and then Knudsen pounded him on the back in a very unmilitary manner. "Congratulations, Commander," he said.

Brent was taken aback for a moment. Then he realized

he had won the pool. "I'm the big winner—the big winner," he laughed.

"Correct, Sir. We'll have a big party."

"A big party," Brent said, disconnecting his leads and stretching.

In a few moments, the weary crew left the plane.

Chapter VIII

When *Shady Lady* landed at Gibraltar, the crew was met on the tarmac by two Land Rovers. While the flight deck crew and two forward gunners struggled through the bomb bay, Brent Ross, Efrayim Mani, Roland Knudsen and Oren Smadja had already slipped out of the rear door.

The flight deck crew was just beginning to appear when the first British officer greeted Brent. "Colonel Sean Townsend, here. I say, smashing to see you again, Commander." He whipped his right hand to his peaked cap in a quivering palm—out salute. Brent returned the salute. Knudsen, Smadja and Mani looked on curiously.

It took a moment for Brent to place the officer, and then he began to recall their one meeting. The year before Colonel Bernstein, Lieutenant Elroy Rubin, and he had been ferried to Gibraltar in a Libyan Constellation after the ill—fated conference with Colonel Moammar Kadafi. At that time, Townsend had met them at almost the same spot. Townsend's young aide, whose name eluded Brent, stood at attention behind the mustachioed colonel. Brent returned the salute and then grasped the Colonel's hand. "Been a long time, Colonel," he said.

"Right you are, Commander, just before the ruddy dust-up at Rabta." Gesturing at the young officer standing behind him, Townsend was discreet enough to provide the officer's name, "You remember my aide, Lieutenant Wesley Watkins?"

Now it all came back to Brent. Both officers were with SIU, Special Intelligence Unit, that had been establish by British Intelligence especially to track Arab units, ascertain strength and attempt to predict intentions. It was rumored that SIU had several operatives in Libya; some, perhaps, in Kadafi's "tent." Their accomplishments rivaled those of Mossad. Townsend had provided intelligence and had acted as their guide and liaison with the RAF. He had even arranged transportation to *Yonaga* in two incredible antique "Stringbags;" a pair of Fairey Swordfish torpedo bombers that dated to the early years of naval aviation.

Brent answered Watkin's salute and grasped his hand. "Of course. Good to see you, again, Lieutenant." Brent quickly introduced the British officers to the three gunners standing behind him.

He began to wonder. Felt uneasy. Did the British know about his debacle back in Fort Lauderdale? If they did, he knew they would be too gentlemanly to mention it. Certainly it had been reported on radio and television. At that moment, Colonel Ware walked up with the cockpit crew, nose and turret gunners.

Devora stopped close to Brent. The great brown pools caught his eyes and for a fleeting instant their gazes merged. Not a word was spoken, yet suddenly there seemed to be a magical contact between them. The barriers were gone, and the desire he had first seen glimmered again. For the first time, Brent did not regret making a fool of himself.

"Thank you, Commander." she said softly into his ear so that the others could not hear. Two of the men stared curiously.

Brent, embarrassed, disliked even thinking about the incident. But a man could drown in those eyes. "Ah, I made a foolish mistake."

"No, don't say that . . ."

She was interrupted by the British officer who approached the pilot. "Ah," Townsend said, "Colonel Ware. A pleasure, Sir."

"Likewise, Colonel." The officers exchanged salutes, spoke in hushed tones for a moment and then the crew was ushered into the two Land Rovers.

Seated in a conference room in the terminal's VIP section, Brent sagged back and sipped his coffee. They had finished a meal of roast beef with Yorkshire pudding and boiled potatoes—traditional bland British cuisine. However, the linen was sparkling white and eleven pieces of silverware had been formed like a platoon on parade around his plate.

Now, Colonel Ware and Townsend were standing on a dais in front of a chart of the Mediterranean. Townsend swept a pointer from Gibraltar to a location south of Sardinia and then curved southeast to a position midway between Sicily and Pantelleria. "May I remind you, you must not stray over 'Eytie' territory. Of course, this

97

stretches your run a bit." He tapped the pointer, "A thousand-mile run to this point. Limit of the Grumman FX-1000."

"Yes. We know about the Italians," Ware said bitterly. "First to shoot off their mouths and the last to shoot off a weapon." He stabbed a place between the Peloponnesus and Libya. "Israeli fighters can pick us up here, leaving a 500-mile gap where we will be unescorted."

Lieutenant Horace Burnside spoke up, "I say, Colonel Townsend, escorting us will be an overt act of war by the Americans. Up until this lot, they've supported us but stopped short of mixing it with those pommy bastards."

"Right you are." Townsend stared uneasily at Colonel Ware. "But this is not the first time Americans have intervened with their armed forces, yet stopped short of declaring war. Vietnam is a bloody good example." Ware, Brent and Roland Knudsen stiffened. Townsend rolled on, showing off his knowledge of history, "Interventions over the years in Central and South America have gone on since the last century. And don't forget the Lend–Lease of Franklin Roosevelt. Pulled our knickers out of the twist, he did. And, by Jove, kept the Empire in the war. And American destroyers escorted convoys to Iceland before Germany declared war on America in 1941." Then Townsend showed an extraordinary, detailed knowledge of history that took Brent by surprise: *"Kearny* torpedoed and badly damaged, *Reuben James* sunk with heavy loss of life and both destroyers torpedoed *before* December seventh."

"Yes, I know," Ware said impatiently. He waved his hand at the chart in a sweeping gesture, "I want to know about enemy fighters, their numbers, bases, types, patrol

98

areas." He stepped close to the chart and ran the rubber tip of his pointer over the "gap." "We'll be in easy range of their bases, here."

Townsend's face flushed and he tugged on a spiked tip of his heavily waxed "Colonel Blimp" mustache. "Of course, Colonel Ware." He raised the pointer and circled Israel. "The enemy is stretched thin. Most of his air force is concentrated here, on the Israeli front, and at least six squadrons of fighters are with his carriers. Since your show at Rabta," he tapped a spot about 60–miles inland from Tripoli, "at least four squadrons have been stationed there and a half dozen more are in the Marianas. However, he does keep an eye on the Med. He has two fighter strips here." The pointer moved to the coast and stopped on Benghazi. "Maybe two squadrons, ah, 24 to 30 aircraft—Me–109s, a few 'Spits', even a handful of P–51s." The crew shifted uneasily. "And his destroyers run anti–sub patrols constantly. You could draw AA fire from them."

Brent moved to the edge of his seat. "Rosie?" he blurted.

All eyes moved to the American. Everyone knew he was asking about the renegade American pilot, Colonel Kenneth "Rosie" Rosencrance and his feared Fourth Fighter Squadron. It was rumored Rosencrance had over sixty kills, his wingman, Lieutenant Rudolph Stoltz, twenty. Townsend shifted his eyes uneasily. "As you know, the Fourth is Kadafi's favorite—all picked pilots."

Remembering Rosencrance's slaughter of his friend Colin Willard–Smith in his parachute, Brent spat out, "Picked killers! Butchers!"

Townsend wrinkled his nose and the massive mustache

worked up and down with his lip. "Right you are Commander. Nothing but bloody killers." He raised the pointer. "Here. We've got it on good authority the bloody bugger and his 'Fourth' is based here at Derna, on the coast, a new fighter base."

"They could be waiting for us," Ware warned grimly. "Certainly, by this time, they must know we're coming."

"Got to consider that possibility, Colonel." The Englishman tapped the floor with his pointer. "Kadafi moves the buggers around. Uses them in, ah—sensitive areas."

."*Shady Lady*'s a 'sensitive area'," Ware growled. Townsend nodded gravely while some crewmen shook their heads, others exchanged hushed remarks.

Brent found another menace, "The three enemy carriers?"

"They're still here." The English colonel pointed at the southern end of the Red Sea, "Based at Aden."

"Out of range of this show," Lieutenant Burnside said. "Takes those six squadrons out."

"Right you are."

Brent heard Smadja mutter, "Those carriers are out of range of Israeli aircraft, yet able to move either north or south at will."

Townsend added, "Bloody good strategic disposition. They've got great tactical flexibility and the Israeli Air Force can't reach them."

Ware interrupted, "Right now I'm concerned about *Shady Lady*'s flexibility. Is there anything else, Colonel Townsend?"

"Yes, Colonel." He handed Colonel Ware a sealed envelope. "From Mossad, transponder setting, frequencies to be guarded, suggested altitudes, rendezvous point with Israeli fighters and a review of your flight plan." He gestured to several boxes piled in a corner. "And there are the flak jackets you requested. That's the whole lot."

"Bull" glanced at the boxes, while opening the envelope. Scanning the contents quickly, he nodded to himself and said, "Everyone get a couple hours rest." Another glance at the documents and then at his watch. "We'll take off at 0700. That way we'll make our run in daylight. If we're intercepted, I prefer to engage them in daylight, not their night fighters." He pointed at the boxes. "Remember to grab a couple flak jackets—one for your chest and one for your balls!" Flushing, he looked at Devora and only managed to compound his embarrassment by muttering, "Oh, damn." The copilot smiled and looked at her long fingers.

Grinning, the crew nodded and exchanged glances. Brent wondered if the colonel's gaffe was deliberate, a ploy to relax a tense crew. Then, he stood with the others and walked to the cots lining the walls.

Chapter IX

The growing dawn light had snuffed out the stars as *Shady Lady* climbed away from Gibraltar's small runway. The air was astonishingly clear. The soft morning blush colored the sky pale blue at the horizon, deepening as Brent looked up until it became indigo overhead. As he turned his eyes to the east, it faded to turquoise and then beyond the low–hanging sun, to a shining buttermilk. Brent had never seen anything like it, it was an exquisite morning. A beautiful day to kill men; or be killed.

Brent shuddered when he thought of the assigned altitude of 30,000–feet. It was felt the high altitude would at least minimize the possibility of visual sighting. But as Ware had warned, "Arab radar won't be blind." Then he pointed out another possibility: "We could come within range of Arab destroyers." High altitude would make AA fire more difficult to range, but, remember, those 5–inch guns could reach us easily."

As *Shady Lady* climbed steadily Brent felt a growing disquiet, an atavistic sense of predestiny and budding menace. He shifted his weight, rubbed the mask that clutched his face like a sticky wet glove and checked the fasteners of his vest–like flak jacket. Then he moved his boots on the uneven surface of the jacket under his feet, trying to find a stable position. "Could guarantee the pleasure of countless maidens," Knudsen had joked as he helped Brent place the jacket.

"Could you believe 20,000?"

"Like stuffing a basketball." They had both laughed.

Now, with the short jerky sailor's scan, Brent searched the cloudless sky, the sea, and the coast of Morocco to the south. Algeria was beginning to appear ahead under the right wing.

Then he saw the Grumman FX–1000s. High above he caught a flight of fighters flying in the usual American two elements of two. He knew that 12 of the vicious new fighters had taken off just before Shady Lady. However, from his position he could see only the one flight. They were magnificent, a thrilling sight. Americans. He tingled with pride.

As the four aircraft banked and swerved over the bomber in an elongated figure "S," he caught a clear view of the sleek design. Small like the Zero–sen, its cowling housed an enormous 4400 horsepower Pratt and Whitney double Wasp engine. Thirteen–foot, four–bladed propellers had forced the designers to "gull" the wings like the F4U Corsair. The fuselage was long and narrow, canopy short and raised like a glistening soap bubble. With its incredible power plant, it was able to carry awesome firepower; four 20–millimeter cannons in its wings and a 30–millimeter cannon that fired through its propeller hub. It could carry 2–tons of bombs or two torpedoes on its wing crutches.

Brent heard Knudsen curse. "Goddamned contrails. Wouldn't you know it. We're advertising over the whole goddamned 'Med'."

Brent's stomach sank as he stared at engines Three and Four. Thick white vapor like endless bandages were unfurling neatly behind them. The air was so cold the water vapor in the exhausts was condensing. There was no secrecy now. All of North Africa could look up and see them. He added his curses to Rollie's.

Uneasily, Brent checked the Browning again and caressed the belt of 50–caliber bullets. All was in readiness. He felt some reassurance.

Devora's voice: "Thirty–thousand–feet, Colonel."

Wind that felt like it whipped off the polar cap ripped through the gun ports and swirled around the gunners. Brent hunched down and turned his rheostat all the way up. He continued his search. It was a cruel, exacting job. His goggles were tight, mask irritating, oxygen fetid like burning copper, flight clothes and flak jacket cumbersome and impairing his movements. But their survival depended on their alertness. Occasionally, he caught a glimpse of their escorts, but he knew fighter escorts did not form a visible umbrella.

"Bull" had warned them just before take–off, "You've got to understand this, you won't see a blanket of protection around us. Fighters must range freely, use the sky to their advantage. They're hunters stalking hunters. The worst way to use them is defensively—to force them to fly close to us, limit their tactical options. Hermann Goering made this mistake during the Battle of Britain. The 'Spits' cut 'em to pieces."

From 30,000–feet, Brent could see over 200–miles.

They were leaving Morocco behind and Algeria was clearly visible. They had passed Oran and Algiers had come into sight. Glowing white in the harsh sun, neither city looked very large. He could see inland for over 100– miles. Coastal regions gleamed emerald in short spurts, but inland the brown terrain was harsh and mean. Dry and virtually treeless, hot sand baked in the sun. Hills jutted upward in ridges and rows showing all the colors of earth; bright yellow for the peaks and ridges where the sun glared, brown on the slopes, blue and purple in the valleys that appeared like cracks in cooling lava.

Brent wondered about his enemies; the people who lived in this incomprehensibly hostile, parched earth. Arabs were a distinctive breed, as cruel as the land that bred them—a vast land that ran from North Africa into the dismal reaches of the Pacific Ocean. Theirs was that crushing part of the world where men could not master the earth. It was not difficult to see why they had embraced Islam and its fatalistic outlook. So harsh, so brutalizing were the forces of nature that those people imprisoned upon it were convoluted into forming a society where pitiless barbarism was commonplace. He had seen it time and again, raged against it, fought it, but still wondered at its power. Brent had learned in negotiations and in battle that he was dealing with a mad society that was virtually uncontrollable. This made the Arabs very dangerous enemies, indeed.

Brent patted the breech of the machine gun, tugged gently on the cocking handle. He knew what he held in his hand was the only argument an Arab could understand.

Shady Lady droned on steadily into the east. They had travelled east over half the world. Ishmael pursued Moby

Dick eastward from New England to be submerged in the sea, where he finally grasped his connectedness to the world. Would he find his "connectedness" at the bottom of the sea in a wrecked B-24?

Ware's voice calling for a station check interrupted Brent's musings. All was well. Boredom tried to creep in, but Brent banished the fighting man's worst enemy with the power of his concentration. He moved his head, focused his eyes to infinity until they ached.

They were nearly 4-hours into their flight with Sicily to the north and Tunisia to the south, when the FX-1000s left. Wheeling and turning, they formed a loose formation of six pairs. Then sweeping low over *Shady Lady* in a final salute, they headed back toward Gibraltar. Never had Brent felt so lonely, so vulnerable; like a child abandoned in a dark alley in the worst part of town.

Ware's voice: "We're on our own, kids, and will be for almost two hours. Keep your eyes peeled and I want you to report if you hear a seagull fart. Now, all stations, check in and then keep the intercom clear of chatter."

Each man reported with brevity and a new seriousness. An unusual kind of discipline was on the intercom, a discipline that came from experienced military men who sensed the nearness of the enemy. There was silence in the earphones as everyone waited and watched.

Almost in an attempt to match Brent's mood, nature began to darken hers. They began to pass dense, small clouds like dirty stray sheep that had wandered away from the main flock of clouds closing in below and from the east. To the south a huge forbidding thunderhead humped its camel's back over the horizon. Swirling with grays and black, it flashed with lightning, rolled with

106

thunder. Somewhere in the desert terrified bedouins were huddling under the furious onslaughts of a *khamsin*. Most ominous was the weather above. Gray clumps of cirrus, like dirty laundry, began to dim and occasionally blot out the sun. Here was the ideal cover for the lurking fighter.

But none appeared. *Shady Lady* bored on steadily through the "gap" for almost an hour and a half. Tension began to ease. *Maybe we'll make it,* Brent thought.

Ware, obviously sensing the relaxation, spoke into his throat microphone: "Keep your eyes on those clouds above us and Smadja, stay awake in the cellar. They could sneak one up our butt. We're not out of the woods, yet."

"Yes, Sir."

Then the shock came, the tail gunner, Corporal Efrayim Mani making the first sighting. "Two fighters— five o'clock high. Diving!"

Immediately, Ware commanded: "Fine pitch, full rich, emergency boost. Pour the coal to her. Give me every- thing she has!"

The great engines bellowed out their new power with thunder to match the storm. The bomber surged with new speed and Devora shouted out, "Air speed three– hundred–seventy–eight, Colonel, but the turbos can't hold emergency boost for more than five–minutes. Pres- sure's at max now, pushing 10 on the turbos, Sir."

Ware's voice calm and evenly modulated: "I know. Watch your instruments, especially the cylinder head temperature, and gunners, watch your discipline. Don't waste a round."

While Ware spoke, Brent searched the sky above and to the rear. Quickly, he found them, two tiny crosses plunging down out of the sun like darts unwinding endless white streamers. *Shady Lady* was the dart board. Immediately, he felt his nerves tighten and crawl like poisonous insects upon his skin. The old familiar drumbeat of fear was back.

He could fight it. Always had. Grinding his teeth and swallowing despite the lack of saliva in his mouth, he swung the Browning to the sighting. It was very hard to focus on them in the glare. His eyes watered. He blinked. Turned away. Raised his goggles. Wiped his eyes with his gloves. Pulled the goggles down and brought the first fighter into his ring sight. It was red; a solid blood–red Messerschmitt Bf–109. And his wingman was black–splotched with big yellow marks. Shark's teeth adorned the oil cooler and the underside of the cowling.

Rosencrance and his wingman Rudolph "Tiger Shark" Stoltz. Kadafi's two favorite killers. Hatred catalyzed fear into rage. The two butchers would kill him, kill his friends. His stomach was still hollow and cold, heart beating to the frantic drummer, but his hands were steady, mind alert and computing like a new IBM.

There must be a bounty on *Shady Lady*. Certainly, the Arabs must know he was on board and his scalp was worth a million dollars American. Whoever shot down the bomber could collect a fortune. And besides, this pair enjoyed killing. To them, the big lumbering B–24 must appear as an easy target. Certainly, much more inviting than fighters. He glanced at a chart glued above the port. Found Bf–109, wingspan 32–feet, 6–inches. Wingtips to the second ring would give a range of 400–yards.

Michael Shaked's voice: "Top turret, two more fighters at one o'clock high. Diving."

Brent heard Rollie, "Shit! Two up our ass and two up our nose. We're on the anvil."

Philipe D'Meziere's voice: "Nose gunner. I have *les deux bandits.*"

Ware's voice: "No thousand–yard miracle shots. Four–hundred or less! And, goddamnit, D'Meziere, use the clock and speak English."

"Oui, commandant!"

"Ah, shit!"

Brent shouted, "Mani, this is the right waist. I have the red one!"

"Roger. This is the tail gunner. I've got his wingman—the one with the crazy paint!"

Brent watched the red Me–109 grow in his ring sight. He knew the fighter carried two 20–millimeter cannons in the wings and two 13–millimeter machine guns in the hood and was at least a 100–miles–an–hour faster than the bomber. The Me's wingtips touched the inner ring. Too far. Grew slowly. Then Brent realized Rosencrance was diving at reduced throttle. He was going to make a leisurely run. Pour his armament into them. He couldn't believe it. Certainly, the renegade knew the B–24 was heavily armed. He was overconfident or too eager to collect his reward. In any event, Rosencrance had made a mistake.

Suddenly, Rosencrance's wings and hood blossomed with petals of fire. Brent held his fire, watching as tracers like long white strings of party lights unravelled all around him. There were two thumps, sharp and ear–piercing, as if someone had struck the fuselage with the end of a bull whip. Thirteen–millimeter slugs, punching through aluminum like tissue paper. Then the bomber jolted and vibrated as Efrayim Mani opened fire on Stoltz with his two tail guns.

Brent aimed directly for the shimmering disk of the fighter's propeller and then raised his sight slightly to allow for bullet drop. Holding his breath, he watched the fighter's wingtips touch the second ring. He pressed down gently on the trigger.

The big machine gun jerked to life, stuttering like a chain saw cutting through a nail—studded timber. The belt racing through the breech, hot cartridges flying out of the ejector in a golden stream, striking his right arm, chest, shaking his whole body. His tracers arced high; too high. He raised the handles slightly. Rosencrance's propeller seemed to devour his tracers. There were orange flashes and bits of ripped metal flew out of the 109's exhaust manifold fairing strip. Brent shouted with joy, fear gone, blood smoking with fighting madness.

At less than a hundred yards, the Me accelerated and dropped off and below, out of his sights. Frantically, Brent came up to his full height, depressing the Browning, trying to track the Me for a canopy shot, but the automatic governor silenced the gun as he swiveled into the B-24's tail. Brent cursed and then heard Devora cry out, "Ball turret!"

Brent shouted, "Rollie, take him!" as he frantically shifted his sights to Stoltz. But the garishly—painted fighter had already flashed beneath them into the fire of the ball turret. Now Knudsen, the upper turret and the nose guns were firing. Snaps, cracks, thumps and more whipping sounds as *Shady Lady* took more punishment from the fighters making the head—on pass.

Brent saw a chunk of wing the size of a book cover fly

off into the slip stream and then a black Messerschmitt attacking from the front flashed into view. The fighter was banking away and then, surprisingly, the pilot half–looped and snap–rolled in a tight Immelmann, charging the bomber and opening fire trying for a cockpit shot. He was close. Very close, his wings actually extending beyond Brent's second ring.

Burnside's voice: "Kill the bloody bugger! Kill him!"

Brent and the top turret opened fire simultaneously. Three streams of tracers converged on the attacking fighter. For a spilt–second, bomber and fighter were connected by a cat's cradle of tracers. More thumps, a flash and a large hole appeared above Brent's head. Something struck his flak jacket under his armpit like a small child wielding a hammer and his left cheek stung. A graze. He ignored it. Felt near sexual heat as his tracers ripped into the fighter's right wing, reaping bits of shattered aluminum and leaving glistening rents. Then, with its retraction jack shot out, the fighter's right wheel dropped out of its well.

Shaked was scoring, too. Tracers cycloned into the cowling hood, shot off the antenna, auxiliary cooling intakes, blew off a supercharger intake. A thin ribbon of smoke unravelled from the engine. The Me slowed, pulled into a near vertical climb, began to roll away, wheel flopping like a broken leg. He would give the bomber his belly.

Sensing a kill, Ware shouted, "I'm turning to the right and climbing!"

Banking and climbing, the big plane turned in a near semicircle around the stricken fighter which had climbed above it. Ware's maneuver would expose the enemy to the fire of at least five 50–caliber machine guns. Brent was stunned by Ware's verve and audacity. A bomber was actually attacking a fighter, probably the first time in history.

Frantically, the enemy pilot kicked rudder, dropped off on his right wing before his plane stalled, trying to nurse his damaged aircraft out of range of the charging juggernaut. A mistake. As he dropped, the whole top of the aircraft was unmasked. Shaked got off a long burst from his top turret. However, thrown off balance by *Shady Lady*'s sharp turn, his fire went wide.

Ware's voice: "Think, gunners, think!"

Now it was Brent's turn. Bringing the Browning up, he aimed ahead of the fighter, allowing a half–length for deflection. It was an appalling gunnery problem, compounding deflective lead with the geometry of two desperately maneuvering aircraft. Although *Shady Lady* was no longer climbing, she was turning at high speed and banking. The Messerschmitt was dropping almost vertically, twisting and accelerating. Calling on the power of the great muscles in his arms and legs, he swung the Browning, intuitively compensating for the intricate ballistics. Then, rotating the gun against the turn of the B–24, he allowed the fighter to drop through a long burst as the enemy dove past his port.

Brent saw his tracers march the length of the Me, tearing out chunks of aluminum like a plow ripping hard pan, tracers sparkling and beading like a magic show. Jerking the barrel hard right, he yelped with joy as at least four slugs punched through the canopy. All were good, striking the pilot's head from behind, shattering it like a dropped egg. Immediately, brains and blood sprayed the inside of the canopy like aerosol paint and the fighter corkscrewed toward the sea. A thick black scarf of smoke marked its obituary.

Brent cheered. The whole crew cheered. Bringing the bomber back to its base course, Ware shouted, "Good shooting." And then he warned, "Here they come again!"

Maddened by the loss of their comrade, the three surviving fighters charged from the front, left side and rear. *Shady Lady*'s defenses would be spread thin and she was outgunned. Knudsen swung his gun and his hip struck Brent's. "Get your ass out of the way, goddamnit!" the corporal screamed at the commander. Silently, Brent stepped away, allowing Knudsen more room. At this moment there was no rank, no seniority, no distinctions at all. Just ten people fighting for their lives.

Devora's voice: "We have a leak in our right wing tank, Colonel." Brent saw a thin mist trailing off from the hole in the right wing. The hole was as big as a small throw rug.

Ware answered: "Roger. I can feel the drag. I'm trimming it out. You and Burnside monitor the leak and let me know if any fumes collect in the bomb bay. We have plenty of fuel, but I would dislike blowing up. Could ruin our whole day."

Brent was amazed by Ware's aplomb. He had never met a man like this.

More tracers smoked past and the whip lashed *Shady Lady* again. The plane shook, D'Meziere opening fire from the nose. Then Knudsen and Mani, from his tail turret, joined in. More cartridge casing sprayed and rolled across the floor. There was a loud "bang," and a shattered fire extinguisher flew across the waist and clattered across the floor into the bomb bay. Then Brent's emergency oxygen bottle exploded like a grenade, a 13-millimeter bullet hurling it across the waist, bouncing off a stringer and onto the floor.

A large fragment tore into the left side of his flack jacket like a scythe through gauze, jolting him with the impact. In a sudden shock of dread, Brent grabbed his side. No blood. He was lucky. Another close one. The jacket would never stop a 13-millimeter slug. More wind. There were three holes above his port and another to the left. The smell of gasoline was suddenly very strong despite the draft.

"Commander Ross! Coming over the top," Knudsen screamed.

Dropping to his knees, Brent raised his sights just as Stoltz shot past like a crazy-quilt missile. Brent sent a short burst after him. He saw some fabric rip loose from the rudder structure and the D/F loop fly off like a spinning horse shoe. "Get a taste of that, you fagot prick."

D'Meziere's voice: "He is coming over, right side."

Shaked fired a long burst from the top turret before Brent had a shot. Without even speaking, he pushed Knudsen, who was crowding him, and swiveled his gun forward. A black Me trailing a white haze of glycol pulled up sharply and banked away with Shaked's tracers hounding him. Brent got off a short burst, but obviously, the Messerschmitt was badly hit and out of the fight. The fighter dropped down into the cloud cover.

The ball turret yammered beneath their feet. Smadja was shouting, "Two of them. I can't take them both!"

Ware banked hard to the left, hoping to give Knudsen a shot. Suddenly, there were thuds, bangs, ripping sounds as heavy slugs punched through the corrugated floor.

Dust, ripped aluminum, cartridges and debris flew into the air and were immediately swirled by the wind, clattering and eddying with the motions of the plane. The floor looked like a trash bin. Suddenly, there was a scream and Knudsen slapped Brent across the back of the head with his right hand.

"What the hell?" Brent turned and saw the gunner's hand and most of his arm drop and bounce off his shoulder and land on the floor. Knudsen was screaming, grabbing the stump of his right arm just above the elbow and rolling across the floor. He grabbed the shot–off arm and clutched it to his chest, disbelief numbing his eyes. Arterial blood squirted, red, steaming hot and thick, coagulating quickly in the dross littering the floor.

"I have a wounded man in the waist," Brent shouted into his microphone.

"He'll have to wait."

"His right arm's been shot off, Colonel. He'll bleed to death."

"A tourniquet. Quick. It won't take much. The blood'll freeze. But your gun comes first."

Brent dropped to his knees and looked at the stump. Ware was right. The bleeding had almost stopped, but a small stream was still spurting. Still conscious, Knudsen stared plaintively at Brent and keened softly under his breath like a wounded animal that could not comprehend the painful punishment that had been inflicted upon it. Whipping off his scarf, Brent looped it around the stump twice, cinched it tight until the bleeding stopped, and tied it. Knudsen winced and twisted, moaned, but there was gratitude in his eyes. Brent reached for the first aid kit, but it, too, had been smashed and its contents scattered across

115

the floor. Hastily, he searched in the rubble for a syrette of morphine. He was interrupted by the Devora's calm voice: "Fumes in the bomb bay, Colonel."

"Crack the bomb bay doors slowly and watch the trim." There was a hum and more cold air whipped through the aircraft. The strong smell of gasoline vanished.

Devora's voice: "I think the enemy's gone, Colonel. Can't see them."

Shaked's voice: "I can. Two of them. Four o'clock high. Swinging around our tail."

Both Shaked and Mani shouted, "Here they come! Five o'clock high and seven o'clock high."

Dropping to his knees, Brent looked up and found them high and in the distance. The fighters had split, Rosencrance attacking from the right rear, Stoltz from the left.

Ware's voice: "Top turret take the one at seven o'clock!"

"Roger."

Squatting on his haunches, Brent elevated the Browning to its maximum. He grunted with satisfaction. The red fighter was in his sights, streaking down at over 400–miles–an–hour. Rosencrance had learned. He was at full throttle. It would be a short burst. Tracers streaked by and the tail turret began to fire. Again, Brent sent his rounds into the shimmering disk.

There were crashing, banging sounds as *Shady Lady* took hits. Slugs raged through the bomber, ripping an inflatable life raft to pieces and shattering a 110–round box of 50–caliber ammunition just to the left of Brent's foot. As Rosencrance flashed past, Stoltz dove below the bomber while out of range and pulled up sharply for a belly shot.

Ware's voice: "Brent, left side!"

Brent turned. Knudsen was sprawled behind his gun, eyes wide with shock and pain, gasping into his mask. He knew what Brent must do. There was no time for tenderness, compassion and they both knew it. Grasping the wounded man under his arms, Brent pulled him forward, careful not to yank his leads loose. Knudsen screamed into his mask and fainted.

Guiding his own leads, Brent grabbed the handles of Knudsen's Browning and pushed them up. Stoltz had curved up from his dive and had opened fire. Smadja was firing back down from the ball turret. Stoltz was slowing, approaching stall speed. He was a good target. Brent ripped off a two-second burst that struck the wing and fuselage of the fighters like little blinking red lights. But Stoltz had guts, he hung on his propeller, still firing.

In two-and-one-half-seconds the twin Rheinmetall Borsig machine guns mounted on top of his engine unleashed 50 thirteen-millimeter bullets; the two Mauser cannons in the wings each fired nine twenty-millimeter shells. The shells went wide, but at least ten bullets punched through the floor and the ball turret.

Smadja's scream was heard throughout the intercom as the first bullet struck the young Israeli's left leg, shattering his thigh-bone. He flung his head back, lost control of the turret which rotated back to its central position, arched his back, screamed again as bullets perforated the flesh, hacked and smashed his lower spine, splintered his pelvis and chopped through the great veins and arteries it protected. Two of the last three rounds coursed up through

117

his abdomen, missing his liver, penetrating the stomach, breaking a few ribs. The last bullet struck him directly under the chin. The entrance wound was small, but the big round exited in an gush of brains, bits of teeth and splintered bone, carrying off most of the top of his skull. The power of the big bullet punctured the lid and sent a small geyser of gore spurting into the waist, spraying Knudsen and Brent.

Screaming with horror and frustration, Brent held the trigger down. But Stoltz had rolled under the bomber to the right side. Again, Brent scrambled across the midsection, grabbed the right waist gun. It was too late and he knew it. Stoltz was diving far out of range. He was headed south at full throttle. The American punched the breech.

Suddenly, Brent felt the pulse of the engines slow. Ware's voice: "Israeli fighters ahead. The enemy has broken off the attack and is headed home. Lieutenant Burnside, assist Commander Ross with Knudsen and Smadja."

"Smadja's dead. His brains are all over the waist."

"Check him, anyway, Commander Ross." For the first time, the pilot showed emotion, "We owe him that much."

Brent knew Ware was right. Smadja must be checked. He moved to the cover of the ball turret while Burnside made his way down the narrow catwalk in the bomb bay and settled down next to Knudsen.

Holding his breath, Brent unlocked the cover and opened it slowly. The young gunner was curled fetus-like with his arms thrown wide. His jaw and the top of his head had been blown off, white bone and blood bubbling.

The yellow—red contents in what remained of his skull settled in the basin like detritus discarded by a butcher. One eye had been blown out, but the other was already filming over with the white coating of death. Reversed and resting on his shoulder, his left foot had been flung up next to his ear. Blood, splintered bone and chunks of brains were spattered over the remains of the shattered ball turret, freezing on the breeches, ammunition belts, clothing, and Perspex.

Brent felt his guts coil with an amalgam of revulsion and sorrow. Swallowing hard, he said thickly, "It's definite, Colonel. Sergeant Smadja's dead."

"And Knudsen?"

"Badly wounded."

"Help Lieutenant Burnside tend to him. There's morphine in your first aid kit. And Lieutenant Burnside will man the left gun."

Brent moved closer to Knudsen. Burnside had found a syrette and injected the wounded man.

Ware's voice: "Check his bleeding. When we descend, the warm temperature will start it again."

Burnside had already unzipped his flight suit and pulled his belt loose. In a moment, Brent had slashed Knudsen's sleeve with a pocket knife and the two men had tightened the belt above Brent's scarf. The oozing stopped.

"Here they are!" Shaked shouted.

At that moment, six P—51s with Israeli markings flashed by. Splitting into three pairs, they circled above the B—24 protectively.

Brent looked at the unconscious Knudsen and the

grisly head of the dead ball turret gunner. The young, brilliant engineering student was just another corpse. The garbage of war. "A little goddamned late!" he cried out bitterly. The intercom remained mute.

Chapter X

"*Shady Lady* has landed at Ben Gurion Airport, Admiral," Rear Admiral Byron Whitehead said. "I just decoded a 'Blue Gamma' transmission."

"Thank the gods and Buddha," Admiral Fujita answered from behind his desk. He patted one of a bank of phones near his right hand. "But I know, it just come over from Communications."

"Fleet Code?"

"No. CNN."

"CNN? I'll be damned." Obviously chagrined, Whitehead shifted his bulbous bulk on the thick cushions of his chair. The aged American rear admiral occupied a special niche with Fujita. While *Yonaga* was ice–locked in Sano Wan for all of World War II, Whitehead had fought in fourteen battles. He knew more about carrier warfare and invasion tactics than any other man on board; arguably, more than any other man alive. Notwithstanding, there was a dark side to the man; he had been sunk six times. "Barnacle Byron," "Neptune's Nipper," "Deep Six," "Torpedo Bait," "Scuttle Ass," were just a few of the more polite sobriquets that had been applied to Whitehead by his fellow crewmen. In fact, near the end of the war, droves of officers applied for transfers whenever he reported aboard a new carrier. To the superstitious Japanese, his presence was especially ominous. Most believed dark *kamis* haunted his every step. But not Fujita. He respected Whitehead and found him indispensable. This was enough to quell any complaints before they could be aired.

"Damn. They were barred—all media were barred from the airport," Whitehead rued.

Fujita's deep wrinkles slanted upward in a suggestion of a smile. "True, Admiral Whitehead. They still had the exact moment of landing and the news of a great dogfight."

"Details?"

"None." The old Japanese spread his shriveled hands on the desk, knuckles rough and withered like a row of walnuts. The intense black eyes pierced the deep blue of the American's. A hint of anxiety broke the usual unruffled facade, "Casualties?"

"No official report, yet. But two of the crew were taken from the bomber on stretchers. But Commander Ross is alright. We know that—it's confirmed."

The oriental sighed, a long wheezing sound, and slumped into the shroud–like folds of his uniform. Weaving his fingers together and making a temple of his knobby knuckles, he said, "Hachiman San has smiled again." He glanced at a small paulownia wood shrine on the opposite bulkhead. Built like a small open cabin with a peaked roof, it contained a collection of icons. Hachiman San, the God of War, was represented by a small exquisitely carved jade archer astride a charger, bow armed and stretched. Fujita bowed his head twice and said, "Oh great Hachiman San, watch over your faithful, those who would protect the Son of Heaven, and accept our gratitude for shielding our fellow samurai."

"Something worked for us," Whitehead conceded. "The enemy had an excellent chance to shoot down *Shady Lady*—should've killed them all."

Fujita nodded and said matter-of-factly, "Your three-headed Jesus?"

There was no sarcasm or malice in the voice. It was a nineteenth-century Asian mind working. Whitehead said, "The Father, the Son, the Holy Ghost?"

"Yes. Why not, Admiral? An omnipotent triumvirate in the west. If you combine our religions, many powerful gods combine their strength in our cause."

Whitehead answered the ludicrous statement with a straight face. He knew in the oriental's mind the contention was perfectly logical and free of contradictions. "True, Sir, faith is not limited by geography."

"Only the prejudices of men." The old man tugged on the single white hair trailing from his chin. "You have more details? I feel *Shady Lady* was ambushed."

"I cannot verify an ambush, but we have confirmed *Shady Lady* was attacked by the Fourth Fighter Squadron."

"That murdering dog, Kenneth Rosencrance!" Fujita spat.

"Yes."

Stiff fingers used the desk top for a drum. "It makes no sense."

"No sense, Sir?"

"Yes. The way Kadafi moves the Fourth around." He

motioned at a wall chart of the Pacific. "He should be gathering his strength in the Western Pacific. By now the whole world knows we are massing landing craft, pulled our two divisions of assault troops out of the Canary Islands—knows we are preparing to make an amphibious assault on Saipan and Tinian."

"Or the Tomonuto Atoll, Sir. And keep in mind, Admiral, the *fatwa.*"

"Kadafi's death decree against Commander Brent Ross?"

"Yes, Admiral Fujita. And remember, Sir, a million dollars has no little appeal for a mercenary like Rosencrance."

"I cannot understand how a man can fight for money. Where is the honor, the glory. These men are nothing but *yakuzas*—gangsters—" He waved a hand in an enveloping gesture. "And why ambush one bomber when there are strategic imperatives to be met on the other side of the world?"

Shifting his corpulent bulk, Whitehead adjusted his overburdened belt downward so that it no longer bit into his bulging stomach. As the senior Naval Intelligence Command officer and personal adviser to Admiral Fujita for four years, he was adept at fielding nearly impossible questions from the old "Iron Admiral." To him, Fujita still saw the world through a window colored by the values and traditions of the East. Relieved by the lowered belt, Whitehead released his pent-up breath with a sibilant wheeze and said, "According to our informants and Colonel Bernstein's, too, Kenneth Rosencrance's influence is growing with Kadafi. He seems to be able to sway the dictator when no others can influence him."

"More than Sheik Iman Younis?"

"I would say as much, but different."

"What do you mean?"

"Sheik Younis is an adviser, a diplomat, a politician, while Rosencrance is a field commander."

"Younis has Kadafi's ear constantly."

"True, Admiral Fujita. But, remember Kadafi admires the warrior, the man in the field—considers himself a man of action, a fighter."

"But Rosencrance cannot have his way regardless of military expediency, favorite or not."

"Not in everything, Sir. And, remember, since the conference in Libya last year, Kadafi has had a particularly venomous hatred for Commander Ross. We must factor that in, too."

Fujita nodded agreement. "Yes. And Colonel Kadafi is still basically a terrorist, thinks like a terrorist, but now on a grand, global scale."

"I agree, Sir. Personal assassination is not beneath him."

Fujita snickered caustically. "What is beneath him?"

"Can't think of a thing, Sir."

Both men chuckled humorlessly. Fujita glanced at a large brass ship's clock on the opposite bulkhead. "It is time for the staff meeting. My staff must be waiting in Flag Plot now."

Slowly, the "Iron Admiral" pushed himself to his feet while Rear Admiral Whitehead waited. The American did not dare offer to assist. He was glad Flag Plot was just across the passageway. It would still be a long, slow walk.

* * *

Flag Plot was a large conference room with a long table, charts covering the bulkheads, and the inevitable picture of Emperor Akihito prominently displayed. Just as inevitable was the shrine filled with glistening Buddhist and Shinto icons hanging on another bulkhead. A near duplicate of the shrine hanging in Admiral Fujita's cabin, it was far more elaborate and contained more icons.

Air Group Commanding Officer Commander Yoshi Matsuhara tapped the shiny walnut of the table restlessly. He had air groups to train at Tokyo International and Tsuchuira, two new bomber commanders to meet. Hundreds of young men from all over the world were enlisting in the war against tyranny and world terrorism. Some would fly from *Yonaga* and *Bennington,* others would be assigned to home defense.

And many would die. That was inevitable. "The garbage of war," he had heard Brent Ross cry our bitterly while standing over a cluster of corpses of the world's most promising. How true! His friend was so wise for one so young.

And what had happened to his best friend, his companion of years of warfare; the toughest, bravest, most violent man he had ever known? There had been puzzling reports of a terrible brawl in a lady's room in the Fort Lauderdale Airport. No doubt, the media had leaped on a minor incident and distorted it to embarrass the "Yankee Samurai." But there was no humor in CNN reports of a long running dogfight over the Mediterranean. Maybe Kadafi had made his *fatwa* good and some gloating killer was collecting his million dollars.

Yoshi tried to shake the morbid mood. But it was no good. It was not just apprehension about Brent Ross that disheartened him. Many monstrous calamities had burdened and bowed his broad shoulders. He had been despondent and *shinigurai*—crazy to die—ever since his beloved Tomoko Ozumori had been savagely violated and hanged by Kadafi's sadistic assassin, Harry "High Wire" Goodenough, the previous year. His third crippling loss. There had been too much tragedy. His entire family had been incinerated in Curtis LeMay's great fire raid on Tokyo and the only other love he had ever known, Kimio Urshazawa, murdered five years earlier, cut down at his side by a terrorist's AK–47.

Yoshi doubled his fists and his knuckles warred each other. He brought death with him, not only inflicting it on his enemies, but luring the foul old woman to those he loved. Maybe, Brent Ross, too, had slipped between her odious loins. "My name is death," he muttered to himself.

"What was that?" came from the gunnery officer and good friend, Lieutenant Commander Nobomitsu Atsumi who sat at his side.

"Nothing. Nothing," Yoshi answered, face flushing slightly. He lapsed into silence, brooding and intense.

Reading the pilot's mood, the gunnery officer smiled and patted Yoshi on the back. "It'll be over soon, old friend, and you can return to your precious airplanes." For the first time, Yoshi smiled and looked at his friend of half–a–century.

Like Yoshi, Atsumi had endured the forty-two-years of isolation in Sano Wan; the break out; the attack on Pearl Harbor and the decade–long war against the *jihad*. Atsumi was much like Yoshi. Both men were in their late sixties, yet, like most holdouts, resisted the inroads of age. His hair was black, skin clear, carriage erect and athletic.

"The lack of tobacco, liquor and women kept us young," Fujita often explained to the curious. There was some truth in the old man's contention. Holdouts from all over the Pacific had shown the same remarkable resistance to time.

Yoshi's eyes wandered over the other occupants of the room. At the far end sat, or rather drooped, the ancient scribe, Commander Hakuseki Katsube. The antithesis of Yoshi and Nobomitsu, time had not passed him by. Indeed, it had plundered him cruelly. Leaning over his pad and brush—Admiral Fujita disdained modern recorders—the ancient officer giggled to himself and drooled, probably enjoying a blithe memory nearly a century old. Yoshi was convinced Katsube was in the advanced stages of senility. Only Fujita's loyalty to his ancient friend kept him on board. He had no family, all wiped out by war and time.

In quick succession Yoshi scanned the executive officer, Captain Mitake Arai, the captain of the *Bennington*, Captain Paul Treynor, escort commander, Captain John "Slugger" Fite, the captain of battleship *New Jersey*, Captain Justin McManus, and the Chief Engineer, Lieutenant Tatsuya Yoshida. Colonel Bernstein and the new CIA man were missing.

Suddenly, the door opened and Admiral Fujita and Rear Admiral Byron Whitehead entered. Everyone snapped to attention and bowed. The newcomers returned the bows and found their chairs, Fujita commanding the head of the table.

"Before we begin this meeting, I want all of you to know Commander Brent Ross arrived in Israel safely," Fujita announced.

"Banzai!" "Hear! Hear!" echoed in the room.

Yoshi felt himself choke on his next breath and coughed into his hand. Atsumi pounded him on the back and shouted in his ear, "No one can kill that 'Yankee Samurai', no one." Yoshi could only nod back while he blinked away the moisture in his eyes.

Looking around perplexed, Katsube decided to join the celebration. Half rising from his chair, the old scribe shouted, *"Banzai!"* and pitched forward, face thumping on his pad. Chief Engineer Yoshida caught him before he could slide to the deck.

Fujita's raised hands restored order. The old man was all business. "As all of you know, Kadafi's reactor at Rabta is still shut down. Our bombers did a splendid job in destroying auxiliary and support facilities."

Chief Engineer, Lieutenant Tatsuya Yoshida said, "I understand the Americans have threatened to supply Israel with nuclear weapons if Kadafi builds an atomic bomb."

Fujita nodded at Rear Admiral Whitehead. Whitehead said, "True. It's official policy. I got confirmation from the State Department this morning."

The escort commander, Captain John "Slugger" Fite, a big, white–haired polar bear of a man came in with a gnawing question, "The poison gas works?"

Whitehead answered, "Our latest intelligence reports all facilities completely destroyed. Also confirmed in this morning's report."

There were excited, happy cries and backslapping.

The executive officer, Captain Mitake Arai, came half out of his chair. A destroyer commander during World War II, his ship had been sunk with terrible loss of life in

1945 by air strikes directed from Task Force 58 by a then young Lieutenant Byron Whitehead. Arai never forgot or forgave. In fact, Yoshi had seen the two old warriors wage the battles time and again. The hatred was mutual and relentless. Yoshi anticipated another eruption.

Arai acknowledged Fite and Treynor and then moved his eyes to Rear Admiral Whitehead. Yoshi was surprised by his congenial tone, "Americans have fought for us and died for the cause and the United States has been generous with some of the older equipment. But the Russian Republics are selling the Arabs everything—two carriers, two cruisers, their latest electronics equipment. Why, four of their six capital ships are Russian. We need more of the latest. More carriers, big-gunned ships, aircraft. The Grumman FX-1000 is the best fighter on earth and we have none. We need more of those great engines that only power Commander Matsuhara's Zero-sen, electronics equipment, landing craft." The conciliatory tone dropped and Arai stabbed a finger at Whitehead, shocking everyone, "You are not doing enough, Sir." His fist struck the table and his words were unprecedented, "You should be doing more, Sir."

The attack struck Whitehead like a thunderbolt. The other Americans stiffened and looked at each other. Yoshi glanced at Fujita. The old admiral had sagged back but was watching the pair warily. The meeting had moved into dangerous, divisive ground. It was time for Fujita to intervene, but he remained strangely silent. Maybe he felt the festering wound would heal better in the fresh air of exposure.

Bumping his ample stomach against the table, Whitehead labored to his feet. "I resent that. Two-thirds of our battle group are American capital ships. The Pentagon's sent us F6Fs, A-1s, F4Us, TBMs, SB2Cs, F8Fs, ships. Where do you get off . . ."

"But not the latest, the best. And the crews! The crews! You have only sent token forces, even for our big ships. The spirits of thousands of the sons of Nippon have entered the Yasakuni Shrine fighting your battles, the free world's battles."

Before Whitehead could respond, Fujita took control. He had let things go too far and knew it. "Enough!" he shouted, waving a tiny fist angrily. "We must stop fighting the Greater East Asia War and concentrate on our current battles." Both men froze but glared at each other with unmitigated hatred.

Glaring at Arai, Fujita growled, "Captain Arai, you are addressing a rear admiral. You will respect superior rank and mind your tongue or I will have you thrown off the ship. And remember, at least one–half of the crews of *New Jersey* and *Bennington* are American volunteers."

Black and glossy, like two bits of polished obsidian, Fujita's eyes roamed the severely discomforted faces of his staff. "We are here to come together in a common purpose, to fight side by side, not against each other." He pointed a finger at the two antagonists. "Let the battles of the past rest in the fathoms with the god of the deep, Watatsumi-no-Mikoto." His tiny fist struck the oak. "If you do not, you will both be seeking new postings."

Both officers dropped into their chairs, throwing grim and baleful looks at each other. Yoshi knew it was not over.

"And remember," Fujita continued, "the two commandments of the Kurozumi—'Thou shalt not be without a constantly believing heart'." His eyes bored into Arai's, "And, 'Thou shalt not yield to anger or grief'." Arai turned his lips under and stared at the table.

A knock interrupted. Fujita nodded and Chief Engineer Lieutenant Tatsuya Yoshida opened the door.

Three officers and a civilian entered the room. They bowed and Fujita nodded back. The first officer was Colonel Irving Bernstein and the second was his young subordinate, Lieutenant Ephraim Sneerson. The third officer was a stranger in the uniform of the Maritime Self Defense Force. The civilian was the blond, youthful CIA agent, Elliot "Ellie" Amberg.

Fujita gestured to Bernstein, Sneerson and Amberg to seat themselves. The stranger, a full commander, remained standing, shifting his weight uneasily. Yoshi knew this was a deliberate ploy by Fujita. The old admiral held the Self Defense Force—he even loathed the name—in contempt.

Yoshi looked the officer over. A short, flaccid man of middle years, his posture was tense, a once handsome face now puffy with fat, pale with an unhealthy pallor and fixed lugubrious expression. Little red veins in his nose and cheeks stood out in vivid contrast to the pallor of his skin. Yoshi guessed the man ate and drank too much. The sight of the officer's stomach bulging against his tunic made Yoshi think of Rear Admiral Whitehead's similar problem. He smiled.

"Lieutenant Sadaaki Mumata of the Maritime Self Defense Force reporting, Admiral Fujita," the stranger said, in a high timbre that squeaked like a poorly tuned *samisen*. He bowed again.

"I expected you yesterday," Fujita snapped.

The little man's eyes bulged like marbles stuck in clay and his puny Adam's apple worked up and down as if a tiny rodent were trapped in his throat. Yoshi grinned at Atsumi who nodded back in amusement. The man was reacting like a condemned soul halted at the gates of the Yasakuni Shrine for judgement. Fujita did that to people. "Ah, I am sorry . . ."

"Do not be sorry, Commander. A samurai does not demean himself with shallow excuses."

Mumata drew his head back. For the first time, he showed a stiffening of his back bone. "Respectfully, Admiral, I am not making excuses. My orders were delayed. I only received them this morning and reported to *Yonaga* two hours ago. Your OD made me wait on the quarter-deck—claimed you were in conference and would not be disturbed."

"That is better and that is true. Seat yourself, Commander." Mumata found a chair at the end of the table while all eyes followed him. The old man hunched forward. "I need all the landing craft you can muster."

"For the invasion of the Marianas?"

The officers exchanged uneasy glances. Some shook their heads. The coming assault was the worst kept secret on earth. It had even been a subject of an American quiz show.

"Correct, Commander."

Mumata pulled a document from an inside pocket. "As all of you know, most of our ships were destroyed in the great raid of 1989." Everyone nodded grimly. The loss of most of the combat ships had been catastrophic. Equipped with useless anti–aircraft missiles and lacking fire power, the Self Defense Force warships had been easy targets for Arab bombers. *Yonaga* had been far to the north attacking North Korean bases and was unable to offer any help. Only frigate *Ayase* and destroyer *Yamagiri* had survived, been rearmed and put on radar picket duty. Luckily, most of the amphibious vessels had survived, though many had been severely damaged.

Mumata continued, "I have good news for you." He stared at Fujita for encouragement. He found cold steel. Clearing his throat, he continued, "Landing ships *Muira, Ojika, Satsuma, Motobu,* and *Nemuro* are ready for operations."

"The landing barges?" Fujita said. "LCVPs?"

Sadaaki Mumata nodded. "Each LST can carry twelve LCVPs."

"You have them?"

"Yes, Sir."

The old man drummed his desk, turned to Rear Admiral Whitehead. The American had calmed. "The American navy has promised us more troop transports, a control ship and attack cargo ships." Fujita waved at Mumata. "We only have the eight transports sent us last year. Not enough. We must land at least two divisions."

Arai arched an eyebrow at Whitehead and snorted into his palm.

Whitehead shot a glance at Arai and said, "Twenty APAs, assault transports, and ten AKAs, assault cargo vessels, have been taken out of mothballs and are almost ready for sea. With these bottoms we can land more than two divisions, complete with support units, artillery and armor."

Yoshi wondered about Fujita's memory. The invasion had been in the works for years and they had reviewed this subject repeatedly. In fact, it had become an obsession. Either the old sailor was forgetful, or he wanted reassurance from the American.

Fujita creaked to his feet and moved to a chart of the Western Pacific. He thumped the Marianas with a rubber-tipped pointer. "We must take Tinian," he said, a hushed, agonizing timbre in his voice that spoke of a lifetime of torment. Tinian held particular horror for all Japanese. From this small, flat island, B–29 *Enola Gay* took off with the atomic bomb that destroyed Hiroshima and vaporized Fujita's family along with thousands of others. For a long moment Fujita stared at the island silently, then covering his mouth he coughed, a thick phlegmy sound.

Everyone stared self-consciously as the old man dabbed at his lips with a handkerchief. Squaring his shoulders, he continued, "We will present our enemies with a tactical dilemma."

"A tactical dilemma?" Whitehead echoed.

With renewed interest, the men hunched forward. "We must take the Marianas, true, but our other target is on the other side of the world."

"Other side of the world, Sir?" Mumata blurted.

Fujita moved to a chart of the Middle East and struck Aden. "Here! At Aden. Three enemy carriers and three cruisers. To speak of an invasion of the Marianas with this force at our backs is imprudent."

Now Yoshi could see through the Admiral's thinking. "Then a feint at the Marianas to draw them out," the pilot suggested.

Fujita nodded. "No, not just a feint, Commander. We will be prepared to make the invasion. If the enemy fleet does not sortie, we will proceed with our landings, taking Saipan first. We hold Aguijan to the south of Tinian. If we take Saipan, Tinian will be flanked, neutralized by our heavy artillery and aircraft. Then we invade her, too. The Arabs know this as well as we do. *Yonaga* and *Bennington* will destroy the enemy's air force, battleship *New Jersey* and Captain Fite's destroyers will shell the beaches."

Leaning on the table, Fujita's eyes searched every earnest face. "But I am convinced the Arab mind will find this untenable, a defeat for the sacred *jihad*. Kadafi should react violently, send his fleet or lose his bases and his prestige as Mahdi. This time we will have them in a vice of their own twisted dementia. Their battle group should come, we will send our amphibious forces into retirement, and then we will destroy his carriers and take the islands. Wipe out the cancer forever!" Slapping the oak with the pointer, a sound like the report of pistol cracked through the room.

"Banzai!"

"The enemy strength in the Marianas?" Captain Fite asked with his usual practical caution.

Fujita gestured at the young CIA man, Elliot Amberg. Green eyes ferreting uneasily around the room, the young man stood. Yoshi chuckled every time he glanced at Elliot's mustard-colored hair. Of moderate length, it stuck out from his scalp as if a storm cloud hung perpetually over the young man's head, electrifying each strand. And, indeed, his glum expression was as dark as the heart of line squall. Amberg said, "I think you all know the Arabs have a full division on Saipan—the Sixth Infantry Division reinforced by the Ninth Parachute Brigade. Sixteen to nineteen—thousand of their best troops."

"Armor?"

Amberg shifted his weight uncomfortably. "A reinforced company, maybe twenty T–62s, Sir."

Bernstein pushed young Sneerson to his feet, "Admiral," Sneerson said, "it is customary for an Arab infantry division to have an armored battalion, three companies, seventeen tanks to a company and the Sixth is equipped with T–72s." The Israeli glanced at Amberg who glared back.

The CIA clashing with Mossad. Another feud that never ended. Time and again Yoshi had seen CIA men embarrassed by Mossad which estimated enemy strength with uncanny accuracy. Everyone knew Mossad infiltrated the enemy with its own agents while the CIA had found little success with spies. Mossad missed nothing. In fact, it was said there was an Israeli whore in every officers' bordello.

Amberg began to retaliate, but Fujita ignored him, addressing the Mossad agents, "Artillery?"

While Amberg fumed, Bernstein said, "The Sixth has four batteries of four 122–millimeter guns each." He shrugged. "But we know they have been reinforced with some heavier guns."

"How heavy?"

"At least two batteries of 152–millimeter guns. All weapons the latest from the Russian arsenal," Bernstein said.

"Of course, our Russian friends," Fujita commented sarcastically. "And Tinian?"

Bernstein yielded to his young aide who was obviously piqued at losing the limelight and the opportunity to taunt Amberg. Sneerson said, "A brigade of infantry, two companies of combat engineers, two batteries of 122–millimeter guns—perhaps five thousand men on Tinian, Admiral. And all units on both islands are digging in and rebuilding old Japanese bunkers."

"You're way off. Our information is indisputable," Amberg objected, anger forcing the careless statement. No agent ever claimed his information was inviolable.

"Ha!" Sneerson mocked. "You were off at Rabta and you're off by at least thirty tanks here and what do you know of Tinian . . ."

Fujita waved the two young agents to silence. "We know the enemy is in division strength with armored support."

Both young men answered, "Yes, Sir."

"And they supply by old *Whiskey* and *Zulu* submarines which are slow, cumbersome and limited."

"True, Sir," the young men chorused.

"Then sit down and cool yourselves." The agents dropped into their chairs. Bernstein gave Sneerson a fatherly pat on the back.

The executive officer, Captain Mitake Arai, eyed Whitehead and then spoke up. "Their base in the Western Carolines, Tomonuto, Admiral. Shouldn't we neutralize it before this operation? There are tankers and depot ships there."

Fujita toyed with the single white hair hanging from his chin. "I have been considering that problem, Captain Arai. We will detach *Bennington*. She will destroy the enemy support groups at Tomonuto and then join the assault on Saipan."

Rear Admiral Whitehead was disturbed. "It's becoming too complicated, Admiral Fujita."

Everyone stared silently. This was not just his feud with Arai. The staff knew Whitehead was always suspicious of the Japanese fondness for intricate planning. A military pragmatist, the American realized the simpler the plan, the better. He knew that battles were beset with the unexpected; surfeits of variables that made a farce of the best laid plans. Once Yoshi had heard him say, "War is a series of catastrophes which result in victory if you are lucky, defeat if you are unlucky."

Whitehead continued, "Sir, we are counting on the favorable outcome of too many imponderables. The great Count Helmut Von Moltke put it succinctly a hundred years ago, 'No plan survives contact with the enemy'."

Fujita showed his own knowledge of the great military minds, "True, Admiral Whitehead. Remember, von Clausewitz said, 'No other human activity is so continuously or universally bound up with chance. And through the element of chance, guesswork and luck come to play a great part in war'."

Silence as palpable as the acrid stench of cordite filled the room. Circling the rubber tip around the Marianas, the old Japanese continued, "I am aware our best laid plans are only hopeful contingencies predicated on the courage and resourcefulness of our men." He smiled. "But we have the men, the best men in the world who have never failed to carry out their orders."

"Banzai!" Katsube waved a hand, half–rose, but was pushed back into his chair before he could fall out of it. Everyone ignored him.

"Then, Sir, respectfully, take care not to become too complex," Whitehead advised.

Fujita's eyes focused hard and long on the American

rear admiral. Yoshi would not have been surprised at a violent outburst of temper. Instead, his voice was poised, nearly tranquil, "You are thinking of Midway."

"Yes, a classic example. At Midway your friend Admiral Isoroku Yamamoto split his forces into six main groups, scattered them all over the North Pacific so that they were unable to support each other. Why, your task forces occupied Kiska, Attu, attacked Dutch Harbor as diversions which only served to split and weaken the main thrust at Midway. And his main battle force trailed Nagumo's carriers by hundreds of miles. If this force had supported the carriers, if the other groups had been concentrated in one great fist aimed at Midway, he may not have lost carriers *Kaga, Akagi, Soryu* and *Hiryu*—could've changed the course of the war, of history."

The Japanese shifted uncomfortably. The great defeat was a page in history none of them enjoyed reading. Whitehead was dragging them through it word by word, teaching the lesson again that should have been learned, but was not.

The American was not finished, "Your *Sho–Ichi–Go* plan for Leyte Gulf. Splitting your fleet into three forces." He described the intricate plan to synchronize the separate attacks on the American invasion fleet off Leyte by sending carriers from the north to lure Admiral William F. "Bull" Halsey's fast carriers and battleships away, while striking simultaneously through the Surigao and San Bernardino Straits with battleships and cruisers.

Fujita grinned, and again showed his encyclopedic knowledge, enjoying himself hugely in his favorite topic; the war he had missed. "And Halsey took the bait, rushed northward to stupidly attack four carriers that carried only 116 planes. They were no threat. And then he was forced to rush back—took your best carriers and battle-ships out of the battle."

Arai could not resist the temptation to taunt his enemy, "I understand some Americans called it 'The Battle of Bull's Run'." The Japanese chortled. Arai laughed bois-terously. It was the Americans' turn to squirm.

Whitehead's face flooded with a sanguine rush and his eyes widened. Ignoring Arai, he addressed Fujita, "But *Sho-Ichi-Go* didn't work, Admiral. Basically, still too com-plex, regardless of Halsey's foolishness."

Fujita scratched his glistening pate impatiently. "Let this "Bull" Halsey rest. Let us not forget, we have a battle to fight in the Western Pacific. True, we must learn from the past, none of us wish to repeat it." He stabbed the pointer at Whitehead, "What would you suggest, Admi-ral?"

"Ignore Tomonuto." The old American turned up his palms, "What does the enemy have there?" He answered the question, "A few oilers, supply ships and his air strip on Barry Island isn't finished. We know that if the enemy battle group attacks us, they will steer clear of Tomonuto, anyway. Fuel in Indonesia. They have bases there. The Indonesians have been licking their boots."

Fujita nodded. "True. True, Admiral Whitehead. I will consider your advice in my planning." His eyes moved to Captain John "Slugger" Fite and the commanding offi-cers of *New Jersey* and *Bennington*. "Your battle readiness, gentlemen?"

Paul Treynor reported, *"Bennington* is ready for sea. Bomb damage repaired, air groups up to full strength, magazines full, and we are topping off our tanks now."

Justin McManus reported the torpedo damage to battleship *New Jersey* repaired and the warship ready for sea.

Fite reported all thirteen escorts ready for action.

"Well done. Well done. Captain Fite, Captain Treynor and Captain McManus. Report to your commands and be ready to put to sea on 24—hours notice. No extended liberties."

"But why, Sir," McManus objected. "The enemy fleet is half—way around the world."

"Do not ask me why!" Fujita snapped. "You are dismissed."

The American captains stood, bowed and filed from the room.

Fujita spoke to Lieutenant Sadaaki Mumata, "You are dismissed, Lieutenant. My executive officer will be your liaison."

"Yes, Sir. Thank you, Sir," the fleshy officer burbled with obvious relief. Quickly, he stood, bowed and exited. Then, the admiral dismissed Sneerson and Amberg but not Colonel Bernstein who tugged contemplatively on his beard.

Slowly and with fatigue spilling across his visage like cold oil, Fujita slumped into his chair. He seemed to have trouble holding his head erect. "Gentlemen," he muttered, his voice crackling like wind through dry leaves, "we will close the meeting for now." He ran a hand over his ridged and crinkled forehead. "But, we will reconvene in my cabin in one hour. I want your reports, but first I have intelligence briefs to study."

Yoshi was convinced the old man was lying. He needed a rest. No one was immune to the years and Fujita was no exception. The continuous warfare had taken its toll of everyone and the old admiral had passed the century mark. Although his brilliant mind was still quick and alert, he had become forgetful and his body had wasted away to under a 100–pounds. How long could this incredible man last? No man could live on willpower alone. And how could he ever be replaced?

From his chair Fujita said, "Gentlemen, you are dismissed."

The officers stood, bowed and left. Only Commander Katsube remained with the admiral, bent over his pad, cackling to himself and brushing ideograms.

Chapter XI

With an hour to wait, Yoshi guided Lieutenant Commander Nobomitsu Atsumi into his cabin. The quarters of a long–dead flag officer, the cabin was large with a wide bunk, desk, table and chairs, and the unprecedented luxury of a small under–the–counter refrigerator. An open port let in air and yard noises. The officers sank into chairs on either side of the table. Yoshi produced a bottle of saké and two small white porcelain cups.

"Ah," Nobomitsu said. "You are clairvoyant."

Yoshi nodded. "After that meeting, I need a drink. I wonder just who is fighting whom."

Atsumi laughed sardonically. "Arai will not allow Whitehead to forget the past and Sneerson and Amberg can't stop fighting."

"Maybe, when we stop fighting each other, we will find time to fight the Arabs," Yoshi said, filling the cups.

Chuckling, the gunnery officer held up his cup with the ship's logo, the Imperial sixteen–petaled chrysanthemum, politely pointed at his host. Yoshi answered the salute and made the obligatory toast, "To the Son of Heaven."

"Yes. To the Emperor." Both men sipped the rice wine.

Atsumi studied his friend. He did not like what he saw. Harsh downward slashing lines from the corners of his eyes and mouth spoke of a personal hell. Slowly, he rotated his cup on the tabletop and watched the clear liquid swirl and crest.

Yoshi spoke, "What is troubling you, Nobomitsu—san?"

"You are Yoshi—san." His eyes studied the pilot's face, the downcast eyes. "You are *shinigurai*—is that not true?"

"Crazy to die? Perhaps."

"Tomoko Ozumori?"

Looking up, the flyer's voice was bruised by pain, "I have brought the wrath of hosts of evil *kamis* and demons down upon all those I have loved." He sipped his drink. "And I cannot inflict my vengeance on that insane murderer, Harry Goodenough."

Nobomitsu nodded understanding. "Yes, of course. A personal revenge, something all samurai hunger for. But those two Israeli women did that for you when they killed him."

"I should have killed him with a wire to the neck." He snorted, "And mere women did it for me."

"I know." Atsumi took a small drink and tabled his cup with a loud thumping sound. "You spent your first fourteen years in America."

"You know I was born in Los Angeles."

"You never mention Christianity. You must have been exposed to it."

Yoshi smirked. "Oh, yes. My American friends considered me a heathen, tried to save my soul."

145

"But it didn't work."

"No. My father brought me up in our own traditions, said Christianity was intolerant, filled with too much nonsense and 'Thou shalt nots'."

"He was very wise." Atsumi tapped his cup with a fingernail, making a high pinging sound. "You have given up on Zen, your prophet, Bodhidharma?" he asked bluntly.

Appearing not to hear the question, the pilot held up his cup and seemed to speak to it, "Tomoko was so much a part of my life that, in a way, I had not even seen her until she was gone."

The gunnery officer nodded. "Then you still believe, you speak Zen."

"Do I?" The pilot threw off his drink and recharged both cups. "True, I have already forged through Buddha's seven rings of hell—have been cut, felt the concussions, wept and burned."

"Then your spirit should be purged."

"No, I found no revival, nothing but my personal demons."

"Then you have no 'self'?"

"Don't say that."

"Why, Yoshi—san?"

"Because I'm what your question turns me into, don't you see that?"

"No, and you're speaking more Zen. Push it further. One should strive to lose his ongoing identity. How else can a man find the Four Holy Truths?"

The pilot rubbed his forehead as if misery were a mask and he was trying to tear it loose and discard it. "Not true. The 'Truths' elude me and I no longer seek them. After she was taken from me, there were no insights, intuitive flashes, enlightenment as Bodhidarma teaches. My meditations became empty and useless." He looked at his friend, face a veil of hopelessness. "There was nothing, Nobomitsu–san, nothing at all."

Propping his chin on his fists, the gunnery officer leaned forward on his elbows. "Yoshi–san, consider this. Man is a part of nature and nature has no conscience. What happens just happens, and none of us are wise enough to know enough to truly decide whether any event is good or evil." He sipped his drink and eyed his silent friend. "We cannot define life by human terms. This is an utterly futile exercise that leaves men continually judgmental and hating life for its injustices."

For the first time, Yoshi smiled. "You've been reading Lao–tzu. There is some of him in your words."

"True. There is much power in Taoism, Yoshi–san. If Confucius and Buddha have failed you, why not try Taoism?"

"I have given Taoism much thought. Studied Lao–tzu's doctrines, Chang Tao–ling's triad, the principal gods—Wan-Chang, the God of Letters, Tsai-Shin, the God of Riches and even called on the God of War, Kwanti."

"Did they serve you?"

"Truly, I do not know."

"What do you know?"

"I know that I must fight my own inner demons more than any other force. We have lived long, fought hard, Nobomitsu–san, and the blood of the men I have killed does not just stain."

"What do you mean?"

147

"It saturates me, feeds my demons. Now I know this is what happens to men of our age who have been opened by blood—lust and battle. Each of us must face an incredibly powerful enemy in this life—himself. They are arrayed against me, my demons, archetypes which are as old as the species. They have been driving me madly across this planet and I never knew them until now. And now I know they exist and can challenge them on a conscious basis."

Atsumi was stunned. Never had he heard his friend speak with such depth, so much passion. "And the teachings of Shinto, our sacred religion—you would cast them aside?"

"Never!" But the gods, the *kamis*, the demons always seek a parity."

"What do you mean?"

Yoshi slapped the table. "The books must be balanced, my friend, and Tomoko and millions of innocents like her have found their place in the ledger."

They drank just one more small cup, talked for a few more moments before the gunnery officer glanced at his watch. "I must return to my cabin before the meeting, Yoshi—san. I have some reports that I should bring." He rose and placed a hand on the pilot's shoulder. "Keep seeking the truth, my friend."

Yoshi smiled up at Nobomitsu and said, "Whatever that may be."

From his chair next to Colonel Bernstein, Rear Admiral Whitehead stared at Admiral Fujita. The hour's rest had served to revive Admiral Fujita only slightly. Yet, as the

148

old sailor looked across his desk into the eyes of his most trusted aides, his voice was firm, if not strong. "Your reports, gentlemen, Engineering Department first."

Chief Engineer Yoshida reported the torpedo damage between frames 86 and 92 completely repaired with frame 89 sectioned and replaced. Two new armored bulkheads between frames 80 and 92 had been installed below the first platform and the damaged oil filler line replaced.

"Boiler Room Number Two was flooded," Fujita reminded him. "Are your repairs complete?"

"Completely repaired, Admiral. We have installed a new boiler, pumps, oil lines, fresh and salt water lines," Yoshida assured him. "And fueling is in progress. All boilers descaled except Numbers 4 and 7 which are receiving new burners, too. Four more days, Admiral, and I can give you 33-knots. Otherwise, my department is ship-shape and ready for sea."

Lieutenant Commander Nobomitsu Atsumi reported barrel replacements on eight of his thirty-two 127-millimeter dual purpose cannons. "But I need six more, Sir. They overheated in our last engagement and the rifling is gone. It's like shooting shotguns."

"They will have to do for now. Production is slow and you know it. Magazines?"

"Full loads, all magazines, Sir."

Fujita turned to Rear Admiral Whitehead. "Communications and Cryptologic Departments ready, Sir," Whitehead said.

For the first time, the old admiral grinned. "You have replaced one of your magic toys with another."

Whitehead grinned back. "Yes, Sir. We have replaced

the electronics warfare unit, AN-SLQ-32, with the complete Mark 38 Suite."

The older Japanese looked at each other. Everyone had seen the new antenna array go up on the foretop and much had been speculated about the new equipment. But Whitehead knew further explanations were due. A nod from Fujita encouraged him. "The Mark 38 is the latest and best Electronics Support Measures equipment available, gentlemen." He described how the antennas covered the entire azimuth, how the digital tracking unit accessed its own computer which contained a threat library, enabling almost instantaneous identification of incoming radar signals. "It can identify the ship, give the skipper's name, wife, children and even," he chuckled, "his mistress." Laughter. "And it's much faster than the old SLQ–32 and has greater range."

"Aircraft?" the executive officer asked.

"The same. Augments our radar, identifies threats, even makes threat evaluations and indicates target priority."

"This equipment was designed for the age of missiles, Admiral Whitehead," Atsumi said.

"Of course, Commander. However, it will be an enormous asset to our Electronic Warfare systems. Gives us greater range, speed and flexibility. That added edge that can make the difference between victory and defeat."

"The rest of your department?" Admiral Fujita asked.

"Ready, Sir. Computers and encryption equipment manned and ready. My cryptographers are all highly trained and efficient."

Everyone nodded. Whitehead's department had never failed them.

Fujita called on Yoshi.

Yoshi voiced a painful truth, "As you know, the attrition of our pilots and air crews has been very high, Admiral." Everyone nodded gravely. "I have nearly two hundred fighter and bomber pilots and crewmen to train and I haven't even met my new bomber commanders."

"They are due to report today."

"Yes, Sir."

"I gave orders that they are to report to *Yonaga*, to me, first."

"But, Admiral, I must start their training."

"I am aware of this, Commander. Engines?"

Yoshi complained about Nakajima's slowness in delivering the new 2500–horsepower Sakae 50 engine which the company called *"Arashi*—Storm." "All of our Zero-sens are equipped with the Sakae 50, *Arashi*," he added. "But, as you know, Sir, our bombers are still powered by the old 2000–horsepower Sakae 42."

Fujita turned to Captain Mitake Arai, "Contact Nakajima at the close of this meeting." He slapped the desk. "I want the delivery of the Sakae 50 expedited. Our bombers have been cold meat for enemy fighters."

"Yes, Sir. With your permission, I will visit the plant personally."

"Granted." Fujita turned back to Yoshi, "The *'Taifu'*, the monster you have in your fighter?"

"Still tends to overheat, Admiral." He shook his head. "It's dangerous to put it into overboost."

Fujita eyed Whitehead. "Nakajima should do better. We need help from the Wright Corporation and Pratt and Whitney."

"Both companies are working to capacity just to build

enough engines for the new Grumman FX–1000 and the new American bombers," Whitehead said.

Arai chuckled out loud and Whitehead shot him an insidious look.

Fujita said to Arai, "Check on the *Taifu* when you call on Nakajima. We are losing the horsepower race to the enemy. This could cost us the war." He knuckled the desk for a moment and then said to Yoshi, "Our American and British fighters?"

Yoshi's face drained of some of his tension. "Our squadron of F6F Hellcats under Commander Elkins are ready for combat now. In fact, all twelve fighters are flying CAP. And our six Seafires are also battle–ready and I am using them in our CAP."

"Well done, Commander."

Fujita shifted to the silent Colonel Irving Bernstein. "Colonel, the Arabs are massing for another assault on the Ben Gurion Line."

"True, Sir. As you know, the Russians are selling arms to everyone, trying to raise cash."

"Nothing nuclear."

"No, Sir. But Kadafi has two new armored divisions equipped with the newest T–72 MBT and we expect an attack."

"You have a fine spy system and the latest electronics equipment, Colonel."

"True, Sir. And in the desert, you can just watch for the dust—hi–tech dust." There was no humor in his voice.

"The prisoners?" Every eye focused on the Israeli. The Arabs held over three hundred Israeli prisoners and thirty-nine of Fujita's flyers. They had been released the day before and there had been rumors of malnutrition and abuse.

"All of the flyers and a hundred Israeli's arrived in Israel this morning. They were underfed, but in reasonably good health."

A sense of relief filled the room, the men exchanging nods and words of thanks.

"Thank the gods." Fujita ran a thumbnail over his bald pate. "But I thought all Israeli prisoners were to be released when we evacuated the Canary Islands. I understood that Sheik Younis agreed to this?"

"True, Sir. But he is an Arab."

"Of course, I continue to expect honor and integrity where none exists."

"Could've been Kadafi overruling him."

Before Fujita could respond there was a knock. Atsumi opened the door. A short, thick-set man of about forty wearing the full stripes of a lieutenant and aviator wings entered. Standing at rigid attention in front of Admiral Fujita he managed to confuse everyone. His face was a living, breathing atlas of the orient and occident. Close cropped, his hair was brown as newly-turned earth, with a hint of a curl. His eyes were round, yet slightly slanted, his skin deeply tanned with a golden hue. Without a trace of an accent, he spoke his name in a stentorian baritone, "Lieutenant Oliver Y.K. Dempster reporting, Admiral Fujita."

" 'Y.K.'," Arai blurted.

The baritone came back, "Oliver Young Kim Dempster, Captain."

The name spoke volumes. Obviously, the man was a Korean-American; an Amerasian. Whitehead was shocked. Xenophobia was as Japanese as saké. This half–breed Korean could spell trouble. And Oliver Young Kim Dempster. How strange. In the fifties, he had served in Korea with an intelligence officer, Captain Frank Dempster. Dempster had been a heavy drinker and lecher. In all Whitehead travels, he had never seen such highly organized and rampant prostitution as that of Korea. And Dempster wallowed in it. It was joked Dempster supported a half–dozen women just to keep his perennial erection under control. Later, Whitehead heard he had retired and gone to work for the CIA, finally winding up as liaison to Admiral Fujita. He had been killed in the great battle in the South China Sea in 1987, most of his head taken off by a piece of shrapnel the size of a dinner plate. And now, another Dempster. Frank Dempster's wild seed? Whitehead shook his head. Fujita must have requested him.

Whitehead could see hostility sparking in the eyes of most of the Japanese; especially Arai's. There had been centuries of bad blood between the two nations. The Japanese occupation of Korea from 1910 to 1945 had been harsh and oppressive, the nation exploited for its resources, workers, and women—who were used as "pleasure girls." Koreans were considered inferior, had no freedom and no rights. Ill–feelings still persisted, especially in the minds of these nineteenth–century men. Whitehead studied Dempster's face, but the man's eyes were unfathomable. Why would this man want to serve in this nest of former enemies? Men who would hold him in contempt? And why would Fujita want him?"

Admiral Fujita nodded an abbreviated bow and said, "Welcome aboard, Lieutenant Oliver Y.K. Dempster, our new Dive Bomber Commander." He gestured to Yoshi, "Your Air Group Commander, Commander Matsuhara."

Yoshi stood, shook Dempster's hand, and returned to his seat. Fujita introduced the remainder of the staff.

Whitehead distinctly heard Arai whisper under his breath, *"Manuke inu-taberu Kankoku*—Stupid dog-eating Korean."

Fujita shot a look that could sear at the executive officer. The old man's hearing was still sharp enough to pick up some of it, or maybe he read the executive officer's expression. The admiral said, "Lieutenant Dempster is the son of our former comrade who gave his life in battle, Frank Dempster of the CIA."

So that was it. Fujita's loyalties fell into a precise hierarchy: his Emperor, his gods, his comrades, and his dead who were revered in the glow of Shinto. Nevertheless, Dempster must be eminently qualified. The old man would never compromise *Yonaga*'s battle efficiency for anything. Everyone nodded and murmured to each other. Dempster remained stony, eyes riveted on the bulkhead above Fujita's head. Whitehead knew the man must be tense and agitated.

Cannily, Fujita partially defused the situation, "Commander Atsumi, Captain Arai, you are dismissed to your duties. Admiral Whitehead and Colonel Bernstein you may remain if you wish."

Both officers indicated they preferred to remain.

"Very well, gentlemen." Atsumi and Arai left.

Fujita gestured and the Amerasian sat. Some of his tension seemed to drain away as he sank into the chair and the door closed behind Atsumi and Arai. Fujita nodded at Matsuhara.

Yoshi picked up the cue, "Your experience, Lieutenant?"

The strange countenance turned toward the Air Group Commander. "I graduated from Annapolis, Sir, in 1975. Got my basic at Pensacola, carrier training at Meridian, Mississippi. Flew A–4, Skyhawk attack bombers until the Chinese laser system rendered them all inoperable. Then we switched to old Douglas SBDs and Curtis SB2Cs. I, also, got in some time in the new Curtis SB3C."

"But no combat experience."

"Respectfully, Sir, not true. I volunteered for the Israeli Air Force in '89 and have flown over four hundred combat missions—all in dive bombers."

A hush filled the room. The man had flown more combat than most of *Yonaga*'s pilots. Fujita beamed.

"Why did you volunteer for duty in Israel?"

"Because the Israeli Air Force bought over a hundred A–4s in 1980 and I was sent there as a training officer. I learned to respect and admire these people greatly, Sir."

Beaming, Bernstein tapped his palms together in a friendly salute. Dempster smiled back at the Israeli. At least one friendship had been cemented.

Whitehead said. "I met your father several times in Korea, Lieutenant. I was in Naval Intelligence and he was in J–2. You were born there—are Korean, correct?"

The almond eyes found the American rear admiral. "I'm happy you knew my father, Sir. He was an unusual man. And true, I was born in Seoul. My mother's maiden name was Heron Young Kim. When my father was transferred back to the states, we lived in Washington, near

156

CIA headquarters. He was a good father, pushed my studies, helped me to enter Annapolis."

Whitehead was pleasantly surprised. Frank Dempster the libertine had another, unexpected side.

Yoshi continued, "And why did you volunteer for *Yonaga?*"

"I am a sailor, Navy trained, Sir." His eyes worked from man to man, wide, unblinking, and assured. "And my father died here." He stabbed a finger upward. "Up there on the bridge."

"You seek vengeance?"

Dempster shook his head. "No. It's more than that."

Yoshi and Fujita looked at each other in wonder. "What could be greater than vengeance?" Fujita asked.

The voice was low and heavy, "Redeeming one's self in your father's grave." The words left them all speechless and wondering.

Fujita finally broke the silence. "Redeem yourself from what?"

"I was home on liberty a month ago." Dempster's jaw hardened, his fists clenched on his armrests. "My poor mother never adapted well to American ways. I felt she was homesick but she never complained. She became reclusive." He sighed self-consciously like a man who felt he was revealing too much of himself. But he continued, "When I entered the house, I found her." He stopped as if his own words were clogging his throat, refusing to be spoken.

"Go on," Fujita insisted.

Dempster took a deep breath, cleared his throat, a deep gurgling sound. "I found her—raped, hanging from the banister with a wire around her neck."

Yoshi leaped to his feet. "No! No! In the name of the gods, Goodenough is dead. Dead!"

The almond eyes widened, stared at the distraught Commander. "Perhaps, Commander. But not his legacy."

Silence as cold as an Arctic gale swept through the room. The men could only stare at each other.

Chapter XII

The first few hours spent in the Israeli Air Force compound at Ben Gurion Airport fled by a dazed Brent, fleeting as the phantasms of a man in a drunken stupor. Voices were disembodied and strange bodies drifted by with names but no identity. He had stood with the survivors and watched silently as Corporal Roland "Rollie" Knudsen was rushed to an ambulance. IV tubes were pouring life back into the gunner as he was carried to the waiting vehicle. But he was unconscious, face ashen–gray. To Brent, he had looked like a dying man. None could watch as the remains of Sergeant Oren Smadja were pulled, lifted and scraped from the shattered ball turret and waist.

After two stiff drinks of scotch, the debriefing had begun; tactful, yet thorough. Brent had watched Devora through the corner of his eye. She was as solid as any man, perhaps better controlled than most. No tears. No dramatics. He had seen this strength in other Israeli women; in Sarah Aranson and Ruth Moskowitz. Despite the persistent droning of the debriefing officer, thoughts of

Ruth came back. Her quick wit, piercing intelligence. Her spectacular body. And, now, she was nearby.

Then he had showered. Peeling off his flight suit, Brent's stomach had wrenched when he saw the coagulated blood. A gelatinous layer clung to the sleeve and entire left side of the suit. How much had Knudsen bled? How could one bleed so much and still live? It was on his goggles and helmet, on his cheek and had run down his neck. Small bits of Smadja's brains were imbedded in the blood like ground meat.

Cursing sudden nausea that sent the taste of sour scotch to burn in his throat, he flung the suit, helmet and goggles into a corner and drank some water, rinsed his mouth. Then, he showered, long and hot. He felt foul; so filthy he could never be clean again. He scrubbed his body, washed his hair, scoured his cheek and neck, over and over again. Finally, he stepped out, toweled until his body tingled and glowed pink and put on his Number One Blues. But the blood was still there. He could not see it, but the stain was too deep. He knew he would never rid himself of it.

Now, looking in the mirror, his mind reeled. Leaning forward, he studied the reflection. A stranger. He was 32–years–old, but had lived a century. There were scars everywhere, invisible to others, but he could see them. They opened him up. He was bared. Maybe Atsumi was right. The gunnery officer had tried to pound his own personal brand of Taoism into anyone who would listen. Leaning close to the glass, Brent saw a man, and through a man, who had spent a decade caught in the hell of war, who had fought his way through firestorm after firestorm only to emerge into his own private inferno.

He had heard Nobomitsu Atsumi allude to this and not understood. Now, at this moment, Brent Ross caught a glimmer, thought he knew. He was a driven man, a man frozen in a killing mentality that had been passed along in the genes of the species since time began. A Buddhist priest had once told him the collective unconscious of mankind all evolved within the soul. But he never found this. He saw nothing but a killing machine, still fighting mammoths with his spear. Cursed to repeat and repeat until he, too, was destroyed by his own personal devils. Now, he had another enemy to fight—himself. It made no sense. But what did?

He spoke to the mirror as if Nobomitsu Atsumi were staring back, "I hope you've found it, Nobomitsu–san—I hope you're right." He tapped the glass, "No event is good or bad, it's neutral, right? It's only how it's perceived by us poor stupid humans that colors it black or white, good or evil." He chuckled. "Yes, that's what you said, Nobomitsu–san." And then seriously, he pleaded, "Please be right, please. I can't go on living with these devils, they're crowding me out."

His Catholic training flashed back. Resurrection! Salvation! Redemption! Immortality! "Thou shalt not kill! Love thy neighbor! An eye for an eye!" He threw his head back and laughed uproariously. "Lot of fuckin' sense that makes," he sputtered into the mirror.

Shaking his head until his hair flew, he tried to drive the maddening thoughts from his mind. It was useless. It was like being adrift. No paddle, no rudder, no anchor.

Then a knock and he heard the impossibly collected voice of Lieutenant Horace Burnside. "I say, old boy. The skipper requests the pleasure of your company in the grand ballroom. Maybe even a spot of tea and a crumpet or two."

The Englishman astounded Brent. He was actually cracking a joke. What solid unperturbable people. The ordeals they had endured in this century alone were enough to give the entire race spines of steel. Burnside had his. Just the man's voice calmed and soothed and pushed the devils into the dark corners. Brent chuckled out loud. What kind of crazy foolishness had filled his head. There were too many religions, too many "truths".

"Coming," he said, squaring his hat. He turned toward the door.

Seated in the debriefing room at a long table with a cup of coffee before him, Brent began to feel reason and control return. His reeling, scrambling mind had frightened him. Now, with the other members of the crew he stared down the table at Colonel C.R. "Bull" Ware. Just the pilot's presence had a calming effect, the stolid, wise parent.

"Well done, crew," Ware said. "I have flown with many crews, but none can match you. *Shady Lady* should have been shot down. Those 109s were designed to kill bombers, had all the advantages. We had one kill and another probable."

Looking down the table, the pilot's face sobered. "I have no further news on the condition of Corporal Knudsen. I'll keep you informed." He shifted uneasily, a note of bitterness creeping into his voice, "We lost one of the best. Sergeant Oren Smadja had a brilliant future. Some of you knew him for only a few hours, but those hours were a lifetime and he gave his to protect his plane, his comrades."

His eyes moved over the three surviving Israelis; Devora Hacohen, Michael Shaked and Efrayim Mani. "Lieutenant Hacohen has volunteered to lead a prayer for him. I know men usually do this. I wouldn't think of infringing on your customs. It's up to you. Are there any objections?" Shaked and Mani shook their heads. Both pulled linen yarmulkes from their pockets and covered their heads. Everyone stood.

Devora placed a small black hat on the back of her head and draped a tallith around her shoulders. Her hair appeared darker, eyes wider and deeper, face as pale as bleached ivory. To Brent, she exuded a beatific, ethereal quality that enhanced her beauty, yet, tempered his usual sensual stirrings for her. He expected a traditional prayer, probably the Kaddish, which was the customary prayer for the dead or *Shema Yisrael*, the last prayer a Jew utters on his deathbed. He got them both. But Devora's opening charge took him by surprise.

Her soft, composed voice contrasted with the stark horror of her words, "For centuries Jews who were being tortured, flogged, flayed, hanged, torn apart, burned at the stake, stoned, boiled in oil, or otherwise exposed to earnest and pious efforts to convert them died with a prayer on their lips." Shaked and Mani smiled grimly, the gentiles looked down at the table. "Of course, more recently, our German friends helped bring us closer to our god, gave six million of us an opportunity to pray in their gas chambers, ovens, killing pits, lime–sprinkled railroad cars, gas vans and a hundred other inventive ways to dispatch us to our reward."

The big eyes like spilled India ink moved from face to face while the silence of a million ghosts chilled the room. She continued in the matter–of–fact tone, "Untold millions found their solace in Deuteronomy, Chapter 6, Verses 4 through 7." Her eyes moved to the ceiling and she began *Shema Yisrael*, "Hear, O Israel: The Lord our God, the Lord is One. And thou shalt love the Lord thy God with all thy heart, and with all thy soul, and with all thy might . . ."

Brent studied her as she moved through the verses, perfectly controlled, yet he knew she must be in turmoil. Finally, she began the last verse. Shaked and Mani joined her, " 'And thou teach them diligently unto thy children, and shalt talk of them when thou sittest in thine house . . ."

Brent watched the supplicants, chanting now in perfect unison. Another world, another religion, three more completely wrapped in a cloak of their own dogma. He was a long way from the theosophy and pantheism of the East, from Atsumi's Taoism. Finally, the prayer was finished, but the three Israelis were not. Brent expected the Kaddish and as if an unseen signal had been given they started the prayer together, "Let us adore the ever–living God and render praise unto Him . . ."

Everyone waited patiently while the short litany was completed, remained standing for a moment and then sat.

Ware had to cough and clear his throat before he could speak. He said gruffly, "We'll remain silent for a minute. Pray for our dead and wounded in whatever religion you may have. If you have none, think good thoughts for them and all the helpless Jews and other oppressed peoples who have been murdered over the ages." And then thickly,

"At least, Sergeant Oren Smadja had a gun in his hand."

"Hear! Hear!" Heads were bowed and the crew remained silent while the seconds crept by slowly.

Then, the military man returned, chasing the ghosts quickly, *"Shady Lady* is badly damaged, but the old bird will fly again," Ware said. Nods. Smiles. "The Israeli Air Force has some special mission planned for her. I don't even know what it is."

"But Colonel, it will take *beaucoup de temps* to fix *Shady Lady,"* Philipe D'Meziere said in his fractured English.

Burnside joined in, "Those bloody bandits poked a lot of holes in the old girl, Colonel. And a new ball turret's got to be brought from the States. Right?"

"Right you are," Ware imitated back, bringing a glimmer of humor into the grim proceedings. He rubbed a three-day stubble of beard like gray grass on his chin. "If we get prompt delivery on the turret, the old girl should be as good as new in six to eight weeks."

Michael Shaked said, "We'll need three new gunners, Sir." He waved at Brent Ross. All eyes focused on the American Commander. "We'll lose our best."

"And he just rode along for the fun of it," Ware jested. Everyone chuckled.

Brent felt warmth not only from the limelight, but in the genuine respect and affection that filled the room. He would miss these people. Near extinction had molded them together as nothing else ever could. "Thanks. Thanks," Brent said softly. "But we were a team, fought as a team, that's why we survived."

Shaked shook his head. "I never saw a shot like the one you made on that stalling Me. He was turning, dropping, we were banking and turning and I missed him completely. But you drilled him—perfect deflection, allowance for turn, speed, bullet drop. Like a computer."

Brent nodded and smiled. There was nothing more to say.

Ware discussed the billeting. The crew would be put up at nearby Air Force barracks. "And, you, Commander," he said to Brent. "An American aviator, a lieutenant, will be here at any moment. I understand he has your orders and billeting assignment.

"Thank you, Colonel. Do you have his name?"

"Sorry, Commander. I wasn't told. The rest of you have been granted a 10–day leave." Cheers and Burnside sang out, "Oh, he's a jolly good fellow . . ." Laughter and back slapping, a remarkable change of mood.

Ware continued, "And if you'll seat yourselves at those tables you'll be served a gourmet meal." He gestured at three tables, two flanking the door to the concourse, the third somewhat isolated in a dim corner.

More cheers and laughter. As the crew moved to the tables, Ware gestured to Brent. The colonel, Devora and Brent Ross sat together at the corner table, Horace Burnside and Kennosuke Torisu claimed one of the other tables, Michael Shaked, Philipe D'Meziere and Efrayim Mani took the last. Each table had full wine glasses and a full bottle of Israel's favorite wine, *Carmel*.

Ware raised his glass. His voice boomed, "Sergeant Oren Smadja."

"Sergeant Oren Smadja!" came back. Everyone drank. Then a toast to Corporal Roland Knudsen.

Quickly, the mood was broken as young enlisted girls of the I.D.F. served brimming bowls of soup. All the girls were excited and obviously pleased for a chance to serve the handsome young men. Hardly a glance was thrown Devora's way.

"Chicken soup," Brent said lifting his spoon.

"Good, Jewish chicken soup," Devora added, mood brightening.

Brent tried his salad. He had expected the usual mixture of chopped cucumbers, tomatoes and a dash of parsley. Instead, he was delighted to find his bowl filled with romaine, tasting of vinegar, olive oil and strong with garlic, sprinkled with croutons. His favorite, Caesar salad. "Was Caesar a Jew?" he quipped.

They all laughed. Freeing a crouton from a trap of lettuce, Ware said, "We'll miss you, Commander." He popped the crouton into his mouth and chewed luxuriously.

Brent said, "You have a great crew, Colonel. I'll miss you." He looked at Devora out of the corner of his eye. "All of you."

Ware refilled the glasses and the remainder of the meal of roast chicken, potato cakes, broccoli and twisted challah bread was consumed in near silence. Just as the trio finished the meal, an Israeli officer opened the door and signaled to Colonel Ware. The pilot excused himself and left.

Brent said to Devora, "I found your tribute to Sergeant Smadja moving."

"Did my little speech upset you, Brent?"

He shook his head. "No, it's all true. If anything, you showed extraordinary restraint."

"Thank you, Brent. You have a remarkable talent for saying the right thing."

He smiled at the compliment. "No, Devora. Only the

truth." He sipped his wine and eyed her over the rim. "You knew Smàdja before, didn't you?" He had to raise his voice to be heard over the laughter of the men and the giggles of the waitresses. Four of the girls had been persuaded to sit at the other tables and drink with the men. Strong flirtations were already underway, Brent and Devora were completely ignored.

Devora turned her wine glass with the tips of her delicate fingers and studied the deep purple liquid. "Yes. We grew up together in Rehovot. He was brilliant."

"You knew him well."

She looked up and smiled at the innuendo. "Not that well."

"You knew those prayers by heart."

"For the dead?" The bitterness returned. "Of course. They're traditional and we Israelis have had a lot of practice lately—especially for the young." She stared down at her hands.

"I want to see you again, Devora," he said, trying to free her of her depression.

Her mood changed color as quickly as a tropical sunrise. Her voice was low and husky, "And I want to see you, Brent—very much."

Her words, the timbre of her voice, brought a long dormant warmth to life. He wondered how Israeli women could be so moody, changeable: one moment sear you with passion, the next chill with the breath of death. A lifetime of war must have twisted them all. He had seen it in many; especially in Sarah Aranson and Ruth Moskowitz. "You'll be staying in a barracks?" he managed in an evenly modulated voice.

"No. I have a small house in Rehovot—my family home."

"Your family?"

Pulling back, her lips became a thin line, voice flat and hard-edged, mood sagging again, "My father was killed in the Yom Kippur War and my brother's at the front."

He did not want to inquire further, but knew she expected it, "Is that it? Your mother?"

"In an institution." She tossed off the last of her wine. Brent refilled her glass. "It's an old story here, Brent. You've associated with Israelis for years. You must've heard it before. My mother's family, aunts, uncles, cousins all went 'up the chimney'." She shrugged. "And now, a half-century later, they've turned her mind to smoke."

She emptied her glass in three gulps. "She just sits and stares. She's out of touch with reality—whatever that may be."

She reached for the bottle. Brent had seen several Israelis drink themselves senseless when confronting the past. He could never forget the night he had held Ruth Moskowitz as she retched and vomited. His hand closed over Devora's before she could grasp the bottle. Startled, she said, "You think I've drunk too much? I've only had . . ."

"Not really. But you could."

"It's the subject. Right?" She pulled her hand back. "You think I'll get drunk thinking about it and that troubles you."

"It troubles everyone." He rubbed the stubble like iron filings on his jaw. "There are 613 commandments in your faith."

"The orthodox, yes."

169

"I just created the 614th."

She raised an eyebrow and smiled, half amused, half quizzical. "And what is that?"

He leaned forward, "Thou shalt not hand Hitler any more victories."

Smiling, she glanced at the bottle and then back to Brent. "You're a fascinating man, Brent—a very wise man."

"I wasn't looking for that."

"I know." She raised a hand as if she were warding off an evil spirit dwelling in the bottle. "I swear I will obey the 614th—the 'Brent Ross Commandment'."

"Very good."

Holding up her empty glass and studying it as if she were examining precious crystal, she gracefully segued out of the painful subject, "Where will you stay?"

He welcomed the change. "I hope the Hilton in Tel Aviv." He shrugged. "But I don't know. I'm on liaison with some armored unit. I may be shipped off to the front tomorrow or sent to a headquarters company, a B.O.Q., or just sit and wait." He turned his hands up in a gesture of helplessness. "You know how war can be—just sit and wait and wait and wait, then hurry to a new assignment to just sit and wait and wait and wait."

"How true. But regardless of your orders, you should get some kind of survivor's leave."

"My fate is unknown to all except god and the General Staff."

"Socrates said something like that."

"He wasn't as practical."

Smiling, she scribbled some numbers on a piece of paper and pushed it across the table. "Will you phone me,

Brent? Come see me? Rehovot is nearby. This is a small country. Everything's nearby." The eyes were warm again, voice low.

"Of course I want to see you. We should have more time together." He stared back. A man could drown in those eyes.

"Yes," she smiled. "We deserve that—quality time." Her fingers touched his hand.

Brent was not sure he was hearing double entendre and did not really care. This lovely creature wanted to see him and that was all that mattered.

The hand retreated. "You've known some Israeli women well, haven't you."

. He lifted an eyebrow. "Ah—I became rather well acquainted with a few in the past decade. And how did *you* know?"

"Men like you attract women. Become very close with many." Brent tried to fathom her look. She was inscrutable. Had he been insulted? Not really. The statement was neutral enough. Complimentary to some men.

"And the last one, Brent?"

"Ruth Moskowitz. Why? Do you know her?"

"No. But I think I've heard of her father, Colonel David Moskowitz. He was wounded last year at *Bren-ah-Hahd.*"

"That's right."

She tilted her glass from side to side and stared at it like a musician watching a metronome. He expected her to pry into his relationship with Ruth. Inquire into how "close" they had been. Most women would. But she surprised him, "Are you in love, Brent?"

"Is there time?"

She laughed humorlessly. *"Touché.* Not in wartime. We bounce off each other like ping–pong balls."

He chuckled. "Picturesque way to put it." He leaned forward. "Have you bounced off anyone lately?"

She threw her head back and laughed boisterously. Her eyes actually sparkled. He was delighted with her new animation. "I've been paddled around a few times, Brent."

"In love?"

"You said it, Brent"

"What?"

"Time? Where's the time?"

"Good answer, Devora."

"It ought to be. It's yours."

Leaning toward him, her hand brushed against his. He traced a single finger across her palm. She stiffened at his touch and the great eyes bored into his, wiping the dregs of old memories from his mind. For the moment, even Ruth Moskowitz was erased from the slate. Her voice was low and husky, "We must see each other again, Brent. You're too precious. I can't let you just walk out of my life."

The mood swings, the double entendre could drive Freud, Jung and Adler to their own couches. But her eyes were mesmerizing. Low and demanding, he felt the visceral heat spread, his loins thicken and stiffen. "We will, Devora. As soon as possible. I promise." For a long moment the noisy room seemed empty and they lost themselves in each other.

An enlisted man materialized suddenly from behind and shattered the moment, "Sir," he said into Brent's ear, "there is an officer here to see you." He pointed to the door. "Should I let him in?"

Brent looked around. Ware was nowhere to be seen. He looked inquiringly at Devora who was nominally second in command. "Of course," she said, answering the unvoiced question.

The door opened and a tall, angular young lieutenant with a DOP patch on his left shoulder and wings on his tunic stormed in. His peaked cap was emblazoned with the gold chrysanthemum of *Yonaga*'s ship's company. It was the Texan, Elroy Rubin.

Spotting Brent, he stopped in his tracks, raised his arms and shouted in his usual disregard for rank, "Why you ol' polecat. Took you a coon's age to finally come back to the old corral." Everyone stared at the young, tall flyer in wonder. Like a morning breeze off the sea, a fresh, bright ambience seemed to pour in with the Texan.

Brent leaped to his feet and clasped his old friend around the shoulders. He mimicked Elroy, "Come a fur piece, ol' saddle pardner. Done got bushwhacked."

"Done heard our ol' buddy Rosencrance made more fuss than the alligator when the lake went dry." Despite the grim memories, everyone chuckled at the outlandish simile. Brent smiled to himself. The brilliant Texan was still playing the country bumpkin to the hilt. He introduced Elroy to the crew and then they sat.

Brent quickly explained to Devora how Elroy had accompanied him and Colonel Bernstein to Kadafi's headquarters on their fruitless attempt to negotiate a prisoner exchange the previous year. He did not mention how Elroy, Linda Crane, Ruth Moskowitz and he had become

173

a foursome, dating, sightseeing like four young, happy tourists.

Devora shook her head. "Took a lot of guts to enter that monster's tent."

"We failed."

"No, you didn't Brent."

Elroy interrupted. "I don' ken that."

"You're both alive, aren't you?"

Brent nodded. "If you put it that way." He turned to Elroy and noticed the two full stripes on his cuffs. "You've been promoted. What's your duty, Elroy."

"I'm still on Colonel Bernstein's staff. In fact, I'm his whole staff—pure and simple."

"But he's back in Japan."

"Sho' 'nuff. But Mossad has a hankerin' for me. Won't turn me loose an' the Colonel wants me to stay put—his personal hombre."

"Got you fenced in, ol' cow poke."

Elroy rubbed his wings. "Been ship's company for nigh on two years an' never set foot on *Yonaga*." He waved his hand over his head. "Should be roamin' that range."

"The wild blue yonder is a mighty big range."

"Not as big as Texas." They all laughed. The Texan reached into an inside pocket and handed Brent a large envelope. For the first time, a military note crept into Elroy's voice, "Your orders, Commander."

Devora looked around and said, "Please excuse me, I have some nose powdering to do."

"This time I won't bust in," Brent said.

"You can hold my hand."

"No, thanks."

Laughing, she left the table while Brent read a single sheet.

He smiled. "I've got a four-day survivor's leave and then I report to *Zahal* headquarters in Jerusalem."

"Nothin' 'bout the First Armored Division?"

"Negative."

"I'll be danged."

"Why?"

"Cause, it come over 'Blue Gamma' direct from Colonel Bernstein that I was to high–tail–it with you to their headquarters—wherever that is."

"Your my aide?"

"Why not? We didn't hog–tie the critter but we did all right in Kadafi's tent, I reckon."

"A good team, I reckon."

"The best. I got you a room at the Hilton, iffn' you want it, Commander."

"Of course, I do. What about transportation?"

"You have a Jeep waitin' for you here at the pool. It's all fixed up for you." A slight smile dallied with the corners of his lips. "I done saw Ruth Moskowitz at Mossad."

"Oh."

" 'Bout a week ago. Asked 'bout you. Told her I didn't know nothin'. She's still a courier—moves around a lot. Told me she had a two-week leave. Was going to Haifa to see her mother. She's real sick. Ruth's probably gone by now, I reckon."

"Her father, Colonel David Moskowitz? He was badly wounded at *Bren-ah-Hahd.*"

"Tougher'n a buzzard's gizzard. I heard he was back at the front."

"Can't believe it."

The Texan ground his teeth and clenched and unclenched his fist. He stared at his hand as if he were watching a strange creature unwind on the table. "Somethin' mighty peecular's a-goin' on, Commander."

"What do you mean?"

"A month ago a Korean lady was raped and strung up on a wire in Washington."

"Christ, no. That was Harry 'High Wire' Goodenough's M.O."

"But that ain't all. They's scuttlebutt that the wife of that special negotiator, Mori Tokumitsu, was done the same way in Geneva."

Brent shook his head in anger and depression. "A copycat killer. Kadafi's sense of humor. He's probably laughing his guts out."

"Got to be. Goodenough's deader'n a door nail."

"The women, always the women."

"They's easier to kill." The Texan unwound his long legs slowly. "Got to mosey along, Commander. Got to report to Jerusalem. They's some orders at Mossad I've got to pick up. I 'spect somethin' 'bout the First Armored."

"Contact me. I'll be at the Hilton." And then as an afterthought, "And Ruth?"

"Bunkin' in the same place. The Maxim Hotel." Elroy stood and left just as Devora and Ware returned.

While Devora seated herself across from Brent, Ware sat with Kennosuke Torisu and Horace Burnside. The ribald laughter and giggles ceased abruptly and the girls began to clear the tables. Ware spread some documents on the table and began to talk with the navigator earnestly. Pouring over a map, they gestured, pointed, measured distances with a pair of dividers.

Devora took Brent's mind from the sadistic killings. "I'll bet he's flying the next mission already," Brent said.

"He's flying something. And *Shady Lady* won't be ready for over a month."

"An incredible guy."

"We need more like him." Again, her hand brushed his, the soft velvet sending a tingle all the way up his arm. "Stay here tonight, Brent? It's late and they have quarters for all of us."

"Got a room at the Hilton."

"You're fatigued. We'll get the VIP quarters. Private rooms, baths, tv, even room service."

"Sounds tempting."

"Drive to Tel Aviv tomorrow, Brent."

"And you?"

"I'm going to Rehovot in the morning. Phone me there. I'll fix you a nice dinner."

"I'll come early. We'll sight see and I'll take you to dinner."

"But I want to cook for you."

"I said I'm taking you to dinner."

"Pulling rank, Commander?"

"That's an order."

"Under protest," she quipped. "But rank has its privileges."

"How many and what are they?"

A slow smile spread across her face. "We'll see." She covered her mouth in an attempt to conceal a yawn.

"Turn in, Devora. You look fatigued."

"I'm enjoying you, Brent."

"You haven't slept for over twenty hours."

"None of us have."

He raised a cup. "I'll finish my coffee and hit the sack."

"We'll have breakfast together?"

"I'll arrange it with the maitre d'."

She chuckled, squeezed his hand, rose and left.

Staring after her, he wondered about himself. He felt a powerful attraction to Devora, yet Ruth crowded back into his mind the moment the door closed behind Devora. What kind of a man was he? The principles of a tomcat, the depth of a layer of paint. Was he attached to anything except war, killing, sex? Some men had families. Children. He had his war. He had his passionate flings. Again, he felt arrested as if he were the perennial teenager, rolling the dice of an infinite war game with squares marked, "Hooray, Another Kill, "Bang You're Dead," "Move on to Your Next Sex Partner." And these Israeli women seemed to be frozen in the same time warp. Like some corny rerun of "Star Trek" where the future repeated the past.

He tossed off the rest of his cooling coffee. Ruth Moskowitz. What was she doing now. Still searching for a boy to love? For sanity in the asylum? He shook his head. Probably alone somewhere. Tossing in her bed. Expecting him to return to her like all the romantic heroes in Harlequin Romances. She had promised without being asked. "I'll be waiting for you," she had vowed. Suddenly, he felt a deep, churning pang of guilt. He knew she would never break the promise he had never wanted.

And an insane, savage, perverted killer was loose. Somehow, this upset him more than the Arab battle group. Rape, sodomy, strangulation. This man wasn't an aberration, he was a mutation. Humans didn't do these things to other humans. A revolting monster. That's what he was, a disgusting, revolting monster.

Chapter XIII

Corporal Ruth Moskowitz raced by Hadera at least one hundred kilometers–an–hour as she headed south from Haifa for Tel Aviv. The official Mossad logo on the side of the old 1977 Chevrolet Caprice helped discourage traffic citations. She was in ebullient spirits. Her mother, Miriam, had recovered from her bout with bronchial pneumonia and had returned to her small house in the fashionable Hadar Hacarmel area of Haifa where her old friend Gavriel Mishulan was staying with her. Her father had healed and returned to his unit. And, she had heard a rumor that Brent Ross was returning. Just the thought of the American caused dewy heat to seep deep down. Squirming, she smiled, thinking of the first night they had spent together. How fatigued she had been after the marathon lovemaking. And sore. She giggled to herself.

What's funny?" the young soldier sitting next to her asked.

Ruth flushed slightly as she answered him, "Oh, nothing, Shlomo. Just delighted with the scenery." She waved at the solid blocks of orange groves flanking the highway.

Ruth had just left the famous Paznon Pancake House after a quick stop for a cup of coffee when she first saw Private First Class Shlomo Granit. He was standing near her car which was parked between the restaurant and the Paz Gas Station. At first glance, he impressed her as being a very unusual looking Jew. Appearing to be about twenty, he was fair–haired, blue–eyed with skin almost milky white. Surprising for a soldier who had just spent four months in the hell of the Negev Desert. But Jews came in all sizes, colors and shapes these days. Even Ethiopians.

In some ways, he reminded her of Brent Ross. Although not as blond, his features were strong and well formed as if they had been fashioned by the sharp edge of a sculptor's chisel. But the chisel had slipped. A livid scar ran from a point just beneath his right eye, down across his cheek and off his jaw. Shrapnel or a knife. Thousands of Israeli men now carried such imprints of war. And this one was so young. Scarred for life already.

And he was as big as Brent, perhaps two meters tall and well over 90 kilograms. Maybe his resemblance to Brent had attracted her to him. Anyway, he had been in a terrible fix when his small Honda had gasped its last at the Paz Gas Station. He was a soldier who had obviously seen his share of the fighting and he was in trouble. She was almost compelled to agree when he shyly asked her for a lift to Tel Aviv. "Got to report to Division in Jerusalem in the morning," he had said in a high whiny voice as thin as paper, blue eyes wide and pleading. "I can catch a bus in Tel Aviv."

She almost chuckled at his timorous naivete, like that of a very young boy who was unaccustomed to speaking to an older woman. *Older woman*, she thought. *I'm not more than four-years older than he is.*

"Your car?" she had asked.

"I'll phone my father in Haifa," he answered under his breath as he carefully placed his heavy canvas duffel bag in the trunk of the Chevrolet.

Ruth was pleased with his company. His conversation was halting and self-conscious, but he did distract her from the loneliness of the long drive. She soon learned he had been born in Israel, but, like herself, had his higher education in America. This accounted for his detectable inflection and clumsy emphasis on vowel sounds. She asked him about his unit.

"Fourth Infantry Division," he answered proudly, voice firming a little. "The Arabs call us 'Rabin's Butchers'." He rubbed his cheek, "Caught a bit of Arab iron, here. Airburst."

She nodded and then decided she had entered the wrong topic. He asked her about her duty and she described them briefly. She was sick of the war. Waving at the orange groves, she changed direction smoothly, "Just smell those orange blossoms."

"Marvelous," he said. "Reminds me of Helen.

"Helen?"

He flushed. "Helen. I dated her. She wore cologne that smelled like that."

Ruth smiled. "Are you in love?"

He squirmed uncomfortably, "Oh, Lord, no. I only dated her twice."

Ruth guessed Helen was probably the only girl he had ever dated. He seemed totally innocent. She had never met a young man quite like this.

Looking around, he said, "We're nearly to Netanya, right?"

"Ten more kilometers."

"Great beaches, there."

"Aren't they mined?"

"Not there, Ruth. No need to and they still get some tourists, you know."

"No, I didn't know." She gestured. "I've hardly seen a car." With the shortage of petrol, very few vehicles had been passed. Occasionally a military vehicle or a bus jammed with civilians and military.

"Say," he said with new enthusiasm. "Let's go for a swim. I'll buy you a lunch, we can picnic. I owe you for the ride."

It was hot and Ruth felt sticky. The thought of a dip in the cool Mediterranean was irresistible. "Why not. I have my suit."

"Mine's in my bag."

"Good. You're on."

He pointed. "Down there—that sign at that intersection."

"I see it. The beach."

Ruth turned the wheel hard right and raced down a narrow road toward the blue carpet of the sea.

After a short stop in Netanya to buy sandwiches, drinks and fruit, they parked just off the road near a thickly reforested area. All around them were stands of large old cyprus, eucalyptus and pine trees that marched all the way to the beach. A rocky stretch, the strip of sand was almost deserted, only a few people visible at least a kilometer to the south. They took turns changing into their bathing suits in the car.

There was a fairly stiff wind blowing off the sea. And the sky had changed in that quick strange way of the eastern Mediterranean. Partially overcast, it dappled the sea with sunshine and shadows. In some places it looked like molten silver, but in other places it might have been a surging mass of dark blood. Shlomo looked around and then spread a blanket in a depression with an outcropping of rocks on the beach side, trees and shrubs on the other. It was ideal, sheltered and private.

She watched him as he tucked the corners of the blanket into small digs. Stripped down to his brief, tight trunks, he even more reminded her of Brent. His shoulders were broad, arms developed and flowing with muscles, waist small, legs powerful. He looked up, caught her eyes and she flushed.

Then he ran his eyes over her body with unabashed candor. She was proud of her figure; large pointed breasts, the flare to her sleek yet womanly hips, hard round buttocks. And her legs, firm shapely limbs that showed the conditioning of years of training in karate and judo. They always caught the male eye.

Her bikini bottom and narrow halter displayed it splendidly. And he found it all, from her tiny feet to her long russet hair. Watching his eyes, they seemed to change. No longer soft and innocent, they narrowed, took on a hard sheen like polished stones, a tiny arrowhead creasing the skin between them. The intensity of the look was unsettling. She had seen eyes like that before, but they were not Brent's. He seemed transformed. His jaw muscles tightened and his entire countenance took on a stony look. Even his scar changed, glowing pink. It was almost as if another being had taken possession of him. Her heart

184

skipped guiltily. She had excited him and had done so deliberately. For the first time she felt a pang of apprehension. What did he expect of her?

Trying to break the mood, she shouted, "Let's cool off!" and raced for the water.

He was right behind her, catching her easily, grabbing her tiny hand in his. Pulling her along, they splashed into the pristine blue water deeper than she wished, until the water lapped at her chin. She looked up and he stared down with remote, icy hauteur, "Please, no further."

"I won't let you drown," he promised, grasping her arm. The voice had changed, low and gruff.

Although she tried to break away, he lifted her and pulled her against him. The feel of his bare body against hers caused her to catch her breath. Then, drifting down, his hands gripped her buttocks and pulled her against him. The innocent young boy had vanished. She could feel his arousal, the animal heat even in the cool water. But there was no rush of passion, electricity charging through her veins as it had with Brent. Instead, she felt dread and revulsion, a grim foreboding that brought on an ominous chill. She pushed against his chest. He ignored her, began to pull her suit down.

"No!"

"Why not?" he sneered.

"It's too soon. I don't even know you." She managed to push herself back, but was unable to break away from those grasping hands, terrible eyes.

His look was as fathomless as a frozen pond. Now it was a frightening look; menacing, determined, unyielding. There was carnal hunger there, and violence, too. She was not accustomed to feeling fear, but waves of panic rose out of some dark place in her soul and she fought to control them. A sense of impending disaster crushed down on her.

"What the hell are you, a goddamned Jewish Queen Victoria?" His thumbs jerked her bikini bottom down almost to mid–thigh.

In near panic, she brought a knee up hard into his crotch. He doubled over, crying out with pain. Pulling up her suit, she raced for the beach. When she finally reached dry sand, she could hear him splashing behind her. He screamed in throaty anger, "If you think you can lead me on and then cross your legs, you're out of your fucking mind. I'm going to give you the balling of your life."

Without breaking stride, she scooped up a thick piece of driftwood like a war club. It was saturated, heavy and partially rotted, but it was a weapon. She raced for the blanket and her bag that held her Walther P–38 automatic. He was close behind her and gaining. She would never make it.

Stopping suddenly and stepping to her left, she spun on her left foot, swinging around, bringing the piece of driftwood whipping in a vicious arc. Taken completely by surprise, he tried to stop, but slid forward in the sand directly into the club. It caught him flush on the side of the head.

There was a crack like the report of small pistol and the driftwood shattered into at least three pieces and a rain of splinters. He was hurt. Staggering, he clutched his bleeding head and cried out in pain. "Goddamned, Jewess kike bitch," he shouted after her as she ran toward the blanket. "You'll pay for that."

Breathing hard, her mind raced. What was this man? No Israeli would ever call her that. Then the true horror hit her. He was an assassin. Like Harry Goodenough. It was all a scheme to kill her. It had been tried before. Terror welled up and she felt as if she would vomit. The pistol. She had to get to her pistol. There was death behind her. She could hear him charging through the sand.

The blanket. Her bag. Frantically, she rummaged in the bag, cried out with joy as she gripped the butt of the 9–millimeter automatic. Whirling, she leaped to her feet and pointed the pistol.

Panting, dripping with water, he looked like a maddened bull. His head was lowered, shoulders hunched, hands fisted at his sides. She was convinced he wanted to charge her, crush her under his feet, destroy anything that came in his way. Blood lust shone in eyes as clearly as the sun glared from the sea. He stopped when he saw the Walther, panting, spittle spraying through his lips. He blinked. Edged forward a step or two, testing her.

Gripping the pistol in both hands, she heard a loud rasping sound filled with terror. At first she was confused. Then she realized it was her own ragged and uncontrolled breathing. "Stop, goddamn you, stop, or I'll shoot your balls off." She lowered the Walther and pointed it at his crotch.

Incredibly, he took another step toward her. He was no longer the smug, calculating rapist she had faced in the water. She had hurt him twice. And now, staring at the pistol he seemed to change again. Rape and murder were still there, but something had happened to him deep inside. Switches had been thrown, new circuits clicking on, new needs and hungers that were more perverted and revolting than he had shown thus far had clicked home in his twisted mind. His demeanor was that of a maniac. His eyes flashed, not icy as they had been in the water, but watery and hot, like a man with malaria. Sweat mixed with sea water streamed down his face. His lips worked incessantly, contorting, twisting, skinned back over his teeth in a weird smile, then puckering into a pout, formed a smirk, then a scowl, then an expression that defied reason. The energy that powered him was from a darker place than the force that had driven him just a few minutes earlier. For one insane moment, she had the panicky feeling it would somehow shield him from harm, even divert bullets.

"You're hot for me bitch, I can smell that kosher pussy from here." He waved. "Why all this crap?" He grabbed his crotch, "I've got ten hard inches here. Better than any of those circumcised dicks of those sheenies you've been fucking." He smirked, a horrible, sick travesty of humor. "Even better than that shit-assed 'Yankee Samurai'."

"I warned you. Stop or I'll circumcise you with a 9-millimeter slug." She lined up the forward sight on his crotch so that even a sharp recoil and kick upward would still send a bullet into something vital. He lunged toward her. She pulled the trigger.

Nothing happened. Stunned, she stared at the pistol. The safety was off, the red dot showing. She had forgotten to chamber a round. Frantically, she pulled the action back, jacking a round into the firing chamber.

With the advantage his, he moved fast. Screaming in horror and panic she brought the Walther up and fired blindly just as he crashed into her. He screamed, the wail of a mortally wounded jackal. His momentum knocked them both down and sent the pistol flying. Crashing to the sand, she landed on top of him. The breath exploded out of him with a flem—ladened whooshing sound. He rolled to his stomach almost to a ridge of rocks and lay still. She leaped to her feet and backed off a few steps.

He lay very still, head resting on the crook of his right arm, left arm flung out. She looked for spreading blood. But she could find none. Must be pouring into the sand. He was very still. She could not detect the slightest movement, not even the subtle rise and fall of breathing.

Dead. He was very dead. She eyed her bag on the other side of the corpse. She had to get out of here. Away from this horror. Cautiously, she edged her way around him between the sandy space and the rocks. The pistol was just the other side of the rocks, half—buried in sand.

Suddenly, he was no longer dead. Levering up on his right arm, he struck out with his left like a cobra, catching Ruth's ankle and bringing her down. Screaming, flailing, punching they rolled over and over in the sand until they crashed into the rocks. Then she realized he was hurt, a bullet hole in his left side, bleeding, smearing blood on her breast, her stomach. But he still had enormous strength—the strength of a maddened animal. He rolled her over onto her back, spit into her face, snarled like a dog and his teeth were at her throat. He would bite her, drink her blood. She worked a fist up his side. Drove her thumb into the bullet hole. It was hot, wet, much like a man driving himself into a woman. Just what he wanted to do to her.

Howling he pulled away and she grabbed her chance, rolling to the side and scrambling to her feet. But, he, too, was standing and the pistol was behind him. Gripping his side, blood seeping through his fingers, true, but still on his feet and menacing.

Pressing the inside of her index fingers with the tip of her thumb, Ruth balled both hands into vicious one–knuckle fists. She went into a crouch. She had a chance. Unwounded, she was a dead girl. But he was hurt. Bleeding.

"Oh, my," he said mockingly. "The great karate expert. Black belt, no doubt. Scares the shit out of me." He stepped toward her. She stepped back. Under no circumstances, could she allow him to close with her, let him use the advantage of his weight and great strength.

He forgot his wound. It no longer bled. She had hoped she had at least punctured a lung. But the bullet had entered too far to the side. Actually, it was nothing more than a flesh wound. Painful, true, but not disabling. Her heart sank as he raised his fists and stepped toward her.

The mood had changed again. Incongruously, his madness had brought on a boisterous, buoyant mood. Smiling almost benignly he said, "You're a tough little bitch, you know that. You deserve a good fucking. I'll see that you're amply rewarded."

Cat–like, she leaped to his left side. With the pain of the wound slowing him, his left arm came up late. Stabbing straight on with her fist, she caught him in the throat.

"Ugh—ah, ah!" he gasped out, grabbing his throat and retching as he wheezed, trying to catch his breath. She followed quickly with a kick to the stomach. It was like kicking steel shutters. If she could disable him, she could reach the pistol. Apparently, he did not know where it was. But he managed to step back and recover much more quickly than she had anticipated.

Before she could regain her balance he was on her. A big right fist caught her on the side of the head. And then a left punched straight on, knocking her back, staggering until she sprawled on the sand. He leaped. She rolled. He reached out. Grabbed her by the hair. Jerked her back half on the blanket. The pain was unbearable. She screamed. Bit his wrist. He slapped her hard again and again, raising himself over her like the specter of doom itself. Blackness swamped her consciousness, split by shooting stars each time he hit her, ears roaring with the rush of blood, mouth foul with the metallic taste of it. Her lips were torn, cheeks lacerated against her teeth. The blackness took over everything.

She was only out for a few seconds. Then she was nude and he was dragging her onto the blanket. "Don't want to get any sand in it. Could sandpaper my dick." He giggled at his wit. He lowered himself between her legs. "Now you're going to get it," he muttered.

"No!

She cried out in pain as he drove himself into her. To her unready body, each thrust felt like a huge flaming brand was being driven deep into her. She cried out again and again. He slapped her twice. "Quiet, bitch, enjoy it while you can."

Finally, the spasms came and he reared up, eyes wide and sightless, crying, "Ah! Ah!" She felt his hot, sticky fluid spurting, flooding her. She thought it would never stop. Finally, he sagged helplessly on top of her. But there was no escape. He was more than twice her weight and she was completely trapped.

Then the perversions she knew were coming. His laughter and taunts as she twisted, cried out in pain and

191

revulsion. Finally, after more than an hour of torture, he jerked her to her feet. She was so sore and weak she could hardly stand.

"What are you going to do?"

His punch knocked her down. This time the massive fist was balled and her jawbone broke with a sound that reverberated in her head like the slamming of a great door. Knocked backward by the blow, she fell spread-eagled and unconscious.

When she awoke again, they were under an old pine tree. There was something tight around her neck and her hands were bound behind her. Wire. No!" she tried to scream, but only wailed and sprayed blood.

"Shut up!' And then like a scolding school teacher, "It won't take long. Just a few minutes and it'll be over. You'll see."

He looped the wire over a branch, lifted her onto his shoulder and the young naive boy returned, "It's been delightful Corporal Moskowitz. Thanks for everything. I want you to know I appreciate your charming company and all that you have done for me."

She gurgled out a, "No!"

"Now stop that," he admonished, waving a finger. "I told you it would be fast. You'll hardly feel a thing."

He secured the wire to the branch with a hard tug and then dropped her off his shoulder like a sack of garbage.

Triple-stranded, the heavy wire dug into her neck, cutting flesh, spurting blood, slashing her larynx and collapsing her trachea. Unfortunately, the jolt was not severe enough to fracture her neck, to paralyze her respiratory and cardiovascular centers and bring on death quickly. She swung and twisted for a while with her feet only a foot or two from the ground; gurgled, blubbered, bit her tongue until it bled, kicked, turned bluish-gray. Her eyes almost bulged from their sockets before she died.

He watched with a contented, happy smile on his face. Playfully like a little boy at a children's playground, he swung and spun the body until he became bored. He looked around. Found large splinters of the driftwood she had used to hit him. Picking up a piece, he moved to the body, pulled her legs apart, and rammed it home with a sharp upward thrust.

"How does that feel," he asked. "Not as good as me but better than that 'Yankee Samurai', I'll bet. And it won't get soft." He rocked on his heels with laughter. Another wildly funny thought struck him and he sputtered through his giggles, "And now you have a dick. No more penis envy." He laughed so hard his stomach hurt, spittle sprayed and his eyes watered. Finally, tiring of the sport, he said, *"Sholom aleichem,* Jewess."

He turned and walked back to the car.

Chapter XIV

After breakfast, Brent walked into the main concourse and telephoned Ruth. There was no answer. "Must still be in Haifa," he said to himself. He began to return to the conference room and met Devora just as he reached the door.

"Be sure to give me a call," she smiled up at him.

He pondered for a moment. "In a couple days?"

"Sure. But what about coming by Rehovot today?" she waved at the phone. "Or do you have a ah—a commitment."

He smiled. "No commitment, Devora." He rubbed his temple. "Why not?"

"Good. You can drive me home in your Jeep. I was going to take the bus."

"So, that's it," he said in mock rebuke. "You're using me. The ruthless woman preying on the naive man."

"Right," she laughed. "I only like you for your car."

"The meeting," he said, taking her arm.

"Right, the meeting. It's time."

They pushed through the doors of the conference room.

The meeting was brief. Colonel Ware quickly reviewed the crews billeting, leaves and training schedule. The news about Corporal Roland "Rollie" Knudsen was good. He was still critical, but had shown vast improvement after the transfusions. Everyone's spirits were raised. When the crew was dismissed, Brent and Devora left together.

Brent's Jeep was a Chrysler Cherokee with a hard top. It was a very tough little vehicle, yet comfortable. Brent liked it the moment he saw it.

Seating herself, Devora said, "It's only a little more than 30 kilometers—I mean, about twenty miles to Rehovot. Would you like to take a little detour to the south, see a little of the country you almost died for?"

He laughed. "If you put it that way."

"Good! Good," she beamed with girlish enthusiasm. "We'll head south for Ashkelon. It's beautiful there and loaded with history."

"Near the Gaza Strip?"

"Right. Just above it."

Brent wheeled the Jeep out onto Route 1, the same road he and Ruth Moskowitz had used for their trip to Jerusalem. But quickly, Devora had him turn south onto narrower, little-used back roads. They passed through vineyards, vegetable farms, citrus groves. Driving through a small town, she commented, "This is Rishon Lezion, Brent, the center of our wine industry. It was actually financed by Baron Edmond de Rothschild of France."

She pointed to a magnificent old stone winery overgrown with foliage.

"Beautiful," he said. "Gallo country."

"Gallo?"

"Vintners—the Gallo brothers, real big in the States."

"As big as Carmel wine, Brent?"

"Much bigger."

She rubbed her chin. "Never heard of them."

They passed through Ashdod, a small man–made port, Ashkelon was only a few minutes to the south. The first thing Brent noticed as they approached Ashkelon was the magnificent white beaches. He smiled when he recalled how Ruth Moskowitz had loved the beach. "I'll build a hut on the beach someday and you and I will play Tarzan and Jane until you're too tired to swing from a vine," she had jested.

Devora's voice like a tour guide jolted him out of his reveries, "Ashkelon was ruled by the Philistines, the Romans, the Arabs, the Crusaders, the Turks and assorted other tyrants too numerous to name. However, they all had one thing in common—none of them suffered from an over–abundance of humanitarianism."

She gestured to the small town which was now clearly in view. It seemed every building was built of masonry or stone. All glared white in the morning sun except for the ruins of a small wall that loomed like a hillock. A few pedestrians were visible, some in western dress, others in the *jalabiyah* of the Arab. To Brent, the *jalabiyah* looked like a baggy nightshirt.

Quickly, he levered her out of the depressing subject, "That wall," he said waving.

"Yes, the Hykos city wall. It's 3500 years old." He

slowed as they passed through the main part of town and she pointed out old Crusader fortifications, Roman tombs and statues, a Byzantine church. "South of here is the Gaza Strip."

"But we won't visit it."

"Not today, Brent. I don't think we'd be too popular. Let's head back north—to my place. We'll stop at a store and I'll buy the makings for lunch—and a bottle of wine."

"Best idea I've heard today." Turning the wheel sharply, he whipped the small vehicle into a sharp U-turn and headed for Rehovot.

Devora's house was on Spinoza Street. It looked like every other house on the block; small, cement-block structures surrounded by a profusion of foliage. The living room was comfortably furnished and Brent sank down into a large plump sofa while Devora hurried to the kitchen with the bag of groceries they had bought at a nearby store. In a moment, she returned with a tray ladened with pita bread sandwiches, cheese, pickles, cucumbers, radishes, tiny carrots, and a bottle of wine. Placing the tray on a small table fronting the couch, she dropped down close to Brent. Pouring the wine, she quipped, "Sorry, no gefilte fish and matzo ball soup."

"I'll come back for the Seder."

"To the next Passover meal," she said raising her glass.

"The next Passover." They touched glasses and drank.

Surprisingly, the flame of desire was not fanned. She was immensely desirable, yet, he actually moved away as he reached for a condiment. Maybe it was Ruth. He knew he would see her soon. Did he actually feel guilty. Was he capable of this? He had never felt guilt after killing a man or bedding a woman. Especially the women. He had told several he loved them and he didn't even know what love was. Were his personal devils devouring him? He wanted to talk, had to talk about anything. He surprised Devora with his question, "You're not much of a Jew, are you, Devora? I've seen that in a lot of young Israelis."

She stopped nibbling on an egg salad sandwich and said, "You know I'm not orthodox, if that's what you mean?" She smiled up at him, obviously challenged by his mood. "And what do you think a Jew is, anyway?"

He hesitated before answering, "Not a race, not even a single religion, just a state of mind, as far as I can tell."

She put down her sandwich. "Well said, well said, Brent. People here don't know what they have in common, except the state of Israel, if that's the state of mind you're talking about." She giggled at her inadvertent pun.

He chuckled. "Yes, the state of Israel." They touched glasses and drank.

Something else came to his mind. "Your street has an interesting—ah, controversial name."

She smiled with delight. "You're very perceptive. Spinoza Street after Baruch Spinoza."

"Yes. The Jewish philosopher, a maverick who died 300 years ago."

"You're filled with unending surprises, Brent Ross."

"I told you once sailors have a lot of time to read."

She nodded and said, "He certainly was a maverick and the orthodox like to blame our troubles on Spinoza. What do you know of him?" She refilled his glass.

"Not much, Devora." He sipped his wine thoughtfully. "In a way, he was a pillar of modern Western thinking.

He spoke out for the rule of reason, the separation of religion and state and the primacy of knowledge over faith." He reflected for a moment while she stared at him in fascination. "He hated the theocratic management of his community and fought for freedom from religious authority over everything, every aspect of everyday life. The old orthodox were good at that."

"Very good, and they still are. You have a lot of I.Q. points to go with those muscles. You're amazing, Brent." She placed her small hand on his. "Spinoza was a very brave man."

"Of, course. He was brave enough to say God was not a personage but exists everywhere, in everything. He could've been killed for that alone."

"He hated the power of the rabbis to control every aspect everyday life and fought against it. The rabbis had him thrown out of Amsterdam for this."

"I can believe that, Devora."

"Because of him Brent, there are Jews who drive cars on the Sabbath, eat pork and do not believe the boundaries of Israel are necessarily ordained by God, yet still consider themselves Jewish."

"They are, absolutely."

"Why do you say that, Brent?"

"Because of 'Brent Ross's Law'."

"And what is that?"

"Ninety-five percent of everything is crap."

She threw her head back and laughed, a deep mirthful sound. "You're a philosopher, Brent Ross." She laughed some more and dabbed at her eyes with a lace handkerchief. Then, scooting closer, she did not stop until her hip pressed against his. The touch of the firm hip and thigh caused him to start, a brief catch in his breath. She ran a hand up his wrist where she could feel the hair. Her palm was soft and hot and he felt a tingle of electricity race up his arm. She turned her face up to him, eyes enhanced by moisture, an arresting deep brown, almost black. "Let's not be philosophers, Brent Ross."

"What do you have in mind?"

"You could kiss me for starters."

He smiled down at her. Spinoza faded.

"Am I too bold, Brent? Too brazen?"

"No. You're just perfect."

She ran her fingers over his cheek. "I told you once you were too precious to lose."

"I remember. I can't let you slip away either, Devora."

"War is full of this, isn't it Brent? People meeting, enjoying each other for a blink in time and then torn apart."

"Like ping–pong balls."

Her laugh was a fresh mountain brook tumbling over pebbles. "My metaphor. "I'm to blame."

"I like it, it's true."

Ruth was gone, Spinoza had vanished. The only thing in the world that counted was this beguiling woman. Suddenly, his mood thickened with need and he began to warm with stirrings of sexual fury. Tightening his arm around her, she came to his lips eagerly as if she had done it a hundred times. Days of being thrown together, of forced restraint and repressed sexual hunger exploded in that moment, blurring out everything. She pulled him down on top of her; mouth wide, tongue hot and probing. He kissed her eyes, her nose, her cheeks, neck, forehead, frantically as if he could not kiss her enough. And the silken hair spilled out like a black halo. He entwined a hand in it, imprisoning her head, his other hand seeking out her breasts, tearing buttons from her blouse in his haste.

She pushed against his chest. "No, Brent, please."

"Why? What? I don't understand."

"I want to shower."

"Now?" He was incredulous.

"Yes. Please. That's how I am."

Breathing heavily, he sat up and she kissed him again, wide and hot. "It won't take long, my darling."

He could only nod as she disappeared down a short hallway. Watching her perfect buttocks move like two small melon halves, caused him to start and feel a boiling frustration deep down. He cursed under his breath in impatience. He heard the shower running.

"Brent," she called. "Come shower with me."

Of course. That's what she wanted from the beginning. He rose and hurried to the bathroom door which was open. He could see her silhouette through the frosted glass of the shower doors. It was a surprisingly large shower for such a small house—for any Israeli house. He was accustomed to meager little ceiling nozzles squirting water onto a cement slab. This one was truly huge and luxurious.

"Put your clothes on a chair in the bedroom," she called over the rush of water.

In a moment, he was nude. Opening the door to the shower, his eyes widened when he saw her. Her body was like that of a model for the cover of *Vogue,* or the centerfold of *Playboy*. He stood for a moment and fed his eyes. And her eyes were busy, too, running over his chest, shoulders, legs, his obviously excited manhood.

Reaching out, she grabbed his hand and pulled him against her under the shower head. "Don't be bashful, my darling." She turned on more jets and water seemed to come from everywhere.

They kissed savagely. Flesh on flesh with the warm water streaming down. His hands ran over her breasts, down to her tiny waist and then clutched her buttocks. She reached down, took him in her hand and guided him between her thighs, squeezing her legs tight together.

Reaching behind her, she found a bottle of green shampoo. She squeezed the thick liquid on his chest, her breasts, hips, legs. "Work it in," she whispered hoarsely.

With short circular motions, he massaged it over her skin, her breasts, lower back, buttocks and then up between her legs.

"More. More, please, darling, higher."

Sliding upward, his fingers probed gently, slipping inside. She was hot and very wet.

Stiffening, she cried out a whimpering sound as his finger found her most sensitive spot. She pulled him back where there was a small marble bench in the corner and turned the main jet with a single swipe of her hand. Grasping her buttocks, he lifted her up and laid her back on the marble bench, opening her legs wide and sliding into her.

They clasped each other and rocked together as he drove into her with deep, steady thrusts. As her sensations rose, her kisses became nibbling bites, and she sucked his tongue as the water splashed over them, making their perspiring bodies ride smoothly together. She began to make small moaning sounds deep in her throat.

She worked her hips more rapidly, cried out, raised her

legs until they curled around his waist, bringing him even deeper within her. Panting, gasping he reached down and stroked her in time with his thrusts. Finally, unable to withstand the soaring sensations, he exploded within her while she dug her fingers into his back and screamed, loud and shrill, over and over. It was almost as if her sensations had tumbled over the bounds of ecstasy and entered the realm of pain. It was the most complete and devastating moment of his existence.

Emptied of strength, they slid from the bench and lay on the floor, legs and arms entwined, unable to move. The shower still ran, now cooling their bodies.

The next morning Brent did not leave until nearly noon. The frenzied night of lovemaking had left him tired and in a sleepy euphoria despite a large breakfast and three cups of coffee.

"Be careful when you drive," she said, standing close to him at the door.

"You damned near killed me last night."

"How do you think I feel," she answered, rubbing her groin.

"Take a hot shower."

She shook her head. "Be too lonely, now. And without you, I'll need a cold shower, anyway."

"We made history in there."

"Yes. I'll hang a plaque from the shower head."

"No one else will ever use it."

"Right. I'll save it for us." She smiled broadly. "I've never enjoyed a shower as much."

"Can't think of a better way to get clean."

"Call me."

"I will. I'll pick you up and we can go to dinner in Tel Aviv."

"Does your room have a shower?"

He laughed. "I'll see to that."

She arched back against his circling arms and looked into his eyes. He expected her to say something about Ruth and she did. "You'll see Ruth Moskowitz?"

"Yes."

"Go to bed with her?"

"Probably. Is that a problem?"

Turning her lips under, she bit on the lower one. "Before last night, no. But now . . ." She shook her head. "But now? Yes."

"It's a problem with me, too."

"I'm glad."

"You have other men." It was a statement, not a question.

"At present, no."

"But you will."

She smiled wryly. "Probably. Is that a problem?"

"We've traded scripts, again."

She chuckled. "I know."

"I understand. And you?"

"Yes. I understand, Brent. It's war and we grab what we can."

"You still want me to phone you?"

"Yes. Take enough showers with me and I'll scrub that woman right out of your hair."

Laughing, he pulled her tight against him, kissed her hard and long. Grasping the doorknob, he said, *"Sholom aleichem."*

She kissed him again and answered, *"Aleichem sholom."* Then, grabbing his arm she dropped her near perfect English, reverting to Hebrew, *"L'hit raot, m'took-a-ti."*

Concentrating on the strange words, he narrowed his eyes. "Ah, you said something about 'meeting again, my, ah . . .'"

She nuzzled his cheek. "You never cease to amaze me, darling. I said, 'Until we meet again, my dear.'"

"Until we meet again," he repeated.

One more deep kiss and he left.

It was late afternoon when three-year-old Chana Furman ran down the beach toward the rocky outcropping and the thick stands of trees. She stopped suddenly and stared up into a large pine.

Face reddened by irritation, her mother ran after her. "Chana! Chana! Come back." Staring into the tree, the toddler appeared to hear nothing. The woman raised a hand and waved it in a spanking motion, "I've told you never wander off by yourself. Don't you ever understand?"

Chana turned. "Mommy," she pointed, "up there. A lady."

The woman stopped next to the rocks and stared curiously. "A lady? I don't see anything."

"No, no, Mommy. Not in the bushes. There's a lady in the trees. She looks funny."

"In the trees?"

"Yes, Mommy. She has a funny wooden thing like baby brother Sol."

The woman moved next to her daughter and stopped

as if she had suddenly frozen. Then she screamed. Screamed again and again. There were shouts and people came running.

Chana clutched her mother's leg crying, "What's wrong, Mommy. I'm sorry. I'm sorry. Please don't spank me."

Chapter XV

Brent did not check into the Hilton until after 1400 hours. Rooms were abundant and he had his pick. He chose the same suite on the seventh floor he had occupied on his previous visit. He loved the magnificent view of the Mediterranean. It took him back to the bracing salt air of *Yonaga*'s bridge.

Entering the living room, memories of Ruth flooded back. They had spent many frenzied, blissful nights together here. He felt a rare emotion—a sting of guilt. Devora. She was still with him. Even the scent of her was on his body.

"What am I?" he asked the silent sea. "A psycho? A depraved gigolo? A man with no conscience? No scruples? The world's greatest hypocrite?" But Devora was the same, in a peculiar way reflecting him. And so did Ruth. Men and women in wartime. Purveyors of death repeating the act of life with anyone; everyone. Maybe it was God's way, nature's way, the species' way—or whatever was in control, if anything—of fighting man's unique talent for killing himself. Kill and create. Interminable, conflicting, insane. They were all schizophrenic. Kill the bad guys because we're the good guys. But everyone wore a white hat. Who could tell the good from the bad? And God was on everyone's side. Maybe, Atsumi was right.

Shaking his head, he carried his small bag into the bedroom. He had just unpacked it when the knock came. It was Elroy Rubin. Brent could tell from his funereal expression that something was amiss. He was carrying a small shopping bag.

Brent said, "I thought you were in Jerusalem, ol' lonesome polecat." He waved the Texan to a chair placed in a group with a small coffee table and a couch.

There was no laugh. Then Brent's suspicions were confirmed when the pilot dropped some of his hayseed facade.

"Got special permission to come here—to see you." He pulled a bottle of rare Haig and Haig out of the bag and sank into a chair. "Have a jolt of white lightnin', Brent."

"Right neighborly of you, ol' saddle buddy," Brent continued to gibe despite his apprehension. He walked to the small kitchen alcove. Quickly, he returned with a tray loaded with the scotch, two glasses, and a bucket of ice. After placing the tray on the table, he seated himself and dropped ice cubes into the glasses with a pair of tongs. Elroy poured the whiskey.

"*Yonaga*," Brent saluted.

"*Yonaga*."

Brent felt impatience mount. "What brings you here? You just couldn't be lonely for my company. You look like you have a burr under your saddle."

Elroy took another stiff drink and wiped nonexistent perspiration from his brow with the back of his hand. He stared at his feet. "It's Ruth." He stopped and coughed as if his own words had gagged him.

Brent felt a terrible iciness coil around his heart. "What about Ruth?"

"Mossad's a—tryin' to keep it hush."

"Keep what hush?"

He stared at Brent the blue of his eyes heightened by moisture. He blurted it out, "Dry—gulched. Dead! She's dead, Brent."

Brent could only stare in disbelief. It seemed it took minutes for the words to penetrate his consciousness, deliver their meaning. He emptied his glass. Elroy recharged it.

"The killer's M.O. was just like Harry Goodenough."

"No!"

The Texan let the horror pour out. The rape, the sodomising, the wire. He described all the details, left nothing out, words slashing like barbed wire, wounding. "They found her yesterday evenin'," he concluded. "Hangin' from a tree."

"Good God! Yesterday afternoon," Brent anguished, gasping as if the room had been emptied of air. "While she was hanging from that tree I was—I was shacked up with another woman." A fist struck the table, pounding out each word, "Balling my guts out."

Whispering reverentially like a man at prayer or a funeral, Elroy counseled him solemnly, "There's no call for that, Brent. You cain't blame yourself for being human. You couldn't do nothin'."

"I know! I know! But she was dying and I was . . ."

Elroy would not let him finish, "There wasn't one gosh

darned thing a body could do. It tears my innards, too, Brent."

Brent punched the table so hard it jumped, bottle clattering. "And there's nothing—no clue."

"Not so."

"What do you mean." Brent leaned forward hungrily.

"This time he was eye—balled."

"Where? How?"

"At a gas station. Big blond dude. An' young."

"There are a lot of big, young, blond dudes."

Elroy ran a finger across his face. "This here critter's branded—got a scar from here to here."

Brent punched the table again. "Good! Good, that's something." He tossed off his drink and poured another. "He's insane."

"Sho 'nuff. Plum loco. That's what I figger."

"Kadafi trained a madman to duplicate Goodenough."

"Right."

"But he outdid Goodenough."

"Bushwacked three women that we knows about. An' he 'peared to be waitin' for Ruth at that restaurant."

Brent nodded, mind refocusing. "The Paznon. She loved their coffee and pancakes. I've been there with her three or four times. He figured she'd stop, had it all set up." His fists warred with each other for a moment. "Must be more than one of them. They studied her—had a book on her."

"Real pros. Trackin' her, sho' 'nuff. Maybe for months." Elroy took a big drink. "An' he always sticks somethin' . . ."

"I know."

"No, you don't, Brent. With Mori Tokumitsu's wife he

done shoved a bottle of sulfuric acid up her and done broke it while she was still alive."

"Oh God, no." With composure slipping again, Brent clutched his glass so tight it shook like a man with palsy, ice cubes clattering, drops of scotch flying. Finally, he managed, "Anything else on him?"

"Nothin' 'cept he was dressed as a private first class and driving a '87 Honda CRX. Pulled the rotor out of the distributor. Them folks at the station said he told Ruth his car wouldn't run. Bummed a ride offin' her."

Brent got a better grip on control. "Figures. Anything on the car?"

"Nothin'. He leased it in Haifa under the name of Private First Class Shlomo Granit, showed identification."

"He didn't steal the car?"

"Negative."

"I'll be damned. Confident bastard. His I.D. was all phony, of course."

"Sho' 'nuff. Phony as a three-dollar bill. But the leasing hombre got a good look—saw the scar, just like them other folks at the gas station."

Brent gulped down his drink. Replenished his glass. "But he'll disguise himself. They're trained for that. Wigs, cosmetics, forged identity papers better than originals." He tapped the table in agitation. "The scar could've been phony, too, you know."

"I was just fixin' to say that."

"He could be anywhere now. Maybe, even Japan, stalking our women."

"Admiral Fujita's done been told. An' they's other clues."

"What?"

"Semen, hair, skin under the women's fingernails. They'se got DNA fingerprints on him with the first two women. Same hombre."

"And Ruth."

"Fixin' to do an autopsy, pronto."

Brent pounded his head with his fists as if scourging the horror with flagellation. "Oh, God. God! She said she was hexed, had a black wreath on her door from the beginning. She was so young, so beautiful."

Elroy put a hand on his friend's shoulder. "She was all them things." He refilled both glasses. "We'll get that rattler, Brent. Kill 'im slow and easy."

Brent's lips compressed into a thin white line and the thick eyebrows seemed to meet above the snapping blue eyes and straight nose. We've got to catch the son-of-a-bitch, first."

"I know."

Brent slapped the Formica table top so hard it stung. A strange raging sound surged through his throbbing throat where a tumult of emotions battled for expression. Finally, he managed to articulate a horrible sound, animal and ferocious, "Kill them! Kill them all! That's the only way!"

Chapter XVI

"Kill them all! That's the only way!" Air Group Commander, Commander Yoshi Matsuhara exhorted from the dais. The Fighter Pilots' Ready Room was jammed with 54 pilots; all young, all staring at Yoshi. Each man had a pencil and clipboard on his lap.

Yoshi continued, stoical face singularly florid, black eyes back–lighted with a frightening flame. "They'll kill you in any way possible—in your chutes, in the water, and if you're captured, slowly and with great artistry. It's kill or be killed. Always remember, Kadafi pays them by the corpse and your enemy is money mad."

A young freckled American from Oklahoma with hair so red it appeared orange, spoke up, "Sir, Lieutenant Scott Wood, here." Yoshi nodded. Uneasily, the young man tensed his jaw and wrinkled his brow and nose so that the freckles gleamed like tiny gold coins. He said, "With all due respect, Sir, I signed aboard to destroy machines, not necessarily men." Pausing, his eyes widened as he saw Yoshi's face turn volcano red. "Please, Sir, hear me out."

"Go ahead."

"I can't accept the murder of helpless men as a viable rule of engagement."

Everyone was shocked by Wood's daring challenge and expected the Air Group Commander to erupt. However, Yoshi surprised them with his control. "I understand," he answered gruffly. "But, Lieutenant Wood, there are no rules of engagement. You have forgotten that you are fighting terrorism—highly organized and well equipped world terrorism. Terrorists recognize no rules, so we who fight them must meet them on their own terms or be destroyed."

Wood persisted, "Sir, I am quite willing to fight them or I wouldn't be in this room."

"Then there is no conflict."

Wood rubbed his nose as if he were trying to erase the freckles. "I ask for one thing, Sir."

"Yes."

"That each man decide for himself if a parachutist or man in the water is to be killed."

Yoshi's eyes were as black and implacable as pools of liquid tar. His voice rumbled like the crack of doom, "You will follow my orders to the letter or be relieved and leave this room now."

"But, Sir!"

"Enough! Decide Lieutenant!"

All color drained from Wood's smooth features and his upper lip and cheeks were covered with a sheen of perspiration. "I'll remain, Sir."

Yoshi pushed hard, "No hesitation? No reservations?"

The answer came in a hushed tone, nearly a whisper,

"None, Sir." The young Oklahoman seated himself. No one was convinced.

The cockney, Pilot Officer Elwyn York, stood and Yoshi nodded. York kept his RAF designation as had most of the foreign pilots, maintaining identification with their own home services. One of Yoshi's superb wingmen, York's inflection spoke unmistakably of London's East End and the Isle of Dogs. His eyes found Wood and he spoke as if his mouth was full of chewing gum, "You'd better swot this up, guvn'r—the whole lot of you new boys. There's no Geneva Convent'un—these bloody buggers we's fightin' get their bags off when they stick one up your kilt. Honor? Ha! It ain't worth a two-penny shit, it ain't. Bullock 'em when you can or they'll come back to stuff a brace o' 20-millimeter up your arse. And that' ain't no bumf." His eyes searched the room. "We lost a boffo lad when that butcher Rosencrance gutted Willard-Smith in his chute. An' more of our chaps . . ."

Haunted by the painful memory, Yoshi intervened abruptly, "You put it succinctly, Pilot Officer York. All of you remember those words." He gestured at a chart of the Western Pacific, "We have some work to do in the Marianas. But this is our first meeting, the first time we have all been assembled as a unit aboard our carrier and the first time some of you have ever landed on a carrier." Almost as if to emphasize the Air Group Commander's words, *Yonaga* took a sudden lurch to starboard and Yoshi was forced to steady himself with a hand to the dais. He said, "But before I continue, anyone else?"

Yoshi's other wingman, Flying Officer Claude Hooperman, stood. Tall, blond, patrician he was the personification of the British gentleman and the antithesis of the short, dark cockney, Pilot Officer Elwyn York. Hooper-man nodded at Yoshi, "With your permission, Sir, I would like to second the sentiments expressed by yourself and Pilot Officer York."

"Of course."

"Daresay, when I first came on board, I had visions of fighting this war like a gentleman—chivalry, honor, re-spect for an injured foe, the whole lot. We had that in the Falklands, you know." He waved a finger over his head, "But those bloody butchers soon relieved me of all honor-able intentions—the whole lot." The lean urbane counte-nance took on a hard aspect. "But I bloody well soon learned that there is no honor up there, no mercy. You can find more chivalry amongst the animals of the African bush." He sat.

While the young men silently mulled the grisly warn-ing, Yoshi's eyes wandered over the faces: six Englishmen, two Frenchmen, a Turk, a Greek, two Germans, thirty Japanese and a dozen Americans. In fact, a whole squad-ron of Americans. All were young, so very young. New faces, but, on the other hand, he had seen the same faces for decades. The bright, the brave, shining with idealism. They never changed. He had led so many into battle; led so many to their graves. The eternal battle. Choose be-tween freedom and slavery and write your answer in blood. His wise young friend Brent Ross had said, "The best are the first to fight and the best are the first to die." The truth of the words wrenched his guts.

And the young faces brought another problem home to Yoshi, as painful and penetrating as the point of a *wakiza-shi*. Once the faces had been all Japanese, the finest, the best, the cream of the Empire. But those faces had all disappeared: most were dead, a few survivors flying slow bombers. He was the only fighter pilot of the original crew left. And he had aged. Most men his age retired to play with their grandchildren while he had become the oldest fighter pilot in the history of aerial warfare, flying the hottest fighter plane in the world and piling up his kills.

The media had harped on this. In fact, one cheap American tabloid referred to him as the "Geriatric Killer." Just before they put to sea, Admiral Fujita had warned again of the incursions of age, warned of grounding him. The old man was in a lyrical mood when he had admonished his air group commander and old friend, "The gods alone have neither age nor death, Yoshi–san. Time decays all other things, as inevitable and eternal as the sea."

But Yoshi had argued fervently and with force. "Still have my reflexes, Admiral," he had countered. Then, with a single swipe of his hand he snatched a fly out of mid–air. Fujita had nodded and acquiesced reluctantly, but not without exacting a painful promise, "You will ground yourself if you slow, become a menace to your men."

"On my honor in the name of the Emperor," Yoshi had solemnly pledged.

But still not satisfied, the old man had called on the death of an early samurai hero as a parting remark, "Remember what the assassin of the great Ota Dokan said as he pierced Dokan with a spear, 'Ah! How in moments like these, Our heart doth grudge the light of life'."

Yoshi was familiar with the life and death of the fabled hero, the builder of the castle of Tokyo. He replied, "And Ota Dokan did not fear death. In fact, he added to the couplet as he died, 'Had not in hours of peace, My heart learned to deftly look on life'."

"You have deftly looked on life, Yoshi-san?"

"Perhaps too deftly, Admiral, but not for too long."

Fujita's countenance was as bleak and stony as a temple Buddha when Yoshi left.

A cough from the back of the room broke through Yoshi's thoughts just as his eyes stopped on the American squadron leader, Commander Steve Elkins. Regaining direction, Yoshi spoke directly to the husky, sandy-haired squadron leader, "On this mission, Commander Elkins, you will not fly combat air patrol."

"No CAP!" Elkins shouted joyously. He turned to his men. "Then we go! Right?" Cheers!

"Affirmative. We will need your Hellcats over the target. *Yonaga* will keep only a small reserve of ready fighters for CAP. *Bennington* will provide most of the CAP for the entire battle group when we go into action."

Elkins said, "Battleship *New Jersey*, Sir? She must close to almost twenty miles to bombard."

"Probably closer than that—much closer. According to the admiral's order of battle, her CAP is *Bennington*'s duty. But we will also share the responsibility. All of you are to monitor her fighter frequency." He struck a chart with the tip of his pointer. "We are here, about 800-kilometers— ah, about 500 miles off the southern tip of Shikoku." He slid the pointer down the Mercator projection in a line slightly east of south. "We will steam this course, 168 degrees, true, for 1600 miles. At our best cruising speed, we should arrive at our launch point here in about five or six days, depending on speed and course changes for training or enemy contacts." The pointer stabbed a point about 200–miles east Saipan. "Latitude 16 degrees, 20 minutes, longitude 150. We will commence launch at 0400 hours."

One of the Germans, *Oberleutnant* Gustav Hoffmann, waved a hand. Yoshi nodded assent and the German spoke in guttural, but distinct English. There was a pronounced Bavarian roll to his diction, *"Kommandeur* Matsuhara, there is a rumor that the enemy has reinforced his *jagerstaffels. Ja?"*

Yoshi picked up a document. "More than a rumor, *Oberleutnant."* He glanced at the document. "According to the latest intelligence, he may have as many as five squadrons of fighters and three squadrons of bombers on Saipan and Tinian. They expect our visit."

"Oberst Rosencrance?"

"As far as we know, *Oberleutnant,* he's still in the Middle East."

"Buggeration," Elwyn York muttered. "I owes that bloody sod."

"We all do, Pilot Officer York."

A Japanese with the face of a schoolboy, raised his hand and said, "Lieutenant Tsunetsugu Munakata, here." Yoshi gestured, Munakata continued, "Commander, just this morning there was a report of another killing in the Middle East."

"There are a lot of killings in the Middle East," Hooperman said. The men grinned.

Munakata looked around apprehensively. "It was a woman—a Mossad agent named Ruth Moskowitz, raped and killed sadistically like Lieutenant Dempster's mother and Ambassador Mori Tokumitsu's wife."

Yoshi stiffened as if he had been punched in the small

of the back. Everyone knew of his loss of Tomoko Ozumori, a loss from which he had never recovered. "I know, Lieutenant," he said, in a harsh, hissing sound.

Tsunetsugu Munakata's jaw worked, and his eyes widened, but he pushed on. "I have a new wife . . ."

Yoshi interrupted with the only correct military response, "Most of the men have women at home. Will we allow this sadistic killer to disrupt our determination? Is that not what Kadafi wants?"

"I know, Sir. But we pulled all of our seaman guards out of Japan when we put to sea."

"The Tokyo police are patrolling, giving extra protection to our women." Perplexed looks were exchanged. It was common knowledge that Tomoko Ozumori was under police protection when she was murdered. No one knew this better than Yoshi who had gone berserk when he found her body and attempted to kill two police officers. Only the intervention of Chief Eichi Nakahashi and Seaman Guard Raitei Arima had stopped the commander. They had been forced to overpower and handcuff him. The men remained silent, no one daring to pursue the topic further except one burly pilot seated in the back of the room.

"Sir," the pilot shouted. Yoshi recognized Lieutenant Yasuo Sakakibaru, a man of about thirty. The son of an old samurai family, he could be sanctimonious, pedantic and harsh, flaunting a superior air amongst men of inferior rank. Aggressive to the point of belligerence, Yoshi saw in him the qualities of a fine fighter pilot and at the same time, a troublemaker. Basically, he disliked the man, but wanted him at the controls of a Zero–sen. "May I say something, Commander," Sakakibaru requested politely enough.

Yoshi gave his permission and regretted it immediately. Sakakibaru waved grandly like the archetypical samurai, "May I suggest, Sir, if any of the men are afraid for their women, let them return to them and hide behind their skirts."

Munakata leaped to his feet, "No one talks to me like that!"

"I do. You are a . . ."

"Silence! At ease! Take your seats," Yoshi shouted.

"Sir," Munakata persisted. "I cannot ignore that insult."

"I know," Yoshi conceded. "But you will wait until this mission is completed."

Both men grumbled but took their seats.

Yoshi cursed himself. Another feud. Amberg and Sneerson, Arai with both Whitehead and Dempster, and now Munakata and Sakakibaru. When would it end? The young men had all grown up in war. It was all they knew. Too much pressure for too many years. The best therapy for this crew would be to meet the enemy, engage in a bloody battle. Nothing pulled men closer together than the heat and sacrifice of battle. And they would have one soon. Camaraderie was honed in that crucible. Maybe they would all die before they realized their common cause.

Fighting his chagrin, Yoshi left the disrupting topic behind by returning to the chart. This time he struck the port of Aden on the Gulf of Aden so hard the rubber tip left a black mark. "Our true objective is here, the enemy battle group."

"Force them out?" Hoffmann hazarded, picking up the new focus.

"Correct, *Oberleutnant*. They know we are assembling a landing force and this strike is being made to soften up their defenses."

"They should sortie and give battle," Yasuo Sakakibaru added eagerly. Munakata glared at him but remained silent.

"That is what Admiral Fujita plans." Yoshi tapped the chart thoughtfully. "Three carriers, two cruisers with escorts." Then he described the enemy ships, information all of the men had digested many times. The carriers were the former Russian *Baku* and *Kiev* and the Spanish *Reina de Iberico*. Big and formidable, the three carriers could operate over 200 aircraft. Both cruisers had twelve 6-inch guns and were fast and well armored.

Yoshi emphasized how the key to world domination rested with these warships. Fujita was determined to engage and destroy them. Thus far, the Arabs had been loathe to commit them. Now, they would engage or lose their Pacific bases, and, perhaps, more important, the *jihad* would lose prestige and credibility with the Arab world. "Kadafi cannot tolerate this. Loss of the bases could cause the Arab alliance, tenuous at best, to collapse," the air group commander concluded.

The young Greek, Lieutenant Styros Paponagas, spoke up for the first time, "The enemy fighters, Sir? Still using the powered-up Messerschmitt 109 as his basic fighter?"

"Some P-51 Mustangs and a few Spitfires, but, basically, yes, his fighter squadrons are still equipped with the Me 109. As most of you know, the new Daimler-Benz *Valkyrie* produces more than 3000 horsepower. The 109 can outrun and out-dive our Zero-sens, but cannot turn with it. It's about even with our Hellcats, but slower than our Corsairs and no match for the Bearcat."

"We need more Bearcats," Paponagas said.

Yoshi nodded. "Rear Admiral Whitehead has been pressuring the Pentagon for more." He shrugged. "But the Americans are busy rearming—claim they need all their production." He turned back to the charts and pounded the Marianas with the rubber tip. "Remember, our primary mission is to protect our Aichis and Nakajimas. They must deliver their ordnance or our mission is a failure. And *all* enemy aircraft must be destroyed."

"Sir, then we may make more than one strike," Hooperman noted.

"True. We will continue to attack until our objective is destroyed or we are all dead."

A hush filled the room, interrupted only by the throbbing of the great engines and the whine of blowers. One of the Frenchmen, a swarthy ensign named Philippe Boncour, bared a concern that had caused anxiety with all hands. "The enemy 'Special Attack Corps', *Monsieur Commandant*. They will crash into our ships, no?"

"Yes," one of Elkins' men cried out. "They have their own *kamikaze* pilots, now. Some of those crazy Shi'ites who are happy to kill themselves to get us."

Yoshi drummed the pointer on the deck and steadied himself as the ship took another hard roll. "True. We encountered some in our last sortie into the Mediterranean. However, they were poorly trained and terrible pilots and did little damage. One hit *Yonaga*'s armor belt and another hit *Bennington*'s bow. However, I won't minimize their threat. Nothing can be more devastating than massed suicide attacks pressed home with skill and the determination of men eager to die. As yet, we have not faced that and there are no reports of Special Attack Corps units in the Marianas."

"We have *bon service de renseignements en* the Marianas, *Monsieur Commandant?*" Philippe Boncour blurted out, in his anxiety reverting to French phrases.

"Yes. In addition to our own intelligence personnel, the natives hate the Arabs and supply us with information." He stared at the Frenchman for a long moment, "And remember, Ensign Boncour, the language of *Yonaga* is English."

"Je regrette, Monsieur commandant."

"You what?"

The swarthy features flushed and Boncour spoke slowly and deliberately as if his lips were shears and he were snipping off each word, "I mean I am sorry, Commander." For the first time, a titter of humor raced through the room.

"That is much better," Yoshi said. He stabbed a finger upward. "Remember, up there on our fighter frequency there won't be time to translate. English! English! English!" The humor vanished.

"I understand," the Frenchman said contritely.

"One more thing, I have posted a CAP schedule on the fighter pilots' bulletin board. Every one of you will fly these missions. These are basically training missions to give you practice in taking off and landing on the carrier's deck. All of you are fine pilots, good marksmen. But you are of no service at all to us if you kill yourself landing or taking off. It is not a difficult thing to do—killing yourself, I mean." The men chuckled. "So, check the schedule."

He looked around. No waving hands, no questions. A new thought struck him. Rubbing his chin meditatively, he said, "Almost half of you are not Japanese. But there are universal truths to be found in Japanese history. In the sixteenth century the great samurai Takeda Shingen had emblazoned on his banner, 'Fast as the wind; quiet as the forest; aggressive as fire; and immovable as a mountain'." He surveyed the sober faces. "Remember these words. They have much to say to fighting men of all ages."

"Kommandeur," Oberleutnant Gustav Hoffman said, coming to his feet. "May I read a piece by Reverend Martin Niemoeller?"

"The U–boat commander of the Great War?"

"Ja, Kommandeur. My granduncle, a war hero and courageous patriot who fought Hitler and was imprisoned." Yoshi gestured approval. Hoffmann pulled a small document from his pocket. His voice dropped octaves and he spoke hoarsely, "My uncle wrote these words for all people of all the ages, everywhere." He read, " 'In Germany, the Nazis first came for the communists, and I didn't speak up because I wasn't a communist. Then they came for the Jews, and I didn't speak up because I wasn't a Jew. Then they came for the trade unionists, and I didn't speak up because I wasn't a trade unionist. Then they came for the Catholics, but I didn't speak up because I was a Protestant. Then they came for me, and by that time there was no one left to speak for me'."

Silence. Hoffmann sat. Yoshi's eyes measured every face. He said, "But now, with men like you speaking for the oppressed, the tyrants may come, but they will find their graves instead of victims."

Cheers. *"Banzai!"* Grinning, Yoshi let the pandemonium reign for a moment. Then with raised hands he quieted his men and said, "Gentlemen, you are dismissed.

Snapping to attention, the young men bowed and, after Yoshi answered the salute, strode through the door. Yoshi noticed Munakata's and Sakakibaru's departures were widely spaced. He knew more trouble was inevitable. "I wish I only had Arabs to fight," he said to himself, suddenly feeling weary.

Scott Wood was the last to leave. He paused, turned and stared at the air group commander.

"You have something to say, Lieutenant?"

"No, Sir." Wood turned and left.

On a southeasterly heading, the battle group steamed under translucent blue skies, the sun dappling the sea with bright flashing sequins like spangles on the gown of an undulating dancer. But the northeasterlies were up, building a running swell that took the ships on their port beams, rolling them gently from side to side. Cleverly, Fujita deployed his ships in a wide dispersal: *New Jersey* flanked by *Yonaga* and *Bennington*, each capital ship protected by its own destroyer escort. This deployment allowed the carriers ease in operating aircraft and *New Jersey* could lend her tremendous fire power in support of either carrier or both.

True to his word, Commander Matsuhara had his air groups practicing take-offs and landings continuously. Luckily the weather held and the exercises were marred by only two minor accidents. One wiped out the undercarriage of a Nakajima, the other tore off the end of an

Aichi's wing when it tumbled into a gun gallery. No one was injured. "The Gods are with us," Fujita had muttered from the flag bridge as he watched the Aichi dragged to the forward elevator.

Nakajima D3A torpedo bombers from *Yonaga* and Curtis SB2Cs and Douglas SBDs from *Bennington* scouted continuously and maintained anti–submarine patrols. Not one sighting of the enemy was made, not even a single long range patrol.

On the fourth day, they crossed the Tropic of Cancer and entered the tropics. All practice was halted. Gradually, the unsullied blue sky changed and there were streaks of high mare's–tail cirrus smeared across it. Penetrating deeper into the tropics, the air itself seemed to change, thick and charged with static that made a man's skin prickle. And the heat bore down, unusual for even these latitudes; heavy, languorous, debilitating. A man's sweat lingered and his thinking slowed. A general torpor gripped the entire crew. It was ominous, as if the gods were moaning warnings through the rigging.

On the morning of the fifth day, the fight broke out on the hangar deck. Yoshi was trying to track down an oil leak in his engine with his crew chief, Chief Shoishi Ota. Knowing his aircraft better than any man alive, Yoshi never hesitated to attack a problem with his own hands. He had disassembled and reassembled the *Taifu*, checked the control cables, stripped down his machine guns and cannons, even tested his instruments and radio. His life and only his life hung in the balance in the cramped cockpit. He always found this adequate incentive for caution. This was one reason why he had lived to become the oldest fighter pilot on earth.

They started with the tank which was intact, so there had to be a defective fitting or cracked line. Two banks of nine cylinders and two turbo–superchargers, all jammed together in a compact mass of cooling fins, pumps, compressors, fuel and oil lines, made the engine difficult to work on. Both men were greasy, irritated and short of patience. The oppressive heat and humidity did not improve their mood and neither did the noise. Although the gigantic compartment was almost a 1000–feet long and had a high overhead, it was crowded with row after row of aircraft being readied for combat. Crewmen swarmed over them, shouting, cursing, banging tools. Adding to the din were the rat–a–tat–tat bursts of pneumatic tools, the rumble of carts and fuel bowsers, and the whine of power drills and grinders.

The dive bomber commander, Lieutenant Oliver Y.K. Dempster, walked past, headed for his mottled brown and green Aichi D3A. He, too, was wearing overalls. Yoshi exchanged greetings with the Amerasian and was pleased to see he was about to work on his own aircraft. Then he was shocked when even over the bedlam, he heard the bellowed insult, "Filthy dog eating Korean pig!"

Dempster stopped as if frozen in mid–stride, and the noise faded away as most of the men put down their tools and turned toward the taunt. It had come from Lieutenant Yasuo Sakakibaru. Sakakibaru, wrench in hand, was walking toward Dempster.

Before Yoshi could say a word, Dempster's fist lashed out and caught the grinning Yasuo on the side of the head. There was a cheer, and the men rushed toward the combatants, forming a solid phalanx around them. Great fun. Two officers in a fist fight. Punching each other on the hangar deck like two lowly deckhands.

Yoshi dropped his tools and began pushing through the wildly cheering throng. He had to stop them. Officers *never* exposed themselves like brawling deckhands. It was bad for morale, made discipline more difficult to enforce, worked against the grain of military tradition. Finally, he shoved through enough ranks so that he could see. He stopped. Yasuo had just grazed the bobbing and weaving Dempster's shoulder with the wrench. However, cat–like, Dempster leaped away and then completely around, lashing out with a foot, knocking the wrench into the spectators. The men cheered and Yoshi paused.

Sakakibaru seemed to be outmatched and Yoshi felt a glimmer of pleasure. He edged forward into the final circles, but slowly. Yoshi knew he should stop the fight immediately, but something held him back. Then he realized he wanted to see Lieutenant Yasuo Sakakibaru take a beating. Lieutenant Oliver Y.K. Dempster did not disappoint him.

Waving their fists before them, the combatants circled. "Come on, Korean dog. Let's see your teeth."

"Even mongrels can bite, oh mighty aristocrat," Dempster taunted back.

Sakakibaru leaped forward, punching straight on for the throat. He was trying to kill Dempster. Yoshi bulldozed forward. However, before he could break through the final ring, there was a great cheer as Dempster stepped to the side and caught Sakakibaru in the midriff with a solid punch. Then a whirl and kick to the chest sent the dive bomber commander staggering back into the spectators. The crowd parted as Dempster followed his advantage with a flurry of powerful punches to the face and stomach. Gasping, Yasuo sprawled out flat on his back while Dempster stood over him.

"Now who's the dog, you filthy swine?" Dempster spat.

"Is there any reason why both of you should not be courtmartialled," Admiral Fujita demanded from behind his desk. "You have disgraced our dignity as officers and fouled the Code of *Bushido.*"

Flanked by Yoshi Matsuhara and Captain Mitake Arai, Lieutenant Oliver Y.K. Dempster and Lieutenant Yasuo Sakakibaru stood at attention before the admiral's desk. Both were bloody, but Yasuo Sakakibaru had a blackened eye, cut lip and numerous bruises on his face and neck. Yoshi guessed his body was equally as punished.

"Lieutenant Dempster attacked me, Admiral," Sakakibaru spat.

"Nonsense!" Yoshi countered. "You insulted him, I heard you and so did a hundred men on the hangar deck."

Sakakibaru threw a killing look at Yoshi, "He's been goading me, softly, when others could not hear. He's jealous . . ."

"And what do you say, Lieutenant Dempster?" Fujita interceded.

"Ridiculous, Sir," Dempster answered. "I haven't spoken to Lieutenant Sakakibaru since our first briefing with Commander Matsuhara. In fact, I have avoided him. I have nothing whatsoever to say to him."

"Liar! Cowardly dog."

"Pull my teeth? Ha!"

"Enough!" Fujita snapped, ending the exchange. Both of you cannot be telling the truth." He patted the *Haga-kure*. "Yamamoto Jin'emon once said to his retainers, 'A person who will tell you seven lies within a hundred yards is useless'." The black slitted eyes pierced both men. "Are you both useless?"

"No! No!" both officers protested.

"Sir," Captain Arai said. "I would like to make a statement."

"Proceed."

Arai cleared his throat. He was about to enter a delicate arena and his nerves showed. "Admiral, with all due respect, I feel the presence of a Korean is a disrupting influence on our crew."

Dempster stiffened, Sakakibaru gloated.

"You would question my judgement, Captain Arai?"

"I have spoken my mind honestly to you for years. Again, Admiral, I am speaking honestly."

Yoshi could not contain himself, "Captain Arai, we have personnel from all over the world. Americans, Greeks, Turks, Russians, Germans and Lieutenant Dempster is an American."

"I know, Commander. But of Korean birth and a Korean is a different kind of animal."

"A dog?"

"I didn't say that, Commander."

"Then what did you say, Captain," Fujita asked.

"They have been our natural enemies, implacable, not worthy of the mantle of samurai, to represent the Code of *Bushido*, the Emperor."

"Sir. I am not all those things," Dempster argued back. "My God, my father was killed on this ship. I was raised

231

in America. True, I am not a samurai, but neither are the other foreign pilots. I just want to be left alone to fight in peace."

No one laughed at the inadvertent oxymoron.

"And you shall," Fujita said. "Your father earned you that right."

"And his performance has been excellent, Sir," Yoshi added.

Sakakibaru said, "Admiral, the Shrine of Infinite Salvation is in the forward part of the hangar deck."

"True. The ashes of hundreds of our honored dead rest there."

"And differences are settled there."

"That is also true, Lieutenant."

Yasuo licked his battered lips. "Then, Admiral, I request that Lieutenant Dempster and I settle this matter there with swords."

"You have been brought up in the samurai tradition. You would have an advantage with the sword, Lieutenant Sakakibaru."

"Respectfully, Sir," Dempster interrupted. "He would not. I would be happy to entertain his challenge."

Fujita shrugged. "If you wish. You may settle your differences there."

"Thank you," the two adversaries chorused.

"But only after this operation is completed." The two officers nodded understanding. "Then you can find your satisfaction."

Again, the two antagonists chorused, "Thank you, Sir."

"And then I will court-martial the survivor and that

man will wish that he had died in the Shrine of Infinite Salvation."

Everyone stared at the little admiral who sat placidly. His grin was that of a death's head. He raised the *Hagakure* and waved it. "There is great wisdom in this book. It teaches, 'Inside the skin of a dog, outside the hide of a tiger'." Yoshi and Dempster chuckled, Sakakibaru fumed. Fujita continued, "It also tells us, 'Victory and defeat are matters of the temporary force of circumstances. The way of avoiding shame is different. It is simply in death'."

"In death, Sir?"

"Yes, Lieutenant Sakakibaru. Death is the great ameliorator."

Everyone stared at the old admiral silently. "Return to your duties," he barked.

The officers hurried through the doorway.

Chapter XVII

For one entire day Brent Ross remained in his apartment; drinking, grieving—enraged at himself and his impotence to exact vengeance, to slaughter the beast who had murdered Ruth Moskowitz. He knew Mossad must be working to apprehend the killer. With the two other murders, Dempster in the U.S. and Tokumitsu in Geneva, the CIA, NIC, INTERPOL and the Swiss police must be involved, too. If any progress had been made, there had been no reports on radio or television to indicate it. Most vexing was the knowledge the killer could be safe in any number of Arab countries that surround Israel. Most likely, however, he was in Libya. Or, perhaps, already stalking another victim.

Devora phoned him a number of times. She was concerned and sympathetic. However, he wanted solitude. Perhaps he felt unworthy. Certainly, he regarded himself a danger to any woman who showed an interest in him. Now he knew how Yoshi Matsuhara felt. "Nonsense," Devora had argued back. "The killer always changes geography, never attacks twice in the same part of the world." Brent knew she was right, but declined to see her.

On the morning of the second day Elroy pounded on the door. "Up an' at 'em, you ol' polecat," the Texan yelled from the hall, loud enough to raise the whole floor. A sleepy, hung—over Brent opened the door and Elroy stormed in. "Got a pass. We're gunna go out an' paint the town red," he declared.

"Don't feel like painting," ol' buddy.

"Shoot! Cain't cotton to that flap jaw talk. Le's go, ol' buddy. Time's a—wastin'. "

With Elroy's prodding and cajoling, Brent shaved a two-day growth of beard, brushed his teeth, combed his close—cropped blond hair and put on his Number One Blues with a fresh white shirt.

"Ready for an all—fired country hoe—down," Elroy said, admiringly.

Brent was smiling for the first time in two days as the Texan pushed him through the door.

After a light breakfast, Elroy took the wheel of his Jeep that was of the same year and model as Brent's. Heading north, he quickly passed through the resort city of Herzliya. Then a relaxing drive through citrus country to Netanya. Waving a hand, Elroy declared, "This here's the diamond—cuttin' center. Biggest in the whole world."

"I know," Brent said, brightening. "Jewish diamond cutters from Belgium and Holland came here to get away from Hitler. And Nathan Strauss put a lot of money into this place."

"Strauss? Who? Oil?"

Brent actually chuckled. "No. He owned Macy's department store in New York."

"Jes' as good as oil, I reckon."

235

"Maybe better."

The Texan drummed the steering wheel. "I heard *Yonaga* done put to sea."

"Couple days ago."

"A rip snortin' barn burner's 'bout to begin, sure as shootin'."

"Fujita's moving on the Marianas. And he didn't take his 'Welcome Wagon'."

"Things'll be fussin' hereabouts, too. A real bust–up of a saloon brawl, I'm a–figgerin'."

"Maybe by the time we reach the front, ol' buddy."

"We're sho 'nuff the luckiest dudes."

"Always."

They swung inland, heading for Nablus, not Jerusalem. Brent knew Elroy would avoid the holy city. There were too many memories there. Neither could ever forget the joyous, carefree outing they had with Ruth Moskowitz and Linda Crane. Entering Nablus, Elroy showed his keen intelligence with his intimate knowledge of the place. "Lots of industry here, Brent." He waved a hand. "Goes way back in history, too."

"I know, Elroy. Abraham entered the Promised Land here and Jacob's Well is nearby."

"An' so's Joseph's Tomb."

They swung south, passing through Ramallah and then turned toward the coast. They drove slowly through Ramle and Rishon Lezion, passing very close to Rehovot. Brent suddenly felt a strong urge to see Devora.

"Sho' could use some vittles," Elroy said, rubbing his stomach.

It was almost evening when they stopped at the Pitango Restaurant which was famous for its French–inspired

236

nouvelle cuisine. "I could use some ol' bust haid," Elroy muttered as he read the menu.

"A drink?"

"Yup. Cain't you unnerstan' plain English?"

"Sorry," Brent said with a straight face.

Before a dinner of exquisite seafood dishes, Brent had a double scotch and Elroy downed a double rye whiskey. Things began to brighten for both men.

Two more drinks after dinner, and most of the problems of the world didn't seem nearly as serious.

Brent had no trouble sleeping that night.

The next morning Brent phoned Devora. "Like to see you. Okay?"

"Oh, Brent. That would be wonderful. You only have two more days of your leave. Right?"

"Right."

"When will you be here?"

"By noon. Okay?"

"The sooner the better. I miss you so."

Brent was humming to himself when he left.

When Devora opened the door, there was no trace of the officer, the coldly efficient copilot, just a young beautiful girl, staring with mist in her eyes. She looked different, almost transformed, years younger like a college freshman. She stood silently for an instant, face lit with an expression of such joy, that he was halted in his impulse to reach for her. Caught by a slight breeze, her long chestnut hair floated gently so that tendrils drifted down on her cheeks—cheeks that were flushed as though she had run fast, and her chest heaved so that she held one hand upon it, fingers spread like a star between those large pointed breasts.

Her tight blue sun dress clung to her like wet satin. Cut above her knees to show off her slender but well-shaped legs, it was pulled in at the waist by a tight black belt not more than 23-inches round. Again, Brent was struck by her amazing body and he tried to gather all of it in his arms. But the kiss was not passionate. Instead, they both exchanged pecks on the cheek and he nuzzled her lustrous chestnut hair.

"God, I've missed you," she breathed, holding him tight.

"You're the best thing since sunlight," he whispered into her ear.

"Dear, sweet Brent," She led him to the couch and sat close to him, clasping one of his big hands in both of hers. "You're in a better mood, Brent," she noted.

"I was in a funk—couldn't help it."

"Of course. It was a terribly depressing thing."

"Precisely what Kadafi wants, Devora."

"He's no dummy."

"*Yonaga*'s at sea, you know."

"Stood out a few days ago, Devora."

"It's started. This front will heat up, too. It always does."

"Yes. I know."

"Your leave ends in a couple days, Brent."

"Yes. At 0800 hours the day after tomorrow."

"Stay here—stay with me."

He drew his fingers down hard over his cheeks and tugged on his chin. "I don't know, Devora."

"We won't mention the war."

"Is that a promise?"

"Yes. And I won't drag you into the shower, either."

His laughter rocked him back and forth and she watched him with delight. "I'm not trying to protect my virtue." He became serious. "It's just that something's wrong—terribly wrong."

"With you and me?"

"That would be impossible."

"Then it's Ruth."

"Of course. She loved me."

"And she was killed while you were, ah—with me."

"You've figured that, too."

"Yes. It had to affect you, Brent." She kissed his cheek and moved so close her hard pointed breast pushed into his side. "I have an extra bedroom. Stay in it Brent. We can be together for two whole days. I'll show you the town, cook for you, wash for you, iron, clean, dance, sing . . ."

His laughter stopped her and then they laughed together like two teenagers on their first date.

He felt strong and vital again. Just to touch the warmth of her and to drink the sound of her laughter was to be rejuvenated. Somehow, the war, the killings, the horror seemed to be fading into the distance like islands drifting into the mists in a ship's wake. "Oh, Lord, Devora. You're such a wonderful girl. I don't deserve you."

"Then you'll stay?"

"Yes."

She gave a elated squeal and kissed him hard on the lips. He wrapped his arms around her and returned the kiss fiercely.

After lunch they changed into their bathing suits and drove to a magnificent beach between Ashod and Ashkelon. They found a deserted stretch as smooth and white as the snows of the Arctic and claimed it for themselves. He lay back on the blanket and watched her as she peeled off her long T-shirt. Then she pirouetted gracefully before him, so that her hips and buttocks caroused brazenly under the thin black elastic bikini. "You like me?"

Laughing, he came to his feet. "Ask me if I like air, life . . ."

She kissed him before he could complete his sentence. Then, pulling him by the hand she began to run. Laughing, hair flying in the wind, she ran like a schoolgirl on a holiday, along the hard wet sand at the water's edge. And he ran beside her. Quickly, they ran the length of the small beach and then turned and began back. She headed for some rocks that tumbled into the sea and formed a shallow clear pool, trapped like a private haven. She pulled him in, and they splashed each other and laughed.

It was then he realized how much Devora was like Ruth. Ruth had been a young woman who had never grown into a world of romance and the carefree pranks only youth could hold. Devora was the same. Rushed by the war from childhood into adulthood without pausing for the teen years, they had both been plundered of a rich, vital part of life. Now Devora, too, was trying desperately to find her own private Elysian fields—that other place free of hate and war where she could be a young girl falling in love.

She grabbed him, rolled over in the shallow cool pool, giggling, her body as warm as bread fresh from the oven. Finally, they tumbled onto the bank in a tangle of arms and legs where she lay on top of him, straddling him. Then she kissed him fervently, pushing down hard. He kissed her back and rolled her onto her side. He felt her leg slide over him and lock behind his knees.

She shuddered. He thought it was passion, but she began to cry. "What is it, Devora?" he whispered into her ear.

"I'm so happy, Brent. So happy."

"So you cry?"

"Yes. You'll be gone and it'll all be over in just a few hours, my darling."

"We'll make the most of it."

"Yes, we will."

That evening they drove to the Hilton where they gathered Brent's few things and returned to Rehovot. After dinner, each of them showered alone. Strangely, passion dimmed and he had to talk. Perhaps it had been the visit to his suite. He and Ruth had first made love there. He felt dampened, weirdly depleted as if someone had opened a vein.

She reacted to him as if she had a window on his mind and they talked, holding hands on the couch. He loved the great intellect that matched that marvelous body. Again, Brent expressed Taoistic questions about conscience and man's determination to set himself apart from nature. "Of course, that's an impossibility," he said.

Devora shook her head and stared into his eyes. "As a good Jewish girl, Brent, I must say it's better to find options than that bondage of cause and effect. It all goes back to Genesis. We choose the good or the evil and pay the price."

"Then I shouldn't eat the apple."

"Not unless I offer it."

He laughed and moved closer. Then, they talked, held

each other far into the night. Finally, Devora showed him to the extra bedroom and kissed him goodnight. He held her. Could not let her go.

"Remember what you said about being platonic?" he asked.

"I hate that word."

"I just removed it from our lexicon."

Laughing with delight, she pulled him into her bedroom.

They fell into her bed and made long and tireless love, both in a sweaty lather. When finally he lay back, breathing hard, limp with fatigue, he marveled in the change in her. The first night it seemed she had wanted him solely for sex, animal gratification. This had been different. True, her climaxes had been shrill and frenzied, but her words had been tender, loving, caresses gentle and lingering as if she truly cherished and adored him. And she refused to sleep.

He watched her as she sat cross-legged on her haunches, body glistening with a patina of moisture, eyes wandering over him. She was not just curious about his body, she was enthralled by it. She examined him like a child unwrapping a new toy on Christmas morning, touching and studying him from the thick cords of his neck to his bulging calves. Without a trace of self-consciousness, she exclaimed and revelled in it, seemed determined to touch and explore every inch. She found the bare tracks through the thick mat of hair that covered his chest. "Phosphorous from tracers," he explained. "Kills the hair follicles."

"Oh, my poor darling." She kissed them, ran her tongue down the grooves, leaving cool traces of saliva. Then the tongue left cools smears on his neck, his abdomen. "I always wanted a rugged man like you for myself," she murmured. Her examination became more intimate. She touched and fondled him. "You're such a man," she whispered in awe. And then slyly, *"Ani rotzah la–a–soat ahava itch, ya chatich, kol kach harbeh ad sh–tmoat."*

Lifting his head from the pillow, he stared at her. There was an elfin grin on her face and her eyes were taunting. He pondered for a moment and hazarded, "Ah, you said something about making love with me."

"Right! And the rest?"

He turned his lips under, repeated the phrases slowly and ventured, "Until I am very tired and I'm a big lug."

She rocked with paroxysms of girlish giddiness, kissed him and said, "Very good. But I was using Hebrew idiom and it would come closer to, 'I want to make love with you, you big stud, until you drop dead'."

Grinning, he said, "I can't let that challenge go unanswered." He pulled her up and rolled her onto her back.

In the morning they returned to the beach, this time to frolic in the pool naked. They had found their private place, their enchanted sanctum. Now there was no one, nothing in his universe except Devora. The horror was all gone, only the joy they found in each other remained. He basked in it, soaked up her magic as if they were exchanging ectoplasm.

"This is such a beautiful place—our place," she said, brushing little waves in the pool with her palms. She took his hands, pulled them under the water and guided them over her sleek body. "It's yours, Brent. All for you Brent. Do you like it?" she asked, eyes wide and searching his.

"That was the most useless question ever asked since man learned to communicate," he answered. Then he

243

told her how beautiful she was. Kissed her neck, her breasts. She stretched and glowed, purring like a great tawny cat. Then she pulled him between her legs.

"In the pool?"

"Why not? What's good for a lady blue whale is good enough for Devora Hacohen," she giggled.

"Maybe you will kill me."

"I'm trying."

"Keep trying. There couldn't be a better way to go."

They made love again.

Most of the day they remained on the beach. Swimming, running, playing in the surf, touching, kissing. They ate their sandwiches and returned to the pool. Made love once more. Finally, as the sun dipped toward the horizon, they returned to her house. It was their last night. They wasted none of it.

In the morning they drove to Jerusalem. "You can keep the Jeep. There are three more days on the permit," he said, as he accelerated past a battery of 155–millimeter guns pulled by 12–wheelers. He was in his blues, she a khaki dress. The magic had almost died, brutalized and obliterated by the guns, the memories, the inexorable forces unleashed by faceless others that pulled them apart. *Yonaga, Shady Lady*, Smadja, Knudsen, Ruth were all back. Their two–day idyll seemed now like a dream, a fantasy of a sailor too long at sea. But Devora sat beside him, still staring at him with those huge glorious eyes. She was real, what had happened was real. Nothing could ever change that. Not war, not distance, not time, not even death. It had happened. That was all that mattered.

Following Route 1, they wound through the Judean Hills until they breasted a small rise and found Jerusalem spread in the natural basin before them. In the morning sun it seemed to glow white as if each building had been whitewashed and scrubbed clean the night before. He remembered the near mystical reaction he had experienced the first time he saw it with Ruth, Elroy and Linda. This morning was different. True, it was still beautiful, this fabled city, the fountainhead of so much spiritual grandeur and bloody misery. But his mind was on the singularly precious girl beside him. In a few minutes she would be out of his life; perhaps forever. A sadistic murderer was still loose. The thought brought him physical pain.

"You'll stay in the BOQ at Lod?"

"I told you I would." She jerked a thumb at the back where her two bags rested on the seat. "My cannon's back there in my shoulder bag."

"Your Webley?"

"Yes. Thirty-eight caliber. Can knock a corrida bull flat on his butt." She patted her right thigh. "And my little-bitty derringer is here, under a garter. I'm armed to the teeth, Brent." She smiled, "Or to the thighs."

He did not laugh. Instead, he grunted and nodded, still feeling troubled. "Be careful when you leave the base. That killer's clever. Can look like anything, anyone. Never let your guard down."

"I promise." She narrowed her eyes and studied him for a moment as he whipped the Jeep past two buses driving in close tandem. Her jaw worked and she bit her lip. "You're the one who'll be in danger."

He glanced at her from the side of his eye and shook his head as he brought the Jeep back into the right lane.

Then she said a ridiculous thing, the kind of thing worried women have said to their men for centuries. "You'll be careful at the front, Brent."

"Very careful."

"I need you."

"I need you, Devora."

"Please, don't get killed."

"I promise. And you, too."

"I had you for two whole days and two whole nights. I sat and looked at you while you slept. Did you know I was watching you?"

"No, I didn't."

She took his hand. "You sleep on the crook of your arm and you draw your knees up."

"Do I snore?"

"No. But you smile, look like an innocent little boy. Did you know that?"

He chuckled. "No, Devora. I've never watched myself."

They both laughed and then she said wistfully, "There was so much comfort in finding you there, in my bed, to turn to, to hold, to find in the morning."

"I know. It was marvelous." He took her hand. "We'll always have that, Devora. The beach, the pool, the nights. And it'll not just be a memory."

"No! No!" There was desperation in her voice.

"We'll be together, again."

"When you come back."

"It'll probably just be a few days. And I'll have a safe billet in some rear echelon," he lied.

"Oh, thank God."

"And then I can worry about you and *Shady Lady.*"

She laughed. "We're trading scripts again."

"Screwed up world, isn't it Devora?"

"Next time let's try another planet."

"Can't argue with that."

She put a hand on his shoulder and leaned close, "Brent, under the azalea on the porch, to the right of the door."

"Yes?"

"A key, a spare key under the pot so that I won't lock myself out. Use it if I'm not home."

He shrugged. "But I wouldn't come over if you weren't there."

"You might. Just don't bring any women."

"You're ruthless."

"That's how I am, insensitive and cruel." They both laughed.

He eyed her slyly through slitted lids, "And what am I to do if you're entertaining a gentleman friend?"

"Show some *savoir faire* and be patient," was the quick response.

"I'll wait until I hear the shower go off."

"Or anyone else."

He laughed. "The French would call that *savoir–vivre.*"

"Right," she chuckled. " 'Good manners', the ultimate good manners." Falling silent, she settled back, head against the headrest, eyes on him. She feasted as if she could never see enough of him.

Entering the main part of the city, he took Ben–Zvi Boulevard to the west side where most of the government buildings were located. In a few minutes he was halted by a sergeant and very youthful corporal at the gate before *Zahal* headquarters. He showed his orders and identification and then Devora showed her identity papers.

"The 'Yankee Samurai'," The young corporal said in awe.

"Right. That's what they call me."

"Welcome, Commander Ross," the sergeant said. Both enlisted men saluted smartly and then waved them through.

Brent pulled into a large parking lot and parked under two large trees. "I'll be in touch as soon as I'm able," he said.

The big brown eyes were brimming. "How long?"

He shrugged. "Not specified in my orders."

She kissed him and he held her. "Goodbye, my darling," he said.

She pulled back and smiled, *"Sholom m'took ati. L'hitraot."*

He narrowed his eyes. "Ah, let me try again." He rubbed his chin. "I know, you said 'goodbye'. And then you said something like 'my dear'."

"My darling," she corrected him.

"Oh, yes. And you finished with, "Until we meet again."

"Correct, you big smart macho brute. And next time I will love you to death."

They kissed for the last time. Then, he grabbed his bag and left the Jeep. She watched him until he disappeared into the building.

Chapter XVIII

Although Commander Yoshi Matsuhara had heard the command, "Pilots man your planes!" hundreds of times, the words still pumped his veins with a tingling brew of excitement and anticipation, spiced with a pinch of anxiety. He bounced and strained along over the flight deck, burdened with his clipboard, sword, inflatable life jacket, and parachute slung under his backside like a cushion. Wearing his padded flight suit, G–suit, "belt of a thousand stitches," two pairs of wool socks, fleece–lined flying boots, *hachimachi* head band, he was sweating and breathing hard.

The foreign pilots could never understand why the Japanese—especially the older men—insisted on wearing their belts and headbands. A dozen times he had explained, "The 'belt of a thousand stitches' was made by my old aunt years ago when I was a cadet. She stood on a Tokyo street corner and solicited a single stitch and a prayer from a thousand passersby. It brings good luck."

"Can it stop bullets?" Commander Elkins had asked just the night before over a cup of tea.

"We believe it can help."

"And the headband?"

"It shows our determination to die for the Emperor."

The American had smiled. "The belt protects you from bullets, but the headband shows your determination to die for the Emperor."

"Correct."

"No contradictions, Commander?"

"Contradictions strengthen a man's *karma*, Commander Elkins."

Then Yoshi had noticed the medal hanging from the American's neck on a gold chain. "Saint Christopher," Elkins explained.

"He brings good luck."

"That's right."

"Can he stop bullets, Commander Elkins?"

Reaching his aircraft, a handler helped Yoshi heave himself up onto a wing and then enter the cockpit with a big, wide sweep of his leg. While Yoshi squeezed himself into the cramped cockpit, Crew chief Shoishi Ota pulled the 6–point safety harness tight and snapped the lock closed. Ota was the kind of crew chief who never trusted any pilot to do things right. Even the Air Group Commander. There was a kind of cabalistic drive to his routine, as if his circumspect ritual would assure his pilot's return. He was sure if Admiral Fujita were in the cockpit, Ota would hover over him with the same imperious concern, rank be damned. Brent Ross called it "The Mother Hen Syndrome." Yoshi never complained. In his mind, there could be an element of luck, a favor from the gods shaped by the inflexible rite.

"Plug in oxygen mask, microphone, and headset, Sir,"

Shoishi Ota muttered. Yoshi drove home the male and female leads. Ota watched while he secured them. Then the liturgy continued, "Mixture full, half–inch of throttle." Again, the crew chief stared vigilantly while the pilot complied.

Yoshi tugged his helmet down and adjusted his goggles on his forehead. Pulling on his gloves, he scanned his instruments. He nodded in satisfaction while Ota's eyes followed his. The crew chief, too, nodded his head in approval.

They continued with a procedure as rigorous and unchanging as a Buddhist *O-bon* service. Check the lock on the open canopy; release and reset the brake by pushing down hard on the peddle; move the control column and watch ailerons, elevators and rudder; drop flaps and retract. All was well. The bird was ready. Ota checked the canopy lock, leaned in for a final inspection, grunted with satisfaction and leaped to the deck. He moved to the starboard side, eyes fixed on his pilot.

A flick of a switch energized the battery and magneto. Instantly, Yoshi's instruments flicked and glowed. Now almost as automatic as a reflex, his left hand found the throttle and mixture control quadrant and checked the settings again. Then his right hand turned the corrugated knob, setting the Curtis constant–speed electric propeller on fine pitch. Just the day before, young Naval Air Pilot Kazuki Aoki had forgotten his propeller on coarse pitch and had plunged off the bow to his death. Totally useless waste of man and machine.

Ota remembered. "The pitch, Sir, pitch," he shouted, cupping his hands around his mouth. "Remember Aoki yesterday!"

"Set on fine."

Ota stabbed a fist upward twice and grinned.

The pilot circled a finger over his head. The crew chief repeated the same signal. Yoshi struck the fuel booster and starter with the palm of his hand. The energizer whined and the eighteen cylinders of the Sakae 43 *Taifu* began to fire erratically—in spurts, bursts, isolated bangs, jerking the four bladed propeller in irregular flurries. The tremendous, erratic power shook the little airframe and the wings rocked from side to side. Finally, there was a roar of unleashed savagery as both banks of cylinders began to fire. The sound echoed from the deck like a thousand furies as the propeller speeded, blurred, and then became a pale gray disk.

Now, perhaps, the most crucial part of the inflexible ritual. Yoshi searched his instruments. Original equipment from Wright Cyclone, they were in clumsy English units: tachometer 1300 revs; oil temperature 96 degrees; oil pressure 45 pounds; manifold pressure 41–inches of mercury; cylinder head temperature 155. He felt a pang of apprehension. Cylinder head temperature had always been a problem with the *Taifu*. He would keep an eye here. Especially in combat when in overboost. Despite the installation of a new cooling fan, he had almost burned up the engine twice. His own engine could kill him faster than the enemy.

He glanced to the left at Pilot Officer York's Seafire and then to the right at his other wingman, Flying Officer Hooperman. Both Rolls Royce Griffons burst into life simultaneously as banks of batteries on accumulator carts flooded the engines with tremendous jolts of electricity.

Immediately, the great V–12 engines added their ear-battering bellows to the roar of the *Taifu*.

Turning his head and using his rear–view mirrors, he could see row after row of Zeros and Hellcats warming while the first bombers were being wheeled from the aft elevator. But four Seafires were missing. Fujita had adamantly refused to release them from CAP despite Yoshi's protests.

"I need them, Admiral."

"Not more than I, Commander," Fujita had countered.

While his engine warmed, Yoshi glanced at his clipboard. They were 300 miles from Saipan and Tinian, not 200. An Arab DC–6 snooper had been shot down by a patrol the day before and Admiral Fujita was forced to change his tactics. In fact, the point option data showed the battle group zigzagging northeastward after launch. This would open the range on both the Marianas and Tomonuto Atoll so that an attack by enemy bombers would be more difficult. More difficult, too, would be the recovery of returning strikes.

Fujita's best bombers were the ten Douglas A1–B Skyraiders on board *Bennington*. With highly sophisticated radar and capable of carrying an amazing four tons of bombs, six of the vicious attack planes had made a shambles of the AA defenses and radar installations at Rabta the year before. This had been done in a low–level attack sneaked in under enemy radar at night. The Skyraiders had returned at dawn when both *Yonaga* and *Bennington* were launching and could not be taken aboard. However, with their long range, the bombers were able to fly to Sicily. This time, there was no Sicily. The Skyraiders would be launched with the other bombers. A remodeled canopy with a new Sperry power turret mounting two 50–caliber machine guns gave the Douglas strong defensive capability. They would need every round of fire power.

Yoshi scanned more items on his clipboard. *New Jersey* would be held back until the enemy air force had been destroyed. It would be sheer madness to send her in against squadrons of dive and torpedo bombers. Even *Yonaga's* sisters, mighty battleships *Mushashi* and *Yamato* which had been the greatest battleships ever built, had been sunk by swarms of American bombers during the Greater East Asia War.

He checked the funnel end of his elimination tube. The stupid thing always iced–up at altitude and a man pissed all over himself. This was especially hard on a man of his age whose growing prostrate forced him to urinate frequently. He never admitted this problem to anyone. The hoary old hospital orderly, Eiichi Horikoshi, had guessed, however. Once he scoffed during a routine examination, "You'll soon need diapers up there, Commander. Or absorbent underwear."

But Yoshi and Ota had solved the problem—he hoped. Just the day before, they had wrapped a heating coil around the tube. "With this masterpiece you should be able to piss a rainstorm at 40,000–feet, Commander," the old crew chief had snorted. The idea had not been original. An electrified tube had been found in the wreckage of a Messerschmitt Bf–109 shot down over Kyushu. The fighter had belonged to the *Vierter Jagerstaffel*. Rosencrance had thought of it first. Looking at the tube, an old Japanese aphorism ran through Yoshi's mind, "Too soon old, too late smart." How true.

Yoshi checked his instruments. Cylinder head temperature in the green, oil temperature and pressure up. He gunned the engine, increasing manifold pressure until his tachometer read 2300. The vibration of the engine was now pounding upon the soles of his feet, shaking his bucket seat so that his buttocks tingled. He cut in his two turbo-superchargers that screamed like tormented souls. Ota nodded approval of the sound. Everything was perfect. The bird was ready for the sky, for the hunt. He throttled back.

Looking around for the last time, he saw the eyes of his pilots were all on him. He would raise the curtain on today's drama. How many would die before the last act was concluded and the curtain rung down? He exhaled noisily, releasing some of his pent up tension. A glance at the flag bridge where Admiral Fujita, Rear Admiral Whitehead, Captain Mitake Arai and Colonel Bernstein stared back down at him. Then he saluted the control officer who stood to starboard just forward of the island on a tall platform. The officer saluted back and jabbed one of his paddles straight ahead like a lance. Go!

Yoshi pulled his goggles down. Then a thumb up to Ota and two handlers pulled the chocks and the pair holding his wingtips released their grips. All four raced for a catwalk while Ota backed off slowly, holding a fire extinguisher. They had learned this bit of safety from the Americans.

A final glance at the ribbon of steam to assure himself it was streaming from its vent in the bow directly down the ship's center line. Releasing his brake, he punched the

255

throttle. The four blades bit into the cool air and dragged the plane forward, accelerating quickly. Forward view totally obstructed by the aircraft's nose, wings blocking his chance to see the deck, he raced forward.

With the deck pitching slightly as the carrier combed the wind and fought the chop, the fighter bounced and rocked as it gained speed. He cursed his inability to see ahead, the rocking deck, the view–blocking wings. "A pilot needs a seeing–eye dog and a white cane!" he had once heard an American pilot complain in the wardroom. Very true.

Anxiously watching his air speed indicator, Yoshi pushed his stick forward, raising the tail so that the huge engine dropped and he could finally see the deck. With the tail no longer dragging, it was as if a large weight had been lifted. Now, accelerating very rapidly, the engine–note altered, booming bigger and harder now that the wings were cutting the air more cleanly.

Yoshi leaned forward, back as straight and rigid as a steel girder. His left hand on the throttle edged forward two more notches and the engine roared its full power, the tires drummed on the deck, an ever–quickening vibration shook the airframe. His eyes, ears and acutely aware senses tracked everything; right hand on the control column kept the tail up, nose level, feet hooked into the rudder–pedal stirrups held her straight, the deck flashing past below like a gray blur, Seafires beginning to roll behind him, the health of the engine in front, the racing judder of the wheels beneath, the wind swirling and whistling through the cockpit.

A glance at the air speed indicator was not necessary. Yoshi could feel the fighter's weightlessness telling him it was eager for the sky. A slight pull on the control column separated the Zero–sen from the deck. The noise and feel of the tires on teakwood ceased abruptly and, with a slight yaw, the fighter swung free into its natural element at last. The elevator, steam jet, staring gun crews, knife–like bow flashed under him and then the endless sea like shining wet steel.

And Yoshi felt it as he always had. Exhilaration! Another take–off without disaster. And he was one with the fighter. He was not piloting it, he was part of it. They would live or die together.

From the first days of his career, Yoshi had learned a fighter aircraft had its own individual relationship with the air about it; especially his modified Zero–sen. He remembered how the lightweight training planes had handled like powered kites, bobbing uncertainly in the skies while heavier bombers cruised regally like ocean liners. But fighter planes were a breed apart. Bred for the specific purpose of killing, they were unnatural creatures, like *sumo* wrestlers or *kabuki* actors playing women. Yoshi always felt every fighter he flew was a manned missile and he sat behind his great engine like a *kami* of death.

Banking slowly to starboard, he pulled a lever and felt two thumps as the landing gear retracted into its wells. A green light blinked off. A quick jerk on the canopy locked it closed and he pushed his goggles up. Close behind, one Seafire was already airborne, the other was racing down the deck. He set his jaw and looked to the west.

Chapter XIX

Flying at 20,000–feet, Yoshi had a horizon of over 160 miles. Behind him three squadrons of fighters were echeloned in wide–spaced groups—the Japanese flying in their usual 'threes', Elkins Hellcats in their customary elements of two, two elements a flight and three flights comprised the complete squadron. Elkins had facetiously claimed the Japanese word for 'cherry' *'Saku–rambo'* for his squadron's radio call because he jested "We're a bunch of 'Rambos'." All of the Americans had laughed, while only a few of the Japanese and foreigners understood the play on Sylvester Stallone's indestructible "Rambo" character.

The fourth squadron, Lieutenant Tetsuya Iizuka's Fighter Two, ranged high above, providing top cover. To the south, Yoshi could see more aircraft; *Bennington*'s Vought F4U Corsairs, Grumman F8F Bearcats, Douglas SBDs, Curtis SB2Cs and the powerful Douglas A–1 Skyraiders. Slightly astern and 4,000–feet lower, were *Yonaga*'s Aichis and Nakajimas, slowing the whole raid as they lumbered along at 160 knots. Compared to the American bombers, they appeared long in the tooth like old men trying to compete in a soccer match with a college team. Over two hundred planes were in the raid.

Yoshi began his eternal search the moment he lifted from the deck. His alertness and uncanny eyes that could still focus to infinity like a Zeiss range finder and detect a seabird winging through a squall at ten miles, had been instrumental in his longevity. Moving his head restlessly, he eyed every quadrant in short, jerky movements, following a set routine: check the space over the wingtips, look left, look right, above, behind and, periodically, he dropped a wing so that he could search beneath him.

It was a beautiful day, one designed for artists and poets. The cloud formations were spectacular, the tropical sky flaunting a full array of clouds. Clumped in white humped-back columns on the southwestern horizon, a cluster of thunderheads paraded through sheets of cirrus which stretched in long, stringy strands like lace and ruffles wrapped around their billowing neighbors. High overhead, thin mackereled stratus glared like illuminated torn silk while below the sea was suddenly obscured by a solid blanket of puffy white clouds stretching almost to the horizon like a ruffled comforter. The sunshine glared from the upper layers of the clouds while the clefts and valleys were painted in infinite shades of silver and gray, some places as dark as ashes. Great painters came to Yoshi's mind: not arabesque enough for Kobyashi Kiyochikau, not as pastel as Migita Toshihide, perhaps only the Europeans, men like Rubens or Tintoretto, could paint wonders like this.

Although his mission was death, destruction, he could not help but feel an eerie presence—a presence of something metaphysical. His years in the sky, the killings, the horror had never jaded him, destroyed his appreciation of the magnificence of this place reserved for so few. Still turning his head as routinely as a security camera, he exulted in it. This was life; this was living on the edge of the world, challenging the gods in their own arena. Here a man clung to life with his hands, his feet, his brain, his muscles, and his luck. Here, more than anywhere else, a man was in touch with himself, tapping his primeval drives for survival—where survival came from his skills, dexterity, cunning and the durability of the flimsy machine in which he defied extinction. Here a man lived life to the utmost, the fullest. And here, not only the enemy could kill you, but the elements as well.

Yoshi revered his Emperor, loved Japan, practice *Bushido* and took pride in his samurai heritage. Yet he knew only the compelling imperative of the mission was the reason for his existence. At this moment, he had nothing to do with victory or defeat, nor was he part of any grand global strategy. This was his work, his alone. He did it because it was given to him to do, or perhaps he did it because he could not bear the shame of being less than the men beside him. The vast vault of the sky, the nearness of the gods made it clear as polished crystal. He fought because they fought; he died because they died. Nothing else was worth recording.

Throwing the switches of his radio, he checked all six frequencies. There was nothing but the crackling of static. He grunted approval. Radio silence was mandatory until contact with the enemy or he broke it. As usual his mask itched and clung to his face. He had gone onto oxygen at 12,000-feet which had been thirty minutes ago. Now a thin sheet of perspiration had formed a bond between his face and his mask. Itching was inevitable. He pulled the mask aside and scratched luxuriously.

And his stomach was rumbling and gurgling. High altitudes always released gases and he was bloating against his G–suit despite the fact he had only eaten two slices of black bread for breakfast. True, he had indulged in the traditional single chestnut and cup of saké drunk by all of the samurai pilots. But that ceremony added very little to the contents of his stomach. And his bladder was beginning to complain. He cursed his stomach, the high altitudes, his bladder, his prostate, the years, an assortment of uncooperative gods, and the invisible enemy.

Adding to his discomfort was the cold. He reached for the heater, which only heated his left foot anyway, and found it full on. He cursed. Told himself it was his advancing age when he saw a sheen of frost forming on his Plexiglas canopy. There was a malfunction in the heater. Probably a simple loose connection. So he would freeze and be blinded. He pounded the heater to no avail. Then, scratching at the frost with his glove, he cleared large enough patches so that he could see. More curses.

Ignoring his discomfort, he set his jaw and settled down to the routine of the long flight. First to take off, he had been in the air nearly three hours already. Although his back and neck had begun the nagging aches that come with cramped quarters, freezing temperatures, and age, he forced himself to remain alert. Those magnificent clouds could provide cover for lurking enemy fighters. Certainly, the Arabs must be aware of the massive raid approaching. Their snooper aircraft's frantic signals had been read by *Yonaga*'s monitors. Frost began to cover his canopy again.

A quick angry kick and the heater came on. Yoshi smiled with delight as the canopy cleared. His first victory of the day. He looked down through the broken clouds at the sea. No landmarks there. Only his clock could help him estimate his position. He glanced at the clipboard strapped to his knee and scratched a line on a small chart taped to it. Then he continued to search anxiously as the great armada pressed on closer and closer to the target. He searched ahead, the Marianas should be ahead under the cloud cover. A finger to a switch turned on his high–frequency monitor, immediately assailing his eardrums with the high–pitched screech of interference. His dead reckoning was accurate. He was listening to the electronic sounds of Arab air–search radar. They were on the scopes, now, and enemy aircraft had to be scrambling or face destruction on the ground.

But the clouds obscured everything. Nothing of the enemy but an undulating screech. He turned off the receiver and almost immediately a red light glowed. His drop tank was nearly empty. Switching to his fuselage tank, he pulled a lever, felt a slight jar and the tank fluttered away from his belly. A quick correction with stick and rudder adjusted the change in trim. Then he noticed tanks raining from the other fighters. He nodded approval. The auxiliary tank was a drag and he never entered combat with it, empty or not.

Enemy formations were near—he felt it in his heart, the way the back of his neck tingled. It was his sixth sense. Yoshi could not define it, but had an intimate acquaintance with it.

"The sixth sense is only the other five senses attuned to threat," Admiral Fujita had said more than once.

It came with a shift in the rhythm of the surrounding formations that opens your eyes. A shudder in the pattern of cloud shadow. The hint of some new sound that brings your head up. And the energy; you can feel it. A squadron of stalking fighters hidden by the clouds gives off an energy, tangible and penetrating.

Uneasily thumbing the cover off of his firing button, Yoshi broke radio silence, "This is *Edo* Leader. Be alert everyone. They have us on radar. The welcoming committee should arrive at any moment. Clear your guns."

He threw a switch and a 100–millimeter pink reticle glowed on the transparent plastic just inside the 90–millimeter armorglass windscreen. Pushing the firing button, he felt the airframe jar and shudder as the two 20–millimeter cannons in the wings and the two 7.7–millimeter machine guns in his hood fired short bursts. He nodded with satisfaction. A quick glance brought a hail of tracers into his vision as his flights followed orders.

There was a double click on the radio as Elwyn York touched the transmit button: *"Edo* Leader, this is *Edo* 3. "Me cock's up. Them bastard's on the block."

Hooperman's voice. "It's always up, you randy Cockney. Twenty whores couldn't deflate that thing."

"Your mother could, your nibs."

"Radio discipline!" Yoshi roared into his microphone, working hard at being military.

Suddenly the curtain opened as several scenes of the drama unfolded simultaneously. The cloud cover ahead parted dramatically, as if pulled aside by a pair of impatient gods and the rugged, mountainous island of Saipan, the flat island of Tinian and the tiny sheer green spire of Aguijan were all visible in the distance. Clouds still clung to the islands as they always did in these latitudes—great slab-sided gray cumulus that sat upon them, overshadowing the land like a roof. Then Lieutenant Tetsuya Iizuka's cry from above, *"Edo* Leader, this is *Okami* Leader. Many fighters, high, diving from my eleven o'clock—230 true. Am engaging."

Looking upward so suddenly his neck pained, Yoshi saw a cloud of black specks hurtling down on Iizuka's twelve Zeros of Fighter Two. As usual, they were taking advantage of the blinding glare of the sun and diving out of a bleary white patch of back-lit cloud. He acknowledged and then shouted, *"Sakurambo* Leader, this is *Edo* Leader. Enemy fighters at eleven o'clock high. Support Fighter Two. Intercept!"

"Roger, *Edo* Leader. This is 'Rambo' Leader. We're going upstairs to greet the new kids on the block."

Yoshi did not understand all of it, but he knew his orders were understood as immediately the twelve Hellcats roared upward at full military power. And a half-dozen Bearcats from *Bennington*'s air groups were also climbing at an incredible rate. He could not expect more. *Bennington*'s fighters were spread thin; CAP for the battle group took at least two of her squadrons. Only eighteen F4Us and the six Bearcats comprised the bomber escort. But Yoshi could see at least sixty Bf-109s streaking down. Top cover was outnumbered by at least two to one. He cursed, intelligence had been far too conservative. Obviously, the enemy had been reinforced and alerted.

But where were his bombers? Either they were still parked on the fields—which was stupid—or they must have taken off long ago and circled far to the north or south to avoid the attacking squadrons. Probably to the south; to search for the battle group. If they failed, they could fly on to Tomonuto. Even with a partially completed strip, Tomonuto was a better choice than being caught on the ground.

But his problem was not the enemy bombers, protecting his own bombers was his mission. He spoke into microphone, calling on his squadron and Yasuo Sakakibaru's Fighter four which trailed him, *"Edo* Flight, *Kentōka* Flight, this is *Edo* Leader. Engage any fighters that break through top cover. Follow my lead and then individual combat."

Yoshi knew Iizuka, Elkins and the Bearcats would not stop all of the enemy fighters. Sheer numbers were against them. Already the sky above was being grazed by wildly intersecting streaks of contrails and a smoking embroidery of tracers.

Frenzied voices came through the fighter circuit. Elkins: "Bryant, two of 'em on your tail."

"Give me some help you guys. They're on my ass. I can't shake 'em."

"Got one. Burn you bastard."

Scott Wood's voice: "Bryant, for God's sake dive!"

"Diving! Diving!"

The heavy accent of Ensign Philippe Boncour: *"Hourra!* Killed a *chien. Tu reduires en cendres, chien*—you burn to ashes, dog!"

"Tomagawa, under you. A belly shot. Turn, roll, by the gods, don't fly level!"

"Tomagawa's burning."

There was the unmistakable white-hot glare of igniting high octane gasoline, and a white Zero streaked downward like a meteorite. As it passed Yoshi, it began to disintegrate, the left wing sheared off and then the aircraft broke into tumbling, sailing smoking pieces no bigger than the hood of a Honda, the largest piece the engine. No parachute.

Elkins' voice: "Nailed the bastard. Have a piece of tail all the way down, you prick!"

A Messerschmitt, engine vomiting blobs of oil and balls of flame, twisted by whipping a strange tail behind it. It was the pilot, parachute tangled in the tailplane, flailed madly all over the sky like the end of a whip.

"Banzai, you dog!"

A burning Zero arced high like a pyrotechnic at the *Kando Myojin* festival, began its dive and exploded in a great burst of white–yellow flame and flaring rubbish. An explosion obliterated another 109. A Zero spun down followed by a F6F with half a wing blown off. A Messerschmitt limped off trailing white misty coolant. Almost casually, a Bearcat whipped after it and blew it apart with a short burst of cannon fire. Another 109, wing blown off at the fillet, flipped wildly like a wounded teal, wrenching, whirling, tearing itself apart, swirling downward like trash buffeted by the wind. Perhaps, eight more planes tumbled and twisted toward the sea, shot to pieces or piloted by dead men. Two left black plumes to mark their epitaphs. Parachutes began to dot the sky; white marking Yoshi's pilots, yellow the enemy.

Yoshi had no time to study the horror raining from above. He knew another two or three Zeros had fallen and at least one Hellcat. The rest were black and needle–nosed. He must protect his bombers.

Punching the throttle through the emergency gate, the *Taifu* bellowed into overboost. Bracing himself, Yoshi hauled back on the stick and kicked rudder. With the engine at full power, superchargers howling, the controls were so stiff that it took both hands to budge the stick. Every rivet, stringer and frame groaned and the wings bent as the Zero whipped into a ferocious turn, leading Fighter One back toward the bombers.

Yoshi hated and feared the effect on his body. It grew worse with age. His mouth stretched wide open like elastic, straining to drag breath into lungs that felt flattened by the leaden vise of G–forces as he continued to drag the plane into a circle so tight he felt nailed to the seat and his vision threatened to fog out. His stomach pushed against the G–suit, eyes watered, sinuses throbbed. Dust swirled from unseen nooks and crannies. Luckily, he pulled out of the turn without graying out and thanked the American who had designed the G–suit.

He expected a rain of Me–109s to strike the Aichis and Nakajimas. Looking into his rear–view mirror, he saw Yasuo Sakakibaru's Fighter Four following as he streaked toward the bombers. He still had twenty-four Zeros to provide a second line of defense for the bombers. But he could count at least thirty of the enemy who had broken through the top cover and were lancing down.

Strangely, the enemy did not strike down directly on the Japanese formations. Instead, their commander decided to dive to the south to avoid Yoshi's two squadrons and come up beneath the bombers for a belly shot. This was where they were most vulnerable. Yet, he was giving up the priceless advantage of altitude to Yoshi. This man was not a 'Rosencrance.' He must be an Arab. Only an inexperienced, stupid leader would choose such a tactic. Perhaps he had been unnerved by his severe losses to the high–flying Japanese squadrons. Apparently, he had been surprised by the appearance of the vicious Bearcats which could out–fly and out–shoot anything in the sky.

Yoshi called Sakakibaru, *"Kentōka* Leader, this is *Edo* Leader. Enemy trying for a belly shot on our bombers. Follow my lead."

The acknowledgment was quick and crisp.

Now the lead elements of the enemy had plunged past the bombers and were already curving out of their dives. Yoshi called his bomber leaders, *"Ken* Leader and *Norishi* Leader. Take evasive action—dive! Dive and skim the water. I am coming through!"

The clicks and then Dempster's calm acknowledgment followed by the tense high voice of the new torpedo bomber commander, Lieutenant Akira Terada. Immediately, forty-one Aichis and forty-three Nakajimas nosed down toward the sea. Only the sea could protect their bellies. At least, their single 7.7–millimeter swivel guns and forward firing fixed machine guns gave them some defensive power, but only above and ahead.

The unexpected tactic had given the enemy a temporary advantage. The lead Messerschmitts opened fire. One Aichi staggered as twenty–millimeter shells ripped off huge chunks of aluminum from it wings and belly. Then the cockpit exploded and, crewed by dismembered corpses, it dropped off into its final tight spin. Another, its 300–kilogram bomb struck by a shell, detonated in a final supernovan season of glory, consuming its killer in its closing act of death. A Nakajima, tail shot off, flipped and gyrated like an insect maddened by a candle, hurling out its gunner and radioman. Only one white parachute opened.

Yoshi pounded his instrument panel in anguish as if his fists could force more speed out of the fighter. His air speed indicator already showed 420 knots and climbing. The brute of an engine pounded his ears like a hundred thunderclaps.

Elwyn York's voice. Yoshi knew what was coming. "You're opening up you arse, *Edo* Leader."

Hooperman: "Can't cover you, *Edo* Leader."

"Roger, Two and Three. Do your best." Looking down, he realized he would be forced to dive through his own bombers. The enemy flight leader was not as stupid as Yoshi had first thought. His own nervous gunners could fire on him. All fighters looked the same to terrified men. It was time to dive.

Yoshi pulled his nose back and watched a fluffy cloud on the horizon tilt and drop away like a lace tablecloth pulled from a table. Then with two squadrons streaming behind him, he split–essed down, half–rolling into a power dive. His world was upside down now, the table cloth a gray–white ceiling on which the twisting fighters above crawled and wove. He felt his guts sink and push against his G–suit, bladder ache. He cursed as he hurtled down on the tightly–bunched bombers. Within seconds, five more bombers were shattered by blizzards of tracers from below. The 109s were in a feeding frenzy.

Steepening his dive, the white needle of the airspeed indicator flirted with the slower red danger line. Vibrations told him the airframe was in jeopardy. In a blink Yoshi plunged through the diving bombers and found spread beneath him squadrons of black fighters. Most had stalled out and were dropping off toward the sea to regain speed. But altitude was short, and the enemy was caught in a box of his own making.

The enemy's speed was so slow, Yoshi was forced to throttle back. He almost reached for his flaps, but the Me 109 was a natural diver and the new 3,000 horsepower Mercedes–Benz *Valkyrie* engine gave it tremendous acceleration. But not enough to escape the avenging eagles from above.

Bracing his feet, he pulled back on the stick with all his strength. He could feel a dull pain in his stomach, his legs became lead. The pressure of his head forced him down in his seat and bent him over. There was some clouding of vision, but fortunately the slowing aircraft had reduced the effects of G–forces.

Shaking his head to clear the miasma, he brought the glowing reticle of his electric sight to the tail of a 109 not more than two hundred yards ahead. Zero deflection and the wing tips touched the circle. A perfect killing angle and his vision was as clear as polished glass. He pressed the red button. Harmonized for three hundred yards, the pair of 20–millimeter cannons and two 7.7–millimeter machine guns raked tracers along the black fuselage instead of pinpointing a single area. The effect was devastating. Aluminum molted from the airframe in sheets, flashed in the sunlight, and then folded back in the slipstream like the discarded skin of some great black snake. The strikes pounded forward into the cockpit and a snowstorm of Plexiglas blurred through the aluminum as the Galland–style canopy exploded along with the pilot's head.

Increasing throttle, Yoshi swerved to avoid the tumbling dross and brought his sight to another enemy who was forced to pull out or crash into the sea. His decision only decided his manner of death. A short burst from three hundred yards concentrated four shells and eighteen bullets directly into the cockpit. The pilotless 109 burrowed into the sea like a Tokyo commuter train into a tunnel.

A Seafire hard on his right fired a short burst. A Messerschmitt hit the water flat like a pancake, skipped and soared erratically, landing gear dropped and twisted, part of one wing and most of its tail surfaces gone.

York's voice: "Sorted that bugger's hash!"

Just before stalling out, the Messerschmitt whipped into a damaged, low–flying Aichi, smashing the bomber's wing with its own.

York's voice: "No! No! Jesus Christ, no!"

Jesus did not help. Tilting like a high–wire acrobat losing his balance, the bomber finally flipped over on its back and dove into the sea. The 109 swerved in the opposite direction and found its own grave.

"Shit! Shit! Goddamnit to hell!"

Young Munakata's voice rasped like a file: "I'm hit!"

"Bail out!"

Yoshi caught a glimpse of Munakata's Zero pulling up sharply, half rolling and dropping the pilot's body free. In a moment a parachute opened and the young man began to oscillate toward the sea.

Hauling out of his dive beneath Munakata, Yoshi pulled up hard. Airspeed and engine temperature were frighteningly high and again he was mashed down into his seat by G–forces. The grayness returned and this time his nose not only ran, it dribbled blood. Mists clearing, he licked the blood from his upper lip, wiped with a glove and snuffled it up his nose. Then superchargers screech-

271

ing he caught another black fighter trying frantically for altitude. But nothing in the air could climb with Commander Yoshi Matsuhara. A quick squirt and the 109 blew up, a flicker of incandescence that pulverized the pilot in the time it took to draw a breath.

"Banzai! Three kills in less than thirty seconds. Who's old, Admiral Fujita?"

There was no order, no organization to the dogfight. It was tumbling, burning, savage carnage, interlaced with tracers and swinging parachutes. Every man for himself. Yoshi screamed with rage and horror as a passing Me–109 shot off both of Munakata's legs just before the young pilot splashed into the sea. Yoshi was too busy staying alive to chase after the murderer.

Eight of Elkins' Hellcats, seven of Okami's Zeros and all six Bearcats from *Bennington* streaked down. Some of the enemy tried to flee to the west. Still in pairs, the small Bearcats mounting four M2 20–millimeter cannons shredded four of the fleeing enemy on the first pass. Then whip–like turns and they charged back through the enemy shooting down two more. But there were brave men at the controls of some of the 109s. Perhaps, they felt doomed and would take some of Yoshi's men with them. Certainly, by now they knew they had been poorly led.

At least twelve, a full squadron, pressed home their attack on the bombers, while six more tried to fight off the attackers. Still more enemy fighters, survivors of the dogfight with Iizuka's top cover, streaked into the fight. Apparently, they had fled Iizuka and Elkins and experienced a change in heart. In any event, they had returned to try to help their comrades. The odds were almost even, now.

The bombers were skimming the sea—perhaps seventy

of them—so low it was impossible to dive beneath them. The 109s dove down, now facing closely bunched aircraft, and seventy 7.7–millimeter guns. Two more bombers were shot down before the enemy pulled up to face the avenging Japanese fighters.

Yoshi's earphones were staccato with warnings, curses, questions. A 109 chased a Hellcat into his vision. He ripped off a burst at full deflection that made it leap, but missed. He heaved the fighter onto its side in an effort to drag it around and track the enemy before he could shoot down the Hellcat. Again, the strain drained strength from his arms and legs and dimmed his vision for an instant. This was what he dreaded most, weakening for the one second that it would take an enemy to catch him and blast him. Luckily, when his vision cleared the 109 was directly ahead of him. A flurry of shells and bullets pounded the 109 amidships for two seconds. The fighter flew apart. It was like a flimsy house struck by a cyclone. It seemed to implode and then explode. The pieces scattered and Yoshi pulled up hard to avoid the wreckage. No parachute.

"Banzai!" Four kills. And he still had at least twenty seconds of firepower left.

Wriggling his shoulders, he loosened his shirt now sticky with cold sweat. And he dared to flick a glance across his instruments. He was heating, approaching the read line at 285. He cursed but did not touch his throttle. It would be death to slow down. He would ride the hot beast until it burned. His blood lust was up and his thirst to avenge Munakata insatiable. Let the God of War, Hachiman San, worry about the instruments.

A Seafire with a 109 hot on its tail whipped downward

to starboard. Hooperman's impossibly unruffled voice, "I say, anyone. I have some unfriendly company close by. Appreciate a bit of help."

York's frantic voice: *"Edo* One. Chivy the bugger! I'm tangled!"

Yoshi threw everything into the corner and rolled brutally after the two plunging fighters. The sea was so close, Hooperman was forced to pull up. The Arab was closing in for the kill, but so was Yoshi. Hooperman broke left. The 109 skidded to the left, too, but Yoshi anticipated, eased a couple degrees so that he turned inside him.

At one-quarter deflection and from slightly above, Yoshi opened fire. With his mask off, cordite fumes drifted up and made his nose twitch. But the Arab turned hard left and Yoshi missed. Pushing the stick and kicking rudder, Yoshi brought the Messerschmitt back into his sight. The Zero shook. He saw white coolant bubbling out of the enemy's exhaust. The man twisted his head, a white young face. He saw the whole aircraft flare and swell until it filled his gunsight, and then his shells and bullets set off the tanks and the enemy became a ball of orange flame with only a couple of wingtips sticking out of it. The plunge into the sea was short.

Hooperman's voice: "Thanks terribly, old boy. Got me out of a bit of a sticky mess."

Then, suddenly, the sky was empty of enemy fighters. One moment bloody, flaming carnage, the next a peaceful sky. Wisely, the few surviving Me–109s, perhaps ten, had fled to the west under full power. He eased his throttle back.

Then he noticed. Their target islands were very close. He looked from side to side, craned his neck back and stared up into the fast vault of the sky. Nothing. Not one enemy fighter. They must be trying for their bases. But there was no refuge. Guam was nearby but American, and closed to them. And it was heavily patrolled by the new peerless Grumman FX–1000. The Messerschmitts would be forced to give battle again or land on Saipan or Tinian. If they landed, they would be destroyed. If they gave battle they would be destroyed. Yoshi knew what he would do: choose death in the sky. But, then, he wasn't an Arab.

He called his bomber commanders: "*Ken* Leader and *Noroshi* Leader. Climb to attack altitude and deliver your ordnance when ready."

Lieutenant Oliver Y.K. Dempster and Lieutenant Akira Terada acknowledged. Dempster had 32 Aichi dive bombers left, Terada had 31 Nakajimas. But closing in from the south were *Bennington*'s air groups. They were almost intact. Fifteen Vought F4Us remained and at least twenty Douglas SBDs, the same number of SB2Cs and ten A-1 Skyraiders. They were about to deliver a tremendous tonnage of bombs to the enemy airfields on Tinian. Yoshi's bombers were to drop their loads onto Saipan's old Aslito Airfield and any other strips they could find. Also, shipping in Tanapag Harbor was to be attacked.

While the bombers climbed, Yoshi reassembled his fighter squadrons and roared upward through scattered clouds to provide a protective shield. His squadrons had taken heavy casualties. His own Fighter One had lost two Zero–sens, Iizuka's Fighter Two was down to half its strength; Sakakibaru's Fighter Four had lost three Zero–sens and Elkins' Fighter Three had was down to eight Hellcats and Elkins, himself, seemed to be in trouble. Still, with *Bennington*'s Bearcats and Corsairs, Yoshi had over-whelming supremacy. He pulled above and ahead of the Aichis and Nakajimas. The bombers had their umbrella.

The first clusters of AA greeted them ahead as Arab radar–directed guns began firing through the clouds that had thickened as they approached the islands. The ugly black cauliflowers of smoke were below them and to the north. But they would correct. Charged by adrenalin, Yoshi was keyed up to full alertness, mind reckoning and computing like a machine. He changed course to make the radar plotters think he was avoiding action. The ruse worked, the next salvos were far beneath them. But, Yoshi knew he could not fool them for long. And, anyway, they were flying into clear sky and the enemy gunners would have them visually.

Now the dive bombers were queuing up in single file. Flashes leaped from the islands as AA gunners worked their pieces furiously. The greatest danger was from the bombers and here they concentrated. The streams of bombers seemed to be flying into a mattress of black hanging smoke. A puff touched an Aichi and almost miraculously a wing bent up like wet paper and flew off. In an instant what had been a perfectly functioning aero-nautical design, was twisting, plunging junk. A SBD ex-ploded, a gigantic flash of yellow–white light that filled the sky. Nothing more was left than a spider shape of gray smoke, its ever–lengthening gray legs made of smoking debris falling into the sea. Another limped off, bomb dangling from a single crutch. But the bombers pressed on. Then the first one nosed over.

The next few moments were filled with plunging dive bombers, explosions, erupting hangars, flaming fuel dumps, and the Vesuvian eruptions of ammunition dumps. While the dive bombers plunged, the Nakajimas fell into gentle glides and released their bombs from nearly horizontal patterns. At the same time, SBDs and SB2Cs smashed two airfields on Tinian.

More bombers fell as they dropped so low anti–aircraft machine guns sent sheets of tracers to greet them. The A–1 Skyraiders held back, circling over the two stricken islands. Then when all of the other bombers had delivered their loads, they swung casually over the target. But no more targets remained at the airfields. Instead, the big bombers swung over Tanapag Harbor and the small port of Tinian Town and blew three small transports to bits. Then, they dropped the rest of their bombs on docks and warehouses.

Yoshi stared down at Tinian, mind filled with old memories. This had been the biggest B–29 base during The Greater East Asia War. From this island the *Enola Gay* had taken off to bomb Hiroshima with the first atomic bomb. No Japanese would ever forget. Now the concrete strips were pockmarked with craters, fuel and ammunition dumps burned and a few aircraft that had been sheltered in revetments had been destroyed. The bombing had been overwhelming, but very few enemy bombers had been on the ground. He felt uneasy.

The voice of the Greek, Lieutenant Styros Paponagas, shocked him. "This is 'Rambo Green'. Enemy fighters, high at 270 true."

Styros had taken command of Elkins' Fighter Three when the squadron leader had limped off with a hole in a fuel tank, leaving only seven Hellcats. Looking up, Yoshi saw a flurry of black specks diving through Fighter Three.

Bennington's Fighters were to the south covering their own bombers over Tinian. For a moment, Yoshi's air groups were vulnerable.

"This is *Edo* Leader. Intercept fighters at 270!"

Going to full power and pulling his stick back, he could count thirteen of the enemy. Courageous men. They had no chance. They had decided to die fighting. Fighter Three met them, but outnumbered almost two to one, they could not stop the attack. Two black fighters concentrated on Lieutenant Scott Wood.

Wood met the attack of the first head—on, damaging the fighter and then turned to pursue and make his kill. He heard Paponagas scream, "Wood, break left!"

Wood stared in amazement as his instrument panel splintered before his eyes. The 13—millimeter bullets had enough energy to bash through the armored oil tank just in front of the fire wall and release a flood of oil and hydraulic fluid which spilled across the floor. Then a furious hammering bounced sparks all over his engine cowling and the Grumman lurched and staggered. The propeller vanished, hurled off into infinity and the un-leashed engine screamed with an excess of energy. Hot black oil mixed with gasoline washed back over the canopy and filled the cockpit with its stench.

Then he saw the black silhouette of his killer, magnifying like a fist to the face. Then it was over him and gone. Already his fighter was losing strength, feeling dead in the controls. Flames poured from his exhausts pipes and cooling gills, igniting the spraying mix of oil and gasoline so that it raged alongside the fuselage. The engine was still screaming in agony so he switched it off.

"Bail out! Bail out!" Paponagas screamed.

Wood pulled the black ball and the canopy flew off. Hot oil and hydraulic fluid sprayed his face. He pulled the single release on his safety harness, unclipped the oxygen tube, jerked the radio lead free. He stood up, but the Zero whipped sharply, dropping him back into his seat, pinning him against it. Again, it flipped wildly to the left and he levered his shoulders up and head out. He had no idea if he were climbing or diving. Then through the smoke and spray he saw islands ahead and the horizon and he realized he was diving at a high speed.

Gravity, centrifugal force, air pressure, all worked to shove him back down, pinning him to the back of the cockpit. He seemed powerless. The islands grew, wind howled, smoke and fumes gagged so much he tasted vomit. He was going to die. He knew this now. Then the plane jerked to the side and his boot inadvertently slammed the control column. The Zero performed a slow roll and he dropped out. A pull on the ring and the white canopy popped open above him. The sudden silence was so profound, his ears ached. He was alive. He felt euphoric.

Pulling his shrouds, he guided the parachute toward the southern part of Tinian which was covered with small farms and appeared peaceful. He was very low, too low to make friendly Aguijan. Then the first tracer climbed toward him, slowly at first, accelerating as it passed. He stared in wonder. Where did it come from? Then another and another. "Hey! That's not fair!" he shouted.

Staring in horror, Wood watched as a stream of tracers rose to meet him. The first 13–millimeter slug tore off his right leg just below the knee. He screamed, reached for the bloody stump. The next smashed into the left side of

279

his chest, breaking three ribs and punching through his lung and out his back, taking most of one shoulder blade with it and spinning him like a doll at the end of a string. He never conceived of such pain. Vomited blood in a wide circle. Tried to free his pistol but only managed to drop it. Two more of the great slugs ripped into his abdomen, coursed upward, shredding liver, intestines, stomach, severing arteries. And then another punched into his chest and exited from the back of his neck, cleanly severing his spine. The young Oklahoman was dead long before he hit the ground.

Screaming with anger and pounding the instrument panel, Yoshi watched the butchery of the young pilot. He had expected it, but was not prepared for it. There was nothing he could do. His first duty was to protect his bombers. He continued to climb hard with Fighter One close behind. But he never fired a shot. Bearcats, Corsairs, Hellcats and the remainder of Iizuka's Fighter Two destroyed the remaining enemy fighters in less than two minutes. Then he noticed three yellow parachutes drifting down.

"Kill them, kill the enemy in the chutes!"

In one pass, three of Sakakibaru's Zeros shot the enemy pilots to pieces.

"*Banzai! Banzai,* you dogs! That's for Wood and Munakata."

Filling his lungs and expelling his breath in several large gulps, he composed himself. Then he spoke into his microphone, ordering all groups to return to the carriers.

As the squadrons formed up and turned to the east, he called *Yonaga,* "*Saihyosen,* this is *Edo* Leader. Mission accomplished." He gave a brief but complete description of the carnage inflicted. As usual, he did not report his own casualties. Then he reported the lack of bombers, "Not more than a dozen enemy bombers destroyed."

There was a brief acknowledgment but no position report. This would come later, if necessary. But Yoshi knew the battle groups had turned west and was steaming at forced draft to their recovery point.

He looked around at his depleted squadrons and suddenly felt fatigue. He had taken a terrible battering to complete the mission, his unprecedented five kills. There was no elation. Many fine young men had died hideously.

He was so weary, he felt lightheaded. He expected it. Cranked up by the cruel and extravagant demands of air combat, at times his pulse had hammered at twice its normal rate, skin been drenched with sweat, lungs rancid with pure oxygen, brain had been sometimes starved of blood, sometimes swamped with it. His arms and legs ached with weariness, the stiff controls taking their toll. He had taken another physical and emotional hammering and there would be more. Fujita's warning came back. "Geriatric Killer," came back. He was growing old. Now he felt it, knew it, despite his five kills. He had lost his vision at least three times, twice when it should not have happened. He found a new depth of depression.

Flying at reduced throttle, on a lean mixture, and with his blades opened wide, he led his squadrons toward the rendezvous. He was just settling back and beginning to relax from the high pitch of tension, when Yonaga's unexpected transmission jarred him, "*Edo* Leader, this is *Saihyosen*. Rendezvous at Point Juliet. I repeat, Point Juliet. Acknowledge! Acknowledge!"

Yoshi acknowledged and glanced at his point option

data. Point Juliet was at latitude 10 degrees, 10 minutes, longitude 150. This was far to the south of Point Echo, the first designated recovery point. Why the change? And it was late. Must be the weather. Could change in a wink in these latitudes. In fact, now, from his high altitude he could see a dark gray mass swelling up over the northeastern horizon. He felt uneasy. Point Juliet was within range of Tomonuto Atoll.

He turned to the southeast and the massed squadrons followed. "And where are the enemy bombers?" he asked himself. He rubbed his cheek through the mask and continued to wonder.

Chapter XX

"Radar reports many aircraft approaching from 285 true, range 190, Admiral," the talker, Seaman Naoyuki reported.

"IFF?"

"Unidentified, Admiral."

"Speed?"

"SOA about 160, Sir."

"Alert *Bennington* and the CAP," Admiral Fujita shouted back.

"Must be the missing bombers Commander Matsuhara warned us about," Rear Admiral Whitehead said. "Too close to be our own air groups. And they're approaching on the reciprocal of our course."

"Correct, Admiral Whitehead," Fujita said curtly. Usually, the prospect of battle enlivened the old admiral, seemed to take years off of him. But this morning was different. Maybe it was age. He had been in a rankled mood since the air groups took off. And now with his battle group in harm's way his exasperation was growing.

As one, Rear Admiral Whitehead, Admiral Fujita, Colonel Irving Bernstein, Captain Mitake Arai raised their glasses to the sighting as if they could see over the curvature of the earth and find the threat. Nothing, not even a sea bird. Dropping his glasses to his waist, Fujita looked at his watch. "Combined closing speed about 190. About an hour's run," he mused. Then, he made his decision, shouting at Seaman Naoyuki, "Sound the General Alarm! Set Condition Zed! Stand by to launch fighters!"

While every man on the bridge reached for his helmet and life jacket, *Yonaga* resounded with organized bedlam. Immediately, claxons hooted and there was the sound of thousands of boots on steel decks and ladders as crewmen dashed to their stations. Men shouted excitedly and steel rang on steel as gunners rammed shells into the breeches of thirty-two 127-millimeter dual purpose cannons, mounted in galleries lining the flight deck. Hundreds of other gunners shouted and cursed, loading and cranking their triple mount 25-millimeter machine guns upward. Water tight doors in the bowels of the ship were slammed shut and "dogged," sending banging sounds all the way to the bridge. At the engine room master control board, Chief Engineer Lieutenant Tatsuya Yoshida threw a master switch and the whining of every blower in the ship died away. Crewmen quickly shielded the now silent vents with steel plate. *Yonaga* had drawn in her breath and was holding it.

More shouts and a cannonade of power on the flight deck, the engines of the ready fighters raging to life. There were only six; four Seafires and two Zeros. Four other Zeros with engine trouble were still on the hangar deck frantically being repaired.

Burdened pilots labored across the deck and were

pushed and pulled by anxious handlers into their cockpits. Then, the fighters shook and wobbled, warming engines gunned and tested for take-off.

Reports began to pour in, "Engine room manned and ready, CIC manned and ready, Damage Control manned and ready, pilot house manned and ready . . ." While Naoyuki relayed the flood of reports, Fujita shouted, "Flag bridge, make the hoist at the dip, 'Anti-aircraft formation'!"

As fast as signalmen could bend on flags and pennants, the signal was hoisted, but stopped just short of the yard-arm.

Every pair of binoculars on the bridge scanned the formation. In a moment a lookout reported, "All ships answer, Admiral."

"Admiral Whitehead?"

"Confirmed, Admiral Fujita," the American answered, fastening his helmet strap.

"Very well. Two block!"

The bunting was snugged up to the yardarm. "All hoists two blocked, Sir.

"Very well. Execute!"

Immediately, the hoists were whipped down and the entire flotilla tightened, the two carriers moving close to *New Jersey*'s massive firepower while the inner ring of destroyers closed in on the capital ships.

Talker Naoyuki, his head now covered by his huge bucket-sized helmet, turned toward the admiral, "Sir, Commander Yatsashima reports fighters ready for launch."

"Wind?"

"Force Three, from 335."

"Very well." Again the signal bridge was called, a flurry of flags and pennants, and the entire battle group turned into the wind. It was a precise, perfectly choreographed turn of fifty degrees. In minutes, *Yonaga* launched her six fighters and *Bennington* her remaining F4U Corsairs. In all, eighteen F4Us, four Seafires and two Mitsubishis were airborne. They circled to the west but remained close to the ships. The battle group resumed its base course of 285.

"Radar. Enemy formation?"

"Range 130, SOA still about 160, Admiral."

"Any friendlies."

"None, Sir."

"Sacred Buddha! Where is Matsuhara?"

Whitehead said, "We launched him from 300 miles, Sir, and then opened the range to almost 400 before we hit that storm." He threw a thumb over his shoulder.

"I am well aware of that, Admiral," Fujita snapped. He turned to Captain Mitake Arai, "Range to Saipan?"

Anticipating the question, the navigator already had his dividers split along his latitude scale so that he could measure nautical miles. "Two–hundred–eighty, Admiral."

"In the name of the gods, Matsuhara is an hour behind the enemy." He turned to Naoyuki, "Radio room, contact *Edo* 1: 'Enemy raid. Fighters to return to battle group with all possible speed. Expedite! Expedite'!"

Naoyuki spoke into his mouthpiece, waited for a moment and reported, "Sent and receipted for, Admiral."

"They'll be low on fuel and ammunition, Admiral," Whitehead cautioned.

"I do not care about those things, Admiral Whitehead. They can ram, is that not true?"

"True, Sir." Arai turned from his chart table and giggled at Admiral Whitehead. Whitehead blustered but said nothing.

Fujita was in a terrible dilemma and even the youngest seaman knew this. He must recover his air–groups before they ran out of fuel, yet fight off a massive raid. There was no escaping the attack, so the old man used his pragmatic sense of tactical imperatives and continued racing toward the Marianas at full speed. This would bring him under attack sooner, but the onslaught was inevitable anyway. There would be one compensation; Matsuhara would reach him in less time, too.

At over 30 knots, the great carrier rode with the following swells, bobbing and dropping stern and bow in a slow seesaw motion as the troughs and crests passed her by like hills and vales. Whitehead gripped the top of the windscreen with one hand and held his glasses with the other. Although behind them the storm bubbled and swirled darkly over the northeastern horizon, the sky to the west glared so blue his eyes ached. With less than two–tenths cloud cover, it was almost empty of clouds. He saw nothing. Then a sharp–eyed lookout high on the superstructure cried out, "Aircraft, bearing 350 relative, elevation angle 20!"

Whitehead heard the rumble before he saw them. A peculiar phenomenon of the tropics. They were low on the water like a swarm of bees, a mass of aircraft apparently attempting to avoid radar. Now they began to climb. A strange assortment, indeed. The expected Junkers Ju–87 Stuka dive bomber with its ridiculous fixed landing gear was there in numbers. Also, the AT-6 Texan, powered up and converted to torpedo bomber. A strange unexpected silhouette began to emerge in Whitehead's lenses, but he could not make it out. He moved to the bridge telescope, a powerful instrument mounted on a tripod and welded to the deck. He put his eye to the rubber eyepiece.

The fine lenses brought the distant aircraft into clear focus. He could make out at least a dozen big, clumsy, mid–high winged aircraft with knobbly fuselages, stringing along in a sloppy formation. They appeared ludicrous with a high greenhouse canopy, windows low on the fuselage and a high tail with the horizontal stabilizer almost at the top of the fin.

"My God. What's that?" Bernstein muttered, studying the ungainly aircraft through his glasses. "It looks like it's more likely to annoy the air than pass through it."

Fujita's eyes were better than anyone suspected. Staring through his glasses, he snapped, "It is big, and it is a bomber, and I do not find that humorous, Colonel Bernstein."

"Sorry, Admiral."

An old memory revived and Whitehead shouted, "It's a Fairey Barracuda torpedo bomber. My, God, where in hell did they get those?"

"Your question is academic, Admiral Whitehead. They are here. They are attacking and we must destroy them or they will destroy us. This is not time for nostalgic reminisces."

"Of course, Sir." Whitehead returned to the windscreen.

"Is it a good bomber?"

"Slow but better than the Texan. Much tougher."

"Very well."

"Range 20, elevation angle 25, Admiral," Arai reported.

Fujita swept the entire horizon. He was strangely deliberate, looking for another group that could have stolen in low on the water. A favorite tactic—attack from opposite directions. Put the carriers on the "anvil."

A young lookout on the wing of the bridge shouted, "More of them, Sir!"

"Bearing? Elevation angle?"

"Bearing 265, elevation angle 30, Admiral."

Whitehead brought his glasses up and was rocked on his heels by another shock. "Impossible," he muttered to himself. He squinted and refocused. A frightening array of fighters; three P–51 Mustangs, four Supermarine Spitfires and six small planes with huge radial engines that looked like truncated P–47 Thunderbolts. Then he recognized them. The fabulous Focke–Wulf 190. The whole mass of fighters was sweeping in on the approaching bombers, high, to provide a protective screen. He reported the sighting to Admiral Fujita.

"Sacred Buddha," Fujita said. He glared at Colonel Bernstein and Whitehead, "We had no word, not one hint from intelligence about the presence of these aircraft."

"Could be from Tomonuto," Captain Mitake Arai injected. Then glaring at Whitehead with obvious contempt, "We should have bombed it."

Whitehead's florid face turned furnace red, "Who in hell said they're from Tomo . . ."

"Enough!" Fujita shouted. He waved. "It makes no

difference! They are here, that is all that matters." Then to Naoyuki, "CAP intercept!"

Immediately, the battle group's fighters screamed to the attack. Wisely, twelve of *Bennington*'s Corsairs curved high and to the south to intercept the enemy fighters. The remaining dozen fighters tore into the bombers like wolves into sheep.

The Seafires proved how wise Fujita had been to deny them to Matsuhara. Stable platforms with contrarotating propellers driven by a 3100–horsepower Griffon engines and mounting four Hispano cannons, they ravaged through the enemy bombers like hell unleashed. On the first pass, two Barracudas and a Ju–87 were blasted out of the sky. Then the Zeros struck, claiming an AT–6 and another Ju–87. In pairs, the Seafires had already turned and were nipping at the trailing bombers before the Zeros had completed their runs. More bombers smoked, dropped off, crashed. Yellow parachutes began to drift down.

The dogfight between the Corsairs and the enemy escort was a stand–off. However, a deadlock worked in the enemy's favor. The Seafires and Zeros could not shoot down all of the bombers and they could not expect any help from the Corsairs. Although a ton heavier and faster, the big American Voughts were learning just how deadly the Focke–Wulf was. One Corsair dropped off into a spin within seconds. It was quickly followed by a smoking P–51 with its engine shot to pieces. Wisely, the bigger, heavier Corsairs dove through the enemy and with their tremendous speed and climbing ability shot back down for another run.

Whitehead was too busy to watch the dogfight between

the fighters. His whole attention was focused on the enemy bombers, the Seafires and the Zeros. The massive battle was already in range of two destroyers in the first ring of escorts. They withheld their fire. Three of the Focke–Wulfs and a Mustang had broken through the Corsairs and had shot down a Zero and sent a Seafire limping off to finally splash in a flat belly landing.

Whitehead cursed under his breath. This was the first time in the decade–long war that the Focke–Wulf and the Barracuda had been seen. International arms dealers. German. British. American. Turkish. God knows whom. Even Japanese. They'd sell anything to anyone to make a bloody profit. It had gone on since time began and would continue until the last man was killed in the final battle. He spat a bitter taste out of his mouth.

A cheer went up as a Focke–Wulf exploded, the enormous blast acting as a propellant that hurled the huge BMW engine ahead like a boulder out of a volcano. But the surviving Japanese fighters were fighting for their lives. The last Zero flamed into a tight barrel roll and died as spectacularly as the Focke–Wulf. Another Seafire circled lazily toward the sea, its Griffon retching gobs of black smoke.

Now, with the interception disrupted, the surviving enemy bombers rumbled toward the carriers. Whitehead counted four AT–6 Texans, four Ju–87s, and three Barracudas, all at about 6,000 feet. The target would be *Yonaga*. *Yonaga* was more than a carrier, it was a symbol—a symbol of the spirit of free men all over the world. It was an ideal cast in steel, eternal, mythic, nearly surreal to freedom loving men. It was the magnet, the binding force that fused their fighting spirit. It must be killed.

Two *Fletchers* began firing, their 5–inch, 38–caliber cannons sending flames leaping from the bulky gunhouses. Fed by loading machines, each ship's main battery fired over a hundred shells a minute, flaming long yellow tongues like a dry pine forest in a summer fire storm. Black puffs pocked the sky. Within moments, 40–millimeter machine guns joined in, sending hundreds of 2–pound shells smoking upwards, slow and arcing, self–destructing fuses sullying the sky with hundreds of black bursts.

Then *New Jersey* unleashed her own enormous anti–aircraft batteries. Brown smoke bellowed and drifted behind her. An AT–6 was neatly severed just aft of the cockpit. The two pieces swirled away, torpedo sailing free like a big shiny cigar. More destroyers began firing. The bombers plowed on, heedlessly.

Naoyuki said, "Fire control reports enemy raid within range of main battery, Sir."

"Commence firing!"

"Our own fighters, Admiral!"

"They know the risks."

Every man on the bridge clamped his hands over his ears. Whitehead held his breath. Still, the report of sixteen 127–millimeter guns firing as one struck like a sonic boom from an old *Concorde*. Brown smoke billowed up from the port side galleries, and the burned solvent smell of cordite seared Whitehead's nostrils. Fed by sweating gunners, the big dual–purpose cannons set up a continuous thunderous drum roll. Two more bombers were destroyed but the others closed fast; three Barracudas sweeping to the starboard side, three AT–6s to port, while the two surviving

Stukas formed a single file, dive brakes down, propellers on full coarse.

Naoyuki shouted over the din, "Admiral, radar reports friendlies. One is far ahead . . ."

"Belay that!" Fujita roared. "All ahead flank! Gunnery, stand by to depress main battery for sea bursts when the torpedo bombers begin their runs." Then, Fujita shouted the battery designations of one–half of the 127–millimeter guns.

Whitehead felt the pulse of the four great engines pick up, the whole bridge vibrating with the strain. Then, in staccato, stammering bursts, dozens of 25–millimeter machine guns began firing. The sky was filled with tracers, black and brown explosions. It seemed impossible that even a fly could weave its way through. A Barracuda didn't. Hit in the cockpit, it tumbled into the sea. It was followed by a Texan that did a half roll and pancaked belly up into the ocean, spraying a solid sheet of white water spangled fleetingly with the colors of the rainbow.

The two Stukas dove together. Both seemed to be coming right down Whitehead's throat. This was how it always was to men under dive bomber attack. He gulped, controlled the terror that threatened to consume him, send him scurrying under the chart table like a frightened mouse. Instead, he bit his lip and looked upward, perspiration beading on his forehead like tiny pearls.

And *Yonaga* was on her own. Her fighters were still involved in a sprawling dogfight and her sister ships had ceased firing. They could hit the great carrier.

Two dive bombers, two torpedo bombers to port and two torpedo bombers to starboard. All attacking together. The worst kind of nightmare. Depressed to negative elevation, eight 127–millimeter guns to starboard and eight to port fired salvoes of shells ahead of the approaching torpedo bombers. Super–quick contact fuses shot towers of water skyward ahead of the AT–6s and Barracudas. Many were duds that hit and ricocheted off wildly, appearing like tumbling blue bottles. Undaunted, the bombers bored on through the mist and spray.

Suddenly a red, green and white Zero flashed out of the sun and shot a Barracuda to pieces. Then with another short burst, the other Barracuda was forced to veer off.

"It's Commander Matsuhara!" someone screamed.

"Cease fire to starboard!" Fujita screamed.

"Thank God for the cavalry," Whitehead said.

"For the what?" Bernstein shouted.

"Oh, nothing."

With Matsuhara's tracers hounding it, the last Barracuda crashed. Now with the threat to starboard gone, Fujita shouted into the voice tubes, "Left full rudder!" He would turn into the Texans, the best tactic against torpedo attack.

Both torpedo bombers dropped their torpedoes simultaneously. Carefully, the admiral conned the great ship, finally slashing precisely between the approaching tracks. A shout went up. One of the Stukas had been hit. Gull wing tearing loose at the fillet, it flopped over and over, twisting into the sea. The other dropped its bomb and pulled up sharply, directly into a storm of fire from Matsuhara's Zero. With a dead pilot, it made its final dive. The bomb exploded harmlessly to starboard.

"*Banzai!* Hurrah!" Whitehead was ecstatic. Not one ship damaged. Not a single casualty. Unbelievable!

294

"Cease fire! Cease fire!" Fujita reduced speed and brought the carrier back to its base course.

"They're gone! Gone!" an excited lookout yelled.

"What is gone?" Fujita shouted.

"The enemy fighters, Sir."

Whitehead brought up his glasses. He found them. Disappearing to the south and east. Tomonuto. Or, they were trying to make Fujita's force believe they were headed for Tomonuto. Fujita wasn't convinced, either. "Radar. Track enemy fighters."

Whitehead looked up. Matsuhara's Zero was circling low and well out of range of the ships. Then he noticed the smoke—white smoke streaming back from the enormous engine. Yoshi had overheated. Strained the *Taifu* beyond its endurance. A samurai, Matsuhara had no choice. Now he might pay with his life. As the rear admiral watched, two Supermarine Seafires swept in low and then climbed to flank the ailing Zero. Hooperman and York. The faithful, loyal wingmen who would die for their leader. Whitehead felt a swelling in his throat and found it difficult to swallow.

Moving his glasses, he focused on the remaining fighters of the CAP. They had paid the price. There were only eleven F4Us and three Seafires remaining. Some must have been damaged, but they were all airworthy. Not one call of distress on the fighter frequency, not one flare had been fired. They resumed circling the force just as a dozen Hellcats and Bearcats stormed into view, flying very high.

"Radar reports many aircraft approaching from 275, range 120."

For the first time, Fujita seemed relaxed, almost tranquil. He had to be pleased with the results of the battle. "IFF?"

"Friendlies, Sir."

"Very well. Must be the bombers. Handlers, prepare to receive aircraft."

The big carrier plowed on regally toward her approaching eagles. Whitehead felt the usual excessive fatigue all men feel after a battle. He gripped the windscreen with both hands and looked at the far horizon. He felt strangely depressed. Only half the battle had been won. There was always another enemy over that horizon. A "pop" high in the sky raised his head. Matsuhara was backfiring and the white smoke seemed thicker.

"Sir, Matsuhara's in trouble."

"How do you know?"

"He's smoking, Sir—backfiring."

Fujita raised his glasses. "Sacred Buddha. Call him, Admiral Whitehead."

Whitehead pulled a microphone from a rack of four and threw a switch. Immediately, their was the hum of a carrier wave on the bridge speaker. *"Edo* One, this is *Saihyosen.* Damage report!"

Matsuhara's voice crackled back, *"Saihyosen* this is *Edo* Leader. I have a hot engine."

"Can you remain airborne."

"On 16 cylinders and with the help of Hachiman."

Fujita grabbed the microphone. "We are not depending on the gods today. I am coming into the wind. Land immediately when I two–block Pennant 2."

"There could be more enemy aircraft up here, *Saihyosen.* A straggler or two."

Fujita's eyes widened, and he sprayed spittle into the

microphone, "*Edo* One obey my orders! Expedite! Expedite!"

"Aye, aye, *Saihyosen*. *Edo* One landing immediately when you hoist Pennant 2."

Followed closely by the Seafires, the red, green and white Zero circled slowly astern. Now the white smoke had thickened, unraveling behind Yoshi like a shiny strip left by a skywriter. Occasionally, a black blob poked a hole in the ribbon.

Fujita shouted more orders. Hoists were made and the behemoth swung into the wind. Colorfully clothed handlers rushed to their stations and the fearsome steel–mesh barrier was cranked out of the deck amidships. Any plane that overshot would be crushed like a swatted fly.

The red, green and white Zero approached the stern at over a hundred knots. Matsuhara did not have his usual precise control. He was too high and wobbling. Whitehead expected him to be waved–off. But, instead, the control officer, convinced the pilot had one shot, flattened his paddles in frantic downward motions and the Zero dropped sharply. Caught by the third cable, it was jerked down to the deck and brought to a stop so violently part of the landing gear collapsed, the port wing striking the deck and one blade of the propeller bending. Whitehead saw the pilot's head snap against his headrest and he sagged forward.

Led by old Crew Chief Shoishi Ota, white–clad crewmen rushed to the aircraft and smothered the smoking engine with foam. Ota was the first to jump up on the wing. Quickly, he reached in and literally pulled Matsuhara out of the cockpit and onto the wing, completely off–balance. Then, they both fell off and crashed onto the deck in a heap, the crew chief sprawled on top of his pilot.

"Sacred Buddha," Fujita said. "He survives a great battle and then his own crew chief kills him."

Quickly, old Chief Hospital Orderly Eiichi Horikoshi and two assistants rushed to the pilot who was sitting up. Matsuhara refused a stretcher and came to his feet while a crestfallen Ota supported him. Whitehead noticed Matsuhara was gripping his right wrist. Then, unassisted, the pilot walked toward the island. Quickly, the barrier was dropped and the damaged Mitsubishi dragged to the forward elevator and struck below.

While air groups poured over the horizon and the roar of engines increased, Fujita stepped to the chart table and stared at it with Captain Mitake Arai. The old admiral traced a line. "I am going to give you the deck, Captain," Fujita said. "After we have recovered our aircraft, retire on this course," he drew a line with a fingertip, "065 at sixteen knots for one hour and then reverse course and run the reciprocal."

"Condition of readiness, Sir?" Arai was forced to raise his voice, the sounds of aircraft engines now becoming thunderous, actually shaking the chart table. The first bomber landed.

"Condition Two. That strip on Tomonuto may be operational. I will signal *Bennington*. I want a complete reconnaissance of Saipan, Tinian and Tomonuto by Skyraiders. They are to be escorted by Bearcats and Corsairs.

Every Japanese on the bridge stiffened. The admiral was admitting his own antique Aichis and Nakajimas were inferior. This was a bitter draught, a chink in the iron face of the samurai. Although the admiral was a proud samurai, he was a military pragmatist above all else. He

298

turned to Naoyuki, "All bombers and fighter to be re-armed and refueled. Nakajimas to be bombed–up as before. Each carrier will maintain a six–fighter CAP." The talker spoke into his headpiece.

"A second strike, Sir?" Arai asked.

"And a third and fourth if necessary."

"Aye, aye, Sir."

"And I want a casualty report as soon as possible."

"Aye, aye, Admiral."

Fujita said to Naoyuki, "Pass the word to Commander Matsuhara, he is to report to my cabin immediately. The bomber commanders are to report to me as soon as they land. If they are casualties, the senior surviving officer." He turned back to Arai, "Inform me immediately in my cabin if we make contact."

"Aye, aye, Sir. I relieve you."

The two officers saluted each other and then the old man walked slowly from the bridge. Whitehead noticed he was limping and his stoop had increased. His whole body spelled exhaustion. He wondered how such a dynamic, vigorous mind could occupy such a ruined body. How much longer could that body endure?

Standing in front of Admiral Fujita's desk, Commander Yoshi Matsuhara tried to hide his fatigue. But his ordeal had been chiseled on his visage; face deeply lined, eyes bloodshot and darkly underscored like bruises. Where his oxygen mask and goggles had pressed against his face there were dark stains of engine smoke and gun powder outlining them. The effect was bizarre, tracing precise silhouettes on his forehead, curving down from his nose and jaw like a wide-eyed creature lurking in a shadowy forest.

Fujita read the tiredness at once while concealing his own. He gestured to a chair. Dropping into the chair, the air group commander gripped his tightly bound wrist.

"You were wounded?"

Yoshi shook his head. "No, Sir. Chief Ota sprained it when he fell on top of me."

"Has Chief Hospital Orderly Eiichi Horikoshi seen it?"

"Yes, Sir. He has treated it." Yoshi did not tell Fujita of the terrible argument he had with the irascible old Horikoshi. "You are grounded!" Horikoshi had said, with his usual contemptible sneer.

"And I'll break your back."

"We shall see."

Fujita said, "You hit all of your targets."

"Yes, Admiral. In fact, The Skyraiders ran out of targets."

The old man ran his hand over his pate, bending down the scattering of white strands still remaining. "Enemy aircraft?"

"They fought well but were poorly led. We destroyed every enemy plane we could find, on the ground and in the air."

"And you, Yoshi-san?"

"I'm not sure, Sir. My crew chief is checking my camera now."

"I hope he does not fall on it."

Yoshi chuckled. "I believe I had five kills."

The old man came erect. "Very good." He hunched forward. "Your reactions must still be good."

"Never better, Sir."

"And you did not black—out, become groggy in the stress of turns, dives. You have a powerful airplane."

"No, Sir," Yoshi lied.

The old man studied the blank face in front of him and saw through it as if he were shopping a store window. "You are not being truthful."

Yoshi waved his hands in frustration. "All men feel some stress in high—speed maneuvers, Admiral."

"Especially old men." He tugged on the nub of a nose. "You are called 'The Geriatric Killer' by some American media. Did you know that?"

"I know. Stupid sensationalism."

"You remember your promise."

"I will not jeopardize my men, Admiral."

"You cannot fly with that wrist and you know Horikoshi will recommend you be grounded."

"That old *roba*—donkey. Sir, I am quite capable of . . ."

Fujita waved him off. "You do not fly until that wrist heals." There was finality in the voice that choked off any further objections. The old man leaned forward, "The enemy still has some flyable aircraft. A few fighters escaped."

Feeling defeated, Yoshi said simply, "Yes, I heard, Sir."

"Four or five Focke—Wulf 190s were amongst them, Yoshi—san."

"Yes, Sir. I know, Sir."

"Very dangerous fighter."

"We can handle it, Admiral." Yoshi narrowed his eyes. "Sir, we have changed course."

"Correct. We are retiring while *Bennington* conducts a reconnaissance. We will reverse course soon."

"To continue the assault?"

"Yes. *New Jersey* will bombard Saipan."

"There is nothing left to bombard."

The old man held up a grid map. "Our operatives have provided us with precise information about the enemy's works—camouflaged pill boxes, observation posts built just above the old invasion beaches. They know we will be forced to assault the same beaches the Americans attacked in 1944."

"With sabot charges, *New Jersey* can hit them from 80 kilometers."

The old man chuckled. "Captain McManus will close to five or less."

Yoshi came erect. He had never been convinced the great ship should be risked in close-shore bombardments. To him it came from Captain McManus, a relic of a tactic used by the Americans during the war. It could be effective, however, it had also cost them many lives unnecessarily. He said, "I knew you planned on a close bombardment, but over open sights?"

"Why not, Yoshi-san?"

"It's not necessary. And *New Jersey* could be hit by shore guns. We know they have some heavies." He leaned forward, "Sir, it has already happened here. During the war, the *USS Colorado* came in too close off Tinian Town and was badly punished by shore guns she could have easily outranged."

Fujita showed his own vast knowledge of the Greater East Asia War, "Her captain was stupid, snagged a reef. Now these waters have been well charted and Captain McManus is a master seaman. And do not forget, Yoshi-san, we want the enemy batteries to reveal themselves.

302

You know that. We are preparing our air groups for a second strike."

Fujita would never alter his order of battle and Yoshi had known this for years. He was so tired, every muscle in his back, arms and legs ached. It became worse after every dogfight. He suddenly yearned for his bunk and sighed long and soft, the exhalation releasing some of his tension.

"And any samurai knows it is to one's profit to intimidate the enemy," Fujita continued. "Let him feel your contempt." He patted the *Hagakure*, "Remember, the book tells us, 'The Way of the Samurai is the practice of death, finding the most sightly way of dying, and putting one's mind firmly in death'."

"True, Sir, but respectfully Captain McManus is a fine seaman, however, he is not a samurai."

"But I have given him a copy of the 'book' and he is learning *otoko no michi*, Yoshi—san."

Yoshi smiled. "The 'manly way' of the samurai." Fujita nodded. The old man gave the *Hagakure* to all of his American commanders. Yoshi doubted if any of them ever read it.

"Yes, Yoshi—san, the 'manly way'. And remember, such a close, punishing bombardment should jar the enemy—help prod him into sending his carriers."

There was a knock. Yoshi opened the door and the dive bomber commander Lieutenant Oliver Y.K. Dempster entered. He was followed by the torpedo bomber commander Lieutenant Akira Terada. Both were dressed in their brown flying suits and their faces wore the same dark outlines of goggles and masks carried by Yoshi's. Terada's head was still wrapped with his *hachimachi* head band.

They appeared as fatigued as Yoshi. Terada wore a particularly harried expression. His eyes moved in short jerky movements and he was breathing hard as if he had been frightened by a monstrous creature in a dark forest and was still trying to catch his breath.

Yoshi was disturbed by Terada's appearance, wondered about the young man's courage. He had shown no lack of it during the strike. Yet, every man had his own reservoir of bravery, a finite amount. With some, it drained very quickly, leaving nothing but a trembling shell, incapable of action or reaction and a menace to comrades. These died quickly and easily or were grounded before they could be killed or kill others. Yoshi had learned long ago to weigh "cowardice" and "bravery" on a discreet scale. Courage was more of a matter of a measure of depleting strength than an inherent characteristic of weakness. He had seen this confusing phenomenon time and again in men of all nationalities, samurai or not.

All men knew fear; brave men controlled it. He had known men who screamed into their oxygen masks to vent fear yet performed mightily. Who urinated into their flight suits but fought to the last bullet. Who carried out their orders with calmness while churning with panic. Who were pushed beyond the bonds of reason and always came back. Was Terada one of these? He had his doubts.

The newcomers bowed and Dempster said, "We just received your orders, Admiral. We were the last bombers to land."

The old man nodded and gestured to the chairs. The pilots seated themselves. "Casualties?"

Dempster's face was grim. "I have twenty-seven flyable Nakajimas, Sir."

"You lost half," Fujita said matter—of—factly. But Matsuhara knew the old man felt the pain of death with each man.

Terada set his jaw and said, "Twenty—six of my Aichis are airworthy, Sir."

Over half of Fujita's bomber strength had been destroyed or put out of action, but his only detectable reaction was a slight turning of the thin lips under. A phone buzzed, the Admiral listened for a moment and slammed the receiver down. He said to Matsuhara, "You lost eleven Zeros and five Hellcats. All of your squadron commanders survived."

"I know Commander Elkins was hit, Admiral."

"His fighter was damaged, but the commander is unhurt."

Yoshi felt a great surge of relief and gratitude to the gods for the survival of the likable, brave American. But, like Fujita, managed to maintain his impassive visage— the look of the emotionless commanding officer. Both were performing well for the young bomber commanders.

Fujita said, "Your groups are being rearmed, fueled and bombed up."

"Another strike, Sir?" Terada asked incredulously.

"Of course."

Yoshi expected the young man to complain about casualties. However, Terada took him by surprise, "But we ran out of targets."

"*New Jersey* will move in for shore bombardment—a close shore bombardment. You will orbit, take out any shore guns that engage her."

Terada seemed not to hear. "But, Sir. We hit all targets."

"You are repeating yourself, Lieutenant. You never take out *'all targets'!*" Fujita pounded the grid map. "We have some hard targets remaining. Pill boxes, observation posts and other works built of reinforced concrete. These targets are best destroyed by naval gunfire. And Captain McManus will also seek out targets of opportunity." He toyed with the hair dangling from his chin. "And remember this, some enemy guns could be emplaced on reverse slopes and hit her with plunging fire. These guns would be out of reach of *New Jersey*'s high–velocity guns. And you know some enemy aircraft are still operational." He gestured at a chart on the bulkhead, "Besides protecting *New Jersey*, I want you to return to those airfields, seek out and destroy any aircraft in hidden revetments. Then we may have a stand–down."

Terada's eyes were very wide, perspiration beading on his forehead like rows of raindrops. "My casualties, Sir. They have been . . ."

It was obvious Fujita had been concerned with the young man's state. Yoshi suspected he had deliberately pushed him to the brink. He had to be tested. Thumping his desk with the end of pencil to emphasize each word, he said, "You are not required to fly this mission, Lieutenant."

Waves of conflicting emotions worked across Terada's face. "I am quite capable of leading my eagles." A sudden icy composure deepened the timbre, "If you order it, Admiral, I will lead them through the nine rings of hell."

Fujita leaned forward, eyes narrow and glinting, "You

are sure, lives depend on your leadership, your judgment under fire."

"On the sacred spirits of my ancestors, Sir."

"Two reside in the Yasakuni Shrine."

"Yes, Sir. My grandfather and great uncle. Both died for the Emperor during the Greater East Asia War."

"I knew your grandfather, Commander Tanashiro Terada. He died a splendid samurai's death at Midway on carrier *Kaga*."

"He was her XO, Admiral. He refused to be evacuated, went down with her, Sir," Terada said pridefully.

Fujita nodded, but Yoshi knew he was still skeptical.

Dempster spoke up, "Sir, all of our bombers are underpowered. It was glaringly obvious when we engaged the enemy fighters. We are still powered with old Sakae 42— only 2,000 horsepower. Sir, we need more power, we need the power to carry heavier armament. Two 7.7 Nambus against 13–millimeter and 20–millimeter guns is a terrible mismatch, Sir. Respectfully, Sir. I sacrificed some of my best . . ."

Fujita waved him off. "I am aware of the situation and you know I have been in contact with Aichi and Nakajima concerning this matter. This situation will be corrected, but your discussion of this matter at this time is ill–advised and ill–timed. We are in the midst of a battle and will attack with whatever equipment is at our disposal—we would send gliders if that was all we had."

"Of course, Sir," Dempster said. "No disrespect intended. However, I feel compelled to call this to your attention in light of our experience during the first strike." He drew himself up. "I can assure you, Admiral, my

307

eagles are ready." He smiled. "And, Sir, we would fly those gliders for you."

"Said like a samurai."

Terada spoke up, "Tomonuto, Sir?"

Possible. We may fly against it—bombard it. We are reconnoitering it now." The old man moved his eyes from man to man, tiny fists clenched and resting on the *Hagakure*. "Remember what this great book teaches." He quoted one of his favorite passages, " 'If your sword be broken, strike with your hands. If your hands be severed, attack with your shoulders. If your shoulders be severed, tear open a dozen throats with your teeth'. His eyes rummaged every face. "That is courage, that is *Bushido*."

Dempster smiled and said, "It also teaches, Sir, 'By dying one avoids shame, unless one has allowed himself to die without having tried to achieve his objective'."

Fujita beamed. "You have been studying, Lieutenant Dempster."

"Of course, Sir. That was your order."

The old man said, "Lieutenant Dempster and Lieutenant Terada, you may return to your duties."

The two young men stood, bowed and turned to the door. Fujita stopped them with a shouted, "Lieutenant Terada, what does the 'book' say about death?"

Both men turned. "Many things, Admiral. That is its favorite topic."

"And what was your favorite passage?"

The dive bomber commander pondered for a moment. "I would say two, Sir. 'Death is as light as a feather', and, 'if you die, die facing the enemy'."

The old man seemed satisfied with the young men. He

watched them as they closed the door. Then, turning away, he blew his nose.

As Yoshi stared after the young men, he remembered a passage from Shakespeare he had heard Brent Ross quote several times after a hard night's drinking: "Golden lads and girls all must, As chimney-sweeps, come to dust."

Shakespeare must have read the *Hagakure*, he thought. He snorted to himself humorlessly. Then he sank back and stared blankly at the door.

Chapter XXI

Night in the Negev Desert reminded Commander Brent Ross of night at sea. With the air free of pollutants, the vault was black sable, stars stabbing brilliantly through the blanket, the dark buffer of the horizon distinct. Relaxing in the passenger's seat of his old American Jeep—so old it actually showed Willys-Overland on its I.D. plate—Brent could not help but chuckle as he surveyed the alignment of the fourteen tanks of *Aleph* Company.

Aleph Company was the most advanced unit of the First Armored Division. In fact, it was more than five miles beyond the southern sector of the Ben Gurion line that extended nearly east and west from Be'er Sheva to Sedom. Coinciding with Fujita's assault on the Marianas, most of the front had been active, the Israelis launching fierce attacks from Al Karak to Al Khishniyab. The borders with Egypt, Jordan, Syria and Lebanon flamed with armored clashes and bloody air battles. However, the southern sector had been quiet.

The Negev was ideal tank country, and to conserve manpower, the tactics were different. *Aleph* Company was dangling like bait deep in the desert, ostensibly to scout, ascertain strength, engage and destroy if attacked. Actually, the company was to engage the enemy and then withdraw at high speed, hopefully pulling the enemy into a cross–fire of anti–tank guns emplaced on curving Subieta Ridge almost three miles to the rear. Dug in along the ridge, the rest of the First Armored would add their fire to that of the anti–tank guns. There was nothing new in these tactics. General Irwin Rommel, "The Desert Fox," had used them repeatedly a half–century earlier.

Aleph Company had already suffered its first casualties. To the south he could see the burned out hulk of an antiquated M–48 tank. It lay on its side like the carapace of a long dead beetle. And out of his vision in the opposite direction were the blasted remains of two old half–tracks. All three vehicles had been destroyed by mines early in the afternoon while they swept the area clear for *Aleph* Company. Four men were dead and three wounded. The three surviving half-tracks had been ordered to clear a sector to the east.

The casualties had brought the hot hand of wrath to rankle Brent's guts. The vehicles were expendable but the men were not. Revenge. He wanted it. Always wanted it. It was always this way. The killing and then more killing to balance the scales and then the cycle began again, repeating and repeating. When would it end? Deep down he knew it never would. It was like being caught in quicksand. The more you fought it, the deeper you sank. Eventually, a man would only wind up with sand in his mouth.

His eyes wandered to the tanks. They were an unusual amalgam of American, British and Israeli thinking. Originally M1A1 Abrams, they had been modified by the ingenious Israelis and given the hybrid name, M1A1 *Sepharad*. The American main gun had been removed and replaced by the superb British 120–millimeter L–11 rifle. The tube was fitted with a fume extractor and thermal sleeve which prevented over–heating and bending. New spaced and laminated armor was fitted over the reactive layer protecting the glacis and a 60–millimeter mortar and infrared searchlight welded to the turret roof. Even some of the fire control equipment and periscopes had been replaced with Israeli and British gear. In all, the low hulking machine represented the best in American, British and Israeli technologies. Shaking his head, Brent wondered at the genius and resolve of the Israeli people.

When the sun had been snuffed out by the abrupt desert darkness, the company commander, Captain Yaakov Shapiro, had resorted to tactics that dated back to the American frontier, pulling his fourteen *Sepharads* of *Aleph* Company into a circle for 360 degree security. The Jeep was parked in the middle. Brent remembered the innumerable Westerns he had watched as a youth where John Wayne, Ward Bond, Randolph Scott, Gary Cooper and a score of other Hollywood heroes had done the same thing to protect helpless settlers from rampaging Indians. He wondered if Captain Shapiro had seen the same movies.

The identical thought was running through the mind of Lieutenant Elroy Rubin who leaned against a fender, checking the 20–round box magazine of his M–16 rifle. "Cap'n Shapiro sho' done pulled his wagons into a circle, Commander. Not even Sittin' Bull could sneak through this here defense, I shit you none."

Brent chuckled. "Custer could've learned from him, that's for sure."

"For danged sure, Commander."

Captain Shapiro, a short dark officer wearing the tank and wreath patch of the Armored Corps, hurried toward them. With skin of sun-seared brown, he was tall and appeared nearly emaciated as if the desert sun had begun to mummified him. Like most men who had spent years in the desert, he was ironic, bemused and fatalistic; a man who had been purged by the iron rod of war. He disliked having the Americans attached to his unit and had made that clear from the beginning. Observers always gave a field commander another responsibility—another problem when the demands of battle were enough to overwhelm a man's ability to make clearheaded decisions.

The man had annoyed Brent Ross from their first meeting. Like most Israeli officers, he seemed to be blind to rank. In fact, he had gruffly refused Brent's request to act as a gunner in one of the *Sepharads* despite Brent's SEAL training and the fact he was replacing a tank company commander, Captain Uri Afek.

"No chance at all," Shapiro had said in his precise, Sandhurst-polished English, so perfect it almost seemed like a tape from a Berlitz course. He had thumped Brent's dossier with a closed fist, "You trained in an old M-60 and the M-1. They're antiques, now." Then, waving at his tank, "We use new British and Israeli electronics and target acquisition gear. That tank's more complicated than your carrier's CIC. It would be a jungle to you and you would have to learn all four stations. That would take months and we move up tomorrow."

Brent protested. He knew he could operate the heat

imager and range finder and fire the gun. Any idiot could. But his arguments were useless. "I'll tag along in a Jeep," he had finally said.

"Suit yourself, take your chances. It's your life, Commander," Shapiro retorted, walking away.

Now watching Shapiro approaching, Brent knew what was coming and had his answer already prepared. He slipped out of the Jeep and stood next to the door, M–16 slung over his shoulder. He faced the Israeli officer.

Shapiro said to Brent, "Intelligence reports a strong column of enemy tanks moving against this sector, perhaps battalion strength. They're probably scouts for the main force. I would suggest you make a discreet withdrawal to Point *Resh*. You know I can't guarantee your safety." He gestured at a machine gun mounted on a post behind the front seat of the Jeep, "You would be almost helpless in an armored battle. That M–60 is just a peashooter and you know it."

Brent scratched the bristle on his chin. Encased in three feet of reinforced concrete, Point *Resh* was battalion HQ back on Subieta Ridge. "Battalion strength, about thirty-five Arab tanks," the American mused.

"That's right, Commander," Shapiro agreed, obviously piqued. The Israeli waved in a long sweeping gesture to the south at a berm that extended for almost four miles along their front. "Somewhere over that rise reconnaissance has reported at least three regiments of tanks, a motor battalion and a mechanized infantry brigade in support."

"The Fourth Armored Division, Captain." Brent offered.

"Correct, Commander."

Rubin said, "I unnerstan' their C.O.'s crazier'n a loon, plain an' simple."

"Major General Shafeek Shabra. He's a Shi'ite."

"One bad hombre."

"Yes, he is known to be very bold, sometimes reckless. And, I repeat, if we engage, you will be ah—exposed. I suggest you withdraw to point *Resh*. This is no place for a sailor and a pilot. I warned you before."

"I'll make that decision, Captain!" Brent shot back. "And keep your warnings to yourself."

Shapiro stiffened. It was obvious superior rank meant little to him. He was commander in the field and he never let anyone forget it. "As field commander it is my duty to tell you if they break through, if we even engage in a running battle, you're dead men. They won't bother with prisoners."

Brent squared his jaw and stared down at the tank commander. "I know. I've been fighting them for ten years. Keep in mind, I'm here to observe and I can't observe hiding behind three feet of concrete. Can you understand that, Captain?"

"Yes. I can understand. You are being very foolish, Commander. I've heard samurai were suicidal, but this is redicu . . ."

"Mind your tongue!" Brent interrupted harshly.

"It's my duty!"

"And I have mine." Brent turned to Elroy, "If you wish, you may withdraw, Lieutenant."

The Texan smiled, "I ain't hankerin' to miss no rip—snortin' barn burner, no—how, Commander."

The Israeli shrugged, a hopeless gesture. He spoke resignedly, "Suit yourselves." He stabbed a finger at a shallow hole hacked into the hard pan behind a small outcropping of boulders. "Then dig in deeper if you can, have plenty of ammo, and be ready to evacuate at a moment's notice." He waved at a *Sepharad* with air identification stripes, the ubiquitous Star of David, and "163" painted on its turret. "Watch me. If I retreat—and I'll back out, not turn—get in that Jeep and get out of here as fast as you can or that hole will be your grave."

"Cut an' run like a bat out'a hell," Elroy said.

"Good analogy, because this could very well become hell—the very bowels of hell where even a bat couldn't survive." Without another word, he turned on his heel and stalked off to his tank.

"Sure got a burr up his ass, Commander."

"That's his problem." Brent glanced at his watch. Almost midnight. He shivered. Although the desert could exceed 120–degrees in daytime, temperatures could drop 70–degrees or more at night. This was one of those nights. He gestured at the hole. "We'd better get some shut–eye. This place could become very noisy before dawn."

The two men shouldered their rifles, picked up canteens and bandoleers of ammunition and grenades and walked to the hole. Grunting and groaning, they slipped into a pair of sleeping bags, stretched on top of air mattresses. Both men pulled in their M–16s to keep them free of the desert dirt.

"Keep that M–16 clean, Elroy."

"Shoot, Sir, my shootin' iron's cleaner'n a hound's tooth an' slick as a virgin pussy."

Brent chuckled at the colorful similes and tried to make himself comfortable. He distrusted the M–16. It was light and fast, but it jammed easily. With no piston, the gas was

316

injected directly into the bolt carrier, pushing it backwards and then escaping through small vents. The system of lugs, locks and vents was complex and did not adapt well to the fine sifting sand of the Negev. A dirty breech could lead to jams. He found himself continuously cleaning and oiling the weapon.

However, it had its merits. With little recoil, it could fire 800 rounds a minute with great accuracy, and the small 5.56–millimeter bullet could kill at five hundred yards. The year before at *Bren ah Hahd* he had killed five Arabs with it. Slowly, he wrapped a hand around the bolt and caressed the cocking handle with his thumb. "Don't let me down, baby," he whispered.

"You awake ol' saddle buddy?" Elroy said softly.

"Sho' 'nuff," Brent quipped.

Sighing, the Texan said, "If I had my 'druthers, I'd have a slick little Texas filly in this here sack with me instead o' this cold piece o' iron. It's been a coon's age since I had some o' that fine shaky puddin'."

Brent chuckled. "Can't argue with that, ol' buddy."

"Fix you up with some when this hoe–down's over, an' I ain't just a–jawin'."

"That's a deal. Now go to sleep."

"Is that an order, Commander?"

"I'm a–feared it is, Lieutenant."

"Not a body to disobey a superior officer, no how."

Elroy rolled over and fell asleep almost immediately, but Brent was restless. Clasping his hands behind his head, he stared up at the stars. They were so bright, it seemed he was looking up at a dark blue panoply, perforated with lights shining through the holes. How incongruous. How could such a merciless killing ground lie under a mantle of so much beauty?

However, the desert was not usually beautiful. He had learned much about it at observation post *Bren ah Hahd*. But the terrain at *Bren ah Hahd* was different. True, the earth was sun baked, hard as petrified wood just like the Negev. But there he had seen an abundance of plants, stunted and scrawny, true, but still covering much of the terrain. There had been jujube bushes, sprawling burnet, skinny tamarisk, marjoram and the prickly camel's thorn shrub. Here, in the southern Negev, only an occasional camel's thorn seemed to survive. And there was no shortage of scorpions and snakes. Flies, too, seemed to follow the troops, almost as if they knew there would soon be bloated corpses to feast on.

Despite the differences, all the hellish obstacles found at *Bren ah Hahd* were to be found here several times over. There was no water. It had to be trucked in or carried on the backs of men. Most of the men of *Aleph* Company were so dehydrated, they urinated infrequently and their skin appeared as parched as the flesh of beef dried in the sun.

In fact, all logistics were a nightmare for supply officers. And the desert knew how to torture. Not only were the temperature fluctuations wild, but wind-whipped sand as fine as talcum powder clogged weapons, seeped into engines, lungs, could blind men caught without goggles. And there were the mirages.

He chuckled. He saw Devora, but she was no mirage. Again his sailor's mind bent by too many lonely years at sea, was playing tricks on him, conjuring up erotic memories. He grumbled oaths, twisting and turning in frustra-

318

tion. Devora persisted, smiling up at him, long hair spread over a pillow. He could feel her warmth, her arms tight across his back, fingernails digging into his flesh as she reached climax after climax. It was torture.

Then a new thought wrenched him. The assassin. The Goodenough copycat. DNA samples of semen and hair had proved he had killed Ruth Moskowitz. He felt a chill and it wasn't the desert cold. Was Devora safe? She had promised to stay at the BOQ at Lod. Then he remembered—the killer always moved fast, covering vast distances before he struck again. He was probably on the other side of the world. But he still felt uneasy.

He chased the worries with new happier thoughts. Fujita had struck in the Western Pacific, hard and devastating. The latest reports told of overwhelming air strikes on Saipan and Tinian. And battleship *New Jersey* had bombarded Saipan. There were rumors that Tomonuto Atoll was under attack. And Fujita's strategy seemed to be working. At least the Arab battle group was reported to be putting to sea. This was what Fujita wanted—the final showdown. The final decisive battle all samurai craved.

This was crazy. He should be with them. Yoshi Matsuhara, Admiral Fujita, Rear Admiral Whitehead, Colonel Bernstein. Maybe they were all dead now. The randomness of the Russian roulette of war. He twisted so that he rolled onto the sharp corner of the M-16's box magazine. Cursing, he turned away. Suddenly, he yearned to feel *Yonaga*'s deck heave beneath his feet, feel the wind-whipped spray on his face. He didn't belong in this desert. Sleeping with this plastic toy of a gun. He was out of his element. He was suddenly desolate. He had lived with death too long and he didn't want to die here. Not with the sand, the snakes, scorpions, flies. Bedouins to pull the clothes off his corpse. If he were to die, he deserved the clean depths of the Pacific. Hundreds of his comrades waited for him. The Marianas Deep. That was the place. An ideal place to sleep the final deep slumber. He drifted off.

It seemed minutes later Elroy awakened him with a hand to his shoulder. "Brent, ol' buddy, somethin's a–stir-rin'."

It was still very dark but a faint blush on the eastern horizon hinted at the approaching dawn. Yawning, Brent said, "What's up?"

"I hears somethin'."

Sitting up, Brent cocked an ear. "Nothing. Nothing at all."

"No. No, Brent." Elroy put his ear to the hard ground. "Some heavy stuff's a–movin'. You can hear it."

Brent pressed his ear to the ground and heard a faint rumbling sound like a precursor of an earthquake. Strange, he thought, with all the modern, sophisticated equipment, sensors, computers, lasers, an old Indian arti-fice could reveal approaching danger. "Captain Shapiro! Captain Shapiro," he hissed.

A dark figure detached itself from the shadows of a tank and approached. "Yes, what is it?" Shapiro answered, obviously irritated. "Keep the noise down."

"Something big, mean and ugly is headed this way."

"How do you know?"

"Put your ear to the ground."

"Ear to the ground? Ridiculous."

"Captain! Captain!" a tanker shouted. "We have

something on our heat sensors." Shapiro whirled on his heel and ran back to his tank.

Elroy chuckled. "Even a blind hog'll root up a log, now an' then. These here fancy tank soldiers have a lot o' learnin' to do. All them fancy doodads ain't for shit iff'n you cain't learn from some old Indian."

Brent was on his feet. "Come on, ol' buddy. Let's get ready to haul ass."

"Never disobeyed an order, Sir."

The two men grabbed their sleeping bags, guns, canteens and hurried to their Jeep.

Captain Yaakov Shapiro grabbed the track guard and pulled himself up onto the back of his tank, *Shofar Aleph* 6. Raising his head up through the hatch, his gunner, Corporal Yitzvak Ami, cried out in a high shrill voice, "Captain, I'm picking up armored–vehicle movements on our thermal imaging system."

"Where?"

"To the east. Five–thousand meters. Coming down the berm."

Shapiro pondered. "Could be the half–tracks."

Now, both men could hear the low rumble of diesels. Heads popped out of all the tanks and men climbed out of their sleeping bags and stood. Some tank commanders stood on their turrets with binoculars to their eyes. "Those aren't half–tracks," Shapiro said. "They make a much higher sound."

"T–72s, Sir," Ami said.

"How many?"

"Twenty plus, Captain."

The news sent a cold shock up and down Shapiro's spine, heart beating so fast he could feel the blood pounding in his temples. With an effort, he steeled himself, forced himself to concentrate on his enemy. The T–72 was the best tank the Arabs had. He had never engaged them before. However the *Sepharad* had advantages. The maximum effective range of the T–72's 125–millimeter gun was about 2,500 meters while the M1A1 could shoot twice as far. Another advantage was the *Sepharad*'s fourth man, a loader who manually loaded the main gun. The Russians designers of the T–72, determined to reduce the number of crewmen to three, had installed an automated reload machine. This automatically elevated its gun and took it off target after firing each round. Shapiro's M1A1, with its fourth man, could hold its gun on–target during reload, allowing for a rate of fire almost twice that of the T–72; about twelve seconds for the T–72, six seconds for the *Sepharad*.

However, Shapiro's greatest advantage lay in the *Sepharad*'s fire control system, the most sophisticated in the world. Gyro–stabilized, it fed data into a 32–byte ballistic computer interfaced with the gunner's and commander's laser sights, the thermal imaging system, and the gun control equipment. Target range was computed from either Corporal Ami's or Shapiro's laser range finders, while the target's angular rate was automatically fed in as the target was tracked. The entire gyro–stabilized system was as accurate at 70–kilometers–an–hour as it was at rest. On the other hand, according to Mossad, the T–72 relied on old–fashioned optical range finding. And they had to stop to fire. Shapiro prayed Mossad was right.

Dropping down through the hatch and onto his padded seat, Shapiro kept his head exposed so that he could see over the turret and under the bulky 50–caliber machine gun at the commander's station. Adjusting his helmet and microphone which bridged around his jaw like a bent twig, he switched on his battle circuit and intercom. *"Shofar Aleph* this is *Shofar Aleph* 6. Tanks! Tanks! Direct front. Form battle front on me! Come on line. Come on line."

Engines started all around him. His driver, Sergeant Eherd Sprinzak, hit the starter and the Avco Lycomig gas turbine whined to life. Shapiro cursed. He had a problem. Many problems. It takes a M1A1 *Sepharad* about forty seconds to warm up before it is ready to fight. And to use the thermal imaging system, it takes about two more minutes for the system to cool down, since it locates and targets heat sources.

He looked around and raised his voice to God. The rumble of the approaching enemy had increased to low thunder, but not one tank of *Aleph* Company had moved. He pounded the 50—round ammunition box of the machine gun. They were still in their warming up, cooling down process. It would be minutes before they were ready to fight. Then a tank moved, then another and the front began to form, tubes pointed at the berm.

"Two—thousand—four—hundred—meters," Corporal Ami called out. They had lost their range advantage and the sky was brightening. There was a clanking sound inside the turret and Shapiro realized his loader, Private Itmar Rabinovich, had rammed an APFSD shell into the breech of the gun without the order. Because of accidents, they were never in "battle carry" condition—a round chambered in the main gun—until it was actually ready to fire.

Then the most frightening call a tanker can hear, "They're traversing, Sir."

They had been spotted. Time to button up. He hit a lever and his seat dropped, lowering him into his battle station. After securing the hatch, he settled behind his computerized fire control system. He was jammed into a jumbled, confining maze, nose assailed by the usual stink—the acrid smell of hot plastics and electrical circuitry, fuel, and unwashed bodies. Overhead was a ring of six fixed–angle periscopes to give all–round vision, while to his left a television monitor repeated the exact red, orange and yellow heat image Ami was tracking. It was clearly a T–72.

Breathing in short quick gasps, he put his eyes to his panoramic sight which allowed him to see through a full 360–degree in azimuth and 70–degrees in elevation without moving his head. He wiped perspiration from his forehead and quickly switched to 10.5 magnification. Again, he assured himself the export model of the T–72 did not contain the latest Russian electronics equipment. He should have an advantage. He would soon learn.

Pressing the laser activating button, he brought the cross hairs of his range finder to the lead tank and watched impatiently as data flashed in the sight's right eyepiece—position of the vehicle, sight and gun axes. Fire–control information from the computer and laser flashed in the left eyepiece. He sighed, he had a steady track.

Now, to release the laser button. The computer took over. Immediately, he heard whirring and whining as the computer traversed and elevated the gun. The whole turret turned. Then the yellow "Ready to Fire" light illuminated in his sight. Finally, he released his breath with a loud hissing sigh as the gun coincidence indicator glowed red. He threw the intercom switch, "Fire!"

Corporal Ami, eyes to his own range finder, squeezed the trigger and there was a dull whooshing sound and the gun kicked back in recoil. Immediately, the smell of cordite mixed with the pungent odor of the turret. Rabinovich rammed another round into the breech.

Shapiro watched as his APFSD round hit low on the hull of the lead enemy tank. The incredible Armor–Piercing Fin Stabilized Discarding Sabot projectile with its depleted uranium penetrator was the most devastating anti–tank round in the Israeli arsenal. Like a hot poker through butter, it punched through the enemy's armor, setting off the ammunition. The tank exploded with such fury, the turret was hurled high into the sky and tumbled end over end into the desert.

There was no time for self–congratulations. He shifted the aiming mark left to the next target. In less than eight seconds he shouted, "Fire!"

Another hit. Another fireball. And now all of *Aleph* Company was firing. Sprocket, return rollers and idler wheels were blasted from one T–72, skewing it around and sending its tracks flying. Foolishly mounted fuel cells lining the right track guard of another burst and enveloped the tank in flames as if it had been hit by a flame thrower.

Now the T–72s were firing. "This is *Shofar Aleph* 16," the shrill voice of First Platoon Leader Lieutenant Arye Deri piped in his earphones. "I'm hit. Left tread's blown off. Am abandoning."

Shapiro caught a glimpse of Deri and three of his men

running from the disabled tank toward another *Sepharad*. Before they could grab a handhold, a burst of machine gun fire cut them down in a squirming heap.

Shapiro's stomach churned as if it had been brought to a boil. "Kill them! Kill them!" he shouted thickly, shifting to another target.

Then a horrifying cry, "More of them, on both flanks," came over the radio from *Shofar* 5. "And infantry!"

He shouted to the gunner, "Corporal Ami, you have the gun."

"I have the gun, Sir."

Ami fired again and again. The berm was lined with flame–spewing blow–torches. Shapiro put his eye to his periscope. Low hulking shapes now clearly visible in the growing light not only on the berm but moving in from the left and right. And he could see squads of infantry, some clinging to the handholds, others running behind the tanks. Shafeek Shabra had sacrificed some T–72s on the berm to spring his trap. The Arab general was making a major move of his own. Who was trapping whom? At least a dozen T–72s were firing, maybe more.

A voice screamed in his earphones, "I'm hit!" Shapiro recognized the voice of Sergeant Moshe Naiman, the commander of *Shofar Aleph* 22. "I'm burning." Then with his transmit button still open, the screams, long and heart–rending like a tortured animal. Icy horror clutched and squeezed Shapiro's guts and he could feel his heart pounding like a mallet against his ribs. He hammered the side of the turret with a gloved fist. Fortunately, Naiman's radio fell silent within seconds.

There was a clang and something hard and vicious hit the glacis of the turret. It bounced off. A HESH round.

They would have to do better than that. The enemy was fully committed. It was time to retreat, pull the Arabs back with them. They would have to fight their way out. Head for Zabib Pass.

"*Shofar Aleph*, this is *Shofar Aleph* 6," Shapiro said into his microphone. "Pull back! Back out! And watch your flanks. Enemy tanks and infantry."

Keying the intercom, he shouted at the driver, Eherd Sprinzak, "Eherd, back out—full speed. The hell with the terrain. We'll be surrounded in a minute. We'll try to make Zabib Pass."

The turbine whined as Sprinzak called on all 1,500 horsepower and the tank jerked into reverse. Shapiro had just caught a glimpse of the old Willys–Overland Jeep crazily racing across his rear, when the HEAT round hit. The uranium–tipped conical shell focused the explosion into a high–speed jet of molten metal that penetrated the armor just below the turret. Fragments sprayed through the tank. A piece of steel plate the size of a frying pan struck Ami like a guillotine, severing part of his scalp neatly just below the right eye and above the left ear, flinging brains, gore, and chunks of splintered bone onto Shapiro's face and chest. The eye rolled onto his lap like a billiard ball, trailing the optic nerve like a white string.

Slapping and scraping the bloody horror away, the captain cringed under the stinging rain of hot metal. The tank was still in reverse at full speed, but he was choking on the thick smoke and trying to wipe pulverized brains and detritus from his face. Sour gorge welled and scalded the back of his throat. Choking it down, he threw the blower switch. Nothing happened. The circuit was broken.

Rabinovich was crying out in pain, howling, keening. But the smoke was so thick, Shapiro could not see any of his men. Too much was happening, too much for one man. He had to get out, get his men out before the tank blew. "Abandon tank! Out! Out!" he shouted into the intercom.

He was reaching for the hatch when the ammunition exploded. All he could remember of the last milliseconds of his life was a low rumble, some shaking. *"Kedosh Yisrael!"* he screamed. And then an engulfing flash like a 1,000 suns at noon, heat, followed by a cloak of darkness as infinite as the universe.

With Elroy Rubin at the wheel, the Jeep bounded over the desert like a wild mustang breaking for free range. Brent clung to the stock and pistol grip of the M–60, fighting to keep his balance. It was quite bright now, the sun breaking free of the horizon and glaring down from a blood–red sky. Behind him, flames and black smoke from burning tanks shot skyward, reminding him of a burning oil field. There was so much smoke, the entire southern desert was obscured.

Brent was shocked by what he had seen. He had expected a short, sharp skirmish and then a quick withdrawal to lead the enemy into the anti–tank guns. A simple maneuver for Elroy and himself to observe, take notes and withdraw. Instead, he was in the middle of what appeared to be developing into a major battle. Indeed, Major General Shafeek Shabra had attacked with much more strength than Yaakov Shapiro had anticipated. So much strength, the Israeli tanks were in danger of being annihilated. Who had been trapped? There would be no lure if *Aleph* Company was wiped out.

The survivors of *Aleph* Company were hard pressed to escape. Looking back, Brent could see only eight *Sepharads* turning and racing away from the berm at high speed, firing as they ran. The rest were adding their funeral pyres to those of at least twenty T–72s scattered over the berm and down its slopes. But other enemy tanks were closing from both flanks. *Aleph* Company was hopelessly outnumbered.

As Brent watched a *Sepharad* was hit low in the tracks by a big 125–millimeter shell precisely at the moment the Israeli tank was tilted to the side by an outcropping of boulders. The blast flipped the 60–ton vehicle up onto its side, its opposite tracks turning it slowly like a wounded elephant unable to right itself. Another round punching into its soft underbelly set off its fuel and ammunition, a series of blasts that blew chunks of metal and men into a 100–yard radius.

"We've done been dry–gulched!" Elroy shouted, fighting the wheel of the careening Jeep, which he was trying to keep on nothing more than an old camel trail.

"Put the spur to her, Elroy! Head for Zabib Pass!"

"I am, Brent, and I'm puttin' iron right up her ass!"

The *Sepharad*'s ability to fire while running took a devastating toll of the moving and halting T–72s. The Arab tanks presented targets that could not be missed. Within minutes, nine more enemy tanks had been put out of the fight. A few black–clad crewmen could be seen running or diving behind boulders for shelter. Three crewmen boiled from a burning T–72. All were flaming torches. Screaming, they ran wildly, jumping, staggering, rolling, beating

329

at the flames with their arms and hands. A *Sepharad* cut them down with a single burst from its coaxial machine gun. "Merciful," Brent muttered. "Should've let 'em burn."

"*Aleph* might make it!" Elroy shouted.

Brent did not answer. He had seen two half–tracks loaded with infantry racing around their flanks. At first they had been accompanied by tanks, but the tanks had been pulled into the fight. The half–tracks pushed on. In his mind, there could be only one mission for the flanking half–tracks—they would attempt to lay mines to the rear. Probably on the approaches to Zabib Pass. The pass was a clear wadi like a funnel between two rocky ridges that acted like natural tank barriers. And the ground was sandy and soft. The T–72s would herd the Israelis into the mine field.

There was no chance a deep, thick mine field could be laid. However, if one or two Israeli tanks could be mined, the others could become confused, hesitant, forced into the narrow track in the middle of the pass. Here, they could be cut to pieces. It was a reckless plan, a tactic wasteful of men and machines and very chancy. Especially without armored escort. But typically Arab; typically Shi'ite, and if it worked, *Aleph* Company was doomed.

Brent had an advantage over the half–tracks. The Jeep had a hopped–up V–6 engine. It was capable of almost 60–miles–an–hour on the highway, perhaps thirty to thirty-five on 4–wheel drive in the desert, if they didn't hit a rock. This was much faster than the half–tracks. Brent figured no more than fifteen miles–an–hour with their heavy loads and rough terrain. Already, the battle was fading far behind and Zabib Pass with its flanking rocky ridges loomed ahead.

In a few minutes Elroy shouted, "Men! Up ahead!" He raised his windshield.

Brent saw them. A six–man mine–laying detail digging holes with mines stacked alongside the trail. Combat engineers. No doubt about it. What appeared to be an old American M–9 Personnel Carrier was parked nearby. A single gunner manned its machine gun. He was seated next to it, smoking, despite mines stacked all around him. The Arabs did not seem concerned by the approaching Jeep. Obviously, they thought Brent and Elroy were Arabs. And Brent had no choice. It was either fight his way through these Arabs or die. He ground his teeth together until his jaw hurt and tightened his grip on the stock of the M–60. He shouted, "Slow her down, Elroy. I can't hit the side of a barn at this speed."

"They're a–figgerin' were Arabs. They ain't 'spectin' an Israeli Jeep out here, no–how."

"I think so. Get closer, slow down or we'll be in those graves Shapiro told us about. When you get to twenty, thirty–yards, stop. We'll open up then."

While Elroy slowed and closed on the enemy, Brent sat with forced casualness next to the M–60. His stomach compressed and ground on hot stones, heart battered against his ribs. He hardened his jaw and exhaled loudly. One hundred yards. Fifty yards. Twenty-five yards. Elroy stopped the Jeep. The Arabs stopped working. A burly sergeant pointed. Two of the men reached for AK–47s. The man in the half–track, cigarette still in his mouth, came erect and grabbed the machine gun. He seemed hesitant. It cost him his life.

331

Leaping to his feet, Brent levelled the M-60 and put his shoulder to the stock. He brought his sights down onto the enemy machine gunner. A short burst and six 7.62 millimeter slugs punched through the gunner's chest, puffs of his last drag spurting from his mouth, nostrils and holes in his chest. At the same time, Elroy was firing his M-16 over the hood of the Jeep. At twenty-five yards, he could not miss. Three of the Arabs tumbled and pitched across their mines.

The sergeant and a private tried to flee across the desert to a scattering of boulders. But there was no cover. Bravely, the sergeant whirled and fired a burst from his AK-47. Slugs whined over Brent's head and then punctured the spare tire bolted to the rear. Frantically, Brent swung his weapon. A short burst from the M-60 and the sergeant stiffened like a statue momentarily and then dropped as if his bones had turned to water. Elroy caught the private with a hail of slugs. He fell forward and rolled over onto his back, arms outflung.

"Let's haul ass!" Brent pointed. "To the right. There should be another detail working that side of the pass."

Elroy whipped the wheel to the right and roared off in third gear. There was no track, however, the bottom of the pass had been eroded by wind and rare rainstorms. It tended to be sandy and smooth. He accelerated while the sounds of the battle grew closer. It was like approaching thunder, loud and reverberating in the pass. Yet not one tank was visible.

"Put the spurs to her," Brent yelled.

"I am."

Within minutes, they found the other half-track working the other side of the pass. Six men, widely scattered.

Digging with mines stacked. Brent sighed with relief. Obviously, the sounds of the battle had muffled the gunfire. Anyway, the Arabs were not alerted. Instead, they were working furiously to bury their mines. The sandy bottom of the pass made their task easier. Again, Elroy slowed while Brent assumed an unmenacing pose. But the Arabs were dispersed. Tougher targets. "Let's kill as many as we can and head for Subieta Ridge."

"They've laid some mines, I reckon."

"I know. We can't do anything about that. Slow down and get as close to that half–track as you can. I want to put a grenade into her."

"No call for that, Brent. That's plum loco. We'll go up with them mines. They won't be able to tell us from hog shit."

"The driver's compartment. I want to disable her."

Slowing, Elroy approached the vehicle. The gunner stared curiously. Brent waved and he waved back. Two other Arabs digging nearby next to a camel's thorn bush, stood erect and waved. Brent and Elroy returned the wave. When only a few yards from the half–track, the gunner straightened and reached for his gun. "He's made us!"

Brent cut him down with a short burst. Elroy stopped, swung his M–16 with one hand and shot the two Arabs next to the camel's thorn bush before they could reach for their weapons.

The other three Arabs went to ground. And Brent wasn't sure where they were. "The half–track!" he shouted, pulling the pin from a grenade.

"Be careful of them mines!"

Elroy lugged ahead in low gear and Brent lobbed the grenade into the driver's compartment. "Haul ass!"

Racing through the gears like a madman, Elroy headed the Jeep for the center of Zabib Pass. There was a muffled blast and flame and smoke erupted from the front of the half–track.

Both men were cheering when the two Arabs rose on the right hand side like apparitions. Their AK–47s were real and spurting fire. There were hissing sounds over Brent's head like a basket full of angry snakes, three or four banging, thudding sounds as bullets hit the Jeep. Frantically, Brent swung the M–60 to his right and pressed the trigger. With the Jeep moving at high speed, his bullets were sprayed like a loose garden hose. But one Arab was bowled over and the other threw himself to the ground.

The firing stopped and suddenly they were free. But the Jeep was weaving and slowing.

"What the hell's wrong," Brent shouted, scanning the desert. In his excitement and confusion, the sailor came back, "Mind your helm!"

No answer. He looked down. A cold blast of horror froze him. Elroy was slumped over the wheel.

"No! No!" Brent cried as the Jeep rolled to a halt. He jumped out and ran to the driver.

"Sorry, ol' saddle buddy. Done stopped one. Gut shot." The Texan toppled over onto the passenger's seat.

Gasping and crying with rage and frustration, Brent eased the limp form into the passenger's seat. Then he jammed the Jeep into gear and raced for Subieta Ridge.

Now the battle was close behind. Six *Sepharads* were entering the pass at high speed, leaving huge clouds of dust boiling behind them, turrets turned, firing. Shells burst around them, orange–white eruptions, flinging sand, dust and rocks in wide circles. Swarms of T–72s forming a rough semicircle and working hard on the flanks, trailed by 1,000 to 1,500 yards. Far behind, infantry in squads of nine or ten men tried futilely to keep up with the battling steel giants.

Cannon fire boomed and echoed through the pass, bouncing from the hard rocky surfaces of the ridges on either side. It was deafening. Then a new sound broke through, familiar and terrifying. Engines. Glancing upward Brent saw four dive bombers, three Ju–87s and a single Curtis SB2C, already in their dives. Almost as one, they dropped their bombs, pulled out and skimmed low over the desert. The three Junkers missed, but the Curtis' 1,000–pound bomb grazed the glacis of a *Sepharad* and drove into the ground. The front of the tank was over it when it exploded. An enormous blinding flash, dirt, boulders, spare treads, water cans, track guards, bedding were flung hundreds of feet into the air as everything attached to the exterior of the tank was stripped or torn by the blast. Hurled up and over by the explosion, the 60–ton vehicle was flipped on its back like a child's toy. Incredibly, its tracks still turned at high speed.

It looked like a turtle hopelessly trapped on its shell. The turtle was easily killed. Struck by at least four shells at once, its treads were blown off and then it was gutted into flaming chaos. Miraculously, a single crewman escaped. Clothes smoking, he staggered after *Aleph* Company. He was looking for a second miracle to save him. None was forthcoming. A T–72 casually fired a short burst, breaking his spine. He toppled backwards like a broken twig, flopping and twitching. A second burst ended the agony.

Fearfully, Brent looked overhead for more bombers. The Jeep would be an easy strafe. But there were none. Then he saw the fighters. Israeli P–51s and Spitfires, high, streaking to the south where several specks were hurtling in. Enemy fighters and bombers. Ignoring the developing air battle, he riveted his eyes to his front, on Subieta Ridge.

The hell with the battle. Elroy was bleeding to death. There were medics ahead. He pounded the wheel in frustration. If he had listened to Shapiro instead of playing the indomitable samurai, Elroy wouldn't have a bullet in his guts. Even Colonel Bernstein had tried to talk him out of it. Fujita was against it, too. He had listened to no one. He had to be at the front. In the middle of it. In the line to show everyone how brave he was. Now, the hell with *Aleph* Company, the hell with the Arabs. The only thing that counted was Elroy Rubin. He floored the accelerator, steadying his unconscious friend with one hand.

Brent saw the rest of the battle through a daze. The track to the ridge was straight and climbed steadily. He speeded for the summit where he knew battalion HQ was located. Nothing was visible, but he knew it was just to the left of the track which vanished into a shallow depression.

Suddenly, Subieta Ridge blossomed with leaping motes of fire. Brent had no idea the battle was so close behind. Four–thousand yards or less. Perhaps a hundred tank and anti–tank guns were firing down range, directly over him. He could feel the muzzzle blasts, was nearly deafened by sharp, piercing barks. His eardrums pained as if they were being poked by a hot pin. Groaning, he shook his head.

High–velocity shells snarled, rustled and hissed just over his head. The larger shells made hollow, tearing sounds like canvas being ripped as they bored through the air.

Turning to his left, he was out of the line of fire at last. He threw a glance over his shoulder. Only four *Sepharads* were about a mile behind him. And now at least thirty T–72s were in close pursuit. But, Israeli artillery was decimating the enemy. Within thirty seconds, at least ten exploded. The others stopped. The infantry vanished behind rocks and bushes. High in the sky and far to the south, the dogfight raged. Contrails, burning aircraft, parachutes.

Then, in huge clouds of dust, First Division tanks burst from their redoubts and stormed down from the ridge like an old–fashioned calvary charge. The T–72s reversed.

Brent screeched to a halt behind the ridge. The entrance to the huge rounded concrete bunker was to his left. Before he could pull his companion from the Jeep, four medics rushed out of the bunker with a stretcher. Quickly but gently they lay the unconscious Texan on the stretcher and carried him to the bunker. Brent walked alongside, holding his friend's hand, staring at the blood–soaked shirt, the ashen face. Coldness settled in his chest, the coldness of dread.

"I did it. Goddamnit! I did it. The great fearless 'Yankee Samurai'. Stupid, bull–headed son–of–a–bitch." He ducked into the entrance.

The interior of the large bunker was crowded with officers and communications personnel. Some stood at ports, studying the battle through binoculars, others had their eyes glued to monitors and radar screens. Still others spoke into microphones, repeating orders to artillery and tank units. Everyone was in a jubilant mood, back-slapping, shaking hands, offering prayers.

Elroy was carried to one side where a small aid station had been set up in a corner that protruded from the bunker like a thumb. The Israelis thought of everything. With their usual efficiency, it was elaborately equipped. Luckily for Elroy, the first casualties from the battle had yet to be brought in. Quickly, a master sergeant stripped the Texan's shirt and examined the wound while two other corpsmen started IVs; one with plasma and the other a solution of dextrose and antibiotics in distilled water. Brent tried to crowd close, to see the wound. A hand to the arm and a private gently but firmly pulled him away, muttering something in Hebrew that Brent did not understand.

"Speak English. Can't you see they're Americans?" the sergeant barked gutturally without turning from the patient.

Obviously confused, the private remained silent, but a corporal spoke in the coarse yet clear English Brent had found commonplace, "Respectfully, Sir, this is no place for you. Please stay out of our way if you want your friend to live."

"I understand. Sorry."

"We understand, too, Sir."

Pushing his helmet up, Brent rubbed both his temples hard. He had never felt so frustrated, so helpless. However, he was astounded and reassured by the medical knowledge of the corpsmen. He had heard they were the best trained in the world and now he believed it.

The master sergeant muttered, "A single round entered here, low, broke a rib or two, nicked the sternum and it looks like it punctured the upper lobe of his left lung when it exited."

"Bleeding?" the corporal asked.

"Not too bad. It doesn't look arterial."

"Good. Thank God we got one break." He handed the sergeant a stack of sterile pads and the sergeant doused the wounds with disinfectant and then tightly bound the pads over them.

"That should hold it," the sergeant said. He turned to Brent, "He'll be evacuated in the first medivac chopper. He's got to have surgery immediately."

"I understand." And then goaded by the devils of doubt, impatience and fear, "What are his chances?"

Coming erect, the sergeant shrugged and turned his palms upward. "Can't say, Sir. Sorry."

Abruptly, through the fading sounds of battle, Brent heard the whirling, thump, thumping sound of a descending helicopter.

"That's it," the sergeant said. "Put him on the stretcher."

Quickly, Elroy was lifted to a stretcher. The sergeant handed Brent one of Elroy's IVs. "Here, Sir. You can help." he said, smiling for the first time.

With Brent carrying an IV on one side and the private holding the other, Elroy was carried to the waiting helicopter.

Chapter XXII

Brent could not drive directly from Subieta Ridge to the Mordecai Military Hospital in Tel Aviv where Elroy had been flown. Instead, he had to report first to I.D.F. Headquarters in Jerusalem, make a report, both written and oral, make a copy for N.I.C. and then request permission to visit his wounded comrade. For some unknown reason, a typical military tangle of snarled red tape delayed him an hour more. However, he was able to phone to discover Elroy was still in surgery. And the operator was harried and abrupt. Wounded were pouring in. He slammed the receiver down in disgust. Finally, he was handed three-day leave papers and a chit for a Jeep Cherokee.

Rushing to the motor pool, he was forced to wait again. He fidgeted and cursed in frustration. "Typical goddamned army, everyone's goddamned army. Hurry and wait." He phoned the BOQ at Zod and asked for Lieutenant Devora Hacohen. More frustration. "Sorry, she drove to Rehovot this morning."

"She went home?"

"She requested the pass for personal business."

"When is she due back?"

There was a pause. "Tomorrow morning at 0800."

Brent phoned Devora's number but there was no answer. He slammed the receiver down.

Finally, his Jeep was ready and he sped off for Tel Aviv. Except for ambulances and military traffic, Route 1 was almost barren of vehicles. Brent made good time, arriving at the hospital in less than an hour. Helicopters were landing and taking off, ambulances unloading. Wounded swathed in field dressings were being carried in. Some had splinted legs and arms. Others did not have legs or arms.

It was like a Tower of Babel, voices rising and clashing in a variety of languages. However, English seemed dominant. Brent had heard the majority of the professional staff was made up of foreign volunteers. Apparently, most of them were from America.

Bounding up the wide stairs of the entrance, he paused at the main desk long enough to learn Elroy's room number, 223, and then he ignored the bank of elevators and dashed up a single flight of stairs to the second floor.

The hall was crowded with hurrying doctors, nurses, inert forms on gurneys—some being pushed by attendants, others pushed against the walls. He jumped aside as a big nurse's aide bulldozed a cart loaded with medications down the middle of the hall. There was no attempt to avoid him or anyone else. Muttering to himself, he stepped close to the wall without breaking stride. He strode past the nurses station where two nurses were working on records and medications. A third was studying x-rays. He headed for Elroy's room.

But before he could enter, a nurse halted him with a,

"Sir, please, Sir." There was a distinct New York flavor to her diction. Probably the Bronx.

Quickly, she overtook him and stood in front of him. She was a lieutenant, beautiful, with blond hair tucked up under her cap. Every plane and curve of her sleek, trim body were accented by a white uniform which fit disturbingly tight. Large blue–green eyes looked him up and down from dirty combat boots to tangled hair peeking out around his wrinkled field cap. She was striking, arresting, and very sexy. Her name tag read "Lt. P. Jacoby."

For the first time, Brent felt self–conscious about his filthy desert fatigues, of being unkempt, unshaven and unwashed. He said brusquely, "Commander Ross to see Lieutenant Elroy Rubin in Room 223." He made a move to step around her.

She blocked him. "Please, Commander Ross—ah, you're the Yankee Samurai."

"Yes, yes. They call me that," he answered impatiently.

Her professionalism returned, "Lieutenant Rubin has three broken ribs, a punctured lung, and has lost a lot of blood. A single round from a AK–47."

"I know that. What's his condition?"

"Critical. He's in our ICU unit."

Brent sighed. "May I see him?"

"He's unconscious."

"Oh, Lord."

"Oh, no, Commander. We had to take him out of the Recovery Room sooner than usual. It's still the effects of the anesthetic. It'll wear off. We're getting a big case load from the Battle of Zabib Pass."

"You've already given it a name."

"Yes. We have a lot of battles, a lot of names, a lot of

casualties." She gestured, "Please, just stay a few minutes."

"Thank you."

Brent walked down the hall and entered the room. There were four beds in the room, two near the door and two flanking the room's single window. Against one wall, three attendants sat behind a long desk, watching telemetry monitors, making notations and studying charts. Three of the beds were occupied.

A dark graying woman with fatigued rimmed eyes looked up. She appeared to be an Ethiopian. "Commander Ross to see Lieutenant Rubin," he said.

Silently, she nodded at one of the figures next to the window. There were IV tubes in both arms and monitors above the bed showed heart rate and blood pressure. A third tube snaked out from the patient's chest and drained reddish fluid into a plastic container on the floor. Brent walked to the bed and pulled a chair close to his friend. He leaned close. He wanted to hear Elroy breathe. Regular and steady, it was a very satisfying sound.

Brent attracted one of the attendants with a hushed, "Miss!"

The dark woman looked up expectantly. Brent pointed at the tube projecting from Elroy's chest. She spoke in a peculiar dialect, good English but hesitant with a distinct Italian inflection, "Ah, that tube pleura–vacs drainage from his left lung. Standard after—ah, lung surgery. Fluids form and they must be removed or infection can develop very easily."

"Color?"

She seemed to hedge, or she was having trouble forming her English sentences, "Ah, good enough. Does not

343

show much infection." She returned to her work, indicating the conversation was over. Brent did not feel reassured.

Brent studied the Texan's face. It was gray, like a dying man's. At that moment, a new patient was wheeled into the room by a pair of elderly men. Two of the attendants quickly moved to the new arrival and helped to lift him from the gurney to the bed. There was a lot of talking and orders given and obeyed as the patient was hooked up to the IVs and monitors. Brent winced as he watched a catheter inserted.

Although he knew Elroy could not hear, Brent whispered into his ear, "Sorry, ol' saddle buddy. I got you into this. Shouldn't have dragged you along. Played the great samurai—the big hero myself." He pounded his head with his fists. "Damn! Damn! Fuckin' stupid hypocrite!"

A bare whisper from the inert form shocked him. "You said something, Elroy?"

"Closer. Closer, Brent."

Brent leaned over the wounded man, ear close to his mouth. He steeled himself. These might be the last words of a dying man, words to be burned into his memory for the rest of his life, words he would repeat to Elroy's grieving loved ones back in Texas. Elroy's voice was weak but clear, "You're as full o' shit as a Christmas goose, ol' saddle buddy an' you smell bad like a hog waller."

Laughing uproariously, Brent turned three disapproving faces his way. Quickly he silenced himself and muttered an apology.

Lieutenant Jacoby entered, glanced at Elroy's charts and monitors and then moved close to the bed, opposite

Brent. Looking down at Elroy, she put a hand on his forehead. "How's my boy doing?"

The touch seemed to give him new strength, his cheeks even gaining color. "As rambunctious as a horny polecat. What're you doing this evenin'? "

She smiled down at him. "Busy tonight, but I'll put you on my calendar for next month."

"The whole month."

"We'll see," she laughed. She turned to Brent. "Remarkable recovery. Very strong man."

"You ain't seen nothin' yet, honey."

Chuckling, she left the room.

Elroy gestured with his head and Brent leaned close. The Texan seemed disturbed. "They're pouring' all kinds o' shit into me."

"Dextrose, antibiotics, distilled water."

"I'm a'needin' sumpin' else."

"What?"

"When that slick filly, ah . . ."

"Lieutenant Jacoby?"

"Yeah, Lieutenant Jacoby. When she done leaned over me and put a hand to me, my ol' twang didn't even stir. Jus' like a dead snake."

Brent snickered. "What do you expect, you're wounded."

"That don't make no never mind. It quit on me, Brent, just plain and simple quit. First time in my life. Should'a been up there like a flag pole holdin' up that sheet."

"Ready to fly?"

"Yeah, that's keerect. Ready to fly."

"Give yourself time, ol' buddy. Give yourself time."

"Time to leave, Commander," an attendant said.

Rising, Brent took his friend's hand. "See you tomorrow."

"Bring me sumpin'."

"What do you want?"

"Oysters, lots of 'em."

Brent took the elevator down. Nurse Jacoby was also on the crowded elevator. She stepped off with him and he walked at her side. The emotional let down that strikes all men after combat, the wounding of Elroy, and the sheer physical over–exertion of the past sixteen hours, all caught up with Brent. His legs and back ached and he took each step with an effort. He needed a pick–up. "Coffee?" he asked the nurse.

"I'd love to, but I can't, Commander. I've got to report to the Emergency Room. My duty starts there in a few minutes.

"My name is Brent. May I walk with you, then?"

"Of course, and my name is Pam."

"Pam for Pamela."

"Yes."

"You're from The Bronx."

"Passaic, New Jersey."

"Oh."

They entered the main lobby, a huge rotunda–like room with hard plastered walls that echoed sound like mirrors reflecting light. Pam headed for a hallway on the far side.

Suddenly, Brent felt his spirits rise and some of the aching lessened. "Lieutenant Rubin seems to be pulling out of it very well?" he said, probing.

"Yes. The aid station gave him excellent care and he has a good attitude."

"You stimulate him."

She chuckled. "It helps. He has a goal, an ambition that drives him."

He looked her up and down and laughed. "I can understand."

She reddened. "That isn't what I meant. He has a strong spirit, a drive to recover."

"Of course. Sorry."

A high voice shouting, "Pam! Pam Jacoby!" halted them. Brent stared curiously as a thin, harried–looking woman who could have been 25 or 45 rushed up.

"Mildred," Nurse Jacoby said, stopping and embracing the newcomer. Pam turned to Brent and explained, "Mildred and I graduated from nurse's training together back in the States. She worked here until last month when she had her baby. She smiled, "How is little Yitzhak?"

"Fine. Fine." Mildred brushed some stray strands of hair from her shiny forehead. She was obviously distraught. "I hear there's been a terrible battle in the Negev. The tv calls it the Battle of Zabib Pass."

"Yes."

"I can't get any information from I.D.F. They're stupid mules. Have any—ah, any wounded from Yaakov's company been brought here? Sometimes, you hear more from them than the high command and sooner. They can talk a lot when they come out of sedation. I know."

"Yaakov. Captain Yaakov Shapiro?" Brent asked.

"You know him?"

"That's right. I was an observer with *Aleph* Company."

"That's my husband's company. Yaakov Shapiro is my

347

husband." Brent flinched at her use of the present tense. There weren't many survivors in that hell. Then the PA system blared out a call for Nurse Jacoby to report to the Emergency Room. With hurried apologies, Pam disappeared into the crowd.

"Please tell me, tell me what you know," Mildred said desperately.

Brent gestured to a row of chairs and they seated themselves side by side. "I don't know much."

"But you were there." She clutched his arm with claw-like hands. "Is my husband alive? I haven't heard a thing."

Brent answered honestly, describing what he had seen, emphasizing the chaos and confusion of a running tank battle, the racing Jeep, the impossibility of telling who was dead and who was alive. "I honestly can't answer you."

"You won't."

"Not true. I just don't know and you won't really have an accurate count of the casualties for days—maybe weeks. He could even be a prisoner."

"Oh, no."

"There's a worse option."

She narrowed her eyes and the timbre of her voice took on a harsh edge. "You're the Yankee Samurai."

"Yes."

"Yaakov told me about you. He didn't want you along."

"I know. It was my duty."

"Ha! Duty. Don't give me that crap."

"I'm not giving you anything."

"Yaakov doesn't like you, you know."

"I was quite aware of that."

"And you went along anyway, to learn something."

"Yes."

"And what did you learn, Commander Ross?" she asked, voice dripping with sarcasm.

Brent felt anger rising. Quelling it, he sighed, scratched the back of his neck and felt control return before he spoke. "I learned he should have warmed his tanks up periodically. I put it into my report."

"What do you mean?"

"He should've kept his engines and electronics gear in a better state of readiness."

"You're a sailor. What do you know?"

"I know it took *Aleph* Company two minutes and forty seconds to come to battle-readiness. It cost them their range advantage."

"Then you think my husband is incompetent?"

"I didn't say that. He was probably following SOP."

"Standard Operating Procedures?"

"Yes, Mrs. Shapiro. And he was a good leader—a very good leader. His men respected him."

She rose. "I must leave, Commander."

He stood close to her. "I'm truly sorry, Mrs. Shapiro. I know you're going through a personal hell. I didn't mean to hurt you."

"You were honest. That's what I wanted, that's what I asked for."

She turned on her heel and walked toward the elevators. Brent watched her for a moment and then walked to a long bank of telephones. He must call Devora. Quickly, he punched out her number. No answer. Muttering oaths, he headed for the exit. To hell with the coffee.

Chapter XXIII

It was late afternoon when Brent arrived in Rehovot. The sky had grayed and a chill wind had sprung up. He pulled a lined khaki field jacket over his fatigues. Parking in front of Devora's house, he felt suddenly enervated, walking with long sure strides to the front door. It was very quiet. He knocked, but there was no answer. He knocked again, louder. Still, nothing stirred except a dog in the next yard.

Barking a challenge, a big Labrador jumped up, putting his two front paws near the top of the ivy covered fence separating the houses and glared at Brent with brown menacing eyes. "Easy, old boy," Brent soothed. "I come as a friend." The dog sniffed and growled a few times, lost interest, and dropped out of sight.

Then Brent remembered the key under the pot. He began to reach for it when he was suddenly struck with a pang of hunger. He would get a bite and a cup of coffee at a neighborhood restaurant and return. Surely Devora was nearby, probably shopping. She would have to return soon. He was desperate to see her, hold her, hear her voice, her laugh. In any event, he had the time and would wait for her. He could always use the key.

He was just turning to leave when he heard a faint rush of water. Was it a faucet in the yard? A neighbor watering? Then he realized the sound was coming from the house. He leaned close to the door and listened. Water. No doubt about it. The shower. She was taking a shower. With her cap pulled down and all those jets rushing she couldn't hear anything. Visions of what had happened in that shower came back and set a fire stirring deep down. Now he felt impatience. Then a clever thought. He would surprise her.

The key was precisely where he expected to find it. Very quietly he inserted it, opened the door, replaced the key, and closed the door behind him. When he entered the living room, all was quiet except for the roar of rushing water. Smiling, he quietly entered the hall and walked toward the bathroom. He would shock her. Jump in the shower with her, clothes and all. He was filthy anyway.

The door to the bathroom was ajar. A slight shove and it swung open. He stopped, frozen in his tracks, wrenched by horror and disbelief. The shower door was wide open. He saw her. Nude. Hanging from the ceiling jet by looped wire. Buffeted by the power of the jets, she was turning slowly. As if she were still drawn to him even in death, her eyes lingered on him, enormous, inky black, bulging, whites splotched red and purple by burst blood vessels. Her lips were swollen sausages, tongue blue and protruding through broken teeth like a half-eaten snake. Arms and legs hung limp, stomach bruised and bulging. And there were more bruises on her face, torso, thighs. One breast had been torn and hung down over itself, covering the nipple as if it had been bitten by a ravening beast. And she was bleeding, the oozing blood washed away in crimson streams as fast as it ran from her neck where the wire bit in, mouth, breast, groin. A fresh kill.

A nightmare. That was it. This couldn't be happening. Not Devora. Not after Ruth. Not both of them. Please, dear God. But it was real and he knew it. What kind of devil tracked him? What kind of monster could do this? His impulse was to rush in. Cut her down. Cradle her in his arms. Close those terrible eyes.

"Devora! No! No!" he screamed in agony. He started toward her but stopped abruptly. The sixth sense came into play again. The energy of the killer. He could feel it. There was the tingling, the feeling that hairs on the back of his neck were stiffening. The hollow sickness in the depths of his guts. And there was a rustling behind him. Not footfalls, more like the flittering drift of a beast stalking through foliage.

Pulling the Beretta from its holster, he whirled just in time to meet the impact of a fist the size of a roast and as hard as a cement block. The fist knocked the pistol out of his hand and back into the bathroom. Instinctively, Brent ducked, the second blow whistling over his head. Goaded by an insane fury and with adrenaline coursing through his veins, he whipped out two quick blows to the attacker's stomach. Grunting, the man fell back, but surprisingly lashed back with a foot, catching Brent in the stomach. Pain shot around his torso in burning circles and breath exploded from his lungs. He stood for a moment, gasping, recovering.

Obviously feeling the power of Brent's punches, the killer stood a few feet down the hall, panting, staring with the pitiless blue eyes of the predator. Brent had expected a big blond man, with a long scar on his right cheek. The man was young and big—as big as Brent. Shirtless and wet, his body was bulky but muscular. His arms were those of a body builder, bulging biceps, triceps and forearms and he carried no fat on his belly or flanks. It was a body that had been developed and honed by hard exercise. But this man was dark, or streaked dark with black hair and no scar. Or was there a scar?

"The mighty Yankee Samurai," the killer said mockingly. "I've been looking forward to this meeting." Brent remained silent as the man continued to gloat, "Your Jewesses were good fucks. That Ruth Moskowitz was one helluva piece. Ah, got a little sand in it, but it was great pussy." He pursed his lips, kissed his bunched fingers and threw away a kiss like a French waiter describing and entree, "And your Devora—ooh, la, la, *fantastique* in the shower. When I got off, I damn near bit her tit off." His sigh was that of a young boy who had been deprived of a piece of candy. "I'll miss her, yes indeed, I'll miss her."

In one quick motion, he swept a black toupee from his head revealing a close-cropped head of blond hair. Then he rubbed his right cheek with the toupee. A long scar became visible. "Call me Lieutenant Barauch Marzel, aka Private First Class Shlomo Granit, aka Paul Marcel, aka John Higginbotham and more, if you like."

The man was trying to fan Brent's fury, goad him into an imprudent charge. He was good with his feet. Charged by the primal survival instinct, Brent managed to control himself, studying his adversary with a clarity of years of combat, stress that had demanded clear-headed action in the most horrifying circumstances. Every sense was fine—

tuned, hearing acute, vision crystalline. Even his peripheral vision seemed to expand. And Devora was behind him. She was dead. There was nothing he could do for her. Nothing except avenge her. But he would do it on his terms. With his fists, his nails, his teeth. The man had no gun. He had seen a holstered pistol hanging in the bathroom. The assassin had made that one mistake.

With dazzling speed, the killer leaped forward, whirling, foot shooting out toward Brent's head. Ducking and stepping to the side, Brent caught him on the back of the neck with a judo chop and snapped a round-house punch into the ribs with his left. He could feel ribs bend, hear the man's breath explode.

The assassin bounced off the wall, spun and faced him, rubbing his neck. The two adversaries had actually traded places. Now Brent could see Devora's body. She was staring at him. He felt control slipping like a flood bursting a levy, but choked back the rage, bridled the animal. His temper could kill him. He had been warned of this time and again. He stared into the murderer's eyes, yet managed to watch his feet. The feet were the key. A shift of balance was seen there first.

"Very good," the man taunted, apparently not seriously injured. "This will be interesting. Yes, indeed, very interesting."

Brent broke his silence, voice icy calm like the flat sea of the doldrums, "This time, you're not fighting a woman." And then he did his own taunting, "If you didn't rape them, you'd still be a virgin, making love to your fist. What a big stud, you can't get a piece of ass without killing somebody for it."

With a snarl, the man charged, lashing out with both

354

fists. A glancing blow to the head sent Brent reeling backwards, fists and arms raised, warding off the punches. Another hard left broke through, catching Brent in the ribs. Pain shot through his body, startling in its power. He groaned, ducking weaving, giving ground into the living room. Here there was more room.

Brent danced to the side as if continuing his retreat and the murderer took the bait. A two–punch combination caught the killer in the eye and full in the mouth. His head snapped back, spittle and blood flew, water sprayed from his hair. He staggered away. Brent pressed his advantage. With a single hand, the man spun off an end table, sending a lamp flying to shatter against a wall and turned completely around, bringing a leg up.

The kick caught Brent on the upper thigh of the left leg. He staggered backwards, reeling. An explosion of white–hot pain shot all the way up into his chest. He used the couch to lever himself up and regain his balance. Grinning through a battered mouth that looked like he had chewed a mouthful of cherries, the killer advanced. But using the couch and his good leg, Brent launched himself into a counter–punch, hooking with his right under the ribs. Something cracked. A howl of pure agony and the killer staggered back, smashing the end table and crashing to the floor.

Brent was on him, reaching for his neck. He would strangle him. Bite his windpipe. Gouge his eyes out. Choke the life out of him the way he killed Ruth and Devora. But the man was far from finished. He punched back. Clawed at Brent's eyes. Tore open Brent's forehead with long nails. The American cried out, rolled away, blood singing in his ears. But the killer rolled with him.

355

Brent smashed his forehead down on the man's nose and heard it crack. But he dug his teeth into the maxillary nerves of Brent's cheek and drew blood before Brent could pull away.

With blood splattered over both of them, they screamed into each others faces. Punched short ineffective punches. Kicked. Rolled into the television stand and knocked a 25-inch General Electric set to the floor.

Brent brought a knee up into the groin and pushed away as the killer grunted and weakened momentarily. With his free hand, Brent delivered a judo chop to the back of the man's neck, then reached around his head and grasped his chin and pulled, turning his head and neck until he heard cartilage cracking. He would tear his head off. Throw it into the shower with Devora. Frantically, the killer clawed at Brent's hand to break the grip before his neck broke.

Brent increased the pressure, could see the man's tongue protruding, eyes bulging. He had him at last. But the killer was digging his nails into Brent's arm, kicking him in the groin. Then with unbelievable power, he kicked, broke the grip and rolled away.

Brent leaped to his feet, the assassin rising behind him, but slowly. They stared at each other, the murderer rubbing his neck, grimacing, wiping blood from his chin, Brent wiping it from his eyes and cheek. The murderer's neck had been stretched nearly to the point of breaking and his ribs had been punished. One or more broken. Brent was sure of that.

"You're a tough motherfucker," the man wheezed.

For a long moment both men stood silently, measuring each other. The first burst of combat had tired them both.

And they were both hurt. Breathing like a bellows, sweating, bleeding from the corner of his right eye, nose, mouth, the killer looked like a bull maddened by picadores, gathering itself for the charge. His broad shoulders were hunched, and his hands were fisted at his sides. Brent was sure he wanted to charge, destroy everything in his path. But he had been hurt. Perhaps, now, he would use his cunning, wait for an opportunity. One thing was obvious: only one of them would leave the house alive.

Brent looked into the wide blue eyes—eyes of frozen glass. He seemed to see through them into an inferno of insanity. Sweat and blood mixed with water streamed down his face. His swollen lips worked against each other like two loathsome worms, twisting, pouting, grimacing so that broken teeth were exposed, blood and saliva drooling. He sneered, smiled, scowled. Then he giggled, the sound of a lunatic, of a man so thoroughly possessed by madness he was completely removed from reality. And his strength and durability were beyond belief. Maybe he was on LSD. What could account for the power, the ability to absorb punishment and keep on coming? He should have been down and finished long ago.

The cunning was forgotten and the bull rush came. Brent tried to step aside but a big fist caught him on the left ear and sent him tumbling over the couch and toppling it with him. With a shout of triumph, the killer leaped over the couch and landed flat on his stomach and skidded into the wall. Brent had rolled to the side and, bracing himself on the wall, came to his feet. His ear rang, and pain shot on hot needles across his skull. How do you fight a man like this? He seemed indestructible. Immune to pain.

The killer picked up a coffee table by a leg and swung it at Brent's head. Brent leaped away and staggered to the center of the room. Still clutching the table, the man advanced. Another swing and this time Brent stepped inside of the swing and drove a fist into the broken rib. A howl of pain and the table flew across the room, smashed into the wall and fell to the floor, broken and splintered. Brent drew back and lashed out again with a three-punch combination. He had made a mistake. The first landed on the man's ear, but then, a quick twist and a heel caught Brent squarely on the breastbone like a sledgehammer. With the air knocked out of him, Brent sailed backwards and crashed into the overturned couch. His head spun and his vision blurred. With his legs drawn up into a fetal position and gasping and wheezing as if he had been garroted, he appeared to be finished.

Smirking, the man hulked over him. Took the bait. "Gunna wire you, string you up next to your Jewess. You'll make a lovely couple. And it'll be a clean death." He threw his head back and laughed uproariously. He reached down for Brent, grabbed his hair with one hand, his throat with the other.

Brent came off the floor like an uncoiled spring, again driving a fist into the broken rib. This time his fist sank further in than it should, into something soft and spongy. More than one rib was broken. The killer shrieked, spun away, grabbing his side. Brent followed, punching to the body, trying for the wound. Still screaming, the assassin whirled and tripped Brent, sending him to the floor again. He picked up the broken television and hurled it at the American. The set hit Brent on the left shoulder and the tube imploded against his head. He was cut. Bad. He could feel blood streaming down his face, and his shoulder felt broken.

The dog next door began to bark furiously and then there were shouts outside in Hebrew and English. "Devora! Devora! What's going on?" There was pounding, but no one entered. Then Brent realized the door must have locked behind him. Both men ignored the shouts. The blood lust was on them both. One would be dead before this was over.

The killer advanced cautiously. He had been fooled before. It would not happen again. His breath came in very short gasps, blood streamed from his face wounds, and he was slightly hunched by the pain of broken ribs. Brent marvelled. An ordinary man would have been disabled by now. But not this psychopath.

Holding his left low to protect his ribs, the killer lashed out with his right. A classic opening and Brent leaped to grab it. He drove from the balls of his feet, for once able to gather all of his leg power behind his punches. His right fist impacted the man's cheek and Brent heard bone break with the popping sound of a bitten apple. His left punched through the lowered hand and cracked into the broken ribs.

Screaming, the man stumbled back to the entry, grabbed a vase and bounced it off Brent's fists onto his skull where it broke into fragments, adding more deep cuts. Stunned, Brent staggered backwards. Almost doubled over, the hulking killer moved forward. Brent grabbed a brass floor lamp high, just under the light bulbs.

"Chicken shit. I'm going to stomp you to death and then the wire."

"I'm going to de—nut you with this, you stupid shit," Brent said, raising the lamp.

"Try it asshole."

"Devora! Devora!" came from the outside. Several voices. Two seemed familiar. And Brent could hear a crowd now. "The police are here. Open up!"

"Fuck 'em!" the killer shouted. Stooping, he picked up a shard of the vase, one end with edges as sharp as a dagger. Holding it in front of him, he advanced. Brent swung. The man leaped and the heavy lamp base missed. Shouting with triumph, he stabbed the broken lamp at Brent like a fencer delivering the *coup de grace* with an epee. Brent jumped to the side, but not before the sharp edge slashed into his arm. Blood spurted from a deep cut. Ignoring his wound, he regained his balance and swung again. This time the heavy brass base caught the killer squarely on the spine, propelling him head—first into the wall, driving his head through the plaster. He rolled to the floor, face up, white powdered plaster coating his face, mixing with the blood . . .

"Devora!" Brent screamed, swinging the lamp like a broad ax and smashing it into the man's face. Bloody mucus and spittle flew and the nostrils were obliterated, upper jaw smashed. There was the sound of a window being broken and then shouts behind him. Brent ignored them. He ignored the blood spurting from his arm, the pain.

"Devora!" and the base tore off the lower jaw and part of the tongue, crushed the trachea and sent teeth and broken bones flying.

"Devora!" the heavy weapon plunged through the

bridge of the nose like paper and into the eye sockets, bursting both eyes like dropped eggs.

"Devora!" And the blow fractured the front of the skull, ripping off a flap of skin and rounded chunk of bone. Yellow–red mashed brains spilled out onto the carpet.

He raised it again. He could not kill him enough.

A rush of bodies knocked him off his feet and bore him to the floor. Suddenly, his strength drained away like air from a punctured balloon. His eyelids became lead, his thigh was burning as if it were seared by a branding iron and he couldn't take a deep breath. As the blackness closed in, he heard someone shout in a crisp British accent, "I say, call an ambulance! Brent's bleeding to death."

"A tourniquet. Quick!" he heard another voice cry out. "I'll use my shirt." Strange. It sounded just like Colonel J.R. Ware.

Then the black wave washed everything away.

Chapter XXIV

The greenish–blue water was curiously hot and murky. Then he saw the monster rising slowly from the shadowy depths. Bigger than a Great White, it looked part reptile, part prehistoric bird of prey. Its scaly, pebbly body was splotched green and brown, long tail thrashing, claws extended with curved talons like daggers. Its massive head was long with cavernous snouts and two black horns that curved like killing blades above its eyes. As it drew closer, Brent could see its glowing yellow eyes on him, gaping jaws, sharp teeth like rows of yellow–stained triangles, whip–like tongue darting out. It almost struck his face. Frantically, Brent thrashed out, trying to swim away, break the surface, run on it, flee. But the water was gelatine, arms lead. He cried out, "No! No!"

The voice drifted through, sweet and feminine, "Easy Commander. Easy."

Now the monster was gone and the water had turned to mist. Devora was there, smiling, arms open for him, walking toward him. "I thought you were dead," he said.

"I'm back, Brent. I love you." As he reached for her,

she vomited blood, her face collapsed like melting wax, and she slowly sank into a squirming heap of corruption.

"Come back, Devora. My God, what have I done?"

The voice again, "It's all right, Commander."

The killer was there. Advancing. Grinning. Holding the shard of vase before him. "I killed you!" Brent cried. "How many times do I have to kill you?"

"Never enough!" He lunged and the point pressed against Brent's chest.

"No! No!"

"Hold him," a deep masculine voice said, in a familiar guttural accent.

"Maybe we should use the straps," the woman said. "He shouldn't be this strong."

Then the light sifted through the mists. A middle-aged man wearing a white smock was leaning over him. He was pressing a stethoscope to Brent's chest. Over his shoulder, a young nurse with big hazel eyes was staring.

"You're a doctor," Brent said.

"Ah, good. You've come out of it." The stethoscope moved twice, the doctor listened and then he straightened.

"Where am I?"

"Rehovot Emergency Hospital. I'm Doctor Jacob Leibowitz and this is Nurse Yael Arad."

"Devora—Devora Hacohen?"

"Dead, I'm sorry."

"The killer?"

"Very dead. You killed him a dozen times over."

"I ache all over."

"You should. You have multiple lacerations and contusions of the scalp, shoulder and left thigh. Most of the rib cartilage on your right side has been badly bruised and you lost enough blood to kill the ordinary man."

"I'm wearing a turban."

"Right. Of bandages. It took over a hundred sutures to close the wounds on your scalp, ear and cheek." Leibowitz turned to Nurse Arad, crisp and business–like, "Maintain an IV rate of 125ccs an hour and continue with the antibiotics, ancef every six hours. He's still running a fever and he's dehydrated."

The nurse scribbled on Brent's chart. She looked up, "Food, Doctor?"

"Not today. I'll prescribe a diet. Try it tomorrow. Let's see if he can keep it down."

Nurse Arad continued with her notes, "And the visitors? The police and a Mossad man are in the waiting room, Doctor."

"I don't give a damn who they are. Not today. I'll tell them to leave, myself."

"Sedative?"

"Yes. Give him dalmane, 30 milligrams. That should give him a good night's sleep. He needs it." He took Brent's chart from the nurse, scanned it quickly, and left.

Nurse Arad turned to a small portable medication cart and returned with a cup of water and a pill. To Brent, she looked like an angel; creamy–white skin, big hazel eyes, delicate features, brown hair streaked with blond swept up under her white cap.

She helped him raise his head and then gave him the pill. He swallowed it in two gulps and said, "Nighty night?"

"Yes. You need rest, if you want to recover." She leaned so close he could feel her breath on his cheek.

"You're a very tough man. You should be dead, Commander."

He smiled. "Sorry. Not time for that now. There's too much to do." He slowly drifted off. This time, there were no nightmares.

When he awoke, the light was very bright. Turning his head, he saw that he was in a ward with three other beds. All were empty. Not like the crowded Mordecai Military Hospital. He wondered about Elroy. Wondered how he was doing with the sexy blond nurse from New Jersey.

Suddenly, he felt a twinging discomfort deep down. Lifting his head despite a sore neck, he saw it. A plastic tube filled with pinkish–yellow fluid snaking out from the sheets groin high and disappearing down toward the floor. A catheter. Damn!

Nurse Yael Arad entered. "How's my boy?"

Brent smiled up at her. The sight of the pert, attractive nurse raised his spirits, put Devora out of his mind for a few moments. "You're from the states?"

"Not really. Got my training in Boston. We talk English around you, Hebrew with the Israelis, Arabic with the Arabs and even a little Spanish and Italian."

Brent waved. "I have a catheter."

"Of course. You were unconscious for two days."

"Two days?"

"You lost a lot of blood, were badly beaten, even had blood in your urine."

Brent turned his lips under and flushed slightly. "Who put it in?"

She laughed, a delightful sound. "I did. Why?"

He sighed. "We're pretty well acquainted, aren't we."

She narrowed the big eyes and smiled slyly. "Yes. I know you very well, Commander."

"Regular or king-size."

"Now, don't be naughty."

"I'm hungry."

"Good . . . Good."

She left and in a moment returned, carrying a tray. Setting it down on the usual sterile white hospital table, she pressed a button, an electric motor buzzed, and the head of the bed came up. Then she lowered the tray on its stand over the patient's waist. Brent looked at the food: orange juice, a small cup of chicken soup, and a single scoop of vanilla ice cream. "Is that it?"

She laughed. "What do you want, chateaubriand? Let's see if you can keep this down."

"If I do and I get stronger and can walk to the head, you'll—ah, I mean someone will take the catheter out?"

She pondered for a moment. "You took several severe blows to the stomach and abdomen. And I told you there's blood in your urine."

"It's clearing up."

"How do you know?"

"I can see it. It's not pink anymore."

"Well, eat your breakfast and if Doctor Leibowitz okays it, we'll remove it."

Brent ate.

The next day a male nurse's aide removed the catheter and then to Brent's joy, the IV was disconnected. Triumphantly, with the aide alongside, Brent walked slowly and carefully to the bathroom. He would have returned feeling very pleased with himself except he dared to look into the mirror hanging over the sink. He found a stranger—a stranger with a head completely swathed in bandages down to his eyebrows, right cheek bandaged, left ear and eye swollen, bruises on what face was visible, even his neck. He walked back to his bed feeling depressed.

Just as he was helped back into his bed, a police officer and a Mossad agent entered. Quickly, they introduced themselves. The policeman, a short heavy-set man of about 40, was Lieutenant Moses Zuker of the Rehovot Police Department. The Mossad agent was Colonel Aharon Barak. Tall and slim, Barak's hair was white, face creased with deep wrinkles. He walked with a slight stoop.

Both men were respectful, solicitous and concerned about Brent's condition. To Brent's relief, they promised to be brief. They sat close to the bed. Prodded gently by their questions, Brent described the incident in detail while the men took notes.

"Is that it?" Brent finally asked.

"Yes, Commander. I have enough," Lieutenant Zuker said. He glanced at the Mossad man. Barak nodded concurrence. Both men began to rise.

I have a question," Brent said. The men stared expectantly. "What do you know about the assassin?"

The Mossad agent pulled a document from an inside pocket, glanced at it, and said, "His name was Paul Andre Marcel."

"Ah, that's where he got the 'Marzel'," Brent said.

"Yes, to him, Israelizing his name that way appealed to his twisted sense of humor," Barak said.

"French?"

"French—Canadian. He was born in Quebec, 30—years old, in and out of mental institutions from the age of twelve. His mother and father were both heroin addicts.

367

His father sold drugs and his mother worked the streets when she wasn't unconscious. She died of AIDS early in the epidemic and the father overdosed when Paul was sixteen. The boy went out of his mind—what mind he had—killed a gas station attendant in a robbery attempt and served only four years because he was a juvenile. He was raped and brutalized in prison and the last vestiges of sanity were pounded out of him. He had a score to settle with the world. Fell in with a cell of terrorists in prison and by the age of 22 he was a prize student at Kadafi's Tinduf camp for terrorists. There, he met Harry Goodenough."

"They became close friends."

Zuker and Barak exchanged a glance. "More than that, they were lovers."

"Of course. That figures."

Barak continued without glancing at the document, "Goodenough was almost ten years older than Marcel, had already made eight or ten kills. He became Marcel's mentor, his role model. Marcel was an excellent student, became an expert with plastiques, especially Semtex, Kalashnikovs, Makarovs, mortars, incendiaries, even flame throwers. He particularly excelled in personal attacks, garroting, strangling, the knife, poisoning—like Goodenough. He loved his work and was one of Kadafi's best students."

Sarcasm crept into the voice, "Commonplace terrorism was not for him. Other people could blow up airliners, throw bombs into crowded restaurants, schools, and night clubs. He watched Goodenough's career with envy—joy. The close-in kill with the hands, especially of women whom he hated. Then when Goodenough was killed by two women, he was devastated. It was natural for

Paul Marcel to adopt his exact modus operandi and continue the horror, exact his vengeance. He could enjoy himself and avenge his lover, too." Barak shifted his weight and said what Brent expected to hear, "DNA and other evidence confirm he was the killer of Ruth Moskowitz, Heron Dempster and the Tokomitsu woman."

"There may be more Goodenoughs and Marcels around."

"True."

"The fight will never end."

"True, Commander, never." The Mossad man said. And then, abruptly, he segued into another topic, "You know Colonel Irving Bernstein?"

"One of my closest friends. We've served together for over a decade."

"You'll be seeing him soon."

"Yes. I should."

"Oh, you will, Commander. Your orders are cut." The man's knowledge did not surprise Brent. Mossad seemed to know everything. He leaned over Brent. "Do me a favor."

"Name it."

"Tell him his old classmate says, *'Mazel tov hazer vatiq'.*"

Brent smiled and said, "Good luck old friend."

"Very good, Commander. We'll make a Jew of you, yet."

Brent rubbed his good cheek gently. "Colonel, you said 'classmate'."

"Correct." Barak pulled up his sleeve, revealing six tattooed blue numbers. "Auschwitz, class of '45."

"The same alma mater," Brent said.

"Right."

"One more thing, Colonel Barak. Do you know anything about Lieutenant Elroy Rubin. He's in the Mordecai Military Hospital."

Barak chuckled. "Yes indeed. I met him last year when he was an aide to Colonel Bernstein. Severely wounded, but he's improving."

"Fast?"

"Too fast for some of the nurses." They all laughed. The two visitors rose. "It's been a pleasure meeting you, Commander." They saluted him and then he grasped their hands in firm handshakes.

As they turned toward the door, Brent said, *"Shalom alekhem,* gentlemen."

"Alekhem shalom." The two men left.

Passing the departing pair, Nurse Arad entered. "You have some more visitors, Commander. Colonel Ware and Lieutenant Burnside. Feel up to it?"

"Are you kidding? Of course."

She motioned at the hall and Colonel James Robert "Bull" Ware his bombardier, Lieutenant Horace Burnside, entered. Each took one side of the bed and each grabbed a hand. "Bull" tried to appear in ebullient spirits, but Brent knew the death of Devora Hacohen had hit him hard, too. "Great to see you, Brent."

"I'm not very pretty."

"You look better than the killer, old boy," Burnside said.

"You stopped me."

"Yes. He was dead enough and blood was spurting out of your arm." Burnside nodded at Ware. "The Colonel put a tourniquet on you, saved your life."

"Thanks. What were you doing at her place?"

"The three of us were going to meet Philipe D'Meziere at Holiday Village near Ashkelon for dinner," Ware said. "The lieutenant and I were to pick up Devora." He stopped abruptly as if her name brought him pain. He seemed suddenly disconsolate. "I shouldn't have let her go." He pounded his head. "My fault." He waved at Brent. "And so is this."

"Nonsense, Colonel," Burnside said. "She bloody well insisted and you had no reason to restrict her to the BOQ. She'd been home on passes before."

"Of course, Colonel," Brent added. "How could you know? How could anyone know? That killer's M.O. should've put him on the other side of the world."

"I know. I know, Brent." The pilot's jaw took a hard set and his eyes avoided the injured man's. "You took a terrible loss, Brent. You were . . . close."

"Yes. She was a great girl."

Ware looked away. "She loved you, Brent."

"I had more luck than I deserved. I never earned her. She was a gift," he said thickly.

The men nodded. No one trusted himself to look into another man's eyes. Clearing his throat, Brent said, "How's *Shady Lady?* Or is that classified?"

"No," the colonel answered. "She needs a new engine and we're waiting for Pratt and Whitney to deliver it."

"Rosencrance and his buddies poked a few holes into her."

Ware chuckled. "The last count 179."

"And a lost engine and ball turret."

"Right."

"You won't be flying for a few weeks."

"Correct. Maybe months. *Shady Lady* was almost unsalvageable. But those 24s are a tough breed. She'll punch back soon."

"Wish I could go. We could make it for Devora."

"Christ yes," the pilot agreed. "We could use you, Brent."

"I'll second that, old boy," Horace Burnside added.

The pilot leaned close, almost whispering, "Horace has a new toy. The next time we call on our Arab friends, he won't miss, guaranteed hits."

Brent chuckled. "Laser fire control—laser bomb sight. Keep the cross hairs on the target and you can't miss."

The two flyers looked at each other in surprise. "How did you know?"

"Just saw laser sights used by tanks in the Negev. First round hits. You won't surprise the Arabs. You won't surprise anyone, Colonel."

"You don't know our objective?"

Brent laughed. "No, Colonel."

The two airmen smiled and sat back. Ware suddenly became solemn. "Ah, Brent. We—all of us know the next mission will be very hazardous." Brent looked expectantly. "We wrote letters. Devora wrote three." He pulled a sealed envelope from an inside pocket and handed it to Brent. "Commander Brent Ross," was neatly typed across the front. "She left this for you."

Brent took the envelope, stared at it for a moment. Sighed.

"We'll leave."

He looked at the grim faces—faces of men with whom he had shared the most hideous dangers, suffered crippling, heart-breaking losses. He felt the bond tug, the commonality like being roped together. He wanted them to stay, yet he wanted to be alone when he read the letter. He was afraid he would embarrass himself. He nodded. "All right. Thanks. Come back, Please."

"We will." The aviators stood, held a smart salute for a moment, and left.

Just as the visitors left, an attendant entered and busied herself checking the telemetry equipment at one of the empty beds. Apparently, Brent would soon have a roommate. Watching the attendant and hoping she would leave, Brent toyed with the envelope. Finally, when the girl began to change the bedclothes he could no longer restrain himself. He opened the envelope. The letter was handwritten.

My Darling:

You know I'm gone. I had to tell you what you mean to me, what you are. Please forgive my doggerel, but it is the only way I can tell you how I feel about you—the day on the beach, those priceless moments together.

In Life and Death

A special day
Honed for lovers
With surf and sun
Caressing the sand
And clouds
Still unknown
We lay together
And loved again and again
Passion, heat, rapture
You knew where I was empty

You filled me
Sometimes with cool nectar
Sometimes with flowing lava
I love you beyond words
Beyond reason
Beyond conscious thought
Do not guard my tomb and mourn
There I am not
Look to your side
And you will find me.
With love eternal,
Devora

Brent put a clenched fist to his lips, but a small choking sound escaped him. From the corner of his eye he saw the attendant's curious look. Samurai did not cry. Not under any circumstances. Brent gathered a knot of bedclothes and bit down hard.

The attendant watched the still figure for a moment, and returned to her work.

Chapter XXV

Within two weeks Brent was able to return to his apartment in the Hilton. His left leg was still sore and the short stubble of hair failed to hide the new scars on his head. The swelling and bruises on his face had almost disappeared, though, his right cheek was still tender and it appeared he would have a scar where Paul Marcel had bitten him. He was able to rent a Chevrolet Caprice with an automatic transmission and visited Elroy Rubin almost daily.

Rubin had improved steadily and had been moved to a rehabilitation center near the Mordecai Hospital. "That Nurse Jacoby won't have no truck with me," he complained. But Brent noticed the Texan had a giggly young nurse's aide nearby whenever he called. "Slick little filly," Elroy commented one afternoon, watching the large rounded buttocks rotate by. "May hog tie an' put my brand on her, yet."

"You ain't just whistlin' in Dixie, are you ol' buddy?" Brent had kidded.

"You can be sure as shootin' 'bout that, ol' saddle

buddy." Watching the girl leave the room, Elroy sighed, "Put a touch o' spur to that an' that'll be one mean bronc to bust."

"Sho' 'nuff."

Then Elroy inquired about Brent's orders. Brent explained he was to return to Japan as soon as physically able and whenever a Swissair flight was available. An agreement had been reached between the Arabs and the Swiss guaranteeing the safety of Swissair. However, the flights were scarce, and bookings difficult even with the persuasive powers of Mossad. Obstinate and independent, the Swiss dictated, accepted no coercion.

With their usual caution, Mossad and NIC provided Brent with a fictitious identity: Anthony Greenwood, an American commodities broker representing the International Commodities Marketing Corporation. He was furnished a complete set of identity papers; passport, Social Security card, driver's license, credit cards, membership cards in three exclusive country clubs, even snapshots of his wife and two children who lived in Chicago.

Finally, after a six-week wait, he was booked aboard a Swissair flight to London. From there he would be flown by United Air Lines to New York and then to San Francisco. There a Japan Air Lines flight would fly him across the Pacific, stopping only at Hawaii. At last, he would see his old comrades: Admiral Fujita, Rear Admiral Whitehead, Colonel Bernstein, Yoshi Matsuhara, Nobomitsu Atsumi, and so many more. He realized he was homesick. *Yonaga* was his home. Truly, the only home he knew.

And he was needed. The Arab battle group had docked in Surabaya, fueling, refitting, preparing for battle. Fujita was doing the same with his forces at Yokosuka. A showdown was due, the final roll of the dice. He had to be there. Fight at the sides of his comrades, share their victory, or die with them. That was how it had to be.

Elroy was outraged when Brent announced he was leaving. "You cain't whup no one, without this here fastest gun along."

"You aren't ready, ol' buddy," Brent countered. "The doctor said it would be another month or two for you."

"That tin horn don't know his ass from hog shit."

Brent saw "Bull" Ware and his crew for the last time in the cavernous hangar where *Shady Lady* was being repaired. Standing next to the bomber with four young replacements, they all had a drink together. Oren Smadja, Roland "Rollie" Knudsen, and Devora Hacohen were saluted, toasted, and honored with prayers.

The flight back to Japan was long, arduous and boring. Brent, flying first class, kept to himself. Memories of Devora kept crowding back and he tried to banish them by reading, drinking, concentrating on the cloud formations, the sea, the land. But nothing worked. Finally, he was overjoyed when the pilot announced their imminent arrival at Tokyo International Airport.

He was met by Commander Yoshi Matsuhara and four seaman guards. The two saluted and clasped each other. Quickly, Brent found a men's room and changed into his Number One Blues. Proudly, he buckled on the *Konoye* sword and squared his cap. He would return to *Yonaga* as the sailor, the warrior, not the bedraggled civilian. Civilian clothes made him feel weak and ineffective.

Then with Yoshi at his side he walked to the exit. Chatting happily like two old school chums at a class reunion, the pair was driven to *Yonaga* in a black Cadillac limousine. A jeep with four seaman guards led, and another Jeep followed.

"You had a tough fight," Yoshi said, surveying Brent's healing wounds from the rich upholstery of the American car.

"The son–of–a–bitch almost bit my cheek off." He described Devora's death, the terrible fight to the death with Paul Andre Marcel.

"He was Harry Goodenough's protege."

"Yes." Brent became very solemn. "Now we are very much alike, Yoshi–san."

"What do you mean, Brent–san?"

"A curse, foul *kamis* ride on our backs. We bring murder with us."

The aviator sighed, a long tired sound. "Tomoko and your Ruth—ah . . ."

"Moskowitz and Devora Hacohen."

"What kind of men are these, Brent–san, who would kill women?"

"Animals. Beasts of prey."

"You squashed one."

"They stopped me." He felt suddenly overcome by latent rage, control vanished, "I wanted to tear off his head, rip his neck open with my teeth, tear him open, pull out his guts . . ."

"Brent–san!" Yoshi cried out in alarm, grabbing his friend's arm, "It's all right. He's dead. Dead."

"Not enough. Not enough."

Rear Admiral Whitehead, Colonel Irving Bernstein, Captain Mitake Arai, Lieutenant Commander Nobomitsu Atsumi, Flying Officer Claude Hooperman, Pilot Officer Elwyn York, Commander Steve Elkins and a dozen others were waiting for Brent on the quarter deck. He was saluted, hugged, slapped on the back, cheered. *"Banzai* Commander Ross," a group of enlisted men chanted.

Overwhelmed by the warmth of the welcome, Brent's controlled demeanor returned and he basked in the warm glow of the unabashed admiration and affection. These were his shipmates. These were the men who would live or die with him—for him.

"You look like you fell into a threshing machine," Whitehead laughed, pounding Brent's back.

"You should see the threshing machine," Brent quipped back.

Elwyn York shouted over the din, "Bugger all, in 'ears you 'ad a bloody 'ard slog, Commander."

Hooperman added, "By Jove, old boy, bit of a tough go, right? Smashing having you back."

"Right—oh and quite right," Brent laughed back in his crispest British accent.

Then the officer of the deck interrupted, "The admiral wants you to report to his cabin immediately, Commander Ross," he said.

"Very well." Brent, surrounded by his friends, walked to the elevator.

The old admiral was seated in his usual place behind his desk. He was alone, not even the old scribe, Commander Hakuseki Katsube, was there. Like most very old people, Fujita had been so ravaged by the years, the passage of more time did little to alter his appearance. But he did seem smaller to Brent, back not quite as erect. "You conducted yourself well, Brent–san," the old man said. "You brought great honor to *Yonaga* and pride to me."

"Thank you, Sir. You are very kind," Brent said from his chair.

"I understand you found a failing in the Israeli armor. A warm–up time."

"You read my report, Sir?"

"Of course."

"It cost them dearly, Admiral. And my replacement, the exchange officer, Captain Uri Afek."

The mask of wrinkles pulled up slightly into a hint of a grin. "He spent the entire battle in the conning tower."

"Behind twelve inches of steel."

"Correct, Brent–san."

"You can't see much from there."

"True. But you almost saw too much."

"Yes, Sir. I almost lost Lieutenant Elroy Rubin."

Fujita gestured at a chart on a bulkhead to his side. "We will invade the Marianas within six months. We will have the transports and the assault troops."

Brent rubbed the healing scars on his cheek. "There are three carrier, three cruisers and escorts in Surabaya."

"Yes, they will come out—must come out when we move with our amphibious forces against Saipan and Tinian. We have already softened them up once, and we will hit them hard again and put men, good men who will die for freedom on those beaches, stamp out those foul invaders for the vermin they are."

"A replay of the American invasion. It was very costly."

"I have studied that operation. We will improve it, not

make their mistakes—their stupid head-on assault over a barrier reef."

"And my duty, Sir."

"On the bridge with me as my JOD. If I am disabled, you will take command."

Brent was stunned. This was unprecedented. "But, Captain Mitake Arai is our exec, Rear Admiral Whitehead has vast experience and both of them outrank me and have seniority on me. I'm deeply honored, but, respectfully, this would ignore the chain of command."

"Chains are to be broken and if I order it, the links will be cut." He hunched forward, "You will command all units as long as the enemy is engaged. When we stand down, Captain Arai will assume command." He thumped the desk with his tiny fist. "You have proven you can fight in any situation and exact the utmost from your men. This is the kind of leadership *Yonaga* must have."

"Very well, Sir. I am honored and I will do my best."

"I could ask for no more." His voice softened, "You have suffered a great personal loss, Brent-san. You must put it behind you."

"I don't know if I can, Sir."

"You are not *shinigurai?*"

"Crazy to die, Sir?"

"Yes."

"I was responsible for the deaths of two fine young women."

"That is not true. We lost dozens of splendid young airmen in our assault on the Marianas. Am I to take personal responsibility? Did I kill them?"

Brent rubbed his temples with his finger tips. "That's not a fair analogy, Sir."

"It is, Brent–san. How could I function, how could any commander function if he dwelled on his dead. Those women were warriors, took their chances, knew the risks and were casualties just as our lost flyers."

"I know, Admiral, but I was personally involved, led the killer to them. That is how I feel, Admiral."

"Nonsense. I did not lead the enemy fighters to our men, pull the trigger." His fingers drummed the desk impatiently. "You did not answer, Brent–san. Are you *shinigurai?*"

The young man sighed and rubbed his still slightly sore thigh gently. "I do not know, Sir. The test of combat will determine that."

The old man seemed satisfied with the answer. His voice softened, "I suffered great personal losses, Brent–san."

Brent knew the old man spoke of his vaporized family: his wife Akiko, his sons Makoto and Kazuo. "I know, Sir. And you have put that behind you?"

"Yes. It takes time. You will put your losses behind you. Remember, we still have our Emperor, an enemy to be fought or surrender to slavery. We cannot remain with the dead without surrendering the future. A man *shinigurai* serves no one but his enemy."

"I understand, Sir."

"Fujita put his hand on the *Hagakure*. "The book tells us, 'A real samurai is a man who does not hold his life in regret'."

Brent nodded. "Very true, Sir."

"Return to the book."

"I will, Sir. As soon as I return to my cabin."

The old man seemed very tired, but pleased, "Good.

382

Good, Brent—san." The narrow rheumy eyes caught and held the deep blue of the American's. "You must be tired, Brent—san. You are dismissed."

Brent stood, bowed and left the cabin.

The old admiral watched the young man close the door. Then he sighed, pulled open a drawer and glanced at a picture of his family. He focused for a moment on his big strapping son, Kazuo, and smiled. He spoke to the picture, "Kazuo. Kazuo, you are home. Thank the gods."